I0627594

SHAKEN AND STIRRED

Lilly Atlas

All rights reserved. This book or any portion thereof may not be reproduced or used in any manner whatsoever without the express written permission of the author, except for the use of brief quotations in a book review.

Copyright © <2025> Lilly Atlas

All rights reserved.

ISBN-13 978-1-946068-59-0

For Sam <3

Table of Contents

Prologue

Nothing sucked more than being the only underprivileged kid in an elite summer program full of spoiled, high-society rich boys who spent more on a haircut than my mom made in a month.

Nothing.

Unless, of course, everyone in the auditorium *knew* you were the one there thanks to a scholarship fund made possible by the generous donations of their parents, who not only paid the insane fees for them to attend but for my sorry self as well.

It seemed everyone knew I was the only kid who wouldn't be there if it weren't for their rich mommy and daddy's need for a hefty tax write-off.

Yeah, that sucked more.

I could have turned down the scholarship, told the school and its wealthy donors where to stick their money, and turned my back on the prestigious NexGen Innovators Summer Program. I could have spent this summer after my junior year like I had the previous five before it—working the entrance kiosk at the Calum River State Park, handing out day passes to sunburned families and eager hikers.

The job was boring as hell, mind-numbing, really, but it gave me plenty of time to read in the booth between park visitors. So, I could have done that again, and I almost did. We sure as hell needed the money, but I'd swallowed my pride and accepted the slot at NGI along with the full summer scholarship—$20,000. Every student here had paid $20,000 for six weeks of college-level engineering and robotics instruction. I'd swallowed my pride and done the smart thing, even if it meant I'd be working a night job to make up for it. In the fall, when I started applying to colleges, I needed NGI on my application to secure a spot in a robotics engineering program. This was the final missing puzzle piece to ensure I got the future I wanted.

One that didn't resemble my childhood.

No shitty rented house with broken appliances and a landlord who never answered his phone. No fifteen-year-old car that ran less than half the time. No stack of unpaid bills or a host of unheard voicemails from debt collectors.

I refused to live my adult life the same way I'd spent my childhood, and that meant I had to secure a decent-paying, stable job with growth potential. Given that I was already obsessed with technology and robotics and excelled in math, robotic engineering was a perfect fit.

So, there I was, surrounded by nepo babies in their pressed designer khaki pants and starched polo shirts, wearing my wrinkled donation bin's finest. That's right, I didn't even wait for this fit to make it to the thrift store. I looted them right out of the bin.

I was classy like that.

"In five minutes, we are going to break off into our lab groups," the program director said from the stage. He was an average-height man, probably in his fifties, with an awful graying combover and the beginnings of a gut testing the strength of his shirt's buttons. He introduced himself as Dr.

Doaks, an MIT professor who'd been leading this program for years.

"Your lab groups will become your robotics family for the next six weeks. The groups are labeled A through E for now." He smirked, making the laugh lines around his eyes deepen. "Choosing new names once you congregate in your laboratory has become a tradition in the program. Anyway, you can find your assigned group in the folders you received when you checked in, along with your schedule. Lunch is daily from noon to one o'clock for all groups. Feel free to leave the campus to eat if you'd like. No one will check on or monitor your attendance. This is a taste of what it's like to be in college. You are responsible for yourself. Each of you is paying a lot to be here, so we assume that means you want to learn from us."

Someone snorted behind us. "Not *every* one of us," some guy muttered. A chorus of whispered chuckles followed the statement before someone kicked my chair, nearly sending me to the floor. I grabbed the armrests to keep from flying out of my seat.

"Dude, what the hell?" the guy next to me—a real serious type with a bowtie and polished loafers—grumbled as he shifted farther away in his seat.

Great, I was already making friends. More laughter came from the row above. Fuck that shit. These pricks would learn fast that I might be poor, but I wasn't anyone's doormat. I whipped around and glared at the row behind me.

"What are you staring at, freeloader?" A guy with perfect teeth and a damn chin dimple leaned forward with a sneer. His dark hair didn't move at all as his friend, a redheaded girl with too much makeup, slapped his arm.

"Kirk." She giggled as she whacked him again. "Be nice."

"Yeah, Kirk," the guy on the other side of him said in a mocking tone. "Be nice. You can't be sure this is the guy who's punching up."

I shifted my attention to the new mouthpiece and—Christ.

Of course, of freaking course, he had to be a damn Ken Doll come to life. Perfect blond hair swept to one side of his head without a strand out of place as though they wouldn't dare defy him. I took in his tanned skin and set of pearly whites so straight and even that his dentist probably featured them on his brochures. His nose was straight and strong, the kind that had never collided with another man's fist. Lucky guy. Then, there was a set of sparkling blue eyes that the Caribbean would be jealous of. Most likely, he had an entire torso of rippling muscles under there too. This guy looked like the type to be captain of his school's lacrosse team or maybe water polo.

Why? Was it too much to hope for an ogre among the sea of rich perfection?

Money and looks. Some guys had all the damn luck.

Too bad he was a dick.

"Fuck off. You don't know shit about me."

Ken Doll smirked. "We know you're not one of us."

"Thank God for that," I muttered as I spun back and slumped in my seat to the jeering cackle of their laughter. Screw those rich jerks. As much as I'd love to jump up and rearrange those symmetrical faces, I couldn't risk expulsion. Six weeks. I could put my head down and endure their mockery for six weeks. Easy-peasy. Hell, I'd survived worse for longer. Two summers ago, I took a second job to help pay for Mom's medication costs. I spent eight weeks cleaning portable toilets at the outdoor concert arena. There was no way spending the summer getting belittled by rich mommy's boys could be worse than that.

"Okay," the director said as he clapped his hands together once. "I've rambled long enough. The first sessions begin in fifteen minutes. Take your time finding your labs and introducing yourself to the other students in your group. You'll be seeing a lot of each other this summer."

With that, he nodded, then strode offstage to the echo of scattered applause from the few still paying attention.

I grabbed my worn backpack and stood as fast as I could. "Sorry," I said with a wince as my bag smacked into the guy next to me. "Sorry, excuse me." Without waiting for him to move, I struggled to sidestep out of the row between his knees and the row below us.

"What the hell, man?" he grumbled as he tried to shift his legs out of my way.

"Sorry," I mumbled.

"Careful, man," Ken Doll said with a laugh. "You might not have enough money to pay your ER bill if you trip and break an arm."

He had no idea.

Asshole.

The others laughed again.

Just what I needed, those jerks watching me scurry off like a damn frightened mouse.

I wasn't frightened. And I wasn't a mouse.

But I couldn't afford to say what I really wanted and have one of them run to the program director, complaining about the rude, impoverished kid with a bad attitude. Risking my scholarship wasn't an option. They could think whatever they wanted about me. All that mattered were my goals. And I'd only achieve them by working my ass off and getting accepted into a robotics engineering program. Thankfully, I lived in a city with exactly what I was looking for. Even with scholarships and grants, I couldn't afford to go to college out of state or even in another city.

For more reasons than my family's dismal lack of finances.

Only when I reached the hallway outside the auditorium could I finally take a full breath. My lab group met in the

Emerson Lab on the building's third floor. I hoped to make it my future home away from home for the four years of my undergraduate studies.

I jogged the two flights of stairs to the third floor and arrived huffing and puffing. No one had beaten me to the room, so I had my pick of lab tables. As much as I wanted a front-and-center spot to see and absorb every word out of the instructor's mouth, I didn't want to paint a second target on my back. A scholarship kid and a teacher's pet were a bad combination. Instead, I chose a safer option at the center lab table in the third of six rows.

As the room began to fill with summer students, I gazed around at the impressive equipment lining the shelves along the walls. Each table had two laptops, one for each lab partner, and two printed syllabus packets. Hopefully, Intro to Robotics wouldn't be boring since I'd been studying the subject on my own for years. Time would tell.

The click-clack of high heels across the linoleum floor had me glancing up to find our instructor, a graduate student at MIT, according to what she'd written on the whiteboard behind her desk. When she entered, she walked straight to the desk at the front of the room, where she pulled a laptop out of her bag. She wore straight black slacks and a cream-colored turtleneck sweater. Her long, shiny black hair hung down her back, tied away from her face in a low ponytail. After she opened her laptop, she watched her class fill through black-rimmed glasses and a pleasant expression on her minimally made-up face.

All in all, she was a beautiful woman. Though we were well into the twenty-first century, men still dominated the engineering field. I loved that our first lab had a female instructor. It would be fun to watch the rich bros in my class take direction from her.

Most likely, they'd spend their time slobbering over her

instead of learning.

"Good morning, everyone," she said once most of the seats filled up. Her melodic voice floated above the low hum of get-to-know-you chatter, which faded to nothing when she spoke. "My name is Marissa Haverstead, and I'm a PhD student here at MIT. I'll be leading you through this introductory robotics course. Please call me Marissa."

She glanced down at a paper on her desk, then quickly scanned the room.

"Looks like we have a full class this year and one vacant seat right now, which means…"

My stomach fluttered as I glanced at the chair next to me.

Empty.

Awesome. Everyone in the room had a partner except me. My face heated from the stares of the other students focused my way.

"Someone is running late," she said right before a body slid into the chair next to me.

"Sorry," a male voice said without an ounce of the embarrassment I would have experienced at being called out for arriving last on the first day.

I turned to introduce myself to the newcomer—my partner —and my stomach plummeted.

The Ken Doll.

"Hey, FL," he said with a smirk. "Fancy meeting you here."

"FL?" I asked with a frown. What the hell was FL?

"Freeloader." He winked.

If I could have smacked the smug grin off his face without being expelled, I would have in a heartbeat. What a conceited prick.

Why the hell did he have to be so hot? His arrogant smirk would be so much less irritating if it weren't made up of plump lips and accompanied by twinkling blue eyes.

I loved blue eyes. They were so different from my dark

ones. This close, I noticed a small fleck of green in his left eye shaped like a comma. One speck of imperfection in an otherwise flawless face that only made him more attractive.

Damn Ken Doll.

Since I couldn't hit him, I settled for my usual weapon, my caustic tongue. "I suppose you paid for this with your lucrative job?" I snapped my fingers. "Oh no, wait, your mommy and daddy paid for it. Just like they paid for your clothes and your Tesla and whatever else you have that you didn't earn yourself."

I only had two seconds to enjoy the flash of surprise in his eyes before he grinned again. "Dayum, FL has a backbone. All right, I can work with that. Let the games begin. This is gonna be fun," he said as he rubbed his hands together.

Maybe I should tell him I was gay. That would get his future-frat-boy ass out of that seat faster than anything. He was the type of jerk to be afraid of catching sexual orientation if he sat too close to a queer guy like me.

I'd be fine if he dropped out of the program. Completing the assignments alone had to be better than putting up with him.

"Excuse me, gentlemen," Marissa said. She narrowed her eyes at us. "Save the chitchat for the breaks, please."

"Sorry, ma'am," Ken Doll said with a charming tone that probably had his high school's entire cheerleading squad fawning all over him.

I resisted rolling my eyes.

Barely.

"FL here was just asking if he could borrow a fiver for lunch. Poor thing doesn't have much," he added in a faux whisper.

Oh, fuck him.

My ears burned. Why the hell wasn't I born with the ability to disappear on command?

A few of my classmates snickered, but most remained quiet. Marissa didn't get the joke. She had no idea I was there on a scholarship. She probably didn't give two craps about petty high school bullying. "Doesn't matter the topic of conversation," she said with a tight-lipped grin. "Talk on your own time."

What an awful start to my first day. "Sorry," I mumbled like an idiot. Ignoring the murmurs and whispered chuckles of my summer classmates wasn't possible. My face burned so hot my ears had to be smoking.

Kenn Doll didn't seem to mind in the least. "Won't happen again," he said without an ounce of remorse while flashing that charming grin at our teacher.

Lucky for me that grin didn't do a damn thing besides piss me off. It was so annoying, it canceled out his appealing features, like his blue eyes.

Tanned skin.

Plump lips.

Fuck.

"Thank you, gentlemen," she said. "Moving on, let's look at the syllabus. I'll tell you a little about what you can expect in this lab for the next six weeks."

As I slid my syllabus in front of me, Ken Doll leaned over. "Name's Ryder," he whispered, making electricity run down my spine.

Of course it was. Such a rich boy's name.

His breath tickled my ear, which was the only reason I shivered. Warm air unexpectedly brushed across sensitive nerve endings. That's all.

"Alex," I ground out through clenched teeth. I scooted my chair away from him. "You're too close. Back off."

He grunted out a laugh, then finally turned his attention to Marissa as she reviewed the syllabus.

Being a summer program, everyone paid out the ass to

attend. There were no exams or papers, only ungraded projects we had plenty of time to complete and learn from. As I listened to her review our planned schedule, the buzz of anticipation I'd woken up with returned. This is what excited me—computer coding, machine learning, robotics, all the nerdy technology I could get my hands on. I wasn't about to let spoiled idiots ruin this opportunity for me.

Working with Ryder would be fine.

"Grab a pen or highlighter," Marissa commanded. "There are a few important details I want to emphasize.

The spoiled idiot plucked his backpack off the floor and rifled through it. After pulling out a pen, he dropped the backpack on the table—a Prada?—in my space and halfway across my laptop.

"Uh," I whispered. "Wanna move your shit?"

"It's an expensive bag. I don't want it to get dirty on the floor."

This had to be a joke.

"It's a fucking bag."

"Shh. I'm trying to listen," he spoke sideways out of his perfect mouth.

Not that I'd noticed.

Of course, he didn't remove the bag. Instead, he rested his elbow on the table and, every few seconds, shifted it my way, nudging the thousand-dollar bag farther on my laptop.

All the while, he sat there with an innocent expression, staring at the front of the room.

It happened at least four times, and each time, my blood heated another few degrees. Who the hell did this guy think he was? Mommy and Daddy clearly taught him he was better than everyone else because they had fat wallets. Maybe it was time for him to learn their money couldn't save him in every situation.

As slowly as I could, I inched my fingers forward until I

could grab the strap on his bag. Then, with one solid yank, I sent the whole thing, every thousand-dollar bill that bag cost, tumbling to the floor. His shit flew in every direction. His pencils, pens, and paper fluttered to the floor all around our lab table.

"Oh shit," I cried. "Ryder, you knocked your bag down. You'd better pick it up before it gets dirty. Looks like a nice one." I pressed my lips together to keep from laughing out loud. Damn, pettiness felt good sometimes.

I risked a glance at Ryder, expecting the same anger and annoyance on his face that he'd been causing me. All I found was that damn Ken Doll smirk.

"Let the games begin," he mouthed.

Fine, if that's how this was going to be, I could roll with it.

Let the games begin.

Chapter One

The animated thump of house music thrummed through my veins on tempo. Some nights, the music felt like the only thing keeping my blood pulsing and my brain computing. Even the energy drink I'd chugged before my shift couldn't keep me on my feet as well as the heavy pulsing beat. If the power cut out and the music vanished, I'd collapse to the floor in a heap, fast asleep.

Day to day, I balanced graduate school, family drama, and work—three obligations that could have kept my schedule packed individually. Together, they damn near drove me into the ground, but all were essential. School would get me out of this life, my job kept me in school, and my family was, well, they were my family.

"Hey, boo." Trevor, the perkiest and twinkiest of my coworkers, bounced into the staff lounge wearing a beige puffy jacket that reached his ankles and a winter hat with fur trim. "Dayum, it's colder than Parker's balls out there tonight," he said with a dramatic shiver.

I turned from my locker and raised an eyebrow at my favorite coworker and one of my closest friends. "And you know Parker's balls are cold... how?"

He hip-checked me as I reached his locker next to mine. "You know our boss has a heart as cold as ice. It's only fair to assume his balls are just as frosty. Have you tried to picture that man fucking?"

"Ugh, Trev, no, I fucking haven't." Despite owning one of the most popular gay nightclubs in the area and employing a gaggle of guys who worked in nothing more than underwear, our boss was professional to the extreme. He was the last man who'd so much as look at an employee with a lustful gaze.

"Give it a try. It's damn near impossible." He shed the jacket and stuffed it into his locker before tugging off his Golden Girls sweatshirt. His chocolaty brown hair had royal blue tips this week that matched the blue nail polish on his slender fingers.

"You might be onto something. I don't think I've ever seen him crack a smile. How could he possibly let go enough to fuck?" I said with a grunt.

Trevor snorted. "Exactly. 'Oh, yes. Take my long, turgid dick. Is that the spot? Your ass is so very tight.'" He moved his hips in a stilted, awkward thrust that matched his stiff words.

I couldn't help but bust out laughing. The impression was dead-on with the formal way our boss spoke and his stiff mannerisms.

"Well..." I said as I yanked my sweater over my head, "... he's doing something right. Guys come here practically tripping over themselves to get within five feet of him."

"Yeah, he's hot and loaded. Of course, they all want him."

Was it my imagination, or did I hear a hint of bitterness in Trevor's tone?

"Hey..." I grabbed a tube of gold glitter and tossed it his way. "Can you sparkle me up?"

"Only if you'll return the favor," he said as he snatched the tube midair as it flew his way. We'd played this game countless times before. "Actually, I'll do it anyway. You know I love running my hands all over that muscular body of yours."

"Please, we both know I'm not your type." I stepped out of my jeans and shoved them in the locker with my sweater. Thankfully, Parker kept the heat in the staff room cranked up this time of year. With the foot and a half of snow outside, working in booty shorts and a damn bowtie could suck. Five minutes after working the floor, I'd be sweating my ass off, but peeling your clothes off in the dead of winter sucked.

Trevor lost his clothes, leaving him in the tight black shorts we called a uniform. "Sad but true. I don't make much of a secret of my love of older men. I'd say I'm not your type either, but it's been so long since I've seen you with anyone that I forget if you even have a type. You probably forget too."

"Yeah, well, I'm too busy to hook up."

Trevor snorted as he squeezed a dollop of glitter onto his hands. "Girl, please, we work in a damn sausage factory. You could get your dick sucked any night you're here, and you know it. Five minutes in BJ Alley, and you'd feel like a new man."

Ah, BJ Alley, the strange half-hallway around the corner from the restrooms. Twenty feet of wasted space leading to an emergency exit we'd thankfully never had to use. Parker tried for years to obtain permits to block off the area, but the city shot him down every time. It turned out they liked people having a way out in case of an emergency.

Crazy.

BJ Alley had become the worst-kept secret in Top Shelf's history. The hidden nook patrons and staff alike disappeared to for a quick suck or fuck. After the fifth security camera mysteriously broke, Parker gave up trying to keep people away.

Trevor rubbed the glitter over my shoulders and across my chest with slow, deliberate strokes. A mischievous grin curled his glossy lips, and one second later, his thumbnail raked across my nipple. A zing of pleasure shot straight to my dick.

"Seriously?" I asked as I jolted.

He did it again. Shit, maybe I did need to find someone to get me off if Trevor's touch was doing something to me.

I slapped his hand away before he made my damn dick hard. "Quit it with that crap."

His shit-eating grin only grew. "Turn around so I can get your back," he said as he wiggled his shimmering fingers.

"If you even think about touching my ass..." I narrowed my eyes at him.

Laughing, he spun me around. "I'll behave, I promise. Besides, Parker would kill me if you went to work with a gold handprint on your ass."

Two minutes later, I was twinkling and ready for a five-hour bottle service shift. As Trevor disappeared to wash his hands, I slipped into my low, black uniform sneakers and secured my bowtie. Black spandex shorts, black shoes, and a black bowtie—the Top Shelf uniform of champions or bottle service boys looking to score as much in tips as humanly possible.

Trevor returned as I reached the door. "Hey, wait, what about me?"

I pulled the door open, and the volume increased tenfold. "What?" I shouted, pointing to my ear. "Sorry, can't hear you?"

"Oh, screw you." Trevor flipped me the bird.

I waggled my fingers at him and slipped into the hallway.

"You loved that nipple tweak, and you know it," he shouted after me.

Ah, revenge. So damn sweet. Guess he'd just have to

wander upstairs to Parker's office for his rubdown. He could thank me later. Trevor might like to complain about our boss, but he'd been gone for the man since the day he interviewed. Parker was everything Trevor went for in a guy—older, serious, rich, and intense as hell.

Chuckling, I wormed my way through the crowded dance floor to the hostess booth for the night's VIP schedule.

"Hey, Alex." Luke glanced at the computer after smiling at me. The lucky bastard got to wear a suit while the rest of us pranced around in a few scraps of fabric shy of naked. But Luke didn't work for tips, and showing skin brought in the big bucks and the customers. "You're on seven and eight tonight. Seven is booked for the entire night by two different parties. One from ten to twelve and another from twelve to two. Seven is only booked for the first two hours."

The ten o'clock booking gave me a half hour to make sure my area was ready for a group of men to spend an obscene amount of money on alcohol and *the experience*. Thirty minutes to get my game face on and prepare to spend hours pretending I loved the club scene and loved serving rich assholes. I didn't like socializing with anyone, let alone rich partiers. To them, I was nothing more than a fit body who delivered the alcohol and let them slap my ass.

But money was money, and I could bank more working four nights a week here than a full-time job elsewhere. And make no mistake, for me, this was all about the money. As much as I could rack up in as little time as possible, this job allowed me to balance classes, studying, and covering the bills.

Mostly.

"Thanks, Luke. Find me if anything changes." Occasionally, a last-minute reservation would fill the empty slot, or a walk-in would be willing to drop big bucks for some privacy in the VIP section.

He nodded and waved without tearing his gaze from the computer.

Though it was only nine thirty, the dance floor was filling fast. Most guys still wore their shirts, but that would change in the next hour or so. We maxed out capacity every Saturday night. Hell, the doors were open Wednesday through Saturday nights, and we hit max capacity often. Wednesday tended to be the slowest, but it was never empty. Thursday was a go-go night with some of the staff, Trevor included, dancing on raised platforms. Friday always had a theme, and Saturday was Golden Night. We slathered ourselves in glitter until we looked like walking disco balls. Customers got a free shot if they wore gold. VIPs, the section where I worked, received a complimentary golden bottle of Dom Pérignon.

Of course, free was a bit of a misnomer. A table in the VIP section cost two grand for a two-hour reservation, and that bumped to twenty-eight hundred on Saturdays. Each table could accommodate up to eight people. The reservation came with snacks, bottled water, and me. The friendly neighborhood grad student who'd deliver the ridiculously priced alcohol while shaking my ass, waving sparklers, and providing the luxury experience these rich assholes thought they deserved. It wasn't uncommon for a VIP's tab to hit over ten thousand dollars on a given night.

The thought of spending that much money on a single night out boggled my mind, yet I witnessed men drop that much cash every week. And then there was me, the guy who felt guilty for spending three dollars on a coffee at the campus café a few times each week.

"Alex, you good?" Trevor called out as he walked by with an armload of bottled water. "You're standing there with lost puppy eyes."

Shit. I gave myself a mental slap across the face. This was not the time to bemoan my station in life, not if I wanted to earn enough tips to pay for this semester's books. "All good. Just went offline for a second."

Trevor's grin turned sympathetic. "You work too hard, Ally. Maybe you should take a week off."

I snorted. "School's not gonna pay for itself, Trev." Like me, he'd graduated last year but with a degree in political science. He is assisting at his mother's fabric shop a few days a week. Must be nice to have the luxury to dick around for a while. I started at twelve, out of necessity, not desire. Back when my mother could still work, I was able to take the occasional day off. Now, not so much. Every day I missed work hurt my family's ability to get by.

Ugh, why was I so maudlin tonight?

I cracked my neck and shook off the mopey feelings, then headed to grab water for my tables.

The first few hours of the night flew by in the familiar dance of fetching, presenting, and pouring copious amounts of alcohol for my two full tables. Table seven was a group of coworkers from a prestigious local law firm. They were in their late thirties and forties, polite, refined, and a joy to have at my table. Table eight wasn't rough either. A bachelor party with both grooms present and a whole lot of Patrón leaving the bottles.

I smiled, flirted, and did whatever the hell I had to for my tips when working, but damn, I'd rather be home reading or working on my school assignments. At least it would be quiet, and I wouldn't have to act like I gave a shit about customers.

By midnight, my calves ached, and my head throbbed. The loud music might keep me awake, but it got old after a while. I only had five minutes to turn over table eight, so I wiped it down as quickly as I could, then ran from the staff room to the bar to chug a bottle of water. By the time I downed all sixteen ounces, Luke had guided a group of six guys to my table. This group looked like they came straight from the frat house to the club, slapping each other on the back and pointing out guys that caught their eye. They looked about my age, give or take a few years, with slick hair and slicker grins. Diamonds glittered from a few Rolexes, and an earring or two winked at me beneath the club lights.

If I dragged my feet a little, no one had to know. Luke seemed fine, entertaining them for a moment while I slow-walked my way there. These were my least favorite tables. I didn't mind bachelor parties, couple groups, or men in their thirties and up, but single rich guys my age sucked. They were loud, rude, and entitled, and many acted like they'd never heard the word 'no.' Probably because they hadn't.

"Ah, and here is your bottle service boy, Alex. I leave you gentlemen in his capable hands," Luke said with a smile so fake I almost laughed. "Good luck," he whispered as he walked by. "If they get out of hand, I'll send Raphael your way."

"Thanks, Luke."

As he left, I turned to the table and smiled. "Hey, boys," I said with the same flirty tone I used with all my tables. "As Luke said, I'm Alex, and I will be at your beck and call for the next few hours. So, are we celebrating anything special tonight?"

I scanned the faces around the table, looking for the ringleader. Typically, one guy ran the show in a group like this. I played a little game with myself I called Guess the Alpha Douche. I had a ninety-five percent success rate.

Not the first two guys—they seemed laid back. It could be the third, maybe. He had a bit of self-important energy, but—*oh, shit*. The only thing that kept my jaw from hitting the floor was two years of practice schooling my expression in front of customers.

There's no way he was here. No way. I'd survived a

summer program with him, made it through the same undergrad school, and finally found my freedom. What the fuck was he doing here now? He'd left the damn state for graduate school.

I blinked. Maybe I was seeing things.

Nope. The smug grin aimed my way belonged to the one person I truly hated.

My stomach sank.

Ryder smirked. "We're celebrating all kinds of things tonight, Alex."

Chapter Two

If I had to stand outside in the dead of winter one second longer, my dick and balls would ice over. I might never be able to fuck again. Was a little punctuality too damn much to ask? A man's sexual future was at stake.

"Ryder, baby, it's been too damn long!" A heavy hand slapped my back, and then I was turned into a rib-crushing embrace.

"Turk!" A grin spread across my face as I hugged my frat brother. After squeezing the life out of me, he let go, and we stepped apart. "Damn, you look like shit," I said, frowning at him.

A lie—the guy was a damn tank on legs who'd been drafted into the NHL. He now played for Denver, but happened to be in Boston this weekend. He was hot as hell and knew it, so there was no point in me feeding his overly healthy ego.

Turk snorted. "Sorry, man, I've really let myself go." He rubbed a hand over his bomber jacket where, no doubt, a set of stellar abs resided. The guy looked like he chewed tree bark and bathed with sandpaper. He was a tough motherfucker.

"Fuck you." We laughed as I noticed a group of men striding our way. "Yo, Manny!" I charged at my friend, the first guy I'd roomed with at college before we became frat brothers and best friends. "Damn, it's good to see your ugly face." We met and grabbed each other in a tight hug.

"Could never be as ugly as you," he said as he slapped my back.

God, I'd missed this city. These guys. What the fuck had I been thinking when I decided to go to grad school ten states away?

Oh, right—sun, surf, and hot dudes strolling shirtless on the beach.

Freedom from my father's reach.

Too bad his arms were so long.

"Yo, Turk." Manny hugged him next, then turned to the three men I didn't recognize.

"Ryder, Turk, this is Jack, Spencer, and Clyde, three guys from my firm. Ryder and Turk were my frat brothers." Manny had taken over his father's booming investment firm after graduation. He was a nepo baby if there ever was one.

Not that I could talk.

I lifted a hand. "Pleasure."

One of the guys, Spencer, couldn't tear his eyes away from Turk. "You're... holy shit, you're..."

"John Turko," he said with a smirk. "Nice to meet you."

"Christ, Manny, you didn't tell me you were friends with John Turko."

"There's a reason for that." Manny smiled, looking way too pleased with himself. "Surprise."

Spencer blinked. His mouth opened and closed a few times before any sound came out. "Man, your rookie season was out of this world. You... you're incredible."

"Okay, let's get inside," Manny said as he guided his friend toward the door. He'd been born and raised in Argentina and had never quite adjusted to the cold. "You start drooling out here, and it'll freeze on your damn face."

"Fuck," Spencer whispered. "I'm making an ass of myself in front of John Turko."

Turk laughed and then squeezed the poor guy's shoulder. "Nah, you're cool, man. Let's get inside before my nips freeze off."

They all filed through the entrance with Turk taking the rear. As he held the door, he turned back to look at me. "Coming?"

Warmth filled my veins despite the frigid temperatures. Why had I left? This was home. Aside from the past year and a half, I'd lived my whole life in this city. Returning made sense but leaving hadn't. A battle loomed in my future, or at least a bunch of heavy and uncomfortable conversations with my parents, but I belonged here. It felt so good to be back on familiar ground.

"Not yet." I winked at Turk. "But the night is young."

He laughed and bounced on the balls of his feet, either excited or trying to warm up, while I kept him waiting outside. "Now you're getting into the spirit of things. Come on, Ry, there's alcohol to consume and hot men to fuck."

As soon as I stepped inside, delicious warmth seeped through my peacoat into my bones. "Wow. This place is swanky," I said as I tipped my head back to take in the entire lobby.

A glittering chandelier, dripping with long crystals, hung high above our heads, refracting light into tiny rainbows that danced on the marble floor. Walls of deep emerald velvet framed the space, interrupted only by sleek gold accents and mirrors that made the room feel infinite. A concierge station, manned by an attractive host in a designer suit, beckoned us. Behind him, a black façade lit with a single neon sign announced the club's name and tagline—*Top Shelf: Where the*

Vibe is Premium.

"Right?" Manny grinned as his buddy, Jack, walked to the host.

The place was the perfect example of understated luxury—right up my alley.

"How have I never been here?"

"It's newish," Turk said. "Opened about two years ago."

"Ah." Right around the time I'd made the stellar decision to leave the state.

"Good evening, gentlemen." The host stepped out from behind his station. He was on the shorter side, about five feet seven inches, and slim with a snazzy navy-blue suit. Diamonds lined the lapels, twinkling along with the chandelier's shimmer. "Welcome to Top Shelf."

"Hey, man," Jack said. "We have a VIP reservation booked under the last name Hall."

"Excellent. My name is Luke. I'll be escorting you to your table, and Raphael here will check your coats." He gestured toward a beefy bouncer with dark skin, dreadlocks, and a tailored suit that would probably split at the seams if he got into it with an unruly clubgoer.

We took a few minutes to hand over our coats to the man who looked as if he cracked walnuts in his palms.

"Thank you, Raph." Luke smiled at the bouncer, whose arms were now laden with our coats. "Gentlemen, please follow me."

Somehow, I ended up in the lead, directly behind Luke. The man had a nice ass and a pretty face, but he wasn't exactly my type. I preferred a guy more my size or bigger. An equal partner who could match me in the bedroom. Not someone I had to worry about hurting if things turned rough.

Luke guided us to a roped-off walkway leading to the VIP section. As we followed the path, moving bodies on my left caught my attention. The dance floor beckoned like the beating heart of the club. It sprawled beneath a sky-high ceiling, where laser lights cut through artificial smoke, creating an ever-shifting kaleidoscope of color. The polished, obsidian-black flooring reflected the movements of a crowd of men that pulsed like a living organism. Their bodies gleamed under the strobe lights, slick with sweat. Expressions of bliss and lust shone from the faces of men grinding and touching each other to the beat of the music. Most had discarded their shirts, leaving yards of smooth skin on display for eyes and hands to explore.

A state-of-the-art sound system sent basslines rippling through my chest—each beat perfectly calibrated to make it impossible not to move. Along the walls, floor-to-ceiling LED panels displayed surreal visuals—rippling water, blooming flowers, and shifting constellations—all timed to the music.

The bar, an architectural marvel, stretched along one side of the room. Its counter was made of backlit onyx that seemed to glow from within, while liquor bottles were displayed on floating glass shelves that sparkled like jewels. The bartenders were as much performers as servers, wearing only tailored leather aprons on their upper half as they mixed drinks with a theatrical flair, their movements precise and fluid.

My blood began to pump to the music's beat. With each passing second, a missing piece of myself fell back into place. Fuck, I was young and goddamn loaded. Why was I making shit deeper than it had to be?

"Is this place incredible or what?" Manny yelled in my ear over the music.

My smile spread of its own free will. "Fuck yeah."

"We'll be going right over there." Luck pointed ahead toward the VIP section, tucked away in an elevated corner. It was a hidden sanctuary of exclusivity guarded by a velvet rope and an imposing security guard. The space was designed to feel intimate despite its opulence. Circular booths upholstered in dove-gray suede encircled private tables with flickering candlelight, the soft golden glow complementing the shimmering gold of the room's walls. Guests reclined against plush cushions while sipping champagne from fluted glasses or swirling aged whiskey in crystal tumblers. A personal host hovered discreetly nearby, ready to fetch anything with a mere glance. From this vantage point, VIP guests could survey the dance floor below, their elevated position a subtle reminder of their status in this glittering world of decadence.

Men on the dance floor noticed our group of six walking toward the VIP area. Eyes lit with interest, lips were licked, and hungry come-hither gazes were cast.

I loved this shit. What could I say? There wasn't any point in denying I'd been born with a silver spoon in my mouth and a love of all things luxurious.

"Here we are, gentlemen. Your VIP liaison will be here momentarily. His name is Alex, and he's ready and willing to cater to your every need."

Turk whistled.

"Within reason," Luke added with a wink.

Bullshit, within reason. I'd bet my trust fund our *liaison* would have no problem servicing us outside the bounds of reason for a hefty tip. This place probably saw more ass than a no-tell motel. It was nearly impossible not to be swept up in the seduction of the décor alone.

"If you desire a more private, more… intimate experience, Alex will be more than happy to pull the curtains for you," he said, gesturing to a green velvet curtain draped from floor to ceiling.

Manny rubbed his hands together. "If only the thought of fucking one of you guys didn't make my nuts shrivel."

We all laughed. "I'm sure you'll find someone who fits the

bill tonight, Manny," I said.

"True, I ain't worried about it." He waggled his eyebrows.

"Now, I am ready for a drink. What did you say our bottle service boy's name is again?"

"Alex, and here he is right now."

My pulse went haywire at the first glance of the guy who stepped up next to Luke. I couldn't have kept from smirking if my life depended on it. Alex Morgan. Who the fuck would have thought stick-up-his-ass Alex Morgan would look like that in a pair of ass-hugging shorts? Jesus, the man had a body that would feel so good sliding all over mine. Tight abs, toned arms, and an absolutely perfect fucking bubble butt, all covered in glitter that made him practically glow. My cock thickened. Thank God for the table to hide the evidence.

"I'll leave you gentlemen in his capable hands," Luke added before turning away. He whispered something to Alex, then strode back down the walkway. This time, I wasn't even tempted to glance at his ass. My attention was fixed on the man who'd hated me from the first moment he laid eyes on me—Alex Morgan. The uber-smart scholarship kid who'd been my lab partner for a six-week summer program after our junior year of high school. He was focused, driven, grumpy as hell, and a royal pain in my ass. He looked down on every one of us like the fact that we came from money was a transmissible disease.

The only time Alex looked at me with anything other than hatred and derision was when we played our little game. We'd spent that entire summer trying to one-up each other, pulling pranks, and setting out to humiliate the other. I'd never forget the fire in his eyes the first time I'd called him FL.

This night kept getting better.

The moment Alex noticed me, his entire body stiffened, and a familiar burning hatred flared in his gaze. I was helpless to do anything but smirk. I sure couldn't stand and shake his hand to let the others know we were acquainted. Not unless I wanted Alex to see how my body reacted to his practically naked one. I'd never give the grouch that kind of ammo. He could be vicious when he wanted to be.

His shock disappeared after only a few seconds. He placed a hand on his hip and cocked it to the right. "Hey, boys," he crooned, his voice thick with flirty interest that had my jaw hitting the floor.

Holy shit, who knew the man could sound like pure sex?

"As Luke said," he crooned, "I'm Alex, and I will be at your beck and call tonight. So, are we celebrating anything special tonight?"

I had to hand it to him. Had I not known his deep-seated loathing of me, I'd never have guessed. He radiated seductive, flirty, and eager-to-please vibes, all things I knew him not to be. He was as ornery as they came and always willing to fight dirty.

And yet, I'd never been able to help myself around him. "We're celebrating all kinds of things tonight, Alex."

"Damn straight we are!" Turk said with a whoop. "And we're starting with some Reposado!"

"You got it," Alex said with a smile for Turk. "How do you want that? Shots? Margaritas? Saturday is our Golden Day, so we have a signature cocktail called Liquid Gold with Patrón, Cointreau, lime, honey, and bitters. It's topped off with some gold flakes." His eyes flared as though teasing us with knowledge only he had. "Because, you know, why not?"

I pressed my lips together to keep from laughing. Poor Alex. Part of him must die inside each time a customer blew money on gold flakes for their drink.

"That sounds perfect," I said, grinning. "The Liquid Gold thing. For all of us."

His eyes narrowed.

"In fact, I think that might be my drink of choice all night."
I couldn't help myself. Riling Alex up had always been too
damn fun. And seeing the annoyance flash across his face
didn't disappoint. Excitement bubbled up in me, the first I'd
felt in a long time.

"You won't regret it," he said with the fakest damn smile.

"Shots too," Turk chimed in. "I wanna start with a round of
shots."

"Perfect. There's bottled water on the table, and I'll be
bringing a charcuterie board out for you to nibble on. Any
allergies I need to be aware of?"

Turk rubbed his stomach as he glanced around the table.
We all shook our heads. "Nope. I eat everything," he said
with a wink for Alex. "Everything."

Alex's face turned red, and he chuckled. "Careful, John
Turko. I happen to know you caused a bit of a media
shitstorm last month because of your... eating habits."

Well, shit, it looked like Alex was a hockey fan.

Turk's jaw hit the table. He'd been caught by a paparazzi
blowing a guy behind his apartment building last month,
which had landed him in hot water with his team's PR
department.

"Be right back with your drinks." Alex winked.

I burst out laughing as Alex turned and sashayed away,
and I got my first glimpse of his backside. The laughter died
in my throat, nearly turning into a groan. Christ, those shorts
were sinful. Two plump round ass cheeks I'd kill to squeeze,
bite, or sink my dick between shifted side to side as he strode
away from us.

In theory, of course. I'd never actually go after Alex. The
man was pricklier than a hedgehog and didn't do it for me at
all.

Well, his ass did it for me, but my eyes and dick didn't care
who a stellar ass belonged to. The rest of me found his

personality among the most off-putting a person could have.

"Did our server just throw some serious shade my way?" Turk asked, rubbing the back of his neck.

"I think so, man." Spencer chuckled as he shook his head. "He's feisty."

"You have no idea," I whispered, still staring at the man in question.

"What's that, man?"

I blinked at Turk. "What? Oh, no, just wondering when our drinks were gonna get here."

"Dude, give the guy a minute. He walked away like three seconds ago." Turk laughed and then got drawn into a conversation with the other guys, allowing me to continue creeping on Alex.

He said something to a much smaller guy dressed in the same ridiculous uniform, and one of the bartenders. They both laughed, then the bartender said something back that had Alex throwing his head back and laughing so hard I could almost hear him over the music.

Had I ever seen him laugh like that? Hell, had I ever seen him laugh at all?

No. Definitely not. I'd never thought it possible for him to loosen up enough to laugh. The only time he lost the starch in his spine was when he pulled a prank on me, and even those didn't make him bust a gut like that. No, that laugh meant happiness. It was only for those he liked and trusted.

Well, fuck him. He'd judged and found me lacking from day one, so fuck him.

And yet I still watched the way his biceps flexed as he opened the expensive bottle and poured out a round of shots.

"Yo, yo, Ry, tell Spencer about how you accidentally became an OnlyFans star." Turk smacked my chest with the back of his hand.

I blinked and tore my gaze from Alex to face Turk. "What's

that?"

"Your OnlyFans story."

I groaned. Of fucking course, he had to pick that story for me to entertain the table. No one knew the real story behind that epic prank, only the tale I'd told, where I'd spun it so a rival frat took the blame. "Oh, shit. Haven't thought about that in a while. Uh, I had a little too much fun at a party the night after finals week."

"Easy to do," Spencer said, with his green eyes shining. They complemented his mop of red hair perfectly.

"Right? Anyway, I passed out in my bed in nothing but my briefs and woke up to thousands of DMs from an OnlyFans account I did not have."

"Oh shit." Manny laughed. "I remember this. God, it was so damn good."

Fucking Alex. The little shit. I could never prove he'd done it, but he had. I knew it in my damn bones. "I rolled over to get out of bed and got a cold, nasty surprise." I cringed at the soggy, frigid memory. "Turns out someone had broken into the room, gave me a whipped cream bikini, then posted it to OF on my behalf."

The guys bust out laughing. "Oh, shit, who—"

Turk smacked my chest again. "Here come our drinks."

Our heads swiveled to find Alex pushing a golden cart our way. The drinks we'd ordered were lined up in neat rows along with the shots. He also had a tray of food to soak up some of the alcohol we planned to ingest. A gold vase held a bouquet of sparklers that sizzled and popped.

"Hell yeah!" Turk yelled. "Bring it on."

"Who's ready to party?" Alex shouted as he parked the cart near our table.

"Fuck yeah!" Spencer jumped up, pumping his fist in the air.

"Here we go, boys." Alex held out a metallic tray with our

shots.

"You better be doing one with us," Turk said as he cast a leering glance Alex's way.

"I had a feeling you'd say that, so I took the liberty of adding one for myself." Once everyone had a shot glass in hand, Alex stared directly at me.

His gaze burned my skin and made me shiver at the same time.

He lifted his shot glass. "Let the games begin."

Chapter Three

After I downed my drink, I lifted the glass in the air with a whoop alongside the six frat bros. I hated how Ryder would know my party-boy act was just that, an act. Hopefully, he wouldn't ruin my image with the others and thus, my tips. At least they'd never know my shot glass held water. Customers often requested—demanded—I have a drink alongside them. Saying no didn't always go over well, especially with these high-paying customers. Parker knew it and allowed some drinking. Top Shelf's policy permitted one alcoholic beverage every two hours for employees, so his employees didn't get sloppy and act like fools. Sometimes, I'd partake, but even one shot was too much around Ryder. I needed every ounce of sanity and reason when it came to that man. He could charm the damn feathers off a goose. I refused to give an inch where he was concerned.

"Damn, that is by far my favorite tequila," the biggest guy said. I'd recognized John Turko, known to fans as Turk, instantly. We frequently had pro hockey players come into Top Shelf. I'd been surprised by how many out-and-proud players existed and even more surprised by how many of their straight teammates accompanied them to a night out at a gay nightclub. Most were fun guys who tipped well, so I always loved a VIP table full of hockey players.

"All right, gentlemen, here are your cocktails." I distributed the bougie drinks around the table. Ryder accepted his last. I'd never know if he looked at me because I averted my eyes. No, not because I was a chicken but because I hated his smug ass, and he didn't deserve my attention.

Why the hell was his shirt so tight? For fuck's sake, I could see the outline of his damn nipples beneath the white material. And the outline of his firm pecs. Maybe even a hint of abs.

Showoff.

"Damn, this is good." One of the guys, a dude even blonder than Ryder, sipped his drink.

"Right?" I grinned at him. "What else can I get you, gentlemen?"

"Another round of shots, my man," Turk said. "We're getting fucked up tonight."

"Coming right up." I turned my back on Ryder and got my ass out of there as quickly as possible. That would be the goal of the night—excellent service with as little face time as possible with Ryder.

Though we'd gone to the same college, we'd rarely crossed paths in social settings. He was a frat boy, and I was an underprivileged introvert through and through—in school on scholarships and grants, needing to maintain high grades to keep them, and unwilling to rock the boat. Needless to say, I'd rarely seen him drunk, but I'd heard rumors about the sexy party boy with more money than sense. Everyone had wanted him, both male and female, but only one side got his attention, though he was rumored to give it out freely to those who did it for him. I could only imagine his charisma skyrocketed when he drank. A charming Ryder would only piss me off. No one had ever gotten under my skin like this man, and I couldn't risk my tip by running my mouth and telling him what an asshole I thought he was.

For the next hour and a half, I played my role of tip-seeking bottle service boy to perfection. I flirted, I danced, I delivered round after round of high-end alcohol with the luxurious flourish Top Shelf was known for, and I did it while avoiding Ryder as much as humanly possible. He and his buddies bounced between their table and the dance floor, going from sober to tipsy to drunk as our patrons tended to do.

My feet throbbed, my back ached, and my ears rang from hours of pulsing club beats—typical Saturday night. Overstimulation and exhaustion came with the territory, though I think I tended to reach my limits quicker than the average twenty-three-year-old. At least, I usually wanted to tap out long before my coworkers.

"Why do you get the table full of hotties?" Trevor pouted his glossy lips as he joined me in a five-minute water break in the staff room. "Do you see mine? It's a bunch of old men who just came here to drool over barely legal boy toys."

I raised an eyebrow as I lowered my icy water bottle from my lips. "I'm sorry... how many times have you told me you like older men? You should be like a pig in shit right now."

"Excuse me." Trevor gasped and pressed a hand to his bare chest. "The key word there is *older*, not old. Wrinkly balls are not it."

"My mistake." I pressed my lips together to keep from laughing at his horrified expression. "Well, you know what they say..."

His eyes lit up. "What? Tell me. I need to hear something inspiring right now. Give me your wisdom."

"Beggars can't be choosers, my friend."

Trevor's jaw dropped, and a gasp flew from him. "Excuse me?" he asked, pressing a hand to his bare chest again. "You did not just say something so cruel to me, Alex Morgan."

I hid my smirk behind the bottle of water. This moment of connection with my friend was just what I needed after the tension of waiting on a man I hated.

"I better get out and see to my table of hotties."

"Bitch, I do not beg. Men beg me, understand?" He narrowed his black-rimmed eyes at me. If glares were lasers, I'd be dead on the floor.

"Love you, Trev," I called as I hustled to the door.

"Sleep with one eye open tonight, Ally!"

Chuckling, I slipped from the staff room into the low-lit hallway. Immediately, the music assaulted my brain. All I had to do was survive a short time longer, and then I would head home for some peace unless my brother was awake. In that case, I'd most likely be heading home to some drama. And if my mom hadn't fallen asleep, she'd probably need some help.

Was twenty-three too young to be burned out? Some days, I felt like an eighty-year-old in a young man's body. Shaking my head, I started back toward the VIP lounge only to run smack into a hard, slightly damp body.

"Whoa, careful there." On impulse, I reached out to steady the unstable man. Firm biceps met my hands, and a familiar laugh registered, causing me to glance at an even more familiar face.

Ryder. Fuck.

He hiccupped and swayed. "Whoops. FL, how's it hanging, man?" He lifted his fist as though we were friends, and I'd give him a bump.

"Really?" That fucking nickname.

"Don't leave me hanging, FL." His eyes had the glossy sheen of someone who'd knocked back quite a few drinks, and his skin had the glossy sheen of someone who'd been dancing for as his ass off. I pretended I didn't notice the tiny green fleck in his left eye. The one I'd struggled not to stare at the entire summer I suffered through being his lab partner.

Rolling my eyes, I tapped my fist against his only because he'd reached the point of wasted and probably wouldn't remember the encounter in the morning. "You shouldn't be back here. This is the staff area."

He listed to the side, toppling into the wall. "I gotta take a leak. Got lost looking for the bathroom."

Great. Now, he was my problem. "Yes. The neon sign that says restroom is tough to find."

"Don't be mean, FL."

I grunted as my blood heated, and not because he smelled like the expensive cologne a saleswoman sprayed on me at the department store one time but because Ryder seemed to be the same ass he'd always been.

That fucking nickname.

He wore a goofy grin on his stupid, drunk face, completely oblivious to how ridiculous it was to call me a freeloader while at my place of employment.

"Oh, I love this song." He began to sing along in a slurred, off-key rendition that would make anyone's ears bleed.

Rude, oblivious, and drunk. Fantastic combination.

I huffed out my annoyance. "Come on, I'll show you where the restroom is."

"Thanks, FL."

"Fuck it," I muttered.

"You say sompin'?" He tried to step away from the wall, stumbled, and crashed into the opposite wall, where he stayed and laughed as though it was actually funny.

I watched him for a moment as my anger mounted. Who the hell did he think he was coming into my place of business, getting up in my face, and fucking insulting me? I'd taken so much shit from him over the years without a word to anyone. My tongue itched to unload all the hatred I'd stored up.

Maybe this was my chance. He was wasted and would probably miss by a mile if he tried to punch me.

"You know what? I did say something." I folded my hands across my chest and stretched the inch or two I had on him. "How fucking rude are you to be calling me freeloader when I'm here busting my ass, serving you and your drunk-ass friends for hours while you use Daddy's money to fucking pay for it?"

He blinked.

There went my tip. *Way to go, Alex.*

He stared at me wide-eyed for a moment as my stomach clenched, then he burst out laughing. "Oh my God, you're so funny. Busting your ass. This job is awesome. You can drink, dance, and stare at hot men all night. I would love this job."

"Sure, you would." I turned him and nudged him down the hallway. "I bet you've never gotten your own glass of water, let alone served somebody else. You'd quit before you finished one shift."

His face screwed up in drunken indignation. "Nuh-uh. I'd rock this shit. Easy as pie."

Irritation simmered beneath the surface of my skin, bubbling at a low rate but dying to surge to a full boil. Letting it out now would be a waste of my time and energy. He was smashed and had the boozy confidence only someone who'd been pickling their organs could pull off. Nonsense fell out of his mouth at this point. Getting pissed would only waste what little energy I had left. So instead of cussing him out, I shook my head and chuckled. "Say that to my face tomorrow."

"You'll see. I'm gonna come back t'morrow and apply for a job."

"You do that." Top Shelf didn't open on Sundays. I pushed him down the hall, maybe a little harder than necessary.

He'd better forget this damn conversation in the morning. How dare he threaten to home in on my territory?

"And you know what?"

I sighed. Who knew he'd be such a chatty drunk? "What?"

"I'm gonna work here, *and* Imma do a better job than you." He stumbled left, then chuckled as he tried to steady himself. "I'll get more tips."

Don't punch him. Don't punch him.

"The only thing you're gonna get is a killer hangover."

"I'm serious! First night, I'll get more tips than you."

The sad thing was, he probably would earn more in tips than I did. Ryder was the kind of guy who went around turning everything in his life to gold with one touch. The thought of him, a rich jackass who didn't need the money earning more than I did, was enough to have me clenching my fists at my sides. "Bathroom's over there," I said through clenched teeth as I pointed across the dance floor. "Go before you piss yourself."

"Aww, don't be grumpy, Alex." He did something that was probably supposed to be a dance move but looked more like a spasm. On anyone else, I'd be teasing them about their boozy state, but I just wanted him to get the hell out of my face before I did something to risk not only my tip but my whole job.

"I'm not grumpy. Just don't want to get stuck cleaning your piss off the floor."

"This is why I'll earn more in tips. I'm charming, and you're a grump." He tried to bump my shoulder with his but missed and nearly fell on his face, which set off his hysterical laughter. It only lasted a few seconds before panic crossed his face. "Oh shit, I really gotta take a leak."

"Over there." I pointed again.

He wobbled his way around the outside of the dance floor. After the first few steps, I forced myself to turn around. What did I care if he knocked into people or spilled someone's drink? Sighing, I hustled over to clear the empties from his table. The whole group of them were out on the dance floor, so I gathered the empty glasses and mopped up a few condensation rings from the marble table.

The music lowered, and 'last call' blared through the speakers. Immediately, fatigue washed over me. It'd been a long day, as most were, but it would soon come to an end. Cleaning up after the club closed never bothered me. Trevor hated it, complaining that once the customers left, he wanted nothing more than to go home. He called the thirty minutes spent cleaning pure torture.

I liked the quiet and the routine of wiping tables, stacking glasses, and mopping floors. I didn't have to act anymore. No one expected me to perform like a trained monkey for my tips. Closing tasks were always the same, and my overstimulated brain took comfort in that. Fifteen more minutes and the customers would disappear.

Ryder would disappear.

I'd be one step closer to going home and maybe catching a full five hours of sleep before my nine a.m. class.

"Alex!" Turko whacked me on the back with so much force I nearly sprawled across the table. "Sorry, man," he said with a laugh as he pulled me into a side hug as brutal as his back slap. "Don't know my own strength when I've been drinking. This place rocks. Next time I'm in town, I'm bringing the whole damn team." He let me go, then staggered a few feet to Ryder, who'd returned from the restroom. "You, too, Ry, you'll be here too. I love you, man."

The sing-song way he said that had my lips quirking. If I were a shittier person, I'd record it. A clip of Turko drunkenly professing his love to his old frat brother would go viral in minutes. Maybe that would get me more than fifty followers, and I could make a buck that way.

"'Course I'll be here." Ryder patted Turko's cheek. "I'm getting a job here."

"No shit?" Turk turned to me. "He is?"

"No." Over my dead body.

"Yes, I am."

"No, you aren't." The music cut off, and the lights came on to a soundtrack of groans from the remaining patrons. "Joke's over. Go home, Ryder."

Turk chuckled. "*Oooh*, someone doesn't like you very much, Ry."

Ry. I'd never considered calling him that. To me, he was always the formal Ryder, the ultra-rich jerk who made me feel like shit and now wanted to insert himself in my life where he didn't belong.

"Uber will be here in three mins," Turk said. "Come on. Thanks for an awesome night, my man."

"Great to meet you. See you next time." I turned and hightailed it out of there before Ryder could spout more bullshit about working here. Before I could reach my goal for the stock room to grab some more rags, a strong hand clasped my bicep and spun me around.

"What the hell?"

"Why are you being such a dick about me working here?"

"Oh, for fuck's sake. Why can't you let this go?"

"Because you have a huge stick up your ass. What the fuck you acting like I can't handle it? You don't own this damn club. All you do is serve drinks in your fucking underwear. I could do that in my sleep. And better than you."

Something exploded behind my eyes. I shoved him against the wall, holding him in place with my arm across his chest. No doubt, he could have gotten away without much effort.

Instead of fighting me, his eyes flared, and his breathing hitched. "Jesus, Alex, what the fuck?"

"You think I work here for fun?" I snarled as I pushed

against his chest. "Because I'm bored? Because I think it would be fun to hang in a club all night four times a week? Fuck you, Ryder. I'm here so I can eat. So my brother can eat. So we don't have to sleep on the streets. I'm here so I can pay my mo—"

An icy wave of nausea washed over me, and I shoved away from him, raking a hand through my hair.

Jesus. What the hell was I doing?

No one, not a single person, knew how dire my family's financial state was. Not even Trevor, who'd picked me up from my house when my ancient car crapped out a few months ago. I shielded my family's privacy like a lioness protecting her cubs. I sometimes wondered if shame kept my lips sealed instead of protective instincts, but that was something to work out with the therapist I couldn't afford.

Ryder laughed, and I had to clench my fist to keep from punching him in his smug face. At least the alcohol kept my words from fully registering in his brain.

"Touchy, touchy. Such a grumpy bear." His eyes lit up. "Oh my God—"

"No," I barked. "That is not going to be my new nickname."

"It so is."

All I could do was shake my head. "Your Uber has to be here by now. Go home, Ryder. And don't come back."

I walked away to the sound of his annoyed gasp.

Was I rude? Yep.

Had I blown my tip? Probably.

Did I care? Nope.

Mostly.

Okay, I cared about the tip a lot, but that ship had most likely sailed.

I left him to fend for his drunken self as I rummaged through the supply closet for rags and cleaning spray. By the time I made it back to my section, Trevor's was already sparkling clean. He'd gone behind the bar to help stack the clean glasses.

An envelope rested dead center on the table Ryder and his friends had abandoned. It had my name in a typical male chicken scratch. Their bill had been astronomical, but I bet I'd get a hundred bucks max. It's what I deserved for running my mouth, but I'd been hoping for at least eight hundred from this table. Being that I'd copped a major attitude to a paying customer, I'd probably end up needing to hand over the entire measly tip to the bartender and bussers instead of the standard thirty percent Top Shelf required.

I grabbed the envelope with a frown.

Huh, it was thicker than I'd expected.

As I opened it, my heart slammed against my ribcage. "Holy shit," I muttered. "There has to be..." I did a quick count and nearly swallowed my tongue. "Three thousand dollars?" Even giving away thirty percent, I'd still clear two thousand on this table alone. That would cover all my books and groceries and leave some money for new medical-grade compression stockings for my mom.

Were Ryder and his friends always that generous? Had he really left me this much money even though I'd been a dick to him all night? I groaned as a hot feeling of shame washed over me.

He'd always struck me as the type to leave a small tip. Maybe his friends had talked him into it. Turko definitely acted pleased with the service.

Hell, maybe Ryder left such a big tip because he felt sorry for me. Oh shit.

I froze, staring down at the money.

Was this pity money?

Chapter Four

"Will this be a common occurrence now that you've returned home?" My mother breezed into the room with her open robe floating around her like a silk parachute. Even at eight on a Sunday morning, she had a full face of professionally applied makeup and an artfully arranged hairdo her stylist had crafted. With the amount of time and money my mother spent making sure she looked perfect, she could have solved many of the world's problems.

My sister, Vera, who trailed in after our mother, snorted when she caught sight of me. Four years my junior and smack in the middle of college, Vera should have been the one with dark sunglasses, a vat of coffee, and a bottle of Motrin beside her plate of plain toast. Instead, she had a fresh face and sparkling eyes that spoke to a solid eight hours of uninterrupted sober sleep while I suffered.

"Aww, feeling a little hungover this morning, bro?" she asked with the kind of micro-aggressive sweetness only a sibling could pull off.

"I'm good," I mumbled into my coffee.

"Really, Ryder dear, shouldn't you be over this phase of life by now? You're not in a fraternity anymore."

Didn't I know it? The frat had given me a place to sleep that wasn't my stuffy childhood home with my image-conscious parents. I needed to get my own apartment and fast. Three weeks back at home had me losing my mind. Unfortunately, my parents were pressuring me to move into one of the hotels my father owned. Two of their five-star luxury hotels offered penthouse apartments with hotel amenities. They were gorgeous, trendy, and someplace anyone would kill to live. For me, moving there felt like a lateral move. Living in a building owned by my father's corporation would allow him a bird's-eye view of my life and the potential for control— his favorite hobby.

"There's no phase of life. I went out with some friends I haven't seen in a year and a half. We had a fun night. Sue me."

My mother's delicate scoff was the stuff of legends. She didn't yell or make a scene when she disapproved of someone's behavior—someone being my sister, father, or me. Instead, she let out the same grating cluck every time. She had the annoying tsk-tsk down to a science. The sound had an arrogant air of superiority that let us know whatever we'd done to earn the infamous scoff had her frowning down on us from her platinum tower. We lived so far below her that we looked like ants as we committed our sins.

My mother used shiny silver tongs to set a variety of fruit on her white plate. Cora, our family's longtime chef, knew better than to provide my mother with an actual stick-to-your-ribs breakfast. Nothing more than fruit and lemon tea for the figure-conscious Miranda Calloway. It was how she kept her petite frame skinny enough for the society pages.

"So," she said as she joined me at the table. "How are you planning to spend your time today?"

What the seemingly innocent question really meant was, now that you've quit grad school, how long are you planning to embarrass me with your lack of ambition?

"Yeah, big bro," Vera said with a smirk. "What are you planning to do with your life?"

They didn't want to know. They *really* didn't want to know. I'd come out to my parents at age twelve with less dread than I had now. Despite being in the top tier of the social elite, my parents were quite open-minded when it came to my sexual orientation. I think they enjoyed the philanthropy and recognition associated with supporting LGBTQIA+ causes more than they actually supported their gay son, but I couldn't complain. I'd had an easier time in that regard than almost any of my queer friends. Especially those few queer friends in my family's circle who were treated like a pariah or whose parents ignored their coming out and flat-out pretended their children were straight.

However, telling them how I wanted to spend my adult working years would not be met with the same acceptance, or any acceptance at all.

So, I went with a version of the truth. "I'm going to take off this semester, then enroll at Boston University. I've already been accepted for a transfer." To a completely different field of study, in which I'd have to take a few undergraduate-level classes before I could enter the master's program. Luckily, I could do them virtually. My first online class started tomorrow.

"Oh." My mother blinked. "Well, that's wonderful." Surprise and delight transformed my mother's face, which only made my stomach clench, and since I'd already puked up my guts this morning, this was not a good thing.

"Yeah." The word scraped my throat worse than the dry toast Cora generously made for my roiling stomach. "Uh, think I might get a job too." My lips twitched. No doubt, Alex went to bed and woke up this morning praying to the god of alcohol that I forgot my bold promise to work alongside him.

The details might be fuzzy, but the look of horror on his face wasn't. Who could forget that? It would be a blast. Music, liquor, and socializing with sexy men all night? It sounded perfect to me.

"Oh?" My mother tilted her head. "Your father didn't mention you'd be taking a job."

Because he didn't know. Because I wasn't going to be working at his corporation. Of course, in my mother's eyes, there were no alternative possibilities.

"No, uh…" My stomach lurched. "Since I'm taking off the semester, I decided to do something just for fun."

She arched a perfectly shaped light eyebrow. Vera and I got our blond hair from her genetic pool. "Oh?"

"Yeah, I'm going to be working at a nightclub. It's a high-end luxury one downtown."

My mom's shocked gasp met my ears at the same time my sister's eyes flared wide, and she bit her lower lip. I could still see her damn smirk.

"A nightclub?" my mother whispered as though the etiquette police might be listening. "Must you, Ryder? What will I tell people?"

"Are you going to be a bouncer? No, no… a go-go dancer?" Vera's eyes danced with mirth. I scratched my ear with my middle finger, making her laugh out loud.

"Vera, please don't laugh so loud. You sound like a hyena."

I nearly spit out my coffee. Vera shook her head while I shot her a victorious smirk.

"Please tell me this is a joke, Ryder." My mother's face had paled to an ashy gray. "You cannot possibly dance in your underwear for money. I swear, I've never understood your sense of humor."

Rolling my eyes, I pushed my mostly uneaten toast to the center of the table. "I will not be dancing around in my underwear for money. I'll be working the VIP section, serving overpriced drinks to luxury clients."

In my underwear, for money.

My mother frowned at her dragon fruit. "I don't like this, Ryder. This is not what we do. I don't think we should let this information leave the table."

"Oh, man." Vera pouted. "Just as I was getting all jazzed to tell everyone I know."

I narrowed my eyes at her before turning to my mom with a shrug. "You're making too big of a deal out of this. As I said, this is just a fun thing to pass the time until school begins next semester."

A flash of Alex getting up in my face last night spread through my brain like a lightning bolt. He'd been hot, sexy even, dressed in those damn tiny shorts with his nipples on display like two flashing bullseyes. The finer details were muddled thanks to Turk and his love of Reposado. I did remember how Alex had been furious with me, but he smelled so fucking good. Body soap combined with sweat and the scent of tequila.

You think I work here for fun?

What the hell did that even mean? Of course, I knew he worked at Top Shelf to make money. But the way he'd said it, with desperate fury, surprised me. Was his situation that dire? Or had I been more impaired than I realized, and my memories were distorted?

Regardless, if I secured a job working with Alex, two facts reigned. I'd get to see a lot more of his exposed body, and I'd have a blast dodging the death rays he'd send my way for the next few months.

Mom stood, pressing a hand to her chest. "I'll figure something out," she mumbled as though this was a serious problem she had to solve. "Excuse me. I'm late for Pilates." She left the room, abandoning her uneaten fruit plate for the staff to deal with.

"That went well," I muttered.

"What's up with you?" Vera's voice made me jump. She stared at me as she blew on her coffee. Unlike our mother, she had a makeup-free face and her blonde hair in a messy bun atop her head while wearing an old sweatshirt of mine with flannel pajama pants. "You left school, you're getting a job, are you having a quarter-life crisis or something?"

"I didn't leave school. I'm changing schools."

And my degree.

"Hmm." Her eyes narrowed. "Interesting."

I squirmed beneath her meddlesome gaze, then tugged at the collar of my hoodie. Had I gained weight? Why the hell did it feel like it was strangling me? "What the hell does that mean? *Interesting?*" I screwed up my face and exaggerated her tone.

A grin broke out across Vera's face. We share the same coloring, light skin that tanned easily, and blond hair we were lucky enough not to have to pay to achieve. We also shared blue eyes, but hers were darker, almost navy, especially when she was sticking her nose in my business.

"No need to get defensive, big brother. It doesn't mean anything. Usually, people have a reason for the things they do, and I'm just wondering what yours is."

I pulled my plate back to me with too much force, sending the toast sliding onto the white tablecloth. "I didn't realize you'd changed your major from chemistry to psychology." Even I heard how defensive that sounded. Scowling, I stuffed a bite into the toast with enough force to crack a tooth.

I should have asked for pancakes. Cora never failed to rock my favorite breakfast. I'd eaten in five-star restaurants across the globe, but nothing beat her homemade family recipe she'd been making me since I was in diapers.

"Har, har."

We ate in silence for a few moments. I tried to keep from

overthinking, but since I'd left school, the entire month before leaving, overthinking had become my default. There was a solution to it—tell my father why I'd decided to transfer schools. There'd be a blowup like never before, but it would be done, and my poor, overworked brain could finally have a break.

But I just couldn't.

Not yet.

Too bad Vera wasn't a psychology major. Maybe then she'd be able to help me screw my head on right.

"Hey, Ry…" Vera set her coffee mug down as she speared me with an intense look I'd never seen from her. "I know you think of me as the silly kid sister who always annoys the crap outta you, but I'm more than that. We're both adults now, and I want you to know I have your back. Whatever you're going through, you don't have to tell me." She held up a hand to stop me from protesting before the words could leave my mouth. "I just want you to know I'm here if you do want to talk or if you need some moral support. I'm not our parents, and I won't react the same way they would, even if it's something bad."

With that, she nodded once, then continued to work on her stack of pancakes. Maybe Cora had made enough for me. My stomach cramped, reminding me why I'd asked for toast.

I blinked and paused with the toast halfway to my lips, frozen in place by the sincerity in her voice. Was she right? Did I still see her as the girl who used to crush on my friends and steal my shit when she'd become my equal?

"Wow, V, thanks." I lowered the toast to my plate. "That… that really means a lot."

She shrugged as though her simple words hadn't shaken my foundation. "You're my only sibling. We should stick together."

She'd beaten me out in the maturity department, that was

for sure. We'd never been super close, but we'd never had a contentious relationship either. It was more of one where she did her thing, and I did mine. Clearly, she wanted that to change. My insides warmed. Maybe I wanted our relationship to change as well. Now that we lived under the same roof again, for however briefly, we had a chance to strengthen our bond.

Sharing with her might be the best way to do that.

"I, uh, I'm thinking of, well, I have changed my field of study for my Master's." I kept my eyes cast down, staring at the coffee in my mug.

"Wow, really? Will it be hard to work with Dad's company without an MBA?" She didn't sound judgmental or disapproving, only curious.

That lack of judgment had me lifting my gaze to meet hers. "Well, that's the thing. I, uh, I don't want to work with Dad's company, and I definitely don't want to run it someday. I never have."

Her mouth opened and closed a few times before a "Really?" squeaked out.

"Really? That's all you've got for me? Really?"

Her sheepish grin and shrug made me roll my eyes.

"Sorry, I'm just surprised. You've never expressed interest in anything else." She frowned. "Actually, you've never expressed interest in working with Dad either. It's always just been assumed you would."

"Exactly." Not once had anyone asked what I wanted to do with my future. I was a Calloway, so, of course, I'd be taking over the family business.

"Wow, Ryder, this is big." She rested her elbows on the table and gave me her undivided attention. "So what is it you want to do?"

My face heated, and I went back to admiring what now looked like a froth heart floating on top of my latte.

"Iwannabeateacher."

"Huh?" Her voice held a hint of laughter. "Didn't catch that. E-nun-ci-ate," she said, eyes alight with humor.

I sighed. What the hell? Might as well put it out into the universe. Had to happen sometime. "I want to be a teacher. Um, elementary school."

A few weeks ago, I read an article online claiming the core of a star could reach twenty-seven million degrees. Those stars had nothing on the temperature of my cheeks, which rose exponentially with each passing second of silence.

If Vera didn't say something soon, I'd be a pile of smoldering, humiliated ash on my mother's velvet dining chair. Not the way I wanted to go out. Maybe we could turn the air conditioning on. Sure, it was five degrees outside, but in here, it was a damn inferno.

As I opened my mouth to tell Vera it was all a big joke, she finally spoke.

"Hey, Ry, look at me."

If I groaned out loud, I didn't mean it. The noise should have stayed in my head. Still, she didn't sound as though she found what I'd said hilarious and stupid, so I lifted my gaze. Her grin had my heart clenching with hope. Could she be supportive of this idea?

"I think you would be a great teacher. No, not great, incredible."

"You do?" Later, I'd be mortified by the wavering of my voice.

"I do. You've always been good with kids. I recall when you volunteered at the LGBTQ+ youth center downtown during college. Those kids adored you."

"That's where I got the idea. I tried to ignore it, thinking it was just the novelty of doing something new, but it's been years, and I still want to get a teaching degree."

"Then do it." She shrugged. "Simple as that."

I barked out a laugh. "You know that's a lie."

"Okay, so Dad's brain will explode, but I don't think he'd disown you or anything. Oh, wait... is that why you're getting a job? Are you worried he'll stop paying for school?"

"No." Although now that she'd put the unpleasant thought in my head, it would be one I'd revisit and obsess about later. "That's not why. It's really just something to do while I wait to start school again."

"Okay, but why not try to get a job working with kids somewhere? Wouldn't that make more sense? Maybe you should..." Her grin changed from supportive to suspicious, and a chill ran down my spine. "Oh, I know what this is."

"What? There's nothing to know." Too bad my scoff sounded like a performance from a D-list actor.

"There's a guy, isn't there?"

"A guy? What? You're nuts." How did she do that? What the hell was she, an FBI investigator?

"Maybe, but you're a terrible liar. I wonder what it says about me that I'm more excited about your boyfriend than your career change."

That one had me laughing so loud that Cora popped her head in. Seeing us enjoying each other's company as well as her food, she nodded once, then disappeared back into the kitchen. "Pfft. I do not have a boyfriend. There isn't even a guy. At least not one I'm interested in." Shit, I could have slapped myself.

"Ah-ha!" She clapped her hands. "So there is a guy."

"No!"

She snorted, then stuffed a bite of pancake in her mouth. "There's a guy," she said with a mouth so full I could barely understand her.

"Cute. That's real cute, V. With the way you eat, we know no guy is coming after you."

She flipped me the bird, and I burst out laughing. Shit,

when had my sister become so much fun?

"Okay, fine. There's a guy, but it's not what you're thinking. I can't stand him. Or he can't stand me." I frowned. "We can't stand each other. This is a competition to see who the best bottle service boy will be. Nothing more, nothing less." To seal the statement, I took a sip of my lukewarm coffee.

"Ooh." Her eyes sparkled. "Enemies to lovers. My favorite trope."

My sip of coffee slid down the wrong way, ending in a coughing fit that had my eyes watering and nose dripping. "Enemies to what?" I asked as I grabbed my linen napkin.

"*Lo-vers.* There's a thin line between love and hate, Ry. And that line is very sexy."

"Ugh." I shuddered. "Two things. One, there is nothing sexy going on. He's an uptight jackass who doesn't know how to have a good time." A very hot one with a fine set of abs and biceps anyone would want to lick. "And two, you're not allowed to know the meaning of the word 'sexy.' Gross."

Snickering, Vera set her fork down on her empty plate and then stood up. "Gotta go, bro. Loved this chat. Tell me when you want me to meet your boyfriend." Then the little imp darted out of the dining room.

Meet my boyfriend. Insanity. Alex was the last man on earth who'd ever be my boyfriend. But a night rolling around in the sheets? I could sure get on board with that, even though it was hard to imagine him letting go enough to enjoy a good fuck.

"Hey, what the hell is a trope?" I called to her retreating back.

Chapter Five

Morning came too fast as it always did on the nights I worked.

Sunday tended to be my most and least favorite day of the week. I didn't have to work at the club. I had time to focus on my school assignments, and if I played my cards right, sometimes I had a few hours to myself to do whatever the hell I wanted.

On the other hand, the day often fell apart despite my intentions to combine productivity and relaxation. Last Sunday, my mother had a reaction to a new medication, and we spent nine hours in the emergency room giving her IV Benadryl. The Sunday before, my brother didn't come home from wherever he'd crashed Saturday night. Mom was so distressed and worried that I'd spent much of the day driving to his favorite haunts, searching for him without success. He'd strolled in at six in the evening, hungry and furious we had the audacity to ask him where he'd been.

Kenny turned eighteen almost a year ago, and since then, he'd been a nightmare. To be fair, he'd been a nightmare since his first day as a teenager, but now that he was an 'adult,' his challenging nature had grown exponentially. He felt he no longer owed us explanations for his actions, could do whatever the hell he wanted, and was now a 'real man,' one who didn't have a job—well, not a legal one. I was pretty sure he started selling drugs. He didn't own a car, didn't contribute to a bill, and didn't do a damn thing to help take care of our medically complicated mother.

So, I didn't have high hopes for relaxation when I woke up Sunday morning. Typically, I hopped right out of bed the second I woke up, but today, I lingered. If I remained tucked away in my room, under my covers, I could avoid reality for a few minutes longer.

At least I had one thing going for me—there was no way Ryder would apply for a job at Top Shelf. He'd wake up hungover and unhappy and either puke when he remembered offering to get a job with the ordinary people, or he'd forget the entire thing. If that was the best thing that happened to me today, I could consider the day a net positive.

A soft knock on the door had me suppressing a groan. There went my avoidance of reality. "One sec," I called out as I tossed my covers to the side. I kicked my legs over the edge, letting the momentum drag my upper body into a sitting position as I reached for the cup of water on my thrifted nightstand. Then I grabbed a pair of black sweats from the foot of my bed. Sleeping naked wasn't my thing, but I couldn't stand going to bed in anything more than my boxer briefs. Once my bottom half was covered so I wouldn't scare my poor mom, I opened the door to find her sitting in her wheelchair in the hallway.

"Morning, Ma. You okay?"

"Yes, honey, I'm fine." No matter how bad things got, and with her progressive multiple sclerosis, they could get bad, she always answered with those exact four words. She carried a truckload of guilt on her shoulders for being unable to work or fully care for herself and felt like a constant burden, no matter how many times I assured her she wasn't. Maybe always telling me she was fine was her way of alleviating her conscience. If she could convince herself she was okay, it could be true.

We never discussed it beyond her apologizing for burdening me and my refutation of the claim. Neither of us were skilled at delving into our feelings and discussing them. Perhaps it had something to do with growing up without a father and a mother who had to spend most of her energy on simply getting through the day. Or perhaps we had a genetic deficiency—a missing piece of the puzzle that didn't allow us to share our emotions.

Ugh, even thinking about it gave me the ick.

"So what's up? Need some help getting breakfast?"

"No, I'm not hungry yet."

I frowned. One of her newer medications killed her appetite. She'd already lost ten pounds over the last month. I'd have to talk to her doctor about it because she didn't have extra to spare.

"Your brother is sleeping on the couch."

"Okay…" I tilted my head. "At least he came home, right? Why don't you wake his ass up and tell him to move to his bed?"

"Well, because he's completely naked."

Of course he was.

She leaned closer. "And he's not alone," she whispered.

I froze. "Excuse me?"

"There's some woman with him."

Oh, hell no.

"And there is… stuff on the coffee table."

Stuff? Christ, if I had to see his congealed spunk where I liked to eat my dinner, I'd fucking castrate him.

"I didn't want to wake him up and embarrass him. What

should we do?"

Embarrass him? I snorted like a bull about to charge. Embarrassment was the least of what I planned to do to his disrespectful ass.

My mom's eyes, the same shape and color as mine, practically overflowed with anxiety. Why? Why did she treat Kenny with kid gloves, like he was a cute, helpless puppy instead of a man old enough to go to war? Why had I never received the same blasé treatment? I loved my mother with all my heart but didn't understand her. The only thing I could think was that she went so easy on Kenny because she carried extra guilt over becoming sick when he was so young. At least I had a decade with a healthy mother. I could remember the effort she put into Christmas morning, the way she loved to bake us homemade chocolate chip cookies, and how she never missed an event at school. Kenny never even had that much, and what he did have, he'd been too young to recall. To make up for it, she allowed him to do whatever the hell he wanted, leaving me to be the bad guy.

I tried to exhale my fury but only managed to bring it down to severe annoyance. "I'll take care of it, Mom. Why don't you go get ready for church?" I didn't attend, but a neighbor always accompanied Mom to Mass every Sunday.

Her gaze shifted toward our living room. "All right, but try not to make him feel bad."

Heaven forbid he feel a moment of remorse for his actions.

She patted my hand. "We all make mistakes."

"Some more than others," I muttered.

"What's that, honey?"

"Nothing." I grabbed the handles of her wheelchair and rolled her to her room. "You just worry about what you're going to wear to church, okay? And holler for me if you need some help."

"You're such a good boy, Alex. Thank you."

"Sure, Mom." I kept my lips curled upward until I shut the door behind me. Then the smile flipped. This bullshit ended today. I spun toward the mouth of the hallway, bumping my shoulder against the white stucco wall. Why on earth would anyone ever put a wall with hard, pointy lumps in a house? That damn stucco had been responsible for dozens of injuries throughout my childhood. I still had a scar on my elbow from where I'd busted the skin open when I was nine, so I knew how the spurs would dig into my palm as I pressed it against the wall as hard as possible to release some frustrated energy, but I did it anyway. It was either that or punch a hole through the wall, and that would not only alert my mom to my anger but also destroy my knuckles. Not something I had time for. I couldn't carry trays of alcohol all night with bruised and bloodied hands.

As the pain registered in my palm, I blew out a breath. It didn't work. I still wanted to murder Kenny. My pounding footsteps down the hall would have woken the dead, but when I reached the living room, there slept Kenny prone on the couch with his pale ass on full display. "Lovely," I muttered. A second later, I noticed the sleeping female curled up on one end of the couch. Thankfully, whoever she was, she had a blanket over her because the bare shoulder peeking out didn't lead me to believe she wore clothes either.

Waking Kenny would suck. Dread filled my gut. Who wanted to start their Sunday with an epic battle? As I bent to retrieve a tattered sofa pillow to whack my brother, I caught sight of something on the coffee table. Mom's warning about *stuff* came back to me.

I shut my eyes and then rubbed my fingertips back and forth above my eyebrows where the ache was brewing. *Please don't let that be what it is.* Despite my earlier thoughts, Kenny's congealed jizz would have been preferable.

When I opened my eyes, my stomach plummeted, and my

shoulders sagged.

Still there—a burned spoon, lighter, and a length of rubber tubing. The scene was right out of every cop drama ever aired. Cliché and accurate.

Every inch of my skin flashed hot and prickly. I snatched the pillow off the floor and brought it down on Kenny's head as hard as I could. "Wake the fuck up, you selfish shit." I hit him again. And again.

"Jesus, what the fuck?" The slurred words were heavy with sleep and remnants of a powerful high. "Alex? Ow! Stop fucking hitting me."

I whaled on him again. "Doing this shit in Mom's house? What the fuck is wrong with you?" As I lifted my arm to hit him again, he rolled over, giving me a prime view of his junk. "Oh, come on." I tossed the pillow at him instead of hitting him. "Cover that shit up."

"Hey, watch the goods." The pillow landed on his crotch. "You sure you're a gay dude? It shouldn't bug you out this much to look at a dick." He covered the offending appendage with the pillow as he shoved hair out of his face.

I grunted. "I just don't wanna look at *your* pencil dick. Who's your guest?"

"Huh?" He blinked up at me from flat on his back.

"Your guest." I pointed toward the end of the couch, where the girl was still sleeping. Knowing my luck, she'd overdosed and wouldn't ever wake up.

Kenny struggled but eventually got himself sitting. Thankfully, he was kind enough to keep the pillow over his crotch. "Huh. Who is that?"

Seriously?

"You're naked and asleep on the couch with a woman, and you have no idea who she is?"

He shrugged. "Some bitch I picked up last night, I guess."

I smacked his bare shoulder so hard he yelped.

"Ow, what's that for?" he asked, rubbing his upper arm.

"Don't be fucking disrespectful. Since when do you call women bitches?"

"She can't hear me. She's fucking sleeping."

"Kenny…" I pinched the bridge of my nose as I tried to control my breathing.

"Oh my God, you're so annoying." He shrugged, then let out a loud belch. "I'll get rid of her."

I sighed as the muscles in my neck knotted until they practically cramped. Kenny hadn't always been like this. A few years ago, he'd been the damn golden boy of Carson High School. Somehow, despite our mother's neurological disease, no fatherly influence, and my complete inability to catch anything smaller than a beach ball, Kenny excelled at sports, baseball in particular. He'd made the varsity team in ninth grade, the first to do so in two decades, according to the athletic director, and ended up team MVP. College scouts were already talking about him during his sophomore year.

He'd been going places.

Then, one gorgeous, sunny, warm morning of his junior year, the kind of day Massachusetts rarely had in early spring, he flipped over his handlebars riding his bike to school. It was a freak accident that left him with a shattered tibia and ruined dreams. He'd been coasting downhill at a crazy rate of speed, the way only a cocky high schooler could, when a damn black cat ran out in front of him. On instinct, Kenny squeezed his brakes, bringing his bicycle to a jarring halt. Unfortunately, the momentum of the abrupt stop sent him sailing over the handlebars.

Since that day, Kenny had been on a downward trajectory full of apathy, self-pity, and drugs. His body healed, though not well enough for college-level baseball, but he'd never been able to pull himself out of the black hole of despair that losing baseball tossed him in.

"Can you get rid of that shit too?" I pointed to the table where he had his drug paraphernalia scattered around. "Then, when you're done, you owe Mom an apology. She's the one who found you, her, and this shit," I said as I pointed to his paraphernalia.

Kenny paled, and instead of feeling guilty for rubbing his bad choices in his face, triumph surged through me. If the thought of disappointing our mom caused that reaction, some of the old Kenny must be hiding in the shell of my brother. It didn't take more than a second, though. He sniffed and rolled his shoulders as his fuck-the-world mask fell back into place. "Screw you. Stop trying to be my fucking father. I'm an adult, Alex. I don't gotta do shit you say."

I couldn't help laughing. "An adult. Right. An adult with no job, no education, and no prospects, who's living in his mom's house rent-free while disrespecting her every chance he gets. You're one goddamn bump away from an arrest or a hospital stay. Good luck paying for that shit with no insurance."

My voice rose to a shout. The girl on the couch groaned and shifted. "Too loud, baby. 'M tryna sleep." A rat's nest of dark hair covered her face, but I'd guess she was pretty. Kenny always reeled in beautiful girls with his charm and good looks. Apparently, willingness to share heroin didn't hurt among his preferred crowd.

"Baby?" I mouthed.

Kenny shrugged.

This was not how I wanted to spend any part of my time. "Get rid of her," I said in a harsh whisper. "And get rid of this shit. You've got five minutes."

Kenny snorted.

"I'm serious, Ken."

"Yeah, yeah, unwad your panties, bro." He waved a hand in my direction without looking at me.

Enough of this shit. If I didn't leave, I'd burst a blood vessel in my brain and stroke out. I threw my hands in the air and marched out of the living room. What a shitty start to what was supposed to be my one day of quasi-freedom.

At least I still had one thing going for me. There was no way in hell Ryder would be getting a job at Top Shelf.

Chapter Six

The daytime vibe in a nightclub was strange, to say the least. While the décor hadn't changed from Saturday night—the sexy, dark green velvet curtains draped the black walls, elegant gold light fixtures dangled from the ceiling, and the gorgeous bar gleamed with cleanliness—everything else felt off. The space was so quiet that my footsteps reverberated as I crossed the buffed wooden dance floor. Bright lights illuminated every inch of the space, eliminating the shadowed, sexy atmosphere from the other night. The club felt vast and lonely without bodies crammed in every corner, writhing to the beat.

I wanted to turn off the lights, crank up the speakers, and shed most of my clothing.

This was unnerving.

"Unnerving, isn't it?" A deep, commanding voice had me whipping around to find a gorgeous man wearing a suit perfectly tailored to his medium frame. He had dark hair with a sprinkle of salt, giving him the distinguished look of a gracefully aging A-list Hollywood star.

"It is. Not gonna lie, I like it better dark, loud, and crowded."

The man half-smiled. It made his dark eyes twinkle, but didn't erase his grave, almost severe countenance. "So do I, considering that's when I make my money."

I chuckled. "You must be Mr. Hughes." I hurried across the dance floor to greet the club's owner. "Ryder Calloway," I said as I extended my hand.

"Parker, please. I hate the formality of having my employees call me Mister, especially considering what I make them wear to work." He winked, and I laughed out loud.

What a pleasant surprise. On first impression, everything about this man seemed formal, from his Armani suit to his shiny shoes—were those alligator? Nice—to his impeccable posture and even his flawless skin. Parker seemed the type to demand rigid perfection from his employees rather than allowing them to use his first name for their comfort.

But I'd never had a boss, so what the hell did I know?

"Parker it is," I said, shooting him the grin I'd been told charmed many men into my bed. Well, my pants, anyway, most never made it as far as my bed. Club bathrooms and random rooms at a frat house were more my style—quicker and less messy that way.

"Come on up to my office." Parker turned and strode toward a back hallway. "I prefer to conduct interviews up there."

I couldn't help but admire the man's backside as he walked, both his ass and the expanse of his shoulders. I'd bet beneath that very well-fitting suit he had a nicely muscled body, probably sprinkled with the same salt and pepper hair his head boasted. All in all, Parker was a devastatingly handsome man. The man must be drowning in dick, owning the most exclusive gay nightclub in Boston.

Older men didn't do much for me. Sure, I could admire them and my cock had no problem appreciating the view, but I never went after them. I had enough issues with my real father. I didn't want a man thinking he could act like my daddy and tell me what to do.

No fucking thank you.

I followed him up a staircase directly into a large, glamorous office. The office's rear wall was the same obsidian as the walls downstairs, but the front was a semicircle lined with windows. Parker had a perfect view of the bar, half the dance floor, and the VIP section. Somehow, I'd failed to look up when I'd been here Saturday night. Otherwise, I'd have noticed this setup where Top Shelf's king spent his nights observing his empire in action.

"Please, have a seat," he said as he strode to a black wooden desk. "Welcome to my office, which has been dubbed the Bird's Nest by my staff."

I chuckled as I sat across the desk from him in a plush chair, the same green velvet as the curtains. It was luxurious and so damn soft I wanted to strip down and rub my naked body all over it. I'd bet money Parker had fucked in his chair. Or at least sat bare-assed while an eager-to-please man kneeled between his legs and choked on his cock.

I sure would have.

"Thanks. It's beautiful in here. The entire club is gorgeous. You have one hell of a decorator."

Parker grinned with pride. "Thank you. This place is my world." Something about the way he said those words had me tilting my head to study him. There seemed to be an undercurrent of sadness hidden beneath his posh exterior.

Interesting.

And not my business.

I was there to work, hopefully, and show Alex he wasn't the only man who could rake in monster tips.

"So you're interested in a position as a bottle service boy?"

"I am."

Parker leaned back in his leather captain's chair, folding his hands across his stomach. "That position is Wednesday through Saturday nights from nine p.m. until two a.m. After two, we close up, and as soon as the place is spotless, you can go."

"Sounds great."

"Have you been to my club before? As a patron?"

"I have. I was here this past Saturday night."

He nodded. "So you're aware of the uniform. It's... small, but customers love it."

I flashed him a grin. "Not a problem. I was a fan of it myself."

A fan of Alex in it, not that anyone would ever find that out.

"Do you have experience with bottle service or bartending?"

"I do not, but I have plenty of experience paying for it, so I've picked up a few things."

Parker grunted and frowned.

Shit. The man was not impressed with me.

"This job is not as frivolous as it seems, Ryder. Bottle service is not an excuse to party. Customers are often overly friendly and want you to party with them. My BSBs are allowed one drink or shot every two hours. Most don't even drink that much. It gets old. They pour themselves water or apple juice and shoot that as often as the client asks."

That little shit. No wonder stick-up-his-ass Alex was happy to down every round we'd asked him for and never wobbled once. He'd been cheating all night.

"That makes sense. Hard to do your job if you're sloppy."

He nodded. "I also have a strict no-fraternization policy with customers or other staff. At least while you're on the clock or in the building. I don't give a shit what or who you do on your own time, but my club is not a meat market. It's the highest-end gay nightclub in all of Boston for a reason.

Everything we do is a level above, and I hold all my employees to that standard."

Seriously? A bunch of hot guys working in their damn underwear and he thought they adhered to this no-fraternization policy? I'd bet my first night of tips that rule was broken and broken often.

Parker chuckled. "I can see the wheels turning in your head. I'm very aware that sex of all kinds happens here every night. I'd need an extraordinary amount of security to prevent it, and then I'd lose business, so I'm willing to look the other way, but not when it comes to my staff. I will not have my club subjected to bad press because my staff can't control themselves."

"Understood. That won't be an issue."

He studied me for a moment, seeming to assess my believability. More likely to determine how much of a horndog I was and whether I'd follow his keep-it-in-your-pants-at-work rule, which I could. I wasn't there to hook up. I was there to one-up.

"Your timing is perfect," Parker said. He unfolded his arms and opened his desk, drawing out a packet of paperwork. One of my long-time guys resigned yesterday. He's starting an internship and can no longer keep such late nights."

"Oh, that is good timing."

"The first month is a probationary trial. You'll shadow and co-service with one of my guys for a week, then have one table with some oversight from your mentor. After a month, we meet, and if it's going well, you'll have more tables on your own."

A devilish excitement zinged through me. "So, uh, I actually know Alex. I've known him for years. He'd be the perfect one to train me." I gave Parker my most innocent smile.

"Oh, really?" He jotted something on a notepad. "I'm just

making a note of that."

This was almost too easy. Any simpler and it wouldn't be fun.

"Yeah, we go way back. Met at a summer enrichment program in high school."

Parker glanced up from his note-taking. "Well, I've gotta say, you being friends with Alex is the best reference you could have. He is by far my hardest worker. He very rarely calls out, has never been late, and often locks up for me at night. Customers adore him and request his section more than any of my other bottle service boys."

I frowned. Listening to Parker sing Alex's praises threatened to ruin my new job buzz. However, the thought of outperforming him and becoming the apple of his boss' eye pumped me right back up.

"He's so great." Somehow, I managed to get the words past my lips without gagging.

"When can you start?"

"Well, you said Wednesday to Saturday, and today's Wednesday, so..."

"Fantastic." He slid the packet of papers across the desk. "Fill these out, please. There's a section on the application for your sizes so we can get you a few uniforms. I'll have them ready for you when you come back at nine tonight."

"Sounds perfect." I picked up the Mont Blanc pen on top of the papers and got to work. The forms were straightforward, and within a few minutes of silence, I had them filled out and signed my final signature. "All done. There you go." I slid them back across the desk.

"Great, I'll get—"

"Oh, Parker..." A sing-song voice floated up from the staircase. "I brought you some lunch because I'm assuming you haven't eaten, and have been working since six in the morning when you kicked some needy boy out of your bed to come here. Oh, sorry..."

A wide-eyed guy who couldn't have been more than five feet six inches appeared at the top of the staircase, holding a white takeout bag. He had platinum blond hair with blue tips, and I couldn't tell which was tighter, his sunny yellow crop top or his skinny jeans.

Parker sighed. "Trevor, what have I said about unannounced visits during the day?"

The growled tone didn't seem to bother this Trevor guy in the least. A mischievous grin curled his glossy lips. "You said not to. Guess I didn't listen. Oops. If you feel you have to punish me, I suppose I deserve it." His grin slipped into a juicy pout.

I snorted out a laugh. It couldn't be helped. This guy had it bad for Parker and had no problem expressing it.

"Trevor..." The rumbled tone held a warning Parker didn't seem to realize would only encourage his much younger fan. "I'm finishing an interview. Can we please have a few minutes?"

As though Parker hadn't spoken, Trevor sashayed into the room and set the food bag on the desk. Then he propped his bubble butt against it and gave me his full attention. "Hello there, handsome. What's your name, and why do you look familiar?"

Damn, this guy was a firecracker and a half. "Ryder," I said, holding out my hand. "And I was here Saturday night."

"He's replacing Lars. Starts tonight." Parker narrowed his eyes at the bag. The delicious aroma of Mexican food permeated the room. Hell, if he didn't want it, I'd eat it. "Oh, and he knows Alex."

"We go way back."

Not a lie.

A storm cloud moved across Trevor's face, darkening his features. "Wait... you're—"

I hopped to my feet. "Well, thank you, Parker." Shit. Trevor knew who I was. The gig was up. If he told Parker how much Alex hated me, I'd be out on my ass in a heartbeat. Time to go. "I'm really looking forward to working here. See you gentlemen tonight."

I turned and darted toward the staircase without offering to shake either man's hand. If they found it rude, so be it. I could come back from a minor infraction like a rude exit. I couldn't come back from the boss learning that the golden boy of his staff hated my guts. Hopefully, Trevor wouldn't spill my secret. He seemed so smitten with his boss that he'd probably forget about me five seconds after I left him alone with the object of his desire.

Was Parker getting some from Trevor? Did he break his own ironclad rule and bend Trevor over his sturdy desk after hours, or was he as much of a stickler with himself as he seemed to be with the staff? I'd find out soon enough. Workplace secrets never stayed buried long.

As soon as I stepped outside, harsh, frigid wind whipped across my face. Winter in New England meant business, and I hadn't dressed warm enough, something my mother had complained about since I was a kid. I tugged my leather jacket closed as I jogged toward my Range Rover. Once inside with the engine running, my seat warmers kicked into gear, and within seconds, I sat in a cocoon of warmth and comfort. This sure would come in handy on a middle-of-the-night drive home after a shift at Top Shelf.

I laughed out loud. None of my buddies would believe I'd gotten a job serving alcohol in a nightclub. God, I couldn't wait to see the look on Alex's face when he saw me in my skimpy uniform. His head might explode.

My father would also lose his shit if he caught wind of this —another reason to start looking for an apartment. Over the past few days, I'd had fun reconnecting with my sister.

Maybe she and I could get an apartment together near campus.

The more I thought about it, the better that idea sounded. I'd have to run it by her later.

Just as I was about to put the car in gear, my phone rang through the car's Bluetooth.

"Dad calling," the generic female voice announced.

"Answer phone," I commanded my electronic helper. "Hi, Dad, what's up?"

"Hello, Ryder. I trust your day is going well?"

Rolling my eyes, I pulled out of the parking spot. "Yeah, not bad."

"I have a meeting this afternoon with the CEO of a biomedical company I'm considering investing in. I'd like you to join us. The more you get involved now, the easier it will be once you've finished your MBA."

'I'd like you to join us' sounded like a benign offer, but it wasn't. It was a command. He might as well have said, "Get your ass here in twenty minutes if you know what's good for you." And since I'd yet to tell him I had no interest in the life plan he'd been laying out for me my entire life, I had no excuse to bail on him.

"Uh, okay, I can be there in about half an hour. I just need to run home and change." My stomach dropped at the thought of spending the afternoon watching businessmen mentally jerk each other off while trying to screw each other over at the same time. I loathed the whole corporate environment. The thought of commanding a billion-dollar corporation made me want to hurl, while spending my day wrangling a classroom of little gremlins sounded like heaven.

"Excellent. I'll have Cindy print you some credentials so you can access the executive floors. They'll be at the front reception desk before you get here. Proud of you, son. There's nothing I've ever wanted more than to pass on my legacy to my son."

Bile crawled up my esophagus, burning my throat. What the hell was I doing? He'd never accept this. Not in a million years. He had the power to stop me, and I feared he'd do it without losing a wink of sleep.

"Thanks, Dad. See you soon." Each word cut like shards of glass ripping through my tongue.

The phone beeped as my father ended the call.

"Fuck," I said as I pulled up to a red light and slammed my hand against the leather steering wheel.

"*Fuck.*"

Chapter Seven

"I'm not late. I'm not late!" I rushed into the staff room with snowflakes flying off my parka. The snow had started a few hours ago, and I miscalculated how hard it was coming down when I left home. As a result, I'd spent the whole drive stressing about making it to work on time.

Oliver, a go-go dancer who only worked at Top Shelf on Wednesday nights, smirked from where he stood, adjusting his chest harness. "I don't know, man. I think you were due in about twenty seconds ago. Better watch it, or Park will dock your pay."

"Stuff it, smartass."

Oliver grabbed his junk, prominently displayed in his shimmery black jock. "No stuffing necessary. Something you'd know if you took me up on my weekly offer for a fun time in BJ Alley."

I snorted. "Never gonna happen, Ollie. Time to move on." Oliver didn't really want me. The over-the-top flirting was nothing more than a fun game between us. He tended to go for the big, burly types who could throw him around. While I could get on board with a bit of rough handling, I didn't have what it took to manhandle the six-foot-two weightlifter.

Apparently, not many did if his constant complaining about not finding someone who could hold him down and rail his ass like he deserved meant anything.

I preferred someone more my equal. A dude I could fight for dominance and sometimes come out on top.

And other times on the bottom.

Damn, it'd been a while since another man had touched my dick. Too long.

The door flew open, and Trevor burst in, looking like a furry marshmallow in a long white coat with a fur-trimmed hood, white snow boots, and an equally white fluffy scarf hiding everything but his eyes. "I refuse to serve drinks in my damn underwear tonight," he grumbled as he stomped toward his locker. "I don't care if I lose tips. It's too damn cold to be running around damn near naked. If I accidentally brush a bottle against my nips, it'll shatter."

"Buck up, princess." Oliver shut his locker and smeared body oil across his ripped torso. "You know you'll be sweating your scrawny little ass off in five minutes."

Trevor whipped around and gasped. "How dare you!" The swish of his puffy coat took some of the ferocity out of his complaint. "My ass is not scrawny. It may be tiny, but it is a firm, round work of art, you big lug." He yanked his scarf from his face and shoved off his hood. "Take it back!"

I shook my head, pressing my lips together to hide my snicker, but Oliver let his fly free.

"I'm sorry, Trev," he said as he walked over and then kissed Trevor on the cheek. "I take it back. Your ass is spectacular." He slapped said ass, then turned my way, rolling his eyes, and I couldn't contain my snort of laughter any longer.

"Heard that," Trevor grumbled. "But it is spectacular, so I'll let it slide." He sniffed, then began working on the buttons of his long coat.

"All right, I'm heading out before Parker sends a search party. See you boys in the trenches."

"Bye, babe," Trevor said.

I made some noise of farewell.

"Work it for those tips," Trevor added.

"Always do." Waving over his shoulder, Oliver disappeared through the door while giving us a prime view of his muscular ass cheeks displayed by the jock. "You can only stare if you tip, boys," he yelled right before the door hid the impressive sight from view.

I grunted. If I didn't get moving myself, I'd be late, but Trevor had a point. Taking my clothes off on nights like this felt like torture until I got into the swing of serving and worked up a sweat.

"Hey, Alex, I need to talk to you about something."

"What's up?" I shed my coat and then turned to Trevor, who had a worried expression. "Everything okay?"

"Yeah, I'm good. It's not about me." He sat on the bench in front of the lockers and then stood straight up again. "Um, I should have texted you this, but I thought it'd be better to tell you in person. Now I'm wondering if I should have given you more of a heads-up."

I frowned. "Okay…"

"Parker hired someone to replace Lars," he said of the BSB who'd resigned last week.

"Wow, that was fast." What was the problem? "Isn't this a good thing? Less work for us. We were going to have to cover extra tables until he hired someone."

"Yeah…" Trevor shuffled in place. "It's just that he doesn't have any experience, and you're going to be training him."

"Oh." I huffed out my relief. Trev knew training new employees wasn't my favorite task, but I'd done it in the past and knew it would happen again. "That's no big deal. As long as he's not a bumbling idiot, it should be fine. We're not exactly doing rocket science here, Trev. I can suck it up for a few weeks." I pulled my sweatshirt over my head and tossed it into my locker.

"Sure, I know. It's not about training someone. It's more who you'll be training," Trevor said as I drew my T-shirt off. "Try to keep this newfound positive attitude you seem to have developed."

I flipped him off, which made him laugh.

"Exactly. Good job. Anyway, Parker hired R... oh shit."

The door opened, and Parker strode in with his typical commanding posture. "Hey, guys," he said. "I wanted to introduce you to our newest hire. This is Ryder."

I froze, my long-sleeved T-shirt halfway covering my face.

He didn't say Ryder. Tell me he didn't say Ryder.

"Oh, wait, you already know Alex, right?"

In my state of shock, I seemed to have forgotten how to get undressed. I flailed inside my T-shirt like a toddler playing dress-up.

Someone chuckled, and my stomach lurched. I'd know that amused laugh anywhere.

Ryder was standing in the staff room. My staff room.

I finally yanked the damn shirt off and came face-to-arrogant-face with the one person I'd have been happy to go my whole life without seeing.

"That's right, Parker. Alex and I have known each other for years."

He'd done it. He got a job at Top Shelf.

How much trouble would I get in if I punched that half-smirk off his handsome—no, stupid—face? I narrowed my eyes and took a step forward. "What the fu—"

"Hey, I'm Trevor. We met for half a second earlier." Trev slid in front of me, holding his hand out to Ryder and blocking my ability to clock the guy. "Welcome to Top Shelf," he said as friendly as could be.

Traitor.

Or maybe my savior.

Had I really been about to hit the guy right in front of my boss?

"Thanks, Trevor. I'm excited to work with you."

To the rest of the world, Ryder was as chill and friendly as could be. To me, he'd been a giant dick from day one.

"All right, I'll leave you in their capable hands, Ryder," Parker said as he clapped a hand on Ryder's bare shoulder. "You're up for training him, right, Alex?"

Oh shit. How had I not noticed he was already dressed in the Top Shelf signature ass-hugging uniform? If there had been any justice in the universe, he'd have a terrible body covered in gorilla hair and warts. But, no, someone up in the ethos clearly hated me because Ryder was fucking gorgeous —smooth, bronzed skin without any chest hair, just how I liked it. Rolling hills and valleys of muscles were everywhere the eye traveled. Not that mine did. I kept them firmly on his sea-blue eyes. The kind rarely seen without contacts, of course.

One fair eyebrow rose in a perfect arch, challenging me.

Like what you see?

Fuck no, I don't. You're not my type at all.

"No problem, Parker," I managed.

Trevor snorted, so I shot him my second-most-annoyed glare. The first was reserved for Ryder and Ryder alone.

"I'll be upstairs if you need me," Parker said as he turned.

Trevor cocked his head and didn't bother to hide his sigh as he watched Parker's ass stride out of the staff room.

"Got a little thing for the bossman, do you?" Ryder asked with a grin.

"I do," Trevor answered, making my jaw drop. The worst-kept secret in the place was Trevor's ginormous crush on the head honcho, but I'd never heard him admit it out loud. "So keep your hands to yourself."

Ryder lifted said hands in surrender, chuckling. "Not a problem, man. He's not my type. Too intense."

"Exactly." Trevor winked and shivered. *"Exactly."*

I bit my lip to keep from laughing aloud. Ryder didn't need to know Trevor and I were close, or he'd set out to become even closer friends with him. And while I tended to agree with Ryder about Parker's intensity, I'd be keeping that factoid to myself as well. I had enough baggage of my own without having to crack through some mysterious man's walls.

No one said anything else for a few moments. I frowned at Ryder across the silence while he stood there with that shit-eating grin as though he had no idea how I could possibly be unhappy with his presence.

"Uh, okay, well, I'm gonna get my tables set up and let you two get, uh... get started with Ryder's training." Trevor grabbed his bowtie and shoes and ran from the room like the floor was crumbling beneath his feet.

Lucky bastard. I guess I wasn't the only one to notice the thick tension and wish I could be elsewhere.

With Trevor gone, I let my frown turn into a full-blown sneer. I'd play nice-ish around the rest of the staff but had no plans of being friendly when we were alone.

"What the fuck are you doing, Ryder?"

"Oooh." He snickered. "I like how you say my name all snarly like an angry lion."

I walked toward him, stopping when the fresh scent of his expensive cologne invaded my senses. God, that was nice. Why couldn't he smell like shit?

Too close. I needed to step back, but I would rather die than let him think I couldn't handle being in his space. To prove that point, I leaned even closer. "Cut the bullshit. Be real for five-fucking-seconds." Shit, my eyes wanted to roll back from the heavenly aroma. My dick also tried to get involved with a nice little twitch, but I bit the inside of my cheek hard to shut that down.

Ryder shrugged. The movement bunched his round shoulders, showing off his delts. I forced myself to look back at his face, but that was barely better as he had a damn dimple on the right side next to his damn perfect lips when he smiled.

It'd be so fun to stick my tongue—

Nope.

It'd be great to lick some other guy's dimples, and if I survived this night, that's what I'd do. Finding someone to fuck would become priority number one. Maybe I'd even take a night off this weekend and hit up someplace where I could find a hookup.

Though it would really hurt to lose those tips.

"I need something to occupy my time until next semester. And I told you the other night, I think I'd be good at this." He winked. "Better than you."

"We'll see about that. And by the way, you look ridiculous in those shorts."

"You think?' As he peered down his long body, he ran a hand over his abs, stopping right at the waistband of the shorts. He slipped a thumb inside, then patted the area right above his impressive bulge.

For sure, it was too much to hope he had a tiny dick.

"I kinda like how I look."

The simple yet loaded statement snapped me back to reality. "Of course you do." I sighed. We couldn't stand here and go back and forth all night, or we'd—I'd—miss critical tips. Ryder didn't need a single extra dollar. "Fine, if you insist on this insanity, here's how it's gonna go. I will show you the ropes and ensure you have all the necessary information and training, but that's it. We're not gonna make small talk or become buddies, and we won't play stupid pranks on each other like we used to. I've worked here for over a year. This job is important to me, and I refuse to fuck that up because of you, got it?"

"Yes, sir!" He snapped out a salute.

My teeth would be ground to nubs by the end of the night.

"Once you're on your own, that's it. We don't talk anymore. We'll be nothing more than moving furniture to each other."

His exaggerated pout did nothing to ease my mind. "Well, that sounds boring," he said. "What happens when I beat you?"

"What are you talking about?"

"When customers decide I'm better at this than you are. We need some prize, doncha think?"

"No, I don't think. There is no contest, bet, competition, or whatever you want to call it. There's only you working and me working. Some of us have bills to pay."

I turned, giving him my back as I yanked my sweatpants down and stuffed them in my locker, leaving me in my uniform shorts. I might not look like Mr. Muscles back there, but I took care of myself and liked my body. My ass was my best feature, if I did say so myself. A few years ago, I'd gone on a tattoo spree, spending any spare change I could muster on new ink. Guys seemed to like my tattoos. Some even went nuts for them.

Did Ryder?

Nope. It didn't matter.

Once my shoes and bowtie were on, I turned and brushed past him toward the door. "Keep up, newbie," I said in a clipped tone. "I work fast and won't slow down for you."

"Pretty sure I can handle it," he said, his eyes sparkling with mirth. Maybe I could convince Parker to make Ryder wear sunglasses so I didn't have to see that unique green speck in his eyes while I worked all night.

I shrugged. "We'll see."

He snorted a laugh and followed me out the door.

I'd been here ten minutes, and I already hated this shift more than any other.

Chapter Eight

Poor Alex. He'd need Botox before turning thirty if he didn't learn to chill and stop furrowing his brow. Not that those little crinkles he got in his forehead weren't adorable, they were, but most people tended to hate them on themselves, even if they found it appealing on someone else.

Trust me, my mother lived in a world of nips, tucks, and body alterations. Her yearly budget for plastic surgery, creams, and serums was higher than the GDP of most small countries. I knew more about crafting the perfect face than I ever wanted to.

Alex didn't seem to be the Botox type. Maybe I'd gift him some for his birthday. That'd earn me an epic glare, maybe even one of those half-growls he did when he reached his limit. But then, if he did paralyze some of his facial muscles, I might not be able to tell when he was scowling at me, and wouldn't that be a shame? The glower was epic.

Though wary, Trevor didn't seem to hate me on sight like Alex did. Maybe he'd be willing to tell me Alex's birthday. I probably knew it at some point, but it'd long slipped my memory.

The door to the staff room swung open, and Alex

appeared. He had a light layer of sweat across his bare chest, giving him an almost glittery sheen. His face had a light pink flush to it from the hectic past two hours. It was easy to forget the sub-zero temperature outside after a few hours in the club.

"Five-minute break is over. Get your ass back out here," Alex barked.

"On my way, boss," I said, snapping out a quick salute. Jesus, five minutes had never flown so fast. All I'd managed to do was sit on a bench and suck down three sips of icy water. They were refreshing, but not enough. No way in hell would I ever admit it, but these first one hundred and twenty minutes kicked my ass.

We'd been back and forth from the bar to our tables at least five dozen times. Rich, drunk people were demanding as hell. Who knew? Then there was the combo skill of balancing a tray of liquid, waving a lit sparkler, shaking my ass, and hyping a table of shit-faced men that I'd never thought I'd need to master. We weren't just alcohol servers—we were a sideshow, there to provide hours of entertainment while keeping the alcohol flowing.

And, shit, a magnum of alcohol was heavy as hell.

My feet ached, sweat ran down my ass crack, and no less than ten guys had tried to cop a feel. A good few managed it too. On a night out where I was the one planning to drink and hook up, I had no problem with wandering hands and grinding dicks, but while I was trying to learn the ropes at my new job?

Those dudes were annoying as hell.

Alex handled it all like a pro. He smiled, flirted, and dodged grabby hands from horny men with ease. I'd seen him dodge limbs like he was a slalom skier, avoiding every octopus reaching for him. If only he liked me better, maybe he'd clue me in on his secrets.

In less than five minutes, the shock of watching Alex work his tables set in. Who the hell was this man? Certainly not the prickly grouch I'd known for years. It turned out when tips were involved, Alex could crank up the charm with the best of us. He also worked hard as hell, hustling the entire shift.

What I still had to figure out was whether this pace was typical for Alex or if he was trying to run me into the ground.

"Here." Alex tossed me a rag and handed me a spray bottle the second I stepped into the hallway. "We have exactly fifteen minutes to turn over the tables before the next reservation." He practically yelled to be heard above the music.

It's funny how I could love the loud pulsing beat on nights I partied, but tonight, I found it annoying to constantly shout and never get a break from the noise.

"Parker hates, and I mean *hates*, if incoming customers catch us during turnover. Everything needs to be clean as hell and restocked. If there's so much as a ring of condensation on the table, he'll chew your ass out, and no one wants that."

"I'm pretty sure Trevor wants that."

He snorted, and his lips quirked, but the almost smile disappeared before I could appreciate it.

"You go wipe down the tables, and I'll grab the water."

Back to the grind. We'd been so busy, and he'd had so much Top Shelf wisdom to impart that I'd barely had time to get under his skin like I wanted. Although my mere presence seemed to irk him, I preferred a more active approach to driving him crazy.

It's time to up my game.

"Gosh, fifteen minutes to wipe down two whole tables? Do you think I can pull it off? Maybe you need to show me how to work this strange contraption," I said, holding up the spray bottle as I stared at it in mock wonder. "And do I have to wipe in a special Top Shelf way? Clockwise? In figure eights? Zig-zag across the table?"

He rolled those deep brown eyes of his and stormed away, scowling. Each step made his ass cheeks bounce in the skintight shorts. Damn, the man had an ass made for all the dirty things. I wiggled my fingers against the impulse to squeeze and knead those round globes. Not much beat the feel of a thick ass in my hands.

Alex's tattoos had been a complete surprise. He seemed too rigid for permanent ink, but the man had a few on his back, one on his right arm, and a quote of some sort on his ribs. We'd been on the move too much all night for me to inspect any of them, but it was only our first night of many working together.

The only thing that surprised me tonight was how sexy I found Alex. Granted, he'd never been unattractive, but shirtless and with those ass-hugging, cock-cupping shorts, he was smoking hot. We were comparable in height, but that's where our similarities ended. Dark to my light in temperament and coloring, he also had me beat in muscular bulk in the most delicious way. I couldn't help but be drawn to the contrast. Everything about us differed, from our looks to our career paths to our families, not that I knew anything about his family beyond the fact that he hadn't grown up with money. Nor did it matter. This was a fun way to pass the time until I began graduate school. It was just fascinating to note the differences and how my dick had suddenly taken an interest in working with Alex.

I wiped the last spritz of cleanser off the table as Alex strode over with a case of water on his shoulder. I'd done a damn good job if I did say so myself. Not a drop of liquid remained on the table. It was so clean I could see my damn face in the shine.

As Alex set the glass water bottles on the table, my attention snagged on the stretch of fabric over one plump ass cheek.

I nearly groaned.

"Get your eyes off my ass."

Busted. I laughed out loud while shrugging. "You got a good ass, FL. What can I say?"

"Seriously?" He straightened and shoved two bottles of Perrier into my chest.

"Oh shit." I bobbled them but managed to keep them from hitting the floor. Thank God. They were glass, and I didn't feel like scooping wet shards off the club floor for the next hour.

"You've been chasing me around while I bust my ass for hours now, and you still wanna call me a freeloader?" Alex shook his head. "Just put those on the fucking table in the setup I showed you before. If you can manage to remember what I did."

He turned toward one table and began displaying the bottles in the triangular shape he'd demonstrated at the start of the night while I stood there frowning.

The FL had slipped out. To be honest, I'd called him FL so many times in the past that I'd forgotten it stood for freeloader. To me, it was just a stupid nickname, but I could see how he found it dickish. On the flip side, it was just a stupid nickname. The man needed to lighten the fuck up, which was exactly why I teased him in the first place. That and because it was fun, although I wasn't used to the tiny seed of guilt I now had embedded in my gut.

We set up the tables in silence. Well, silence between us. There wasn't any such thing as silence inside the club. As I finished changing the incoming party's name on the digital screen above the table—under Alex's critical watch, of course —Luke walked over, escorting a group of eight guys dressed more for Burning Man than a night out at a luxury club in the dead of winter.

"Here we are, gentlemen." Luke grinned as he gestured toward the table. "Alex and Ryder will be taking care of you tonight. Please don't be shy about letting them know what you need, and I am always available up at the front as well."

A tall, slim guy wearing a fishnet top and what appeared to be leather chaps covered in feathers eyed me up and down. If I had to guess, I'd put him at around forty, with a dirty blond stubbled jaw and a mop of wild sandy hair almost brushing his shoulders. His skin was deeply tanned as though he'd recently spent some time much farther south than Boston. "Two bottle service boys, huh? How'd we get so lucky?"

While handsome in a funky way, I couldn't help but think I'd prefer him with darker hair. And maybe a few tattoos like —

Full stop.

Alex. I thought he'd look better if his body were more like Alex's. What kind of mindfuck was that?

I ran a hand through my damp hair. That was unacceptable —time to get this train back on the tracks. I took the job to show Alex I could do what he did, only better, not to admire his body.

I gave Feathers my most innocent grin. "Well, not sure if you'll think you're lucky in a little while. Today's my first day. Consider me your bottle service virgin," I said with a wink.

Alex muttered something under his breath.

Grouch.

"Well, this night keeps getting better and better." Feathers scanned me up and down with a hungry look while the rest of his group filed into the seats around the table. I couldn't help but play along, knowing how much it would irritate Alex, so I winked.

"What can we get you started with? To drink," Alex said in

a clipped tone when Feathers opened his mouth to no doubt say he wanted my ass served on a gold platter.

Feathers lost all his flirtatious flair when he turned his gaze on Alex, whose jaw looked ready to crack. Interesting.

If I preened a little, who could blame me? Who wouldn't want to be objectified by a sexy older man?

Feathers threaded his arm through the man's next to him, who was dressed in the more typical club attire of dark denim and a skintight silver tank top. "We're celebrating tonight, so let's start with some Dom. A lot of Dom. And I'd like it delivered by you." He turned his attention back to me. "Can I lick it off you?"

Silver shirt squeezed Feather's hip. "You want to celebrate our engagement by licking champagne off the bottle service boy?" He had a slight French accent, and the way he said it—bottle service boy—as though I was only one rung above a cockroach on the ladder of life twisted something in my stomach. I almost frowned but winked again instead.

I glanced at Alex, whose fake smile didn't show an ounce of annoyance with the way Silver Shirt spoke, but I noticed the tension in his shoulders and the slight narrowing of his eyes. I could read his annoyance like a book with the number of times he'd snarled at me.

Did it happen often? Being looked down on by customers? Did Silver Shirt see us as less because we served the drinks instead of ordering them? If so, what a dick. Little did he know I'd never been on this side before.

I frowned. God, had I ever made a hospitality worker feel that low?

Was that why Alex hated me on sight? No, calling him freeloader was nothing more than a dumb joke. The man had a stick up his ass was all.

"A magnum of Dom coming right up," I said with as much charm as I could muster. "And there will be glasses for everyone. You gentlemen get settled in, and we'll be right back with the good stuff."

"Mmm, can't wait." Feathers licked his lower lip as his partner chuckled.

I hustled after Alex as he hurried to the club's enormous walk-in refrigerator to grab a chilled bottle of the requested champagne. "Hey, is that allowed?"

As he pulled the heavy refrigerator door open, the play of muscles in his shoulders and upper back snagged my attention. For a guy who spent so much of his time studying, Alex was no slouch. Those shoulders would look spectacular as he held himself up while I—someone—powered into him from behind.

He spun to face me, placing his hands on his hips. That, too, accented his strong shoulders and upper arms. I guess carrying heavy bottles did good things to a man's physique. "Is what allowed?"

"Huh?"

As expected, the walk-in was damn cold. As soon as we stepped in, my nipples hardened to two chilly points. So did Alex's. They looked good, all tight and pointing out from his hairless chest. Did he like them played with? Sucked or pinched while someone stroked his cock? Maybe the occasional light nip.

Or harder.

I nearly fanned myself. What happened to the cold air in the damn walk-in?

"Hello?" Fingers snapped in front of my face. "Earth to Ryder. You asked me if something was allowed."

I blinked as he snapped again. "Oh, right, sorry. Uh, the guy in the feathers asked if he could lick the champagne off me. If I were down for that, is it something Parker allows?"

"No." He shook his head as he strode across the walk-in to where the giant bottles of champagne were stored. "Parker is kinda strict when it comes to that. We can dance, flirt, obviously, even touch as long as it's nothing overly sexual. But we must keep our mouths to ourselves and customers' mouths off us."

He hefted the bottle off the shelf. Once again, my attention strayed to how his toned upper body flexed and rippled with the effort.

"Sorry to disappoint. He's cool with us getting numbers, though, so you could always hook up with him later. You want the bottle or the glasses?"

I snorted. "Thanks, but I'd rather not have to pull feathers out of my orifices. I'll pass. And bottle. I'll take the bottle." I snatched it from him. Alex, carrying a tray of empty champagne flutes, shouldn't make his muscles pop enough to distract me. "Lord knows where that guy's tongue has been. How dare you think I'd be that easy," I added with an exaggerated scoff.

Alex just grunted.

The giant walk-in refrigerator was one of the quietest places in the club, and though freezing, there seemed to be an unspoken agreement between us to take a second to enjoy the peace before venturing back out into the chaos.

"Bet he sucks a mean cock, though."

"Hadn't thought about it." Alex rotated his head from side to side, cracking his neck and exposing the long, smooth line of his throat.

What the hell was wrong with me tonight? Why couldn't I stop noticing things about this man's body? He was throwing me off-kilter without trying, and I needed the upper hand back. Luckily, I knew just the thing to get under his skin.

I cleared my throat, trying to hide my smirk. "You know who gives a fan-fucking-tastic blow job?"

Alex rolled his eyes. "Oh, let me guess… you?"

God, he was so fun to play with. So easy to rile. I waggled

my eyebrows. "That's right. Bet I give better head than you've ever had."

He folded his arms across his chest, cutting off my view of his perky nipples.

Too bad.

"I highly doubt that, but I guess I'll never know for sure because you are the last man I'd let near my dick."

"Bet I give better head than you."

He snorted. "Not taking the bait, Ryder. Let's go. Feathers is waiting, and you don't want to get on his bad side if you want a good tip."

Something in me thrilled at him using my nickname for our interesting customer. "Not worried about it. I've got that guy wrapped around my finger even though he wants to be wrapped around my dick."

"Lovely. Can we go now?"

I tilted my head and stared at him as the best idea I ever had popped into my brain.

"Move it. We're taking too long," Alex complained. "Not only is the customer going to get annoyed, but Parker will notice too. What? Why are you looking at me all weird?"

"I bet if I sucked your dick, I could make you come faster than you could sucking mine."

He coughed and sputtered. "I... what? What the fuck is wrong with you?"

I shrugged as though talking about him on his knees with my dick in his mouth hadn't felt like a punch to the gut. Good thing it was too cold in there for my core to spare blood for my dick. "What? Just making an observation. Bet I could hold out longer than you because I'm that damn good. Men are powerless against my mouth."

He shook his head and pinched the bridge of his nose. "I'm not talking about this with you."

"Come on. How about this? We give it a shot. You make

me come quicker than I make you come, and I'll stop working here. You come faster, and you're stuck working with me until the next semester starts."

His hand fell from his face, and his jaw dropped. Then, like a switch flipped, his shock transformed into anger. Scowling, he crowded into my personal space. I stepped back until my shoulder blades met the cold refrigerator shelving. He planted a hand on the shelves on either side of my head, boxing me in. Damn, in another plotline this would be hot as hell.

"I wouldn't go to Blow Job Alley with you if my mouth could perform miracles," he said right in my face. The words, spoken in a low, furious growl, should have felt like a threat, but they ran over my skin like light touches, making me shiver.

Okay, even in this plotline, the moment was hot as hell. Too bad it wouldn't end with him dropping to his knees.

He shifted and leaned in until his lips brushed my ear. I shivered and not from the cold. Christ, I was going to get hard despite the frigid temperature.

"I'm too honorable a man to let you make a bet you wouldn't stand a prayer of winning. I'd suck you so good you'd not only unload your balls in seconds, you'd forget your goddamn name." With that raspy declaration, he shoved away from the shelf, yanked the vat of champagne from my hands, and disappeared.

I exhaled as my arms dropped limp at my sides.

What the hell had just happened? Alex had gotten the upper hand and given me the tease of a lifetime—that's what happened.

It was so sexy my dick ached, and my knees quivered. I swallowed a lump as I lifted a trembling hand and ran it through my hair. No way could I walk out into the club like this.

Well, that determined it. We were going to make this bet and test out my theory. And if I had to pull out every dirty trick in the book to get it done, so be it.

My dick would get in that mouth. He talked a huge game, and now I needed to know if he could back it up.

"Goddamn," I whispered over the hum of the refrigerator motor. "Wait... what the hell is Blow Job Alley?"

Chapter Nine

How did he do it?

How did Ryder manage to charm every damn person who worked at Top Shelf as well as the customers? Why was I the only one who saw through his winks, sexy abs, and knuckle taps to the shallow bully beneath?

He'd started at Top Shelf precisely one week ago and already snagged his own table. Not only that, he worked it like a pro, learning the drinks, memorizing prices, and balancing efficiency and professionalism with the VIP entertainment service we provided, which was better than any club in Boston.

He was a model employee, and I hated it.

A chin landed on my shoulder at the same time as two thin but strong arms wound around my waist.

I immediately tensed.

"What's up with you tonight?" Trevor spoke directly in my ear so he didn't have to shout above the music. His sweat-dampened hair tickled the side of my face.

Now that I knew my best friend was the one draped over me and not some plastered customer, I relaxed against him. "You on break?"

"Mm-hmm." On Wednesday, he got a thirty-minute break every ninety minutes when he danced. The dancers used the time to rehydrate, stash their cash in their lockers, and catch their breath. "You didn't answer my question. You've been off today. Everything okay at home?"

"Yeah. It's been a good week. My mom's new medication seems to be helping with her energy levels. She's actually considering a visit to her sister's house in Connecticut for a few days. Her brother-in-law offered to drive up here and pick her up."

"Wow, Alex, that's fantastic. She hasn't been able to go anywhere in ages."

Tell me about it. Between her and my brother, I hadn't had a moment alone in the house for longer than I could remember. How incredible would it be to have even an hour of solitude? "Yeah, she's excited."

"And your brother?"

I shrugged. "I haven't seen much of him, but as far as I know, he's not in jail or the hospital, so I'm counting that as a win."

Trevor chuckled against my ear. "Sounds like all is as good as can be on the home front, and yet you're still all broody."

"Broody is my default."

"Yeah, but tonight it's worse than usual."

My gaze landed on Ryder, where he laughed and flirted with a VIP table full of rowdy college guys who couldn't get enough of him. They hollered and cheered as he distributed what had to be a sixth round of shots. Together, they all downed the shot, Ryder included, though I had a feeling he'd adopted our water trick because he'd participated in every round while knowing Parker's strict rule of one drink every two hours for staff.

One of his customers, a devastatingly handsome guy with the straightest and whitest teeth I'd ever witnessed, slid a hand up Ryder's chest and around the back of his neck. I couldn't help but stiffen as the guy leaned in.

Was he about to kiss Ryder?

Was Ryder going to let him?

"Relax," Trevor said in my ear. "Ryder knows the rules and has followed them so far."

Sure enough, Ryder drew back and managed to extricate himself from the customer's grabby arms without offending the man or risking his tip.

"See?"

I grunted. "He's pushing boundaries, and one of these times, he's going to fuck up and go too far." God, I sounded like a middle-aged father, annoyed he had to wait up half the night for his kid to come home.

Trevor sighed. "He's not that bad, you know. He's early for every shit, works hard, learns fast, and the customers fucking love him. You might find him tolerable if you give him half a chance."

What the hell? How had I missed Trevor giving Ryder his stamp of approval? I spun, dislodging Trevor's hold on me. My friend was kneeling on a barstool, which explained how he'd been able to rest his chin on my shoulder while being six inches shorter than me. He wore his favorite harness, the one he always danced in on Wednesdays. It was funny how, as cute as Trevor was, I'd never looked at him nearly naked and wanted to lick him all over.

"No, I won't. He's an asshole, Trev. The whole reason he sought out this job was to fuck with me. You forget I know him."

Trevor frowned and shifted so he was no longer kneeling but sitting on the stool. "Babe, you knew him in high school. Most people are assholes in high school. Don't you think you're clinging to this grudge too hard?"

"No, I don't think so." Sure, I hadn't told Trevor the details of why Ryder took this job, nor had I mentioned his ridiculous idea for a bet, but the way he sided with Ryder still stung. Trevor was my friend. My close friend and my only one. "I had no idea you liked him so much." Stepping back, I shook my head. "My break's over. I gotta get back to work. Thanks for having my back, though."

With that cheap parting shot, I stalked toward the staff room to stow my water bottle.

"Oh, come on, Alex," Trevor shouted after me. "Don't be mad. I didn't mean anything by it."

I lifted a hand in a half-see-you-later, half-it's-fine wave. Trevor would stress all night if he thought I was truly mad at him.

"You better come to Parker's party Sunday night. I'll show up and drag you out of your house if I have to."

Ugh, a party on a Sunday night. Who wanted to go to a party on a Sunday night? People who worked on all the good party nights, that's who. I'd go, not because Trevor begged me to attend, but because it wasn't healthy for me to have zero life beyond work and school.

"Pink Pony Club" blared through the entire club. I couldn't help but nod along as I went to the staff room, but that was as much dancing as I did without the promise of a hefty tip. This song never failed to have the whole club on their feet, singing and dancing. All the guys at my two tables were shaking their asses on the dance floor, so I had a few seconds before I needed to head over to the VIP section to check in.

As much as I enjoyed the song, the quiet vibe in the staff room had me mumbling out a breathy, "Oh, that's nice," as the door closed behind me. Once I stowed my water in my locker, I spared an extra second to shut my eyes and roll my neck back and forth along my shoulders, eliciting a series of pops and cracks. The tension there had increased over the past week, and it didn't take a genius to guess why. Working with Ryder four nights a week was as miserable as I'd assumed.

But not for the reasons I'd expected.

He didn't taunt or send me those patronizing glances he'd loved so much in high school and college. He also hadn't called me FL since that first night. Instead, he'd let his body do the tormenting for him. Hours of watching him work bare-chested in booty shorts without an ounce of relief was pure torture. The CIA could get gay men all over the country to spill every secret they held by forcing them to work side by side with the half-naked Ryder and denying them any form of release. A few nights of being that hot and bothered, and every single one would crack like a cheap mirror.

After each shift, I'd gone home, stormed into my bedroom, and had my hand down my pants within seconds, jerking with such furious strokes my dick felt raw.

Then, there was his constant offer of a blow job. At least three times a night, Ryder sidled up to me and reminded me of his proposed wager. He'd quit working at Top Shelf if I could make him come with my mouth faster than he could make me come.

I'd have taken him up on the offer if he were any other man. As it was, I was so horny and desperate that I'd nearly caved on Saturday night just to put an end to the agony. The only thing that got me through was knowing I had the next three nights off and could find some relief in a random stranger at a club on the other side of town.

But I hadn't done it. I'd stayed in and touched myself alone in my room.

The music's volume increased for a second, then decreased again, which only meant one thing—I whipped around to find Ryder standing in the doorway wearing a playful smirk.

God, I'd love to wipe that smirk off his face.

I could think of a few ways to do it too.

A good smack.

A solid punch.

A breath-stealing kiss.

Shit.

"Move," I said as the door closed behind him. "My break is over. I gotta check on my tables."

"They're all still dancing. You're fine." He tilted his head, staring at me with an intensity I felt in my balls, probably devising a new way to fuck up my life. "Coupla the guys at our tables seem to have hit it off." He waggled his eyebrows. "Makes me feel like a proud papa to know they may get each other off before the night is over."

He laughed and pushed away from the door as I rolled my eyes. "Yes, if they hook up, they owe it all to you."

"Damn straight. Also means we should get double the tips. Maybe triple. Facilitating orgasms deserves it. Know what I mean?" He turned his back to me as he entered the combination on his locker. We all trusted each other with our belongings, and the staff room door had a keypad entry to keep non-employees out, but once in a while, a drunk patron managed to make their way inside. Items had been stolen in the past, so we were careful to keep our lockers secure.

"Make sure you tell them that at night's end. I hear demanding a bigger tip for acting like a pimp is the fastest way to get on Parker's good side."

Now Ryder was the one rolling his eyes. "God, it was a joke. Why you always gotta be such a stick-in-the-mud? It wouldn't kill you to loosen up and laugh now and again."

"I laugh plenty, and if you ever say something funny, I'll laugh for you."

That had Ryder snickering. "Me-ow. Claws are coming out, I see. I know just the thing to lighten you up." He grabbed his water bottle and then arched one eyebrow my way as he uncapped it.

"Not happening. It's never going to happen, so you can stop wasting your breath and bringing it up every five seconds. I'm gonna start thinking you have a thing for me."

This time, Ryder laughed long and loud before shrugging. "Your loss," he said when he could finally breathe again.

Screw this. Why was I wasting my time arguing with this asshole when I had tables to service. I started to turn as Ryder lifted his water bottle to his lips with his head tilted back. Every swallow had his throat contracting in a rhythmic up-and-down motion. He shut his eyes, clearly loving the relief of the cool liquid. Excess water sloshed out of the bottle, spilling from the corner of his mouth.

A thin river ran down his smooth chin, dripping to his chest where it cascaded over his pecs. I pressed my tongue to the roof of my mouth as it automatically twitched with the desire to capture that escaped stream of water. To lap it off Ryder's chest, then continue sampling every inch of exposed skin. And there were so many inches.

"Shit," he mumbled as his hand went to his torso, where he swiped the water away, then continued to stroke his hand down over his abs in a slow, caressing motion.

My breath caught in my throat. The short break had helped cool me down, but the heat surged again, flushing my skin and making me dizzy.

That damn hand kept cruising down, down, down, smoothing over muscles and tanned skin.

I couldn't look away from how his abs tightened under the touch. And then his fingertips reached the top of his shorts.

But he didn't stop there.

Ryder stroked over his growing bulge, and my cock responded in kind, thickening beneath the tight confinement of spandex. The temperature seemed to rise by twenty degrees, growing too thick to breathe. My skin prickled, and my fingertips tingled with the need to touch. I couldn't figure out if I wanted my hands on him or myself.

A loud snort pierced the air, ripping me from the erotic trance of Ryder's show.

My gaze jerked to his face to find him smirking. "Tell me again how it'll never happen, Alex."

My face flamed so hot I could feel waves of heat emanating from me.

Goddammit. He'd won this round.

And we both knew it.

"Fuck off, Ryder." I turned and stormed out of the staff room to the sound of his victorious laughter. When I reached the hallway, I stopped, bracing a hand against the wall. Air stuttered out of my lungs as I tried to exhale the disturbing past few minutes and give my dick a chance to deflate.

"Are you okay, Alex?" Parker's sophisticated voice had me straightening.

"Yep. All good." My voice sounded strained even to myself. Great.

He frowned. "Your table needs refills. They've been asking for you." He tilted his head and studied me. "You don't usually disappear mid-shift."

The disapproving tone from my boss was enough to kill any remaining embers of desire. Now I was fucking up at work because of Ryder. Maybe I should take the damn bet and suck him so good he'd explode in five seconds and once again be part of my past instead of my irritating present.

I looked my boss in the eye. The man deserved no less than my utmost respect, even when I wanted to stick my head in a hole and die. "I'm sorry, Parker. I'll take care of them right now. Won't happen again."

"Thank you. See that it doesn't."

I scurried away from my boss with the shame of disappointing him flowing behind me like a cape.

For the remainder of my shift, I managed to avoid Ryder

while I stewed in hatred and self-recrimination. How could I have been stupid enough to fall for a juvenile stunt like that? Touching himself to destroy my focus, for fuck's sake.

It sure had worked, though. God must have been having a truly shitty day when he gifted that gorgeous man such a wretched personality.

By the time I arrived home a few hours later, I was tired, horny, and pissed off. My final table's tip reflected the latter emotion, being a few hundred lower than my average, while Ryder could practically fill a tub with his earnings.

Fucker.

I walked into a quiet house. As usual, the outside and foyer lights had been left on for me. Though I was twenty-three and had been taking care of most household duties for almost a decade, my mother worried and never retired for the night unless she felt confident I wouldn't return to a dark walkway.

I shut the lights and locked the door behind me before kicking off my shoes. Sometimes, if I didn't have much homework, I'd watch television until I calmed enough to try sleeping. Wednesdays were a short day of classes, so, as today, I often finished my work before my shift.

Tonight, though, I was too tired to bother with the television, but not sleepy. My mind whirled even as my aching feet and fatigued back begged to be horizontal in my bed.

I padded down the hall toward my mother's room, where a quick peek revealed her sleeping soundly in her bed. She was a loud sleeper, not quite a snorer, but her breathing reverberated through the room. When I was younger, I hated the sound. She'd fall asleep on the couch and drive me crazy. Now, it gave me comfort, knowing I could easily ensure she breathed well. Though she was no longer a functional ambulator, she managed her wheelchair well in the house and could stand for a few minutes without help. She could also take about four or five shuffling steps, which made all the difference in the world. It allowed her to get from her bed to her wheelchair independently and stand at the sink to complete her morning and evening routines, as well as use the bathroom independently.

Someday, she'd lose the ability to perform those activities. I had no clue what we'd do when that time came and tried not to think about it too deeply. Our little family had adopted the unspoken motto of crossing the bridges when we came to them, and it had worked for us so far, though I wished we had the money and resources to plan a safe and secure future for my mother.

Someday. You'll get a good job—a real job—and be able to provide what she needs.

I backed out of her room and shut her door without making a sound, then continued down the short hall to my room, which was the last on the right. As I passed Kenny's room, I glanced in and almost tripped over my own feet. There, alone in his bed, slept none other than my brother.

"Holy shit," I whispered. It'd been months since I'd come home from work to find Kenny in bed before me, which was crazy given my hours.

This meant I could head to my room and go straight to sleep without worrying about anyone.

"It's a miracle," I whispered as I closed Kenny's door.

When I reached my room, I didn't bother to turn on the light as I stripped out of my clothes and tossed them somewhere near the hamper. Then I brushed my teeth and emptied my bladder also in the dark. There wasn't any point in turning on the light only to view my exhausted face in the mirror.

"Fuck yes," I said as I flopped onto my back on my bed, clad in nothing but briefs. "What a night."

What a life. Twenty-three seemed too young to be this

tired. Or this grumpy, as Ryder loved to point out, though he was the only one who brought out the full force of my grouchy side. Maybe I needed a break or a vacation. Well, staycation, seeing as how I couldn't afford to go anywhere. We'd just come off winter break from college, but I worked the ticket booth at a local winter festival on top of my Top Shelf hours to earn money for Christmas presents and afford new snow tires for my car. It didn't count as a break if I was just as busy as when class was in session.

It must be nice to be Ryder and not only have endless piles of money but an entire semester to dick around, offering blow job competitions and treating the world like his playground.

"Stop thinking about him," I muttered into the quiet of the night.

Now that work forced me to interact with Ryder four nights a week, I found my thoughts drifting toward him too often. How stupid was I to fall for his little stunt tonight?

But God, it had been hot. I'd have had to be dead not to react to him rubbing his damn hand all over that stellar body. What was he doing? Spending every hour he didn't work at Top Shelf in the gym? Whatever his workout routine, it was working for the man.

He should never be allowed to wear more than those damn booty shorts. Warmth spread through my limbs as my mind conjured the image of him in our work uniform. It'd be so easy to peel him out of it and have him bare before me. No doubt his dick would be as impressive as the rest of him. He was one of those lucky people blessed by everything in life, dick size included.

And he wanted me to suck him off.

My cock responded with a surge of blood, rising to attention against the black cotton of my briefs. "Sometimes I hate you," I said, even as I pressed the heel of my palm against my hardened shaft. I groaned at the pressure, lifting my hips off the bed to rub against my hand.

Dammit. Was I really going to do this? I'd never fall asleep now that I was hard and aching to come, but did I really want to get myself off to thoughts of Ryder? I couldn't change the script. He was in my head in all his mostly naked glory, and that's where he'd stay until I erupted all over my hand.

"Fuck it." No one would ever know. I'd die before letting this secret escape.

I hooked my thumbs in the waistband of my briefs and shoved them over my ass, allowing my stiff dick to spring forward. Groaning, I wrapped my hand around myself with a light grip and slid up and down my length. Lube would be helpful, but retrieving it required more energy than I had to spare, so a dry hand fuck would have to do.

Luckily, I already had precum leaking from the tip, so I swiped my thumb across it, hissing at the electric zing of pleasure. The fluid eased the sting of friction.

My mind ran away to an alternate universe where Ryder was not only hot as lava but someone I could have. Someone I wanted who also wanted me. Gone was our hatred and rivalry, replaced by roaming hands, hungry mouths, and dirty words. In my fantasy, he tugged my cock with the perfect tension and strength, knowing exactly how I liked a man to stroke me. His hands were strong and skilled. Within seconds, I was pumping my hips into his imaginary grip while reaching for him as well. We jacked each other without words, only grunts and pants.

My hand flew over my cock as my brain brought the fantasy to life. It wasn't long before my back arched and warm spunk spurted from the tip of my dick as my body convulsed with pleasure given to me by fictional Ryder. I wiped my messy hand on my stomach, which already had a trail of cum running up to my sternum.

Shit, that had been good and so necessary. For the first time in ages, my mind felt light and clear.

I closed my eyes, enjoying the floaty post-orgasm sensation surrounding me. In a few minutes, I'd get up and clean myself off. No one wanted to wake up to briefs around their knees and crusted cum on their stomach.

Sleep stole all my good intentions, and within minutes, I slipped into a near-coma, still covered in the evidence of my shameful fantasy.

The last active thought to cross my mind before I lost consciousness was how much I liked imaginary Ryder gazing at me with heat and desire instead of condescension and disgust.

In my fantasy, that look had been even better than Ryder's hands all over me.

"No one has to know," I mumbled, and as I told myself every time, this would be the last time I thought of Ryder while jerking off.

Chapter Ten

"Goddamn."

Everyone knew Top Shelf kept Parker's pockets stuffed, but they had to be overflowing for him to own this kind of property. And this was coming from me, who'd lived in luxury my whole life.

"Impressive, right?"

Trevor's voice had me glancing down to my right, where he stood at my side wearing skintight jeans, his white puffy coat with a fur-trimmed hood, and boots that matched.

"I had no idea Parker was this loaded."

Unlike my parents' home, whose style could only be described as old-money ornate, Parker's place had a fresh, modern style. The foyer, where Trevor and I stood gawking, had at least a thirty-foot ceiling. To our right, a wall of windows offered a gorgeous snowy view of his vast yard, while the left wall featured an enormous modern painting. Music played somewhere in the background, though nothing like the loud beats we were used to at the club.

"Yeah, Top Shelf is his baby, but not his only source of income. He's invested in multiple businesses in Boston."

"Huh." I cast him a sideways glance.

"What?" Trevor narrowed his lined eyes as he peered up at me.

"Nothing. You know a lot about the man, that's all."

He shrugged. "Yeah, I guess. I've been working for the man for a long time."

It was more than that, and everyone who spent five seconds around Trevor and Parker knew it.

"How long?"

He sighed. "I'm twenty-eight, and I've been working for him since the day I turned twenty-one."

My eyes nearly fell out of my head. "For real?"

He nodded, gnawing on his lower lip. "Yep, I waited tables at an Italian restaurant he owned before opening Top Shelf. He sold it about two years ago, wanting to focus more of his attention on the club."

"And the whole time you've been obsessed with him?"

Sighing, Trevor nodded. "The whole time. Pathetic, right?"

"Nah." Heartbreaking, maybe, but not pathetic. "Anything ever happen there?"

"Nope," he said, popping the 'p.' "Not a once. Parker is… complex."

I laughed. "Yeah, I get that impression." As I spoke, I unbuttoned the large buttons on my peacoat. "For what it's worth, I don't think your feelings are unreciprocated."

He snorted. "You know, Ryder, that actually makes it ten times worse." He shrugged out of his coat and cast me a sad smile.

Yeah. I could see that. Wanting someone so badly and knowing they wanted you but couldn't or wouldn't move forward for whatever reason had to feel like a daily knife to the heart.

"Gentlemen, I apologize for keeping you waiting. Please forgive me."

The newcomer jerked us out of our depressing

conversation. He was an older man, probably in his fifties, wearing a perfectly pressed charcoal suit. His snowy white hair had a slight curl he'd tamed into a neat style atop his head.

"I'll take your coats and take you to where Parker and his guests are enjoying drinks."

"Thank you, James," Trevor said as he handed over his jacket.

James, huh? Clearly, this wasn't Trevor's first time, probably not even his tenth, visiting Parker's home.

"Yes, thank you," I echoed as I draped my coat over his waiting arm.

"Follow me, please," James said, turning.

I glanced down to find Trevor looking up at me with an amused grin. "So formal," I whispered.

Nodding, he linked his arm through mine. "That's Parker for you."

We followed James down a hallway, where more impressive artwork filled the walls. It appeared my boss had an extensive collection of paintings.

"Do me a favor?" Trevor asked as we trailed a few feet behind James.

"Sure, what do you need?"

"Lay off Alex tonight." His eyes no longer sparkled at me —they'd gone serious and almost lethal. "Whatever you think you know about Alex, whatever impressions he gave you when you guys were younger, they're wrong. He's a good guy… the best, actually. Now, I happen to think he has the wrong idea about you, too, but make no mistake, my loyalty lies with Alex. And if it comes down to choosing my allegiance, I'll choose him. I'd appreciate not having to do that, so like I said, lay off him tonight."

I'd wondered if Alex had spoken to anyone at work about our dislike of one another. I guess he had. My stomach twisted at Trevor's fierce expression. He might be the smallest guy in the room, but he wasn't the meekest.

"In case you haven't noticed, Alex isn't exactly open to the idea of a truce between us."

Or a blow job. Damn, I wanted his lips on my cock.

"Oh, I've noticed." He chuckled. "But I told you my loyalty lies with him, so you're the one who gets my lecture."

"Lucky me."

He snorted.

"All right, I'll be nice. You know, I don't even hate the guy the way he hates me. He annoys the shit out of me, sure, but it's mostly because he has a giant stick up his ass."

"Here we are, gentlemen," James said as we reached a large room with floor-to-ceiling windows revealing a sprawling landscape covered in snow.

"Thanks, James," Trevor said before zeroing in on Parker, who sat alone in a beige armchair observing his guests. "Wish I had a giant stick in my ass," he mumbled.

I choked out a laugh so loud that all six heads in the room swiveled our way.

"Hey, all." Trevor wiggled his fingers as he slipped his arm from mine. "Miss me?" He practically bounced into the room and over to a plush beige couch. Gone was the man who'd threatened me, replaced by the Trevor we all knew and loved —the life of the party.

"You made it." Parker rose from his spot and strode to where I now stood alone. "What can I get you to drink? I have it all."

I glanced at the tumbler of amber liquid in his hand. "What are you drinking?"

"Whiskey. Johnnie Walker Blue."

"Nice." I rubbed my hands together. "One of those sounds perfect."

"Follow me." I accompanied him to the full bar which had

a white marble top and an impressive liquor stock. It made sense he'd have the best of the best in his home, considering what he served in his club.

"Your place is amazing," I said as he strode behind the bar. I stayed in front, bracing my hands on the stone top.

"Thank you." With the confidence of a man who knew his worth, Parker grabbed the half-full bottle of Johnnie Walker and a crystal glass. "I've lived here about three years now and never plan to move. It's my oasis." After pouring me a double, he slid the tumbler my way. "It's taken me a while to perfect the décor, but I think I'm finally done. Let me see if anyone wants a refill. I'll be right back."

I turned and rested my back against the bar as he left me alone. The first sip of whiskey went down as smoothly as you'd hope and had me grinning. Damn, that was some good stuff. It would warm me from the inside and chase away any lingering chill from the winter air. So would the sizable electric fireplace set into a stone wall on the other side of the room. The only wall without windows, the fire glass gleamed like hundreds of sparkling diamonds. Parker's recreation room was dominated by two large couches and three posh chairs that managed to be contemporary and inviting. A thick white rug covered the light wood floor beneath the couches—the kind you wanted to roll around on naked. The incredible room also had a pool table, a foosball table, and what had to be a ninety-inch television with multiple gaming consoles.

No one would doubt a bachelor lived here, but one with class and a shitload of money—no bearskin rug, cheap beer, or Ikea furniture for Parker. Even with the obvious luxury and high price tag of everything I'd seen so far in his home, he created a comfortable environment. It was the kind of place I wanted to curl up in for hours and watch movies while enjoying the warmth of the fire.

My parents' home, on the other hand, felt like a museum,

even more so since I'd been away for a while. It had a cold, sterile vibe I'd always hated.

God, I needed to get my own place.

Parker hadn't returned to the bar after a few minutes. Instead, Trevor snagged him and dove into an animated story complete with gestures, jumping, and plenty of eye rolls. I smirked at the visible difference in their personalities. For his part, Parker remained stoic and expressionless as he listened, but I'd swear on a stack of Bibles, the heat in his eyes came from desire for Trevor instead of the fire or even the whiskey.

As I watched and tried to comprehend their dynamic, the hairs on the back of my neck stood on end. A shiver ran down my spine, settling at the base in a tingle of awareness. If I believed in ghosts, I'd worry Parker had one who resided in his rec room.

But no, this feeling didn't have a supernatural origin. Alex had arrived—no idea how I knew on instinct, but I did.

A glance to my right revealed my sixth sense had nailed it. Alex stood at the entrance to the room with James, scanning as though hoping to find someone specific. Or, more likely, hoping *not* to find me. He wore a hunter-green sweater that hugged his upper body, paired with dark, straight-legged jeans and winter boots like the rest of us. The cold had turned the tip of his nose red, made more apparent against his paler skin and dark hair that was slightly mussed as though he'd been wearing a wool hat.

My pulse fluttered at the base of my throat. Swallowing did nothing to help.

How was it possible that Alex looked just as sexy with every inch of skin covered as he did working in a scrap of material at the club?

Of course, he wasn't smiling, but he wasn't scowling either, probably because he'd yet to notice me. While I wouldn't describe his posture as relaxed—I don't think he knew how to chill—he didn't seem as tense as usual. No pinch in his forehead, no narrowed eyes, and his facial muscles weren't twitching as he clenched his jaw—none of his typical pissed-off tells.

He looked good. More than good. He looked downright edible.

I blew out a silent breath and adjusted my Henley's collar. I had to fight the urge to fan my face. Maybe the fire was too high.

No one else had noticed Alex yet, so he remained alone after James departed. I shouldn't have been staring so openly. If he noticed me, he'd no doubt scowl and march off in the opposite direction, but I couldn't make my eyes obey. I barely even blinked.

After a few seconds, Alex's gaze settled on Trevor, and a soft smile curled his lips. He shook his head slightly, exasperated by Trevor and his unrequited obsession with our boss—the worst-kept secret at Top Shelf.

I still couldn't drag my gaze from him. I should. Staring was foolish. Any second now, his attention would swing my way, and he'd—there it was—notice me.

As though flipping a switch, his face screwed up and his shoulders bunched. You'd think he was the only one in the room who knew I'd committed a heinous crime with how fast his expression turned hostile.

I sighed.

Keeping my promise to Trevor would be a challenge. The best thing I could do to avoid making a crack that would have Trevor coming for me would be to stay as far away from Alex as possible tonight, especially if we were both drinking. I'd likely say something insulting, and he'd scowl so hard his face would freeze. I could imagine trying to explain to our Top Shelf customers the reason his face had a permanent glower.

Well, you see, I was wasted and trying to get under his skin, so I called him freeloader like I used to when I was a dumb high schooler. After shooting lasers at me with his eyes, he scowled at me, and bam, face stuck.

Parker would fire me on the spot for damaging his golden bottle service boy.

I snickered. It might be worth it.

"Alex! You're here!" Trevor bounded across the room to fling himself at Alex, who easily caught him. He smiled. Actually fucking smiled a huge happy upturn of his lips, complete with teeth and a half-laugh.

Something twisted in my gut.

What the hell? I'd seen the man smile before at work, plenty of times. Not at me, of course, and not those free but practiced smiles for our customers, and real ones for other coworkers.

Asshole.

Why the hell did I care? I'd made it my life's mission to irritate that cranky fuck. His not ever smiling at me meant I'd accomplished my mission. Maybe it was less about Alex and more about the fact that no one had smiled at me that way recently.

Something had been off with me for the past few weeks. I had a huge friend group here in Boston, both from college and high school, but I'd barely reconnected with them since returning home.

I couldn't put my finger on why, but I felt different. It could be the secret I'd been harboring about the change in my education and career plans. No one, and I mean no one in my friend group, would understand why I wanted to become a teacher when I had the chance to take over a billion-dollar empire. And that was okay. No one needed to understand it. Hell, I barely did, but I had a suspicion they wouldn't support me either. And that's the part that had me biting my tongue. I wasn't ready for the criticism and pressure that would accompany the news getting out. My sister's support meant the world, but all the naysayers would drown out her voice.

I turned my back on Alex and strode toward where Luke was chatting with Dominic, one of the bartenders. Dom and I had met but hadn't chatted much beyond drink orders.

"Hey, Ryder," Luke said as I joined them. This was my first time seeing the club's host out of a suit. He dressed down well in jeans and a striped blue and gray sweater. "Dom was just telling me about a customer who followed him home and tried to climb in his window."

"No shit?" I sat on the couch next to Luke and across from Dom, who'd perched on the coffee table as though the thing didn't cost ten thousand dollars. "Was this last night?"

Dom waved his beer bottle back and forth as he shook his head. Dressed in baggy jeans and a band T-shirt with combat boots, Dom was a little gruffer than most of Parker's staff. "This was a few years ago when I lived in Chicago. I worked at a wild place with a very different vibe from Top Shelf. The best part was that the person who followed me was a woman. It was a plain old sports bar, and she had no idea I didn't swing her way. Poor thing got herself arrested tryna catch some dick from a dude who'd rather walk on broken glass than give it to her."

"Amen to that," Luke said as I laughed along with Dom.

"I had a girl offer me two hundred bucks to sleep with her in college," I said before taking a sip of Parker's very nice whiskey.

"Shit, I'da done it for that. Just close my eyes and imagine Idris Elba," Dom said with a snort. "Did you do it?"

"I tried." I shrugged. "Got as far as taking off her bra before I bailed. Tits were not made for me."

Both Dom and Luke burst out laughing, and from there,

the conversation flowed like we'd been friends forever. We laughed and drank, swapping stories and trying to outdo each other for the wildest ones. I hadn't enjoyed myself so much in ages. Even the night I hung out with Turko and Manny, I'd had an odd sensation of not fitting in. Here, with these men I was just getting to know, I didn't feel the pressure of confessing my secret.

After I'd finished my first drink, Luke insisted I have one more. He returned from the bar with my refill just as Parker announced it was time for dinner.

"Come into the dining room," he said, waving us through an arched doorway. "I kept it simple tonight. Just pizza and salad."

I couldn't keep my eyebrows from rising to save my life as I purposely held back to let Alex in first. Hopefully, we wouldn't end up sitting near each other. But I'd scale that mountain if I got there. "I'm struggling to imagine Parker Door Dashing a bunch of pizzas."

Luke laughed at my expression. "That's because he didn't. You'll see."

Sure enough, we trailed Parker into the dining room only to find a long table with a red and white checkered tablecloth. Five platters of pizza, two giant salad bowls, and multiple bottles of red wine were spread out along the length of the table. But not just any pizza. These pies were clearly homemade in a wood-fired pizza oven. A chef stood off to the side in his gleaming white coat and tall hat. All that was missing was the Italian tenor crooning in the corner.

"Good evening, gentlemen," the chef said. "Tonight, we have prepared for you five different pizzas. We have margarita pizza, barbecue chicken pizza, a white pizza with garlic and spinach, sausage and pepperoni pizza, and finally, one with sundried tomatoes, chicken, and pesto. Don't be shy. I have plenty more to serve if you finish these. Please enjoy."

My mouth watered at the sight and smell coming from the table. "Now, this is a dinner party," I muttered.

Dom rubbed his hands together. "Damn straight."

"Dig in, please," Parker said as he gestured toward the table.

Who was I to deny the host his request?

The food was excellent and the company even better. Drinks flowed easily through the meal. I don't think my wine glass fell below a quarter full before being refilled, which meant I had no idea how much I drank.

Dangerous but fun. This was the perfect way to get to know my coworkers. The club was so busy that we rarely had time to wave as we passed each other, running back and forth with giant bottles of expensive alcohol. This dinner allowed us to bond and become friends.

I was having so much fun I'd forgotten Alex was sitting at the opposite end of the table.

Almost.

Toward the end of dinner, I made the mistake of glancing toward Trevor, who was laughing so loudly I couldn't hear Luke next to me. The second I turned my head, my eyes locked with Alex's. He sat beside Trevor, and to anyone else, it appeared he was listening to his friend's story, but I could feel the intensity of his attention to the tips of my toes.

I swallowed a bite of dry crust that abraded my throat on the way down. I barely felt the discomfort. The force of Alex's gaze had me frozen. Like when he first arrived, he wasn't smiling or frowning. His eyes radiated a heat I'd never seen from him. It stole my ability to think or breathe.

The rest of the room faded to a fuzzy background. My dick thickened, and if I'd been in my right mind, I'd have checked to ensure the tablecloth hid my sin. But all I could do was bask in the fire of Alex's gaze. Time slowed until I could mark its passing by the thump of my pulse in my throat.

What the hell was happening?

Did he feel it, or was I lost in my own delusion?

"Anyone up for billiards?" Parker's sophisticated tone sliced through my trance without mercy. I jolted and blinked, only to find Alex talking to Trevor as relaxed as could be while I sat there with my insides churning.

Did I imagine it? The connection from seconds ago? Had I had some kind of wakeful fantasy where I dreamed the heat and electricity crackled across the long table?

My rock-hard dick thought it really happened, but Alex didn't appear a fraction of a percent as affected as I felt.

"If you mean pool, then hell yeah," Dom said, rubbing his hands together. "Last time I cleaned up, and I've got my eye on some heated grips for my bike so I can ride longer."

Trevor snorted. "I'll never understand you motorcycle guys. Who wants to ride around with a thousand pounds of vibrating metal between your legs?" He pursed his lips. "Hmm... you might actually be onto something, Dom."

Dominic winked at him. "Now you're catching on."

Everyone at the table laughed as they stood and began to file back into the rec room while trash-talking Dom's pool game.

I didn't get up, partly because my dick still tented my pants, but mostly I feared my legs wouldn't support me. I'd yet to recover from the intensity of what transpired between Alex and me, whether real or imagined.

"Ryder." I glanced over to see Parker studying me with a tilted head. "You coming?"

I almost groaned—poor choice of words. I couldn't be further from coming, yet now I wanted it, and I wanted Alex to make it happen.

"Uh, yeah," I croaked. *Way to sound normal, Ryder.*

"You okay?"

"All good." My voice still radiated discomfort. "I'm gonna

hit the bathroom first, then I'll be in."

He nodded. "Use the one at the top of the stairs. No one will bother you up there."

"Uh, thanks." How humiliating. He probably thought my stomach was revolting after the heavy meal. I'm not sure if that was better or worse than him realizing I had a boner for another of his employees.

After Parker left, I forced myself to my feet. Thank God no one else lingered in the dining room, eyeing my tented pants with judgment.

I exited the dining room and turned left toward the staircase I saw when I'd first arrived. Thankfully, I didn't run into James or anyone else milling about and doing their jobs for Parker. By the time I reached the top of the stairs, I'd managed to convince my dick to chill the fuck out. Unfortunately, my brain didn't get that same memo. I couldn't stop thinking about the way Alex had been staring at me.

Hungry. Hell, ravenous.

A dozen steps from the staircase, the bathroom was easy to find. A few minutes of quiet and some splashes of cold water on my face would help me get back on track. I opened the door and stepped inside the large powder room with a wall-mounted white stone sink and gold fixtures. A large round mirror hung over the sink.

I shouldn't have peeked. I'd have been better off not seeing the tipsy and horny need in my eyes.

"God, I'm fucked up," I muttered to my image in the mirror.

"You are."

I jumped so hard, I think my heart stopped for a few seconds.

"Alex," I said with a gasp as I spun to face him. He stood in the open doorway, chest heaving and eyes blazing.

My eyes widened. I didn't dare blink as I took him in.

"One time," he said, narrowing his eyes at me. "One time for each of us. If I come first, you can stay. If you come first, you're gone. Out of my life. You never come back to Top Shelf, and if you ever see me out, you turn and fucking leave. Deal?"

Holy shit. Holy shit.

My heart kicked into full throttle, waging a battle against my chest wall. "You mean…"

"You go first," he said, all business as he began unbuttoning his jeans. "Get on your knees."

My cock filled back up so fast I had to reach for the sink to keep from dropping to my knees and cracking my kneecaps.

"Are you drunk?"

He snorted. "Drunk enough not to care that this is a terrible idea. But not too drunk that I can't consent and remember it in the morning."

Well, that answered any questions I had about how he currently felt about me. "Same."

"I want you gone," he said, venom dripping from his voice as though I'd done something monstrous to him tonight when I hadn't spoken a word to him.

He stepped into the powder room, turned, and locked the door. The snick of the locking mechanism dropping into place shot through my body like a bullet straight from the chamber.

Alex's hands resumed their task of removing his belt and unbuttoning his jeans. "You in?"

I lunged forward, shoving him against the door with a hand on his chest. Who would believe Alex was letting me touch him? Who would believe I was about to have his cock in my mouth?

"Fuck yeah, I'm in," I whispered against his ear. "And I'm about to give you the best goddamn blow job of your life."

Before he could fire back with something that would cut

me to the quick, I kicked the small rug where I wanted it and dropped to my knees. Alex had his jeans open and was about to slide his hand into his royal blue briefs.

I grabbed his wrist, stilling his movement. "We start like this." Clothed, so I had the privilege of controlling the reveal of his cock.

His eyes, a darker brown than I'd ever seen and cloudy with lust, flared, but he nodded and withdrew his hand.

"Your watch." I tilted my head in the direction of his left wrist. "Start the timer."

"Right."

If I said it out loud, he'd probably bolt, but I fucking loved that he was so flustered he could barely remember why we were in this position in the first place.

"Three... two... one... go," he said as he tapped the screen of his old model smartwatch.

I shoved my nose into his groin and inhaled. "Let the game begin."

Chapter Eleven

I was fucked.

I was so fucking fucked.

Damn Trevor for making me that third drink. Tequila? What had I been thinking?

I'd been thinking about how hot Ryder looked in his snug Henley and black pants, and how I had to be in the same room with him looking so good without the excuse of work to keep me busy and away.

Down went drink number one.

Then I'd been thinking about how he'd ignored me the entire time with not so much as a hello or a what's up. He hadn't even glanced away from his conversation with Luke and Dom. Did he even know I was there?

I'll take drink number two and make it strong, Trev.

And then I started thinking with my dick, drooling at him across the table and fantasizing about how much I'd rather feast on his cock than the damn pizza. I hadn't even tasted a single bite of the two pieces I'd eaten.

The third drink had disappeared before I knew it, which had to be how I found myself cornering him in the bathroom.

This is a means to an end. If you can keep from coming as long as possible, he will leave your life forever.

Right. At least I still had some rational thinking left. This was a means to an end. Nothing more.

Goodbye, Ryder. I had this in the bag.

I glanced down.

Huge mistake.

Ryder hooked his thumbs in the band of my briefs and shimmied them over my hips and ass, along with my jeans. My cock sprang out with a bounce that had me wincing. I was so damn hard it almost hurt.

"Goddamn, Alex," Ryder said with awe in his voice. He licked his lips. "Your cock is a fucking work of art."

Oh shit. The way he stared at me with abject hunger and appreciation while time ticked away had my balls tightening. He acted like he had all the time in the world. Like appreciating my cock mattered to him more than winning.

And it was so hot I nearly begged him to suck me. Instead, I went with my usual charm. "Keep staring. Let that fucking clock run up as long as you want."

One of his eyebrows arched in a seductive challenge, and I ground my molars so hard, I swear I cracked a filling. I swear the green fleck in his eye grew when he was turned on. "Not too worried about it," he whispered right before wrapping his lips around the tip of my cock and suckling like he wanted to wring me dry.

"Jesus. Fuck," I cried out, slamming my palms against the bathroom door.

Ryder chuckled, and the vibrations almost made me shout again.

Bills.

Spiders.

Toothless gums.

He tongued my slit, and I saw stars. My eyes rolled back so I could no longer watch him work me over, but I'd lost control of them. God, that was my favorite. For whatever reason, I loved it when a guy did that to me. So, of course, he did it again without breaking suction. The combination of pressure from his lips and direct stimulation from his tongue had me crying out.

Paper cuts.

My empty wallet.

Dog shit.

Ryder coasted his lips down my cock, laving every inch with his wicked tongue as he went.

Nothing was going to work. A masked intruder could come in and hold us at gunpoint, and I wouldn't be able to stop Ryder. Distracting myself from pleasure so sharp wasn't possible.

When his nose hit my pubes—because, of course, he could take every inch down his throat—he moaned as though I was the one servicing him.

"Fuck. You." I managed.

He swallowed in response, his throat muscles rippling around the head of my dick with the most perfect, powerful pressure.

As though controlled by an external force, my hand slid to his hair, where I gripped the soft strands and thrust my hips forward even as my one remaining rational brain cell screamed at me to stop.

I'd made a colossal mistake.

Ryder was too damn good at this. He sucked me like he loved the taste and feel of my cock in his mouth. Like this wasn't a challenge to see who could best the other, but like he'd taken me down his throat for his pleasure as much as mine.

Who the hell could resist something so fucking hot?

He sped up, no longer working on strangling my dick with the back of his throat but dragging his tight, wet lips up and down my length again and again. I glanced down, helpless to look away.

His hair, always perfect and unmoving, stuck out in all directions between my fingers. His cherry-red lips glistened with saliva as they stretched around my length, and his face was flushed with effort. He'd never looked better.

I couldn't wait to come. I wanted it so badly. I wanted to watch the way his eyes flared as my cum filled his mouth, his throat flexed as he swallowed me, and his satisfaction as I sagged against the wall, spent and blissed.

No!

Shit. I was losing control, making this real instead of a damn bet.

I bit my lower lip to keep filthy words of encouragement from leaving my mouth. I wanted to ask him how much he loved choking on my dick. I wanted to praise him for his incredible skills with that wicked mouth.

No*!*

My balls were so heavy and full of the load I fought against releasing. Every time my cock hit the back of his throat, my stomach spasmed. I wanted to roar out my pleasure and fuck into his mouth more than I ever wanted anything in my life.

Somehow, as though he knew I stared, he met my gaze. Pleasure, desire, and triumph burned in those blue orbs. He knew he had me. He damn well knew how badly I wanted to fuck his face.

I swear I saw the mischief enter his eyes a fraction of a second before his big hand surrounded my balls. He snuck a finger against my taint and pressed as he dove back down on my cock and swallowed—hard.

That was it. I was powerless to fight against the triple onslaught of sensation to my dick, balls, and that bundle of nerves right behind them.

"You fucking cheat." I gasped as pleasure exploded from

my center outward. My hips left the wall, and I held myself deep inside his mouth as I unloaded every pent-up drop.

Nothing mattered but the incredible pleasure pulsing through my veins, vibrating my muscles, and soaking my brain. No longer was I in my boss' bathroom with a man I hated trying to win a bet.

I sagged against the wall, panting harder than an Olympic runner as the room slowly came back into focus. At some point, I realized I still clutched Ryder's hair and had my hips pressed forward, keeping my cock in his warm mouth.

I forced my fingers to open and release his head. My dick slipped out of Ryder's mouth as he lowered onto his heels with a smirk that should have enraged me, but he'd sucked any fucks I had to give right out of my cock.

He gripped my wrist as I drew my trembling hand back and turned my wrist. "Six minutes and twenty-three seconds," he said, raising an eyebrow.

Shit.

I had my work cut out for me.

Still, I couldn't muster my usual hatred and annoyance. The benefit of a stellar orgasm, no matter who it came from.

Ryder stood slowly, unable to hide the sizable tent in his slacks.

I blew out a breath and ran trembling fingers through my hair. He'd gotten hard, extremely hard from sucking me off, if the evidence could be believed. Even if he swore he'd hated every second and only blew me to win the bet, his body disagreed and had the hard-on to prove it.

The sight made me feel better, slightly. I'd come like a geyser down his throat. He could have gloated and preened like a peacock, which would have killed my post-orgasm bliss, but he didn't.

It was then I realized I stood slumped against the door with my jeans at my ankles and my softening dick hanging out, wet from his mouth.

I cleared my throat, then bent to grab my pants. Ryder kept his hungry gaze on me as I pulled my briefs and jeans over my ass then fastened the button and zipper. Neither of us said a word. What could we say? This situation was weird and stupid as hell, but he'd held up his end, so I wouldn't back down either.

Six minutes and twenty-three seconds of giving head were all that stood between me and never having to work with Ryder again.

The dip in my stomach had nothing to do with the job. I loved giving head, and even though Ryder was an asshole, I could admit my physical attraction to the man. It certainly wouldn't be a hardship to get him off, but for whatever reason, my insides swooped.

Once I was tucked away and somewhat decent, I reached for him only to have my hand slapped away with a snort.

"I don't fucking think so," Ryder said, chuckling.

My face heated, and the anger I'd been missing a moment ago surged. "What the fuck?"

He raised his hands. "Chill. Don't ruin all my hard work getting you to relax for once. I'm not trying to back out or anything." He pointed at the bulge I'd been admiring. "See the state I'm in?"

Ryder's meaning clicked, and I coughed out a half-laugh.

"Yeah, exactly." He ran a hand through his hair, smoothing the strands as he shook his head. "In this state, I'll last twenty-two seconds if I'm lucky. No way am I handing you the victory like that."

What were we doing? This was insanity, and now it had to happen again?

I refused to think about why the idea of another round didn't repulse me.

I sighed. "You working Wednesday night?"

He nodded.

"Fine. We'll do something then." His laughter had me narrowing my eyes. "Well, how would you describe it? This isn't exactly normal for us. Nor do I want it to be."

"Ah, there's the grouchy Alex we all know and love. If you were anyone else, I'd be worried about my oral skills with you getting grumpy three minutes after a big O, but I'm actually shocked you lasted this long without snapping at me."

"You're hilarious." Why did I let him get to me this way? Every time I frowned at him, he patted himself on the back for getting under my skin again. Even with that knowledge, I couldn't prevent my reaction. I really hated the man.

You sure didn't hate his mouth on your cock.

"With the bar set this low, it gives me something to shoot for next time."

"Next time?"

He must have heard the shock in my voice because Ryder-fucking-Calloway blushed like a schoolgirl.

"Whatever. You know what I meant. The point is, you need to lighten up and learn to smile every now and again, especially after someone sucks your brain through your cock."

"You didn't…"

He stared at me, challenging me without words. He knew how good that had been for me. I'd filled his damn mouth to the brim with a gallon of cum. That didn't happen from a mediocre blow job.

I wasn't the type to back down from a challenge, any challenge, apparently, so I held his gaze. The bathroom crackled and fizzed with electricity as the seconds ticked by. I inhaled, but the air felt thick, and as I blinked, I could feel the walls closing in on us, moving us closer. If one of us didn't leave, we'd be crushed. Forced together by the universe, me sated yet curious about returning the favor and him with his cock rock-hard and ready to go.

"All right," I said, but it came out strained and raspy, not with the confidence I demanded of myself around him. "I've had enough of this. I'm gonna go back down and make some excuse to leave. Just wait a few minutes or something so no one gets suspicious."

"No worries there," he said with a wry smile I refused to call charming. He pointed toward his dick, which still strained against his pants. "I'm gonna stay up here and take care of this alone in my boss' bathroom like a serious creep. I figure it's better than going downstairs while I'm pitching a tent. By the time I get down there, I shouldn't need to come up with a lie to leave. Everyone will assume I've been up here destroying Parker's bathroom in a different way."

I couldn't help it. I laughed loud and long.

The way Ryder's eyes widened in shock probably should have felt like an insult, but everything between us had skewed. Instead of sticking around to hear some comment about how I looked when I laughed, I went with the stellar, "See ya," turned and fled.

Thankfully, someone in the universe liked me enough to keep the stairs and hall to the rec room clear of my coworkers or worse, Parker.

"Dude!" a beyond tipsy Trevor shouted when I rejoined the group. "Where have you been? I missed you." He drew out each word as though crooning a heartfelt ballad.

"Wow, drink much tonight, Trev?"

Before I finished the question, I had my arms full of a very drunk, very affectionate Trevor, who had no idea what I'd gotten up to in Parker's house.

Holy shit, I let Ryder blow me in my boss' mansion. *Let*, hell, I practically begged for it. No one could argue I wasn't the initiator, even if Ryder had come up with the stupid bet.

I'm the one who cornered him in the bathroom with a hard dick and missing brain. If only I could blame the alcohol, but I couldn't. The drinks I'd consumed during dinner had me tipsy at best, but weren't clouding my judgment. No, that was the lack of sex and the hot man I hated yet couldn't stop fantasizing about.

"Whasamatter, Ally?" Trevor slurred with a dopey grin.

"Nothing." I shifted, trying to keep him from falling while avoiding getting a mouthful of his gelled hair, but he was determined to squirm around. Whenever he drank, he became worse than a wiggling toddler. "Hey, Trev, I'm gonna take off. I gotta check on Kenny." It was the most believable excuse because it was only half a lie. I should check on Kenny. Someone should constantly be checking on Kenny. And who, if not me? Trevor would have no reason to doubt my intentions.

"You're a good brother." He grabbed my arm and started to lead me in a stumbling waltz, only to pitch us onto the couch. His bony elbow dug into my hip as he giggled.

"Yeah. I'm the best," I grumbled with a wince as I struggled to sit up with a hundred and fifty pounds of Trevor trying to 'help.' At least he hadn't taken us to the floor. "Look, Trev, you're wasted. I don't want to leave unless I know you've got a way home. How about you come with me? I'll drop you at your place."

The offer wasn't as selfless as it seemed. With Trevor in the car, yapping away, I wouldn't be stuck listening to the voices in my head dissecting what happened tonight and why I'd liked it so much.

"I've got him. I'll see he gets home safely." Parker's amused tone had me glancing up to where he stood over us, wearing a frown that betrayed his voice. Everyone knew Trevor had it bad for our boss, but Parker had never been anything but professional, almost overly professional, around my friend. As far as I knew, Parker hadn't crossed or blurred any lines. Trevor's poor heart took a beating every time rumors of Parker's nocturnal escapades made it to our staff room. The man certainly wasn't a monk, but he refused to give Trevor the time of day, no matter how green Trevor's light flashed.

But times like now, with the intense way he stared at Trevor, I'd swear Parker wanted Trevor as much as my friend craved our boss.

Why did all of this shit have to be so complicated?

"You sure, Parker? I don't mind dropping him home. It's on my way." Translated—please save me from myself.

"I'm sure, Alex. Thank you, though. You're a good friend to him." Parker shifted his attention to Trevor, who stared up at him with hearts in his eyes from where he'd sprawled on the couch. "Come on, Trevor. Let's get you some water."

"Okay." Trevor took Parker's outstretched hand and practically floated off the couch. "I'll call you tomorrow, Ally."

"Sure." Chances were, he'd never remember, but I'd check in on him in the morning.

I stood and made the rounds, saying a quick goodbye to the rest of my coworkers. A few protested my leaving early, but a simple mention of helping my family dispelled their arguments.

After retrieving my coat and gloves from James, I left.

Cold, crisp air smacked me in the face the second I stepped outside. The kind of frigid air that seized your lungs when you inhaled and made your breath visible when you exhaled. I loved it. Sure, warm weather where I could run around in shorts and T-shirts was great, but I truly loved these freezing winter nights. Despite the social nature of my job, I preferred to stay home, and nights like these made me want nothing more than to huddle under a blanket on my couch watching a movie.

I'd love it even more if I had someone to join me. A man who would tangle his legs with mine and run his fingers through my hair as we pretended to pay attention to the movie until we were both hard enough that we couldn't ignore it any longer. We'd fuck right there on the couch for hours, maybe even the rest of the night, then fall asleep spent and satisfied. Too bad I lived with and was responsible for my ailing mother and deadbeat brother.

I'd probably spend the next thirty years alone, working my ass off to keep us afloat until I was too old to get it up and no one would want me anymore. Then I'd trudge into my twilight years a grumpy old jackass who had no prospects and a prescription for Viagra.

Jesus, I was getting morose.

Undisturbed snow glittered in the moonlight as far as I could see. Parker's property was gorgeous. I tried to focus on the area's beauty instead of my minor freakout. The stroll down the walkway to my car was leisurely despite the cold and snow. Parker had a heating element under his driveway that melted the snow on contact.

What a life.

I spent two hours yesterday shoveling our small driveway by myself because Kenny never showed up despite promising to take on shoveling duty this time.

I was starting to sound so bitter. No wonder Ryder called me cranky.

"Nope," I said aloud. "Do not think of Ryder." I slipped into my car, shivering as a gust of wind rattled my bones. "Come on, baby," I said as I turned the key in the ignition. "You can do it." It took three tries to get the engine to start. Sometimes, she didn't want to run in the cold, which I could respect, but it made me dread the day she refused to start, even with my coaxing and sweet-talking.

As soon as the car was idling and warming up, I cranked the music until my brain pulsed. Hopefully, I could make it loud enough to drown out my thoughts.

It worked. Kendrick Lamar sang to me the whole way home. By the time I pulled into my driveway, my head ached, but at least I wasn't thinking about Ryder. Not too much, anyway.

"Why did I do that?" I muttered as I killed the engine. My dick twitched as though answering me.

You did it because I wanted it. The man is hot, and his mouth should be registered as a weapon.

"Shut up," I grumbled, staring at my crotch. Then I grunted. "I'm talking to my dick. Fantastic." Shaking my head, I climbed out of my car and back into the cold.

The three steps to our small front porch were slick with ice. I made a mental note to sprinkle salt in the morning. It was too late to hunt around the dark garage for the ice melt at this time of night.

As I was about to shove my key in the lock, a groan came from my right.

"Jesus Christ," I shouted, jumping so hard my neck tweaked. "Kenny? What the fuck?" I rubbed the back of my neck as I walked to the lump huddled on the outdoor chair I'd found on the side of the road last summer. "Were you sleeping out here? It's fucking five degrees."

He wore a thick winter coat—mine, and the one I'd been looking for earlier that day—and had his knees tucked into his chest.

"Couldn't find my key," he mumbled as he unfolded himself and sat up.

I shook my head, huffing out a white puff of air. "So why didn't you knock or call Mom?"

"I did. You know how she is when she's sleeping. An explosion wouldn't wake her." He turned away and mumbled something.

"What was that?"

"I lost my phone. Can you unlock the fucking door already? I'm fucking freezing."

"Kenny, do you know how unsafe it is to sleep outside? Especially if you've been drinking or taking whatever."

"Thanks, Dad, just open the door."

Sighing, I unlocked the door and motioned for him to go first. He ran straight to the bathroom. Five seconds later, I heard the shower run.

"You're welcome," I muttered to no one.

What if I hadn't left early? What if I'd stayed at Parker's a few more hours? Would I have come home to my brother dead and frozen on the front porch? Something needed to be done about Kenny, but hell, if I knew what to do. I wasn't a father, just a twenty-three-year-old drowning under the weight of his life.

And to think I'd been stressed about a blow job.

This was the perfect reminder that my life wasn't my own, and I had bigger things to worry about than Ryder Calloway and his gifted mouth.

Chapter Twelve

"I want to turn our attention to the acquisition under review. We've spent the last few months vetting Synergro Medical Robotics, a promising startup focused on surgical automation. Integrating their technology with our CallCore platform could open new markets and diversify our revenue beyond traditional manufacturing. I believe this move will help us stay on the cutting edge and add significant shareholder value long-term."

I glanced at the rapt faces sitting around the long oval table in the boardroom as my father droned on. The eight board members hung on his every word. Some took notes, some had their assistants beside them, and they scribbled notes, and others merely listened. My father's executive assistant sat to his right, taking a detailed record that would serve as meeting minutes and the basis of the quarterly press release.

My grandfather, Herbert Calloway, founded CallCore in 1980. An engineer who worked in the auto industry, he dreamed of advancing and streamlining auto production for years before leaving his job and branching out on his own. At its inception, CallCore specialized in precision robotics for the automotive sector. In the early two thousands, after my grandfather suffered a debilitating stroke, my father took over. With a grand vision in mind, my father embarked on an aggressive expansion by acquiring smaller robotics shops and pivoting to serve a broader range of industries. We now had divisions for aerospace, electronics, consumer products, and biotech industries. To keep things interesting, my father also owned two prominent luxury hotels. The man was nothing if not ambitious.

Today, CallCore focused most of its energy on AI-driven technology, particularly surgical automation through robotics. Despite sitting in that boardroom with my freshly minted engineering degree, just like my father and his father before him, I had no interest in the exciting and groundbreaking advancements. I was another in a long line of Calloway men destined for this life.

Or so my father insisted.

The meeting commenced twenty minutes ago, and already boredom had me wanting to pull out my hair.

I'd been dead asleep when my father pounded on my door at six a.m., ripping me from a heated dream of Alex's cock tunneling down my throat.

It wasn't a dream.

Maybe not, but this sure had been. In this version, Alex grabbed my head and rammed his cock down my throat, moaning and praising me for sucking him so good. His eyes had been wild, not filled with an exhaustive effort to hold off his orgasm. He'd stared as my eyes teared and asked if I wanted his load filling my mouth.

Of course, my answer had been a resounding yes.

And just as I'd felt the first thrilling jerk of his dick about to give me what I wanted, the hammering on my door ripped me from the erotic fantasy with brutal ferocity.

"Ryder, I'm leaving in twenty minutes," my father had yelled through my locked door. "I assume you remember you promised to come to the board meeting this morning. It would be poor form for my son and the future CEO to fail to show up after I informed the rest of the board he'd be in attendance."

So there I was, wearing a damn suit and listening to him drone on while not having the balls to tell him I wouldn't be living out his dream for me.

Alex would probably jizz himself to be in this room, surrounded by so many great engineering minds. The man lived for this shit and would probably drop to his knees and swallow my cock on the spot if I got him a seat at the table.

Huh, not my worst idea.

"In closing, I'd like to thank each of you for your ongoing support. Our recent strategic pivots have positioned us well to continue delivering strong financial results and advancing our broader mission of promoting industrial innovation. I look forward to your thoughts on the acquisition plan and how we can best align our resources for another successful quarter. Thanks, everyone. Let's take a ten-minute break. Marjorie brought in some pastries. Refill your coffee, grab something to eat, and then Bob will continue with the next quarter's financial projections."

A low murmur of conversation kicked up around the table as the board members relaxed for a few moments. I stood and made my way to the coffee urns for a refill. It gave me a chance to hover on the side for a moment and act busy. For some reason, whenever I accompanied my father to the office, I felt like I had a neon sign flashing *liar* above my head. I could feel the stares of employees and board members, hear them calling me a nepo baby who didn't deserve or even want to head up the company. And that was before anyone dissected my lack of qualifications. What did I know about running a business, let alone a billion-dollar global empire?

Nothing. I knew nothing.

My father would laugh and tell me he wasn't going anywhere for a long time. He'd remind me he learned the same way I would, at his father's side, once he'd completed college. He had an answer for every roadblock I threw in his path.

Damn him.

"Ryder, my boy," he said, his voice dripping with pride as he strode my way. For some reason, he always called me my boy at the office, like he needed to remind everyone of my elite status as the CEO's son.

"Great job, Dad. Some exciting projects on the horizon."

He squeezed my shoulder as he reached for an empty mug. "Thank you, son. There's nothing I love more than having you here by my side." His eyes, the same blue I'd stared at in the mirror my whole life, now had the softness of age crinkling their corners. His blond hair, also a near copy of mine, now had the sprinkling of salt common for a man in his fifties. He'd also lost the athletic build he'd been blessed with after decades of living the life of a very wealthy man. Despite the years showing in his appearance, he still maintained the razor-sharp business acumen that had expanded his father's corporation to one of the most prestigious in the nation, maybe the world.

"I remember the exhilaration of joining my father at board meetings. I loved the feeling of knowing I'd one day take the helm. It's a heady one, isn't it?" Pride radiated from him, hitting me square in the gut.

"Yeah," I croaked as guilt soured the coffee in my stomach. "It's... something."

If he noticed my less-than-enthusiastic response, he didn't show it. Most likely, he was too wrapped up in his fantasy of a father-son empire.

"You by my side is all I've ever wanted, son."

I set my mug down. Another sip, and it would all come

back up. "Thanks, Dad." I had to tell him, and soon.

Or I could switch my major back, get an MBA, take over, and be miserable for the rest of my life to avoid disappointing him.

Again.

My parents had been great when I came out to them at sixteen. They said everything right, donated to LGBTQ+ causes, and hadn't even acted shocked.

Despite both coming from extremely conservative backgrounds, they were smart enough to realize my sexuality wasn't a choice or something they could control. My career path, though? That was a choice, I just had to be willing to go against everything I'd been groomed for since birth. This bomb had the potential to destroy my family the way my sexuality hadn't.

"I'm going to get started up again," my father said, squeezing my shoulder. "I have another meeting immediately after this, but I've arranged for you to spend some time in the R&D lab. Okay?"

"Sure. That sounds great."

He beamed at me, then moseyed back toward his place at the head of the table. "Okay, if you could all take your seats, we'll continue."

I spent the rest of the meeting pretending to focus on whoever spoke while my mind drifted a million miles away. The pressure to slide into a slot I wasn't built for had never felt so crushing. It had always been there, but hovering on the periphery as something to deal with when I finished high school, when I graduated from college, and then when it was time to obtain a Master's degree. I pushed the decision back every chance I had, but now I'd hit the wall. There wasn't anywhere else to hide, no other corners to shove this decision. Hell, I'd decided months ago—now I just had to man up and own it.

And crush the dreams of the father who'd given me everything.

I think if there were a chance my father would react well, my anxiety would disappear. But there was no chance he would take this news well. Not when pigs flew or snowballs formed in hell. Those idioms left a minuscule window of hope. Most considered my father a fair, even-keeled man. Even those working under him described him in favorable terms. He rarely lost his temper and never at work, but I knew it was only because he got his wishes ninety-nine percent of the time.

That one percent?

Well, no one wanted to be the one percent that set him off.

And that's where I lived these days, right in that dangerous one percent of things that would not go his way.

The board meeting finally concluded after two painful hours of statistics, projections, and verbal circle-jerking. I leaped to my feet before anyone could engage me in conversation and darted out the door toward the elevator.

Jabbing the down button a good twenty times, I glanced over my shoulder to the fully exposed boardroom. The rest of the meeting's attendees milled about, chatting and finishing their coffee. My father was nowhere to be seen. He'd probably rushed straight to his second meeting.

No one had followed me to the elevator bank, so when the doors opened, I was able to slip inside alone.

The doors slid shut, and I sighed as I sagged against the wall, staring at the long string of numbered buttons. The button for floor seven, where I was due at the R&D labs, seemed to glow brighter than all the other floors.

I pushed the lobby button.

The yellow glow bounced down from floor sixteen, where I was.

Ten... nine... eight... seven...

My stomach tightened.

Six… five…

My father would be livid when the lab called to ask why I didn't show up. He'd blow up my phone and eventually corner me at the house. By leaving, I'd essentially scheduled a conversation with my father about my future.

No escaping it now.

Speaking of escape, as soon as the elevator doors opened on the ground floor, I shot out and strode across the lobby toward the exit with the gait of a man on a mission. No one stopped me, though a few called out greetings, which happened whenever I came around. Nearly all of the thousand-plus employees knew me by face and name, even if I'd never laid eyes on them.

The second I left the revolving door and stepped into the cold, crisp downtown air, an enormous weight lifted off my shoulders. Despite what I'd thought, someone must have clocked me leaving because my father's valet service had my car idling at the curb.

"Thank you," I said as I accepted the keys from a trim older man in a CallCore security uniform who held my car door for me.

"You're welcome, Mr. Calloway. Will you be back later today?"

"No, I'm done here for the day."

"Very good, sir. Enjoy the rest of your day."

"Thank you… Karl," I responded, reading his nametag.

My Range Rover was toasty warm inside, thanks to heated seats and blasting vents. I adjusted everything to my liking, then pulled out into traffic, heading to the one place that would give me clarity.

Ten minutes later, I parked in the sparse lot at True Colors of Boston, a community center for LGBTQ+ kids and children of LGBTQ+ parents. Unbeknownst to my family and friends, beyond Vera, I'd volunteered here for the past five summers and on school vacations. The YRA had after-school and weekend programs for kids who needed a safe place to land. We provided tutoring services, counseling, mentorship, free meals, and a mountain of activities for the kids to engage in. Volunteering with their tutoring program was what sparked my interest in becoming a teacher.

Today was the first day I'd stopped by since I'd returned home.

The familiar sound of basketballs dribbling greeted me as I walked into the nondescript building. Ahead of me, the front desk, unmanned as usual, made me smile. How many times had I filled in, answering those phones and checking the kids in and out?

Hundreds.

To my left, a horde of teenagers ran around the gym, hurtling basketballs and trash talking while laughing. On my right, classrooms filled with students completing their homework, making up the quieter side of the building.

"Ryder Calloway?" An incredulous voice had me glancing down the hallway to the left of the desk. "Is that you... Oh my God, it is you! Ryder!" Another, then another, followed her screech, and before I knew it, the pounding of excited feet grew thunderous. Teens came out of the woodwork, throwing themselves at me from all angles.

Micky reached me first—a tenth grader whose parents dumped him on his ass when he came out to them. He was a fantastic track star, leading his high school to glory, but all his family could see was who he was attracted to. His gangly arms wrapped around my midsection and squeezed the life out of me.

"Mick, my man. Halle, hey! Jordan, what's up, bro?" I greeted everyone I recognized and nodded or smiled at the new faces hovering on the periphery.

"What is going on out here? Oh, Ryder! Hello." Carmen, the director and most compassionate woman I'd ever met, emerged from her office. "What a fabulous surprise."

"Hope it's okay that I'm here without being on the schedule."

She waved away my concern. "Of course it is. You are always welcome here."

"Why aren't you at school? You flunk out or something?" Devon, a little shit seventh grader, asked. He had a mouth full of braces and looked like he didn't own a hairbrush. Not much had changed since I'd last been there six months ago.

"No, Dev, I did not flunk out. But thanks for the vote of confidence. I'm switching back to school here in Boston. I'll be able to volunteer here a few times a week again."

The kids cheered as though I'd told them they won the lottery.

Why hadn't I come back earlier? This was where I felt the happiest, useful, and appreciated.

I bet Alex would like it here. A few of the kids reminded me of him or the version of him from high school—smart kid with a chip on his shoulder and something to prove. He'd grown into the driven man I couldn't seem to stop thinking about, even during board meetings or here at the center.

"All right," I said, shaking off thoughts of the sexy man who hated my guts. "Whose ass am I kicking on the court today?"

Cheers went up as the kids tugged me toward the basketball court. I hadn't thought to bring a change of clothes, so it looked like I'd be sweating through my Armani suit and playing basketball in dress shoes.

Six hours later, when the kids finally allowed me to leave, I was exhausted, happy, and running late for my shift at Top Shelf. My phone chimed as I jogged from the center out to my Range Rover. If I hadn't been thinking about how fast I'd have to drive to avoid an ass-chewing by Parker, I'd have thought twice about checking my messages. Instead, I swiped the screen, and my stomach dropped.

Where are you?

Why didn't you go to the lab?

How could you be so irresponsible?

This ends now. I want your ass in my office at 8 tomorrow.

ANSWER ME NOW.

Chapter Thirteen

Parker hated lateness. He fully lived by the adage that five minutes early was on time, and on time was five minutes late. I'd say lack of punctuality was his number one pet peeve, but watching Trevor flirt with customers might top that chart, even though he'd never admit it. The tick in his jaw said it all.

So when I parked at Top Shelf with only three minutes to spare, something I never did, I felt justified in my mild panic.

My stupid piece of crap car took a solid ten minutes to start again. If I didn't take it into the auto shop soon, I'd likely get stuck on the side of the highway in a snowstorm, but who had the extra cash for an expensive car repair lying around?

Not me.

Grumbling, I shut off the car and hustled out into a cold, dark Wednesday night. Someone hovered near the rear staff entrance, hunched against the cold, illuminated by the floodlight above the door. Whoever it was faced away from the lot, speaking to someone on the phone.

"Yes, I am taking this seriously." Silence, then, "Okay, I get it." An arm flew up as a huff left the frustrated speaker.

Ryder.

I recognized the ridiculously thick gold ring he wore on his left middle finger. Some dumb family crest he'd worn since the day I met him. It was gaudy as hell, a monstrosity with rubies and diamonds glinting in the floodlight. Exactly the type of thing you'd expect a rich frat boy to wear. Ryder probably rubbed his dick on it to get off.

"Could we talk in the morning, Dad? This is an important conversation, and I'm late for—"

Silence again.

"What do I want to talk to you about? Um…"

I'd never heard anything but confidence crossing into arrogance from Ryder. Not tonight. His voice was hesitant, almost fearful, and it had me feeling like an intruder. I slowed, then glanced over my shoulder. Should I return to my car to give him some privacy? Parker would kill me if I came in late, but this conversation seemed private.

"Well, I want to talk about my future. My plans for *my* future." The conviction in Ryder's voice had me frowning. His future? Wasn't he getting an MBA, then sliding into some high-ranking role at his father's corporation until the day he took over? He'd sure bragged about it enough back in high school.

This silence lasted longer than the previous, probably filled with his father's words. Unhappy ones if the way Ryder curled in on himself was any indication.

"W-what?" Ryder whispered. "What do you mean you refuse to entertain any ideas I have for the future? Yes, I know the plan has always been for me to take over CallCore, but I —"

The abject devastation in his tone froze me halfway between the door and my car. Ryder hadn't noticed me hovering, but he would if I tried to sneak inside. His body blocked most of the door. No way could I go around him without alerting him to my presence, and he'd know I'd heard his half of a conversation I had no business hearing.

"I'm a goddamn adult," Ryder growled into the phone, his voice rising. "I'm allowed to have my own vision for my future."

My heart kicked into overdrive as I glanced at my car. If I started back, I'd be caught. If I moved forward, I'd be caught. So I stood there like a living statue, freezing my balls off as time ticked by, and my shift started without me. We were a solid five minutes into both of our shifts.

"No... I..." Ryder sighed again. The heavy sound twisted my insides.

"This is not a negotiation, Ryder." His father screamed so loud on his end that his voice came through the phone, making me jump.

Shit, that was one angry man.

"Do not fuck me over. You are my son, and you will fulfill your role or find a new goddamn family."

I gasped.

What the fuck? Who dictated to their adult son like that?

Ryder whipped around. The second he saw me, his eyes widened with horror.

We stared at each other, both wearing dismayed expressions.

Shit. Shit. Shit.

I had to be the last person he wanted to catch him in a vulnerable moment. "I... uh... I'm late," I muttered, scurrying around him to get to the door. "Sorry." I slipped inside, leaving him slack-jawed as his father's irate voice still reverberated through the phone.

I dressed, or undressed, as quickly as possible, then rushed out to the floor to set up my tables for the first reservation. When another five minutes passed without Ryder, I paused beside his unprepared table.

Had he left? Would he be a no-show for the shift? If so, it'd be the last one he worked. Parker had very little mercy for guys who flaked on work.

I sighed and then went to the stock room, where I grabbed extra napkins and glasses. After depositing some on Ryder's tables and the rest on mine, I arranged them in the artful way we always did.

The least I could do was help the guy out a little. He was having a shitty night, and he'd sucked my dick, after all.

Do not think about that.

My VIPs were due to arrive in about five minutes, so I jogged to the walk-in for some cold bottles of water. As I rounded the corner, Parker's angry voice had me slowing down.

"You're almost fifteen minutes late, Ryder." Even though Parker's back was to me, I could see the annoyance on his face, and it made me cringe. No one did disappointment quite like Parker.

Somehow, my tardiness escaped my boss' notice—thank God for small favors. Clearly, Ryder wasn't as lucky.

Poor guy. Adding insult to injury was never fun.

Trevor would probably pop a boner at the censure in Parker's tone, but Ryder merely mumbled an apology while his cheeks flamed an intense red. "I'm sorry, Parker. I had a family... issue."

Parker grunted. "The only things I hate more than lateness are excuses."

Ouch.

They stood between the refrigerator and me. Screw it. I could get the water bottles after greeting my VIP customers. I stepped back as quietly as I could, then started to turn on my heel.

"Don't bother, Alex," Parker said, making me nearly jump out of my skin. "I'm done here. Ryder won't be late again, will you?"

"No, sir."

Parker nodded. "Get to work, boys."

He walked away, leaving Ryder and me staring at each other across a span of fifteen feet after I'd caught him in an awkward moment.

Again.

The red stain of humiliation on his cheeks didn't detract from his hotness. In fact, it reminded me too much of the flush he'd worn while on his knees before me.

Fuck, why did my mind always go there?

I cleared my throat. "I've got your table ready. Just needs water."

His eyes narrowed. "Why?"

Good question. I huffed a half-laugh. We sure weren't in the habit of doing favors for each other. Of course, we could count the blow job as the ultimate favor.

Why?

I shook my head as though I could dislodge the memory of his mouth. "Fucked if I know."

He grunted. "You better get out there before Luke escorts your VIPs over. I'll grab the waters."

He abruptly turned and disappeared into the walk-in before I had a chance to thank him. Not that I would have. He hadn't thanked me, though I suppose his return of the favor was his way of saying thanks.

Whatever. This interaction didn't deserve another second of my brain power.

Yet as the night went on and I did my performing monkey routine where I smiled, flirted, served drinks, and entertained men with enough money to blow thousands on a Wednesday night out, I couldn't keep myself from glancing at Ryder every few minutes.

He was off his game. Short with customers, lost in his head, and frowning. He'd even spilled a full glass of Macallan on a smartly dressed attorney I was sure would threaten to sue. Instead, he'd murdered Ryder with a glare and earned his table a ten percent discount.

It was so painful to watch him work tonight that I almost offered to take his table and let him leave early. The only thing holding me back was knowing how humiliated I'd feel if the tables were turned.

Who'd have thought I'd miss his cocky grin and untouchable attitude?

After the third time he fucked up an order, I couldn't take it anymore. We were both due for a quick break, so I motioned to a coworker to keep an eye on our tables, which were empty while the VIPs danced.

"Ryder," I shouted over the pounding music.

He raised an eyebrow, so I pointed to the break room. "Ten-minute break."

He nodded once, then turned and strode away, shoulders hunched in defeat. I trailed a good fifteen feet behind him. If he didn't get his shit together, he'd be out of a job and—

Wait.

Wasn't I supposed to want him gone? Wasn't that the entire reason I'd agreed to his ridiculous bet in the first place? A chance to get rid of him without any fuss?

He slammed through the staff room door with a harsh shove, leaving me frowning as he disappeared, and I realized I no longer hated working with him. Customers loved him, he'd made friends with the staff, and on an average night, he had most of the place laughing. Ryder made work fun.

I treated the staff room door to a much gentler push and slipped from the sensory overload of the club to the muted, almost peaceful staff room to find Ryder guzzling water in front of his locker. He had his chin tilted back, exposing the long line of his throat as he swallowed over and over. The urge to press my lips to his neck and feel those muscles working nearly brought me to my knees.

Before I could do something stupid, like rub my growing dick on him, he lowered the water. "Can't stop spying on me tonight, huh, FL?"

I narrowed my eyes. The return of the nickname had my hackles rising.

"Hope you're not here thinking I'll suck you off again. That shit ain't happening. Besides, it's your fucking turn. Though I thought for a minute there, you might get lucky. Parker might fire my ass before you ever have to bruise your knees."

"Ryder…" What was there to say? Until a few hours ago, I'd thought he'd lived a perfect, charmed life. And maybe he did. Maybe whatever he'd been arguing with his dad about was the ultimate first-world, rich-boy problem. Maybe his black AMEX had a new spending cap, or his Range Rover wasn't his favorite color. Perhaps the alligator shoes he'd ordered got delayed, and dear old Dad had no sway with the delivery company.

But I didn't think so. This felt more, bigger.

Ryder's sorrow felt real, and for whatever reason, I didn't like seeing it on him.

"Leave me the fuck alone, Alex. You know Parker doesn't like two BSBs to take a break at once. And we both know who'll be blamed for it tonight."

"Don't be a dick, Ryder. I'm trying to be nice here."

He grunted. "Why shouldn't I be a dick? It's what you think of me. It's what you've always thought of me. Might as well live up to it."

I pressed my lips together. Years of dealing with Kenny's bullshit taught me to control my temper, but Ryder was pushing it. "Look, I'm sure our problems are very different, but—"

He barked out a harsh laugh, throwing his hands in the air. "Yeah, FL, I'm sure they are. And your biggest problem is going to be me if you don't leave me the fuck alone." He advanced on me as he shouted. Stopping only when we were almost nose to nose. His chest heaved, and his eyes burned with anger. He was so damn close I could smell the expensive whiskey on his breath from the shot he'd done with his table recently.

I could taste it so easily. Just slip my tongue right into his mouth and sample all that smooth whiskey and building heat. My dick sure liked the idea. It swelled, and I couldn't do a damn thing to hide it in the ridiculous work shorts.

"Are you fucking listening to me?" Ryder shouted.

His tone crashed over me like a bucket of ice water, jerking me back to reality.

I scoffed. "You know what? You're right, Ryder. I have always thought you were a dick, and tonight you proved me right yet again." I stepped back. "Go ahead and drown in your shitty mood for all I care. Don't know why I'm trying to save your fucking job anyway."

I spun and shouldered my way out of the staff room. Dance music assaulted my ears and overwhelmed my frayed nerve endings. Screw him. It wasn't my fucking fault if he got his ass canned.

"Whoa," Trevor said as I stomped over to the bar. He sat at the end, sipping a bottle of water. "What crawled up your ass?"

"Nothing," I muttered, which made Trevor giggle.

"Maybe that's the problem, my friend." He leaned on his gold, sparkly elbows and arched an eyebrow. "Maybe you need something to crawl up your ass."

Dom set a water bottle down in front of me. "I'm not one to kink shame, Trev, but I don't think anyone needs anything crawling in their ass."

"You have a point," Trevor said with a laugh as he used a napkin to wipe the sweat off his forehead. I'd never understand how he danced for hours on end, but he loved

Wednesday nights. "My point remains, though." He pointed at me. "You need to get laid. How long has it been?"

If he only knew.

"Ryder was late tonight, Trev," I said instead of answering that very dangerous question.

Trevor's jaw dropped. "What?" He slapped my bare chest. "And you're just mentioning this now?"

"Yep. Parker went all disappointed father on him too."

"Now you're just being mean." Trevor bit his lower lip as he fanned himself with the damp napkin. "I miss all the good stuff when I'm dancing."

"If you promise not to come in your shorty shorts, I'll break a glass in front of him later." Dom waggled his eyebrows as I pressed my lips together to keep from laughing.

Trevor, of course, clapped his hands. "Would you? Dom, you're the best," he practically squealed when the bartender nodded. "I'd do it myself, but I think he's onto me."

"Might have something to do with you bending over and asking if he wanted to spank you last time you broke something."

He pouted. "Porn-fucking-lies," he grumbled, to which both Dom and I cracked up.

I needed to get back to my tables before Parker noticed me slacking. Trevor would probably come on the spot in that case, and I had less than no interest in watching my friend spontaneously orgasm from our boss' stern tone.

"All right," I said, wrapping my knuckles on the bar. "I'm out. Thanks for the hydration, Dom. And Trev, you might want to consider therapy."

He flipped me off and blew me a kiss at the same time while I walked away laughing.

Much better. I owed them a thank you for keeping me from spiraling into a shitty mood after my interaction with Ryder.

"Yo! Alex, my man!" One of my VIPs slung an arm across my shoulder as their group returned to their table from the dance floor. "Shots! We need shots. At least three rounds, right now."

Christ. They were already shitfaced. Three more rounds of shots might make them comatose. "You got it," I said, despite my stomach roiling at the thought. "What are you up for this round?"

"Surprise us."

"Yes! I love surprises." They all started cheering and chanting, "Surprise us," as I shook my head. "Be right back, gentlemen."

One of the most challenging aspects of the job was determining how much was too much. Parker was adamant about not overserving, but the line could be as thin as a strand of hair. Many of the guys who partied at Top Shelf could drink me under the table a dozen times over. They were practically professional partiers who could suck back more alcohol than should be possible on a Wednesday night and get up for work on Thursday. Cutting them off too early could result in an angry review or a bad tip. Letting them drink to excess could result in a fight, vomit, or alcohol poisoning.

Thankfully, Parker was always willing to be the bad guy if we needed to tell a customer he'd no longer be served alcohol.

These guys seemed to be handling the high volume of alcohol well, even if half of what they'd drunk would have put me under.

As I returned with two dozen shots on my tray, I saw Ryder frowning at his table. It looked like his night wasn't getting any better anytime soon.

Whatever. Not my problem, as he so clearly stated.

Unfortunately, that sentiment didn't last as long as I'd

hoped. Trying to ignore him and let him choke on his failure, I couldn't stop casting concerned glances his way. A few times, I even helped him out by grabbing empties off his table or wiping a spill, all without his knowledge, of course.

"Hey, Alex?" Parker's voice had me whipping around where I stood near the bar, waiting on Dom to fill my table's order. "Can I ask you a favor?"

Oh shit. Was he about to ask for a report on Ryder's performance tonight?

"Of course, boss. What can I do for you?"

Don't ask it. Don't ask it.

"Would you be able to lock up for me tonight?" He rubbed at his temples. "I think I've got a migraine brewing, and I'd like to head home early."

Relief hit me. Closing, I could do. "Yeah, of course." I'd closed several times, and aside from having to be the last one to leave, it wasn't a big deal. The task involved a final sweep of the club, locking the external doors, and setting the security system. Nothing to it.

"Thank you, Alex. I appreciate it."

"No worries, boss."

"For fuck's sake," Parker muttered. "What is going on with him tonight?"

My stomach sank as I followed his gaze to Ryder's table, where one of his VIPs was shouting and waving his arms while Ryder stood with a drink in hand. Most likely he'd fucked up another order.

Parker huffed in annoyance and took a step in Ryder's direction.

"Um, Parker?" I caught my boss' arm before he could go and rip Ryder a new one. "Is it okay if I handle this one? He's having an off night, but he's still new. We can probably cut him a little slack."

"Fine. My head aches too much to deal with it anyway. But

if I end up having to handle a table demanding a refund, it's on you."

Yikes. Why the hell did Trevor like it when Parker got mad?

"It won't come to that."

"Better not," he muttered as he turned his back on me and started for his office.

Sighing, I made my way to Ryder's table. He'd probably be pissed I was intervening, but something had to give. There had to be some way to pull him out of his funk tonight.

I stopped halfway to his table as heat flashed through me. Of course, there was a way to fix his shitty night. And Parker had handed me the perfect opportunity for it.

Chapter Fourteen

This day could go fuck right off.

I only made it through my shift without getting fired because Parker left early with a migraine. Who knew what would happen next time I saw him? I'd fucked up everything I touched tonight, including myself, having spilled three, count it, three drinks on my bare torso.

Part of me couldn't wait to get home and slide between my soft sheets. To crawl into bed and let sleep claim me so I could finally stop obsessing about the earlier conversation with my father and dreading the upcoming one. The other part of me couldn't fathom sleeping under his roof tonight.

It'd taken me twice as long to clean my area tonight. My limbs felt heavy and slow while a brick resided inside my chest, weighing me down. To top off my father's refusal to entertain my plans for my future, I'd been yelled at by my boss and multiple customers, all in front of Alex, who I'd treated like shit. I owed him an apology.

A sigh burst forth as I shoved the tight-as-hell booty shorts over my hips, freeing my cock. Those damn things might make my ass and bulge look fantastic, but by the end of a full shift, my cock was screaming for freedom from the extra tight spandex. It hung free and heavy between my legs, along with my balls. The thought of shoving them back into underwear sucked, so I stuffed them in my duffle before stepping into my favorite Moncler sweats. The soft, warm fabric felt like a cozy blanket after the shitty night I'd barely survived. I slipped my T-shirt over my head, followed by the sweatshirt that matched my pants, and bent to retrieve my discarded shorts. After cramming the rest of my stuff in my duffle bag and sliding my feet into my sneakers, I was ready to go the fuck home.

After I apologized to Alex, that is.

Bag over my shoulder, I walked out into the dim light of the empty club. Even though I'd seen Top Shelf deserted this way after every shift, it still felt off to be there in the quiet without hordes of men gyrating to loud music.

It almost felt wrong, like I wasn't allowed to be there, but at the same time, I kind of liked it.

"Alex?" I called as I set down my bag and coat near the bar.

He didn't answer. Part of the closing process involved checking every nook and cranny for random stowaways or guys who had passed out. Apparently, a few months after opening, some guy passed out under a VIP table, and no one noticed. He'd awakened alone in a dark, unfamiliar place and freaked out. Determined never to have that social media nightmare occur again, Parker made sure someone completed a thorough search every night. Alex must have been somewhere he couldn't hear me.

Maybe he'd be more apt to accept my apology if I helped him get out of here faster.

I strode toward the VIP section only to stop dead in my tracks at the sight of Alex standing with his hip propped against his table. Like me, he wore sweatpants, but unlike me, he also wore a tight T-shirt that hugged his muscular chest like a second skin.

My cock immediately reacted to the gorgeous sight, tenting my pants. Without underwear, I had no hope of hiding my erection. If my throat weren't so tight, I'd have cursed.

God, he looked good, dark and serious, without smiling. I'd gotten used to seeing him grim-faced, but he didn't seem mad tonight, which was good. Part of me assumed he'd be pissed at me for taking so long to get out of there, especially after the way I'd snapped at him earlier.

"Uh, hey. Done checking everywhere?" I walked toward him, trying my best to keep my gait casual and not like there was a lead pipe between my legs.

Alex's gaze flicked down before returning to my face. He nodded.

Mission failed.

"Um, look, Alex…" I stopped about a foot away. Too close. I could smell his cologne. It was nothing fancy, but it mixed with his natural scent and the sweat of a long night's work, creating something intoxicating. "I owe you an apology for earli—"

He stepped forward, placing a hand on my chest, and my words died on my tongue as his heat seared through my sweatshirt.

"You had a shitty night." His seductive tone felt like a stroke to my needy cock and a balm to my battered ego.

"Yeah." I swallowed what felt like a mouthful of gravel. "It sucked."

Alex trailed his hand down my abs, which flexed beneath his touch, even with layers of fabric between us. He paused, resting his palm flat against my lower belly, right above my cock, which ached for touch.

His touch.

"Want to end it on a better note?" he asked, tilting his head as he studied my face. His dark eyes held a note of mischief so rarely seen in him but all the more potent for its rarity.

I sucked in a breath.

"Yeah," I whispered. "I really fucking do."

The grin that curled Alex's lips was so fucking wicked that my knees shook. "Then maybe we should get rid of these sweats." He grabbed the waistband and shoved it over my ass. The second he released my sweatpants, they pooled at my ankles. My cock, free of restraints, bobbed in front of my body, curling up toward my abs.

"Commando, huh?" Alex raised an eyebrow in what was quickly becoming my favorite expression of his—inquisitive, impish, challenging.

"After being in those tight-ass shorts for hours, I need the freedom." And if I'd known it would be one less barrier for Alex getting to my cock, I'd have stopped wearing underwear altogether.

"Mmm. Have a seat." He pressed on my hips, ushering me to the side. If I wasn't so turned on, shuffling with my pants at my ankles might have been awkward. As it was, I could think of nothing but what he was about to do to me.

When I made it into position, Alex gently nudged me into a chair at the very VIP table I'd been serving all night. The bead of precum pooling on the tip of my dick came from the knowledge I was about to get serviced.

His dark eyes locked with mine as he lowered to his knees. I assumed he'd dive right in, but instead, he removed my shoes and pants, leaving me clad in my white ankle socks. I couldn't tear my eyes away as he rose to a tall kneel and placed a hand on each of my knees.

Winking, he pressed my legs wide, then settled between them with my cock inches from his mouth.

"Jesus, Alex."

There went the eyebrow. "Look at your watch." His lips were so close to my leaking tip that I could feel his breath wafting across my dick's sensitive nerve endings, torturing me.

Suck me, please.

"Ryder?"

I blinked. "What?"

"Your watch."

"My... wa... oh."

I crashed back to reality as though Alex had slapped me. The entire point of this activity was to time the blow job and see if I could hold out longer than he did.

I was doomed.

"O-okay," I said as I glanced at my watch. "Ready when you are." That was the understatement of the century. If he didn't get his mouth on me soon, I was likely to start begging.

Instead of engulfing me between his plump lips, Alex wrapped a strong hand around my cock and swiped his thumb over the fluid at the tip.

Close enough.

I pushed the start button on my watch's timer as my head fell back on a groan so I didn't see him lean into lick me, but I sure as hell felt the warmth of his tongue circling the head of my dick.

"Oh shit."

I was so fucked.

"Alex." I lowered my head and his eyes met mine a second before he opened his mouth wide. The asshole was out for blood. He didn't tease or torment, and there was no build-up or warning games. He sucked me straight to the back of his throat.

"Fuck!" I shouted. The pressure and heat were almost too much to bear. My hips lifted off the chair of their own accord, and I grabbed onto his hair. Alex grunted, not quite a gag, but close, though he didn't back off even a fraction of an inch. He kept my cock deep as his throat muscles worked around the head, making me see stars.

He finally drew back, inhaling through his nose before diving back down on my dick. Again and again, he drove me out of my mind with the hot tug of his lips along my oversensitive shaft.

"Yes," I cried as he tongued the underside of my head, and shocks ricocheted across my skin. "Fuck, Alex, that's so good. Your mouth is so goddamn good."

He hummed his response to the praise, then continued going to town on my dick. Spit pooled at the corners of his mouth in an erotically filthy sight.

I couldn't fight it the way he'd done the other night, and I didn't want to. I wanted to come. Today had been fraught with too many emotions. I was too vulnerable, too close to the emotional edge, to deny myself something so good. Alex probably knew it. He'd probably chosen tonight, knowing I'd come fast and hard, and he'd win the bet.

As a man of my word, I'd be forced to leave the job. Later, I might hate it, feeling tricked. Maybe I'd even be furious with him, but his mouth felt too damn amazing to worry about that now.

The suction disappeared from my dick, making me groan in protest, only to have Alex chuckle and then take one of my balls into his mouth.

"Oh, fuck, I love that. You found my weakness," I mumbled, to which he hummed a reply that vibrated through my sac.

Why was I telling him these things? I needed to shut up, and, oh God, the suction on my balls had my eyes crossing, but I needed more. I needed the pressure back on my dick.

"Alex…" I gripped his hair and pulled him off my nuts only to direct him back to my cock with a line of precum running from the tip.

"Mmm," he said with a smile. "You've got one hell of a

delicious dick, Ryder."

Holy shit, I almost came right there, blasting his face with my cum. He'd complimented me. He'd let me know he was enjoying this. He wasn't slogging through it to win a bet.

He sucked me back into his mouth, and that was it. Three more slides down my shaft, and I shouted into the quiet club.

"Fuck, Alex, I'm coming. Your mouth is too good." I clutched his head in my hands as I curled over him and trembled with the force of my orgasm. He swallowed around my dick, taking every damn drop as though he couldn't bear to waste any of my load.

So damn hot.

At some point, my hand went from gripping his hair to petting his head, and about the time I realized that, I realized the bet was over.

And I'd most certainly lost.

I released Alex and sagged back against the chair, too fucking sated to move.

He wasn't, though. He smirked and grabbed my wrist. "Four minutes and two seconds." He tsked. "Guess I'm the winner."

We stared at each other. He was on his knees with swollen lips and mussed hair, and I was sprawled in the chair with my legs so wide my thighs were beginning to ache. The air thickened with a different tension than had been there moments ago.

Now what?

My heart thudded. Guess I had to hold up my end of the bet.

I cleared my throat. The words didn't want to come out. It turned out I liked working at Top Shelf. The crew was great, welcoming and friendly, like a little family. I enjoyed working with Alex most of all. "I'll turn in my resignation tomorrow."

Alex stood and, without saying a word, turned his back on

me, walking away.

Fantastic. I huffed a self-deprecating laugh. "Guess that's that," I muttered. Forcing my sated body into action, I bent and retrieved my pants and shoes. After slipping back into my sweats, I sat again to don my shoes. As I tied the final sneaker, Alex approached with a glass in each hand and an obvious flagpole in his sweats.

He held out a glass with amber-brown liquid. "Thanks," I said, though it sounded more like a question.

He sat at the table opposite me and then sipped his drink. "Don't quit."

My eyes widened. What was in his glass? It had to be something magical. I didn't know how to respond, so I nodded, which seemed to be all he needed.

I sipped my drink and let the warmth of the liquid heat my insides. Ah, Macallan. The good stuff and my favorite. Had he known? I'd mentioned it a few times. Was Alex paying attention to what I said?

We sat across from each other in silence. It had to be somewhere close to three in the morning. At this time of night, the darkened, quiet club held a peace that was in stark contrast to the vibrant life during working hours. As we sipped our drinks, the silence changed from awkward and tense to an almost comfortable intimacy.

Or maybe it was all in my head. Regardless, my mouth opened, and words I never thought I would confess to Alex, of all people, flowed out.

"I lied," I said as I rotated the whiskey tumbler in my hand.

Alex frowned. "What do you mean? Lied about what?"

Shrugging, I took another sip. "I told you, I came back home because I wanted to finish my degree here. Because I liked the program here better."

His forehead wrinkled as he absorbed my words. "Okay…

and that's not the truth?"

"It is, but it's not the whole truth, I..." Why was it so hard to say? I was so convinced that everyone I told would have a negative reaction and would react like my father did. I blew out a shaky breath.

Alex sat there patiently, wearing a curious expression but without a hint of judgment.

I almost laughed. He probably already had such a low opinion of me that nothing I could say would drag it lower.

Fuck it.

"I changed my major. The school here in Boston has a stellar master's program for education. One of the top in the nation."

Alex blinked. "I'm sorry, you're gonna have to run that by me again."

Chuckling, I sipped my drink. "I changed my major to education. I want to teach elementary school." That's it. My secret was floating in the universe now as I waited for the man who'd hated me from day one to pass judgment.

"Wow, Ryder, that is..."

I snorted. "Stupid? A waste of my parents' money? A betrayal to my namesake? Laughable?"

"Really fucking brave."

"You think?" I whispered, hating the vulnerability in my tone. "Doesn't feel like it. I knew since high school that I didn't want to follow in my father's footsteps. Took me years of a degree I won't use to muster the courage to do something about it."

He shrugged. "You know how many people end up doing something different than what they thought or planned at eighteen?"

I sipped my drink as I watched him swirl the liquid in his. "No. Do you?"

He snorted. "Okay, not exactly, but my point stands. We

pick a major so young and expect we're going to stick with it. There's nothing wrong with changing your mind and nothing wrong with wanting something different as you grow and mature." He shuddered dramatically. "Ugh, mature, what a word."

The attempt to lighten the mood worked for a second, eliciting a small laugh from me, but I quickly fell back into a contemplative mood. "You didn't change. You've known you wanted to be a robotics engineer since before I met you."

"Yeah, well, my situation is a little different. I need a secure future for my family more than I need a career passion."

"What do you—"

He waved the hand holding his tumbler. "We can dissect my problems another night. I take it the conversation earlier was your dad flipping out about the major change?"

Of course, I knew he'd received scholarships and financial assistance for both the summer session where we met and for college. Hence, the whole freeloader nickname that got me on his most-hated list, but did his family's financial situation go deeper than not being able to pay for college or pricy summer programs out of pocket? I wanted to press, but the set of his jaw told me I'd get nowhere tonight.

Another time.

Did he mean it? Would there be other times when we hung out and talked? Touched? Got each other off?

"Ryder?"

"Uh, sorry." I shook my head and then stared down into the still amber liquid he'd poured me. "He doesn't even know yet. All I said this afternoon was that I wanted to discuss my future career plans. He flat-out refused to discuss it and threatened to cut me off."

"Shit," Alex said on an exhale. "That's… a lot."

I snorted, then tossed back the rest of my drink in one gulp. "Yeah."

He still had half his drink left, which he sipped much more slowly. "Remember Andy from the summer session? The guy who had six toes on each foot."

I chuckled. "Yeah. Though I never saw his feet, so I'm not sure he wasn't lying."

Shrugging, Alex grinned. The smile transformed his whole face from unapproachable to open and warm. This wasn't the first time I'd seen that smile from him, but it had never been directed at me. Trevor, plenty of times, even Dom and Luke, but never me.

I liked it.

"No idea. Anyway, he volunteered at the LGBTQ+ youth center downtown."

"Oh yeah, you're right." He'd volunteered a few nights a week, just for that one summer as far as I knew.

"Whenever I would complain about how much I hated you..." Alex said with a wry smirk that had me chuckling, "... he'd tell me you weren't the asshole I thought you were, that you spent all your free time at the youth center, and you were fantastic with the kids. I remember him being frustrated that he couldn't connect with them the way you could. Once, he told me he wished he'd had someone like you in his life when he was younger. A mentor or a teacher he could trust."

My chest tightened as all the moisture in my mouth evaporated. I swallowed in a vain attempt to correct it. "Wow," I croaked. "That's... thank you for telling me that."

Alex huffed a light laugh. "At the time, I told him he was delusional, but now..." He pushed his glass away. "Well, it sounds to me like you're making the right choice."

This time, his words caused a fluttering in my chest. When was the last time someone believed in a choice I'd made? Hell, I couldn't remember ever making my own significant life choices. This was a first, and the support came from the oddest place.

But I liked it. Alex's simple encouragement without fluff or blowing smoke up my ass finally released the sick tension living in my gut since he caught me speaking to my father.

He stood and reached for my glass. "Fuck your father. It's your life. You gotta live it."

I couldn't help but stare at the way his ass moved beneath his soft sweats as he walked over to the bar. Then there were his arms beneath his T-shirt, not huge, but toned from lugging heavy bottles for hours on end. They rippled and flexed as he washed and dried the glasses.

Occasionally, his gaze would drift my way and linger for a second, crackling with heat, before he seemed to realize where his attention had settled. I felt a twinge in my gut each time he ripped his focus away.

He strode over to me once the glasses were back on the shelf, and fuck, if I could look anywhere but at the swell in his sweats. He'd sucked me off, listened to my problems, and provided advice, all without an ounce of relief for himself.

I stood and stepped in front of him before he could reach for his coat at the table, palming his hard dick through his sweats.

"Shit, Ryder," he said as his steps faltered, and he grabbed my upper arms for support. His pupils grew three sizes. "What... ah... what are you doing?"

"Thank you," I whispered in his ear.

For listening.

For letting me out of the bet.

For your mouth on my cock.

"Ryder... what are you doing?"

"You're hard," I whispered. "I can fix it. Simple as that."

I drew back and met his searching gaze.

He seemed to war with himself, which I responded to with a firm squeeze.

His hips bucked into my hold. "Fuck it," he said with a

groan. "If you want to fix it, get your damn hand in my pants."

Well, damn, bossy Alex had my full attention.

Chapter Fifteen

This was a terrible idea. The bet concluded. We blew each other, Ryder lost, and I told him he didn't have to quit.

That should have been the end, but then he had to go and get all chatty on me. Now I knew things about him. Things others didn't know. Things that made him human and likable. It was one thing for him to be so hot when I hated him. Hot and likable spelled trouble.

And trouble had found me. My dick, in particular, wouldn't let me walk away, no matter how advisable.

He pressed the heel of his hand against my aching erection with the perfect amount of pressure to make me needy as hell. I loved giving head, and sucking Ryder was no exception. It had gotten me hard and ready to fuck. I'd resigned myself to going home and rubbing one out the way he'd done at Parker's, but the offer of another man's hand was too good to pass up.

"Demanding," Ryder said with a smirk as he slid his hand into my sweats' waistband. The second his hand wrapped around me, he barked out a laugh that eclipsed my groan. His hand was warm, strong, and surprisingly rough, considering where he came from.

"Commando, huh?" he asked as he stroked me. The little shit had to be loving throwing that back in my face.

I smirked. A flush of heat worked its way up my torso. Already, after one dry stroke, my knees were wobbling, and my balls were heavy. "After being in those tight-ass shorts for hours, I need the freedom."

He tilted his head back, laughing at how I parroted what he'd said to me.

"Who knew fucking around with you would be so much fun?"

"It'd be more fun if you weren't dry rubbing my dick," I said with a grunt as the friction closed in on sandpaper rough.

"Like I said.... demanding." He withdrew his hand and the loss had me immediately scowling, which only made him chuckle. "Of course, I think this is one demand I can happily carry out." He licked the flat of his palm with a long, slow, seductive slide of his tongue while locking eyes with me, and my damn dick felt it through the ether. "Hmm, not wet enough." He worked his jaw, then spit in his palm.

"Shit," I panted as he returned his hand to my cock and resumed stroking with his spit easing the glide. "You're filthy."

"You have no idea," he whispered against my ear as he increased the pressure on my cock. "We've only scratched the surface."

So far.

The unspoken words reverberated through my lust-soaked brain. Was he thinking of them, too, or was I so desperate to come that I imagined this wouldn't be the last time? It didn't matter. All I could think of was more, more, more.

And Ryder delivered.

He jacked me with a firm, skilled hand that had my eyes crossing and my cock leaking precum. Though better than nothing, spit was a far cry from lube. Ryder swept his thumb across my slit, gathering the fluid and slicking the way for his large hand.

He kept his gaze on my face, watching my reaction as he stroked me. The smug, self-satisfied tilt to his lips told me he knew exactly how much I liked his handiwork.

So I didn't bother to hide it.

"Jesus, Ryder," I said, breathless, as I grabbed for his hips to steady myself.

"You got a really nice dick, Alex," he said as he tightened his grip. "Wanted to tell you last time, but well… you know."

I could only grunt in response. My energy was focused on not coming too soon so I could prolong the incredible pressure of his hand coasting up and down my shaft.

"Fills my whole hand real well. Filled my mouth too."

It did. I wasn't small, and neither were his hands. The memory of him on his knees brought me closer to the edge.

He leaned in and spoke against my ear again as his free hand cupped my balls. "Bet it would fill my ass perfectly. Stretch me so well. Right to the edge of pain. Mmm… it would be so fucking hot."

My hips bucked, and I gasped as his hot breath hit my ear the same time he tugged my balls and squeezed my dick.

Was he telling me he wanted me to fuck him? Is that what those dirty words meant? That he wanted my dick fucking his ass.

His hand sped, sliding along my dick with sure, fast strokes. I couldn't keep my hips still any longer. I fucked into the circle of his grip as I clung to his sides and moaned like a damn whore right there in my place of employment.

"That's it, Alex. Fuck my fist like you'd fuck my ass."

The image of him bent over and writhing in ecstasy as he took my cock in his tight hole bombarded my brain. I planted my head against his chest and cried out as pleasure blasted through me, so sharp and intense my vision blurred.

"Oh shit," I shouted as my body jerked, and I flooded Ryder's hand with my release. He rubbed me through the orgasm, making a damn mess in my sweats, but I didn't care. I sighed and let the pleasure twitch through me until I finally came down from the high.

Eventually, I uncurled my fingers from Ryder's sides and straightened away from him. After one final caress, he withdrew his spunk-covered hand.

"Seems we made a bit of a mess of your sweatpants," he said with that smug grin I was beginning to hate less than I had days ago, especially after coming so hard.

I snorted and ran a hand through my hair. "Yeah. Gonna be a fun ride home."

"I'd say I'm sorry, but..." He shrugged and smirked.

"Worth it." I adjusted my sticky sweats with a slight cringe. Yeah, this would be freezing cold and gross by the time I made it home, but what was a little discomfort compared to a stellar orgasm?

"Hmm." Ryder met my gaze and lifted his hand to his lips. He ran his tongue between his fingers and over his palm, cleaning the evidence of how much I'd liked his hands on me. "Tastes just as good the second time around. Glad my memory didn't deceive me." He winked, and it was so confident and cocky that my spent cock twitched as though it had a prayer of rallying this soon.

How was it possible that something that infuriated me days ago thrilled me today?

"Um..." I cleared my throat. "Seems like you're feeling better."

Ryder threw his head back and laughed. The sound echoed through the empty club, filling the desolate space with a sense of happiness. "Yeah." His grin stretched wide across that gorgeous face of his. "I think it's safe to say my night ended much better than it started. So, thank you." His voice lost any playful inflection. "For real, Alex... thank you."

Conceited Ryder, I knew and could handle. Apparently, I had a pretty good grip on sexy Ryder as well. Tonight proved I could manage my way around Ryder when he needed to vent, but this version of Ryder? This genuine nice-guy routine where he thanked me with sincerity?

I had no idea how to handle that. It made this thing we were doing too real when it should have been nothing more than a bet.

"No problem," I said with a shrug. "What are coworkers for if not to help when your personal shit is affecting your job?"

His frown almost made me cringe, or maybe it was my awkward attempt at lightening the conversation, but I held it back.

"Right," he said, then turned and grabbed his coat. "Guess we should get the hell out of here before our next shift starts."

I snorted a half-laugh. "Yeah. Good idea."

We grabbed our belongings and exited the club in silence. I'd expected him to go straight to his fancy car, but instead, he hovered near the employee entrance with me while I locked the final door.

You don't have to wait.

The words dangled from the tip of my tongue, but I pressed my lips together and kept them inside because, well, I liked having him there with me. This wasn't the first or even the fifth time I'd closed for Parker—each time, I'd been alone. While the task was quick and easy, I hated being the last one to leave. If something happened, no one would know.

"Good to go," I said as I armed the alarm. "Thanks for waiting. You didn't have to do that."

Ryder merely gave me a droll look that conveyed how stupid he found the statement, which did not warm my insides at all. Nope, not a single bit. Because we weren't friends. Hell, I didn't even like the man. He'd been an ass to me at camp.

Eight years ago...

Maybe, but he still took pleasure in annoying the hell out of me. Who wanted that in their lives?

He also takes pleasure in pleasuring you.

Jesus, my inner voice needed to be stomped out.

"Well, guess I'll see you tomorrow night."

God, I was so awkward. Sometimes, I wondered how I ever made a single dollar in tips working my VIP tables.

Ryder half-snorted a laugh. "Yeah, I'll be here." He touched my shoulder, and I refused to believe the tingles came from anything more than surprise. "Thanks again, Alex."

"Sure, no problem."

No problem? Of course, it wasn't a damn problem. We both came. God, I was such an idiot.

Our cars were separated by about five spaces. The distance between us increased as we made our way to our vehicles. Thankfully, we didn't get any snow or ice tonight, so the drive home at the late hour should be uneventful.

"Night, Alex," Ryder called as he reached his electric Range Rover. I almost laughed at the difference in our cars. His shiny and black without a smudge on it, where my old rust bucket was covered in a salt film from driving to and from work all winter. Paying for a car wash was a luxury I couldn't afford.

I should have waved over my shoulder and slipped into my car, but instead, I turned and met his gaze. We stared at each other across the quiet parking lot for a beat while I had the ridiculous urge to ask him to text me when he got home safe so I wouldn't worry.

Thank God I had the presence of mind to keep that thought

where it belonged—in my head and not out in the universe.

"Night," I called back. "See ya tomorrow."

He dipped into his luxury vehicle and started it up without a sound. I'd bet my tips that the interior was warm and toasty within five seconds. That fancy car probably had heated leather seats and steering wheel, whereas I'd spend the next ten minutes begging my hunk of junk to start. If it did, the car would finally warm to a comfortable temperature about the time I pulled into my driveway.

I followed him out of the parking lot, turning left where he turned right. If there was ever a sign we lived in different worlds, that proved it. Luxury vehicle aside, he'd turned toward the rich side of town, whereas I'd steered my car toward the rundown, neglected neighborhoods.

For a short time tonight, I'd forgotten our differences. Sex had put us on a level playing field, but now, freezing my ass off while he was toasty warm, I remembered we weren't the same. We weren't even friends.

As predicted, I arrived home as soon as my car finally hit a cozy temperature. My comfort lasted for less than a minute, disappearing when I opened the car door. When I glanced at the quiet house lit only by the porch and foyer lights, my stomach cramped. Was Kenny home? Was Mom asleep in her bed, or would she be dozing on the couch as she stressed about him? I didn't have the reserves to go out looking for him tonight—this morning—or even wait up until he arrived home.

My boots crunched over a thin layer of snow I'd have to shovel in the morning, and a wave of fatigue crashed over me. Was it too much to ask that Kenny pull his head out of his ass to do one damn chore without me having to badger him? It had snowed ten hours ago, for crying out loud. Mom couldn't help take care of the house, but even she managed to do more than my lazy-as-fuck brother.

Silence greeted me when I stepped into the foyer. No strung-out brother or naked women I didn't know on the couch, and no drug paraphernalia littering the coffee table. My stomach sank. When did finding my brother high off his ass with a random girl become the desirable choice? At least it meant I knew where he was and wouldn't have to worry I'd get a phone call from the cops or, worse, the morgue.

With a heavy sigh that made me feel twice my age, I wiped my boots and then kicked them off next to the door. I removed my jacket, hanging it on the row of hooks I'd installed a few years ago after watching an instructional YouTube video.

Clad in my socks, I padded past the kitchen and down the carpeted hallway, peeking into the first room on the left. My mom slept soundly on her back with her wheelchair lined up next to the bed. Most of the time, she could transfer herself in and out of bed without assistance, but on days she felt weaker, she'd nod off in her wheelchair until I returned home to help her to bed. Today must have been a good day.

The knot in my stomach loosened as I backed out of her room and shut the door. One family member was safe and sound. My room was next to hers, and Kenny's was across the hall, with the lone bathroom across from Mom's room. Having only one bathroom made for an interesting challenge. Mom's equipment occupied much of the floor space and littered the counter. Catheter equipment, a nebulizer, and a basket of medications had to be moved before I could wash my face. I could piss through the opening in the raised commode seat but had to move it to sit. The bench took up ninety percent of the small walk-in shower space. Kenny and I constantly moved equipment in and out of the bathroom, depending on who needed the space. I'd kill to add a second bathroom, preferably an en-suite for my mom's room, but that was money we'd only have if one of us won the lottery jackpot.

Another sigh left me before I reached Kenny's room. I'd have to be more careful with those. My mom tended to bury herself under a mountain of guilt if she thought I was overworked and stressed, which I was, but she didn't need to know that.

My heart kicked up to a full gallop as I reached for Kenny's door handle. It turned with ease, and I pushed the door open wide enough to peek in. Relief at finding him prone and snoring hit me so hard that I almost collapsed to my knees.

Thank God.

I could get myself ready for bed, sleep a whole five hours, and make it to my nine-thirty class by the skin of my teeth.

But as was typical with solid plans, the universe decided my time would be better spent staring at my ceiling for the next two hours, wondering how awkward it would be the next time I saw Ryder.

Chapter Sixteen

"Dude, where the hell are you?"

Sparkly teal fingernails snapped in front of my eyes, making me blink. "What?"

Trevor scowled. "Okay, I know it can't possibly be me because my company is stellar, so what is up with you today?"

Shit. I'd zoned out on him for the third time in the twenty minutes since we sat down for lunch at our favorite café on campus. "Sorry, Trev. It's definitely not you."

He smirked. "I know. I already said that." Today, he'd gone with a black fitted turtleneck sweater and designer denim flares that Parker had given him for his last birthday. He'd rimmed his eyes with a dark pencil and glossed his lips with a light pink sheen. He looked gorgeous, but then Trevor always looked good. He was the epitome of a clothes horse and prided himself on always looking perfect.

"So what is it?"

I set down my spoon and pushed the tray with a bowl of tortilla chicken soup away from me. "It's noth—"

"Nope!" Trevor pointed his fork at me. "Do not tell me it's nothing. You've barely paid me two seconds of attention since we sat down, and you know that doesn't fly with me. Spill so we can solve your problem, then get back to more important topics, mainly me." He winked.

No one would deny that Trevor was high maintenance. Hell, he called himself a diva on a good day, but much of his over-the-top personality was a shield to hide the wounds at his core. One night, after way too many shots, he'd opened up to me about his horrific past. After promising I'd never repeat a word of his story, he'd also made me promise we'd never discuss it again. I'd honored the agreement but hadn't forgotten the awful things he'd confided in me. It made me view Trevor in a new light.

He was a good guy who'd fought tooth and nail for every sliver of happiness he had.

I shook my head as I leaned back in my chair. "Fine. I did something stupid, that's all. I'm just having a hard time shaking it out of my head."

Trevor snorted. The café was crowded during lunch, and the noise drew curious looks from neighboring tables. "You, Mr. Responsible, did something stupid? What was it... you missed trash day or something?" He snorted again, then reached for his iced tea.

"Funny," I said as he took a sip of his drink. "No, I... uh..." I lowered my voice, leaning across the small table. Christ, I couldn't believe I was about to say this out loud. "I sucked Ryder off. And he returned the favor."

Trevor's eyes widened as he inhaled a sharp breath and immediately began to choke on his drink. He set down his cup, coughing so loud a woman ran over from a nearby table.

"Is he okay?" she asked as she whacked his back.

Trevor held up a hand, waving her away as he continued to cough. His eyes watered, and he wiped at them with his sleeve.

"He's fine," I told the concerned patron. "Just iced tea

down the wrong pipe."

She nodded and back-walked to her table, still watching my former friend, Trevor.

My face burned like I'd poured my freshly made coffee all over it. Not only had I confessed my ugly secret, we now had the whole damn restaurant gawking at us.

Trevor's coughing finally waned. He took a sip of his tea, swallowing with care this time. "Okay," he said after wiping his eyes again. His voice sounded hoarse from the hacking spectacle. "You're gonna have to repeat that one for me."

"No way." I gave him my nastiest glare, which had less than zero effect on him. "There is no way in hell I'm telling you again after the dramatic display you just performed."

He sniffed, then cleared his throat. "Well, pardon me for being shocked, but I did not have Alex-slurps-his-sworn-enemy's-dick on my Bingo card for today."

"Keep your voice down, for fuck's sake," I whisper-yelled across the table as I glanced around the café. Thankfully, most customers appeared to have lost interest in us and returned to their meals.

He didn't respond but pursed his shiny lips and stared at me through shrewd eyes as though he could see beneath my skin to the turmoil swirling below.

"What? You want details? You want to know how it happened?" I squirmed in my seat. If he didn't stop looking at me like he knew more than I wanted him to, I was going to walk out.

"Ha," he said with a grunt. "I know how it happened." He shrugged as though it was a foregone conclusion. "Hatred is a passion just like desire... very easy to get it jumbled up. There's a reason hate-fucking is a term."

Fine, maybe he did know.

His damn all-seeing eyes twinkled with mischief.

"You're enjoying this," I muttered as I glanced at a table a few rows over where a chubby toddler was trying to stick her hands in her mother's soup.

"You're right about that," Trevor said with a laugh. "I'm enjoying the fuck outta this. It's not every day I get to see you ruffled over a guy. Actually, I don't think I've ever seen you ruffled over a guy."

"I'm not *ruffled* over anyone. What the hell does that even mean?"

"It means you liked it. It means you liked having his delicious man meat in your mouth and—"

"Seriously? Are you twelve?"

Trevor cracked up, once again drawing the notice of others. I was starting to think he did it on purpose. He'd always been a damn attention whore.

"All right," he said with a wave of his hand. "I'll stop teasing you. Why do you think this has you all spun up?"

Shit, the psychological analysis was worse than being made fun of. I scowled. "Go back to the teasing."

He raised his hands in surrender. "All I'm saying is that maybe you don't hate him as much as... what? What's wrong?"

The back of my neck prickled, and for whatever supernatural reason, I glanced over at the café's entrance, freezing in place as Ryder walked in with another man I didn't recognize.

He scanned the restaurant until his gaze landed on me.

And stuck.

The temperature in the room shot up ten degrees, and my heart rate climbed with it. One peek at him, and I was back in Top Shelf, watching him reach into my sweats and fist my cock. The cock that was rapidly remembering exactly how good it felt and how much it liked to feel that good. Thank God the table hid the evidence, or Trevor would not have been merciful in his attack.

"What the hell are you... oh," he said as he glanced over his shoulder toward the entrance where Ryder still stood staring at me. "Look who we have here."

Ryder's buddy realized he was halfway to the counter alone and turned back. He called and waved to Ryder, who didn't react.

Because his whole focus remained on me.

And I liked it.

"This is ridiculous," Trevor muttered. "We're doing this shit my way."

I blinked. "What do you mean? Trevor, no!" I whispered as he stood and waved both arms above his head like Ryder didn't know exactly where we sat.

"Yoo-hoo!" he shouted in a high-pitched tone over the lunch noise. "Ryder! Over here. Come sit. We have plenty of room."

My heart lodged in my throat. If I could, I'd have slunk down in my seat, slithered under the table, then crawled to the exit, but Trevor would probably jump on my back and beat the shit out of me. The man might be small, but he was scrappy as hell and slightly terrifying when pissed.

Ryder's gaze shifted to Trevor. His lips curled in a smile that had my stomach swooping with discomfort, of course. What else would it be? I didn't want to sit through a super awkward lunch with the man I blew and the other man who knew I'd blown him. The flutter in my chest had nothing to do with excitement and everything to do with dread.

"Yay." Trevor beamed as he sat back down and faced me. "He's on his way over."

"Yes, I can see that."

"Good Lord, Ally, fix your face." Trevor rolled his eyes.

Did I have something on me? I ran a hand over my mouth, but it came back clean. "What's wrong with my face?"

"You have this pinched expression like you're about to

have a root canal, not have lunch with the dude you're smitten with."

It was my turn to choke, but I hadn't consumed anything, so my throat clogged with air. "I am not smitten with anyone," I grumbled. The closer Ryder came, the more my insides vibrated. "This is nothing, Trevor. It was a stupid mistake."

"*Suuure* it was."

Ryder and his friend went to the counter, placed their orders, then made their way to us once they had their food.

"You're staring," Trevor muttered, then hummed the tune to Elvis Presley's "Can't Help Falling In Love."

"I hate you," I whispered as Ryder drew so close I could see the green fleck in his left eye. Couldn't he have the decency to wear sunglasses so I didn't have to see it?

Trevor blew me a kiss. "Oh, Ally, you love me, and you know it. Hey, Ryder!" His demeanor transformed from ball-busting to welcoming in the blink of an eye. "Fancy meeting you here."

"Hey, guys. This is my buddy, Corvin. Corvin, this is Trevor and Alex. We all work together at a nightclub."

"Hey," I said because I had a real way with words.

"Sit, sit." Trevor gestured to the two empty chairs opposite each other at our small square table. I sat there like an idiot. The connection between my brain and tongue seemed to have vanished.

"Thanks. Nice to meet you guys." Corvin seemed nice enough. He had light features like Ryder, but that's where the similarities ended. His blond hair was so pale I'd almost call it white, and where Ryder had ocean-blue eyes, Corvin's were light gray. He was tall and thin, almost waifish, and walked with grace and elegance.

"You look familiar," Trevor said to Corvin as he sat. He propped his chin on his hand, studying the newcomer. "You ever get a VIP table at Top Shelf?"

Chuckling, Corvin shook his head. "I wish. That place is way above my budget. I don't know if you follow dance at all, but I'm a ballet dancer in the program here on campus."

Trevor snapped his glittery fingers. "That's how I know you. I saw you perform a few weeks ago. You had the male lead in Romeo and Juliet, didn't you?"

Corvin beamed. "I did."

Trevor leaned closer, eyes bright. "You were fantastic. Took my breath away."

"Thank you." Corvin removed the lid from his salad with long, graceful fingers. "I worked my ass off for that role. Glad to know it paid off."

"Yes, your *ass* did a spectacular job. I couldn't look away."

"Oh my God," I muttered as Ryder laughed and Corvin turned pink. Trevor might be head over heels in love with Parker, but that didn't stop him from flirting like his life depended on it with anyone who caught his eye.

"So, how do you two know each other?" Trevor went on.

Ryder laughed. "We met at a party freshman year, hooked up a few times, and have been friends ever since."

My insides seized. They'd hooked up?

"Oh really?" Trevor said in an exaggerated tone. "How juicy." He winked at Corvin, whose cheeks might have permanently turned pink, but Corvin didn't notice Trevor's flirty move. His attention remained on Ryder, and the sappy, puppy dog eyes he was giving had bile climbing in my throat.

He still wanted Ryder. Hell, he might be in love with the man whose dick I sucked last night. Thank God I hadn't eaten much of my lunch, or I'd have thrown up for sure.

"Yeah," Corvin said, almost breathless. "We've been really close ever since."

The urge to lunge across the table and punch the guy in his

lovesick face was nearly impossible to resist. I opened my mouth to say who-the-fuck-knew what, probably something that would make me sound like a psychopath, when a sharp pain blasted through my shin.

I grunted and stared across the table at Trevor, whose eyes narrowed at me. He shook his head once in a subtle movement meant only for my eyes.

I slumped back in my seat with my heart pounding an anxious staccato. Christ, what had I been about to do? Lay claim to Ryder? Tell Corvin to back the fuck off because Ryder was mine? The notion was so ridiculous I could barely think of it without laughing out loud.

Trevor saved me from humiliating myself.

I forced myself to avoid glancing at Ryder, but the restraint grew more challenging by the second.

Dozens of questions bounced around in my head. How was he after the drama with his father yesterday? Had they talked?

Do you still fuck Corvin?

I no longer felt the waves of tension flowing off him like yesterday. Maybe he'd had a productive conversation with his father. I was dying to ask, but I wouldn't air his dirty laundry in front of Trevor and Corvin. Plus, we weren't friends. He'd probably find it weird if I checked in on his personal life.

Though what we'd done last night felt personal as hell.

Ugh, why had I crossed that line? I could write off blowing each other as nothing more than us trying to win a stupid bet, but the way I'd let him have at my dick after I sucked him off? I had no justification for that beyond wanting him to touch me and make me feel good.

Stupid.

As Trevor rambled on to Corvin, who kept sending heart-eyed looks Ryder's way, my fists curled under the table, and I had to force my fingers to open. I hadn't punched someone since I was thirteen, when a kid at school insulted my sick mother. It felt great at the time, but the ass-chewing she gave me afterward left me ashamed and promising I'd never use my fists to solve my problems.

And I hadn't.

My gaze finally drifted left, and I found Ryder watching me. I sucked in a breath as the nerve endings in my skin came to life, tingling with awareness. I could almost feel the heavy weight of his gaze like a caress on my sensitive skin.

Or maybe that's just what my subconscious wanted it to be.

I needed to get the hell out of there. But instead of standing and making an excuse to leave, I opened my big mouth. "So, uh, what are you up to today, Ryder?"

He cleared his throat. "Just finished up a meeting with my academic advisor for next semester. And this afternoon, I'm signing a lease on an apartment."

"No shit?" The news overrode the bullshit in my head, and I grinned at Ryder, who nodded. "Well, congrats, man. That's awesome news."

"Thanks. Want to come with me? I can give you a tour."

And we can get each other off again.

The unspoken words reverberated through my brain as loudly as a brass marching band.

Everyone not at our table disappeared. Trevor's gleeful stare was palpable. My friend used every ounce of strength to avoid standing up and cheering us on. Corvin's stare, on the other hand, burned into the side of my head—hot, jealous, and laden with heavy disappointment.

But I didn't care. All I could think about was being alone in an apartment with Ryder, where I could get my hands on him and feel his on my bare skin.

Where I could make him come.

Again.

"Uh, yeah. Sure. I guess I can do that."

Trevor snorted.

My hoodie and jeans went from keeping me comfortably warm to stifling me in a burning inferno. A bead of sweat rolled down the center of my back. If someone didn't change the subject, I'd start panting and might hop up and hump his leg.

Ryder knew exactly what the offer did to me. He smirked the same arrogant grin I'd seen from him and hated countless times, and while it still had a profound effect on me, it no longer enraged me to the point of blind fury. Now it riled me up in a way that had my dick aching.

"I didn't realize you'd found an apartment." Corvin's clipped tone had Ryder frowning his way. "I'd have been happy to join you if you wanted company."

Over my dead body.

"Oh." Ryder cleared his throat. "Shit, sorry, Corvin. I—"

"Actually," Trevor broke in, flashing Corvin his most charming smile. "I was going to ask if I could get a tour of the university's ballet studio after lunch." He batted his eyelashes and scooted his chair close to Corvin, resting his hand on the other man's arm.

"Yeah," Corvin said. "I can do that." He did a shitty job of erasing the disappointment from his face, and if Trevor had an actual interest in him instead of just taking one for the team, I'd hate the man even more.

"Yay," Trevor said as he clapped. "I'm excited." He pinned me with a you-owe-me-big-time look that had me chuckling.

I wasn't sure if I should buy my friend a bottle of champagne for being a stellar wingman or slap him upside his head for enabling my toxic behavior.

The rest of the lunch crawled by in a too-slow blur of stolen glances at Ryder, insufficient blood flow to my brain, and a constant desire to donkey kick Corvin, whose mooning over Ryder bordered on pathetic.

Trevor kept the conversation flowing, drawing Corvin's attention whenever his slobbering over Ryder became too obvious, while I reverted to one-word answers and grunts. If I participated in the conversation, I'd have either blasted Corvin with a verbal assault or begged Ryder to leave now and feast on my cock for lunch instead of his panini.

I snuck another peek at Ryder to find him watching me. My tongue dried up at the heat in his eyes. They'd darkened until I almost couldn't find the speck of green I'd become obsessed with.

I didn't know what the hell we were doing besides playing with fire, but I did know one thing.

I was seriously fucked.

Chapter Seventeen

After serving drinks until two a.m., coming my brains out on Alex's tongue, and jerking him until he flooded my hand, you'd think I'd have passed out the second I got home. Instead, I'd laid flat on my back, staring at the ceiling for an hour, tense. My skin felt sensitive and irritated, as though I'd developed an allergy to sleeping under my father's roof. The thought of spending another night there had me wanting to scream, so I got up, grabbed my laptop, and searched for apartments until the sun came up. As soon as the business offices opened at eight, I called my top five and decided to rent one right then and there. Tonight, I'd sleep in my own apartment in a building my father did not own.

At some point, I would have to speak to him. I couldn't expect to avoid him forever, but today wasn't the day. I needed some time to determine the best way to approach the conversation and assert myself in a way he'd accept and respect. I didn't really think he'd cut me off. My mother would have a fit if he tried, but on the off chance he did, my bank accounts were fat enough to sustain me for years, thanks to investments I'd made once I turned eighteen from money my grandparents left to me.

I didn't plan on running into Alex today, but what a fun surprise. Helpful too. Corvin and I had been friends for years. Sure, we'd hooked up two or three times when we'd met, but he wasn't my usual type, and I wasn't into him in that way. Unfortunately, he felt differently and had expressed his desire for a repeat performance a few times since I'd returned home. Turning him down gently didn't seem to be working. Maybe it was shitty of me, but I hoped he finally got the message after I asked Alex to join me while I signed the lease.

And if I played my cards right, maybe we could get each other off again.

After putting my car in park, I pressed my hand over my cock, which had been half-hard from the second I glimpsed Alex in the restaurant. Feeling his gaze flick my way every few seconds hadn't helped the situation, and I'd had to walk away from the table, holding my winter hat over my crotch. The move didn't fool Trevor for a second—Corvin either by the crushed look in his eyes.

I sighed. That did the trick, and my cock deflated. At some point in the near future, I'd have to endure an uncomfortable conversation with my friend.

Alex pulled his old beater in next to me. He climbed out of his car with the same sour expression I now realized was his thinking face.

"You good?" I called out as I opened my door.

"Yeah." He glanced up at the brand-new luxury apartment building. "Place looks fancy."

I shrugged. "I guess." It looked normal to me. Rarely did I think of things in terms of fancy or not. "Let's go in. The leasing agent is going to meet us in the apartment."

He craned his neck and looked up. "How many floors is it?"

"Sixteen, I think. There is everything from studios to three bedrooms. The top two floors have penthouses."

He frowned. "Ryder, which floor are we going to?" The suspicion in his tone had me glancing his way, and his deep frown made me chuckle.

The guy was clearly out of his element, and I had no idea why I found his discomfort so endearing. I winked. "Guess," I said as I strode toward the entrance.

"Shit," he whispered, hustling to catch up to me. "Maybe I should just go. I don't really fit in here or know how to talk to all these fancy people."

I stopped and spun around on the spot. Alex would have crashed into me, but I put a hand on his chest, halting his progress. "First of all," I said, shaking my head. "You work at Top Shelf. You deal with *fancy* people four nights a week." Then I curled my fingers into his puffy jacket and pulled him so close I could smell his fresh aftershave and feel the heat coming off his face. "Second, I got hard just sitting next to you at lunch, and I suspect you did as well. I plan on doing something about it right after I sign the lease and kick the agent out the door. Don't make me take care of this alone," I whispered as I thrust my re-awakened dick against his leg.

"Christ," he bit out, squeezing his eyes shut. "You play dirty."

"Mmm, I do a lot of things dirty."

His nostrils flared as his eyes opened, so dark and stormy with lust, I almost shoved my hand into his pants right there.

"All right, I'll come... go," he said as though realizing I'd run with that slip. Then he reached down and adjusted himself. "Just... shut the fuck up, or I'm going to scar the leasing agent for life." He shoved me away as he spoke.

My head fell back as I laughed. The times Alex joked were my favorite, especially when he did it in that growly tone. I caught a peek at the noticeable bulge in his worn jeans and swallowed hard. My dick responded in kind. Maybe his jokes were my second favorite thing.

"Let's go," I said as I turned back to the entrance. This was going to be the fastest apartment tour and lease signing in history.

We rode the elevator to the sixteenth floor in silence, standing on opposite sides of the ascending box. I could see him clearly in the elevator's mirrored doors. He stood stiff in his spine *and* those fucking jeans with his legs slightly spread. His eye smoldered, and he breathed low and deep as though working to control his inhalations. Around floor eight, he reached for his denim-covered dick, massaging himself through his jeans.

I groaned. "Fucking tease."

He smirked and continued to fondle himself until the elevator beeped at the penthouse floor. The doors required a code to open at this level, so I keyed in the four-digit guest code given by the leasing agent, making sure to rattle off the numbers for Alex to hear. Never know when he'd need it.

"After you," I said, gesturing as the door slid open.

He grunted a half-laugh. "Don't trust me behind you?" he asked as he strode past.

"I do. I just want to stare at your ass while I imagine all the things I want to do to it," I whispered, which made him stumble.

"Oh my goodness." A petite blonde woman with a sharply angled bob and lavender power suit rushed our way. "Are you okay, sir? Did you trip on something?"

I couldn't help but laugh as Alex scowled my way.

Payback was a bitch.

"No, ma'am, I'm fine. Just clumsy." His face turned as red as the stripe in my Burberry scarf.

"You must be, Charlotte. I'm Ryder." I stepped forward with my hand outstretched to put the poor guy out of his misery, especially since I was the one to cause his embarrassment. No way would I risk pissing him off and jeopardizing my orgasm.

"Yes, hello, Ryder. So nice to meet you." She shook my hand, having short, manicured nails that matched her suit.

"Likewise." I gestured to Alex. "This is a coworker and friend of mine, Alex."

He stepped forward to shake her hand with a nod, then returned to my side. It was nice having him there. It felt nice not to have to sign the lease alone, but also having his presence by my side.

I liked it.

"I know you said you're all in and prepared to sign the lease and pay the security deposit and first month's rent today, but let me give you a tour before we get to that, just in case." She chuckled a light, tinkly laugh. "Trust me, it's much easier to change your mind now rather than after we've signed. So, follow me." She turned and click-clacked her way down the hall in beige, heeled boots.

I nearly groaned out loud. All I wanted was to sign the damn thing and send Charlotte on her way so Alex and I could get down to business.

He must have sensed my urgency because he snorted a laugh. "Chill," he muttered too low for Charlotte to overhear. "You're going to *live* here. You need to at least look at the place. And I'm not going anywhere. You made me some promises I plan to collect on."

"Well, if you're going to be all logical and mature about it..." I strode after Charlotte with the sound of Alex's dark chuckle at my back.

"Holy shit," he muttered as we turned left into a spacious kitchen. "This is insane."

White marble countertops, rows of light gray cabinets, and gleaming Wolf appliances greeted us. Everything screamed brand new, never used, and costly. The space was modern with clean lines and an airy feel. The kitchen opened on one end to a dining area with a six-person wooden table surrounded by windows with a gorgeous view of the snowy city far below. The opposite end of the kitchen flowed into a sprawling den with a massive television, tan leather sofa, and roaring electric fireplace.

The vibe was completely different from my parents' ornate look, which included dark wood, heavy furniture, and patterned wallpaper.

I loved it.

"This place is insane." Alex's eyes were twice their normal size as he did a slow turn, taking it all in.

"It's perfect."

He snorted. "This kitchen is humongous. Do you even cook?"

That had Charlotte and me laughing. "No, do you?"

He nodded. "Some."

Huh. I never would have guessed.

"But never in a place a quarter as nice as this. My whole kitchen could fit in that refrigerator."

I glanced at where he pointed. Yeah, the Sub-Zero refrigerator was quite large.

"And look at that fucking television." He cringed. "Sorry. That freaking television."

"That's quite all right. The place is incredible and requires a strong reaction." Charlotte chuckled, seeming charmed by Alex's awe.

"Now you're going to want to get a TV that big to go there," he said, shaking his head.

Charlotte glanced down at her notebook. "Didn't you say you were interested in the furnished option?" she asked.

I nodded. "Yes, I am."

"Then the apartment comes with everything you see, television included."

I worried Alex's eyes would fall out of his head. "We live

on different planets," he muttered.

The remainder of the tour went the same way, with Alex muttering astounded comments about the differences in our worlds. In the beginning, I chuckled and threw him the occasional wink, but by the third bedroom—yes, I know I did not need three bedrooms, but I hoped to eventually talk Vera into living with me—he'd begun to withdraw and do his grunting thing. It was time to end this charade before I lost him.

"Okay," Charlotte said as she neared the front door from the final bedroom. "That is the penthouse. The building also has an impressive list of amenities, including a fitness center and spa, dry cleaners, a small convenience store, and a restaurant you can have delivered to your apartment anytime between the hours of seven in the morning and midnight." Her sunny smile made me feel guilty for imagining throwing her out the window to get her to leave. "I have to say the restaurant is fantastic. The executive chef is a James Beard award winner."

Alex paled. He jerked his thumb over his shoulder in the direction of the door. "I think I should—"

"Great! Thank you, Charlotte. Where do I sign?"

She chuckled. "In such a rush. Don't you want to tour the fitness center and restaurant?"

"Nope." I tried to flash her a charming grin but, admittedly, didn't know as much about charming ladies as I did about winning over men, especially when drunk and horny. "I am in love with the place and ready to commit. Show me some papers, and I'll sign on the dotted line."

"Dude," Alex muttered. "Go see the other places. Don't be stupid."

"Nope." I winked. "I'm sold."

"Okay, great." Charlotte didn't need as much convincing as Alex, probably due to the commission she'd get for offloading the final space in the building. "Come on over to the table, and we'll review the paperwork."

I faced Alex. "Do. Not. Leave," I mouthed, earning me an eye roll and a scowl, but he nodded and folded his arms across his chest, leaning against the wall by the door. He stood a little too close to the exit for my liking, but I wouldn't push my luck and make him sit at my *fancy* new dining table.

My excitement grew each time she flipped a page in the rental agreement. Every stroke of my pen brought me closer to being alone with Alex and his addictive cock. At this point, I risked chubbing up every time I signed my name in the future. It would bring me back to this moment of thick anticipation and need.

Charlotte flipped the packet closed with a sunny grin. "And that was the last one."

I could feel Alex's spine snap to attention as he straightened off the wall with a gasp.

"Great. Thank you so much for all your help."

"Of course. It's been my pleasure. Do you have any remaining questions for me?"

"Nope. I'm all good. Excited to get settled in." I stood and took two steps toward the door Alex opened, waiting for Charlotte.

Eager much?

"Ah, yes, I can see that." Charlotte's sharp gaze bounced between Alex and me as we stood there like two idiots, staring at each other. Her grin changed from professional and pleasant to sly and knowing. "Well, gentlemen, enjoy the penthouse, and please do not hesitate to contact me if you need anything." With that, she shook my hand, followed by Alex's, and vanished into the hallway.

I stepped up behind Alex as he shut the door behind her. My palms went to the door on either side of his head, boxing him in. "Couldn't wait to get rid of her, huh?" I whispered against his ear.

He shuddered, brushing his delicious ass against my erection. "You're one to talk. You just signed a lease in a building you haven't toured."

"Mmm, so I did." I scrapped my teeth along the back of his neck, eliciting another full-body shudder. This time, I leaned into him, pressing my pelvis to his ass.

"Fuck, Ryder, let me turn around."

I licked where my teeth had been. If my cock wasn't begging for release, I could have spent the entire afternoon enjoying the silky feel of his skin against my tongue while savoring the slightly salty flavor.

"What if I like this side of you?" I pulled one hand off the wall and cupped his ass, squeezing the meaty globe.

He knocked his forehead against the door. "Ryder…" The rumbly growl hit me right in the balls.

"There's something about your pissed-off tone that just does it for me," I said as I continued to fondle his ass.

"Well, you've heard it often enough."

"That I have." I tapped his hip and shifted back half an inch. "Turn."

He did. Our faces were so close we nearly bumped our noses. Our gazes locked. His pupils were blown, almost hiding all the chocolaty brown. I could smell the sweetness on his breath from the iced tea he'd drunk with lunch. My lips tingled as he exhaled against me. What would it be like to kiss him? Would it be slow and sensual, or would we explode in a hungry fight for dominance? I swallowed, and his eyes immediately shifted down to watch my Adam's apple rise and fall.

Had I ever been this hard for someone?

One of our phones buzzed from wherever we'd set them down in the apartment. The noise was just enough to break the enchanted spell that weaved itself around us, but not enough to cut through the lust.

Alex blinked, then his lips curled into a wicked smirk. He looked down as his hands went to my jeans. Three seconds later, he had them open and dove his hand into my briefs.

I jerked as his warm hand encircled my aching shaft. "Shit." Did his hand feel better than any other one that had touched me, or was I so lust-drunk that my brain was making shit up?

"Wait," I croaked as he worked me over with proficient strokes.

His hand stilled but never left my dick. One of his dark eyebrows jumped to an arch. "Problem?"

"Take yourself out. Give me your cock. Let me see how hard you are for me."

His nostrils flared like a bull ready to charge, but he followed my command. As soon as his hand left my briefs, I reached into my back pocket, where I'd had the foresight to stash a packet of lube. Call me an optimist, but I'd hoped this would happen after work again tonight. Who knew we'd run into each other at lunch and find the perfect opportunity for a little afternoon delight?

I shoved my pants to my ankles but didn't bother to kick them or my shoes off. Neither did Alex. Next went our underwear. We had to look ridiculous as hell standing in my new foyer with our pants at our feet and our hard dicks reaching straight out, but neither of us had the excess brain capacity to give a shit.

I held up the lube packet. "Prepared this time."

Alex snorted. "Wow, pretty damn sure of yourself, huh?"

"Is there a reason I shouldn't be?" I ripped the packet open with my teeth, spitting the torn piece to the side.

Alex's head thumped the door as he stared up at the ceiling. "That should not be hot. Why the fuck was that so hot?" His growly mumble was most likely not meant to be answered, but I wasn't one to miss an opportunity to tease.

I chuckled. "Because confidence is hot, and I've got confidence in spades."

His gaze dropped back to eye level as he grunted a laugh. "Don't you mean arrogance?"

As I laughed, I drizzled the lube over my dick, drawing Alex's stare. The cool gel against my most sensitive skin had me gritting my teeth. I stepped forward, bringing our dicks in line and making both of us gasp. "Maybe, but it's still working on you."

He made a noise I couldn't decipher, but it couldn't have been that bad because he reached for our cocks. Before he could get there, I slapped his hand away. "I know it's your turn, but I'm greedy. Keep your hands on the wall, or better yet, my ass."

His teeth sank into his lower lip before he spoke again. "Figures the rich boy who's used to getting whatever he wants would be bossy as hell."

I shrugged. "My apartment, my rules."

"If you don't do something soon, it's going to be your hand, your dick, and only your dick."

I threw back my head and laughed. Who the fuck knew Alex could be so much fun? Did he ever let other people see this playful side of him? I'd known him for years and never knew he could joke and tease in this manner. I loved it. Sex, of any kind, should be fun as well as hot, and this was the perfect combination.

"Now look who's bossy." But I did as he demanded and wrapped my hand around both our dicks. I wasn't stupid enough to buck an order like that.

"Fuck yes," he said on an exhale.

"Right?" There was something so incredible about the slide of two dicks against each other. Sure, I loved fucking, but I would happily get off this way again and again.

My hand wouldn't fit around both of us, but Alex didn't seem to mind. He thrust into my grip as I jerked us with fast, borderline rough strokes.

Alex clung to my hips, sinking his fingers into the sides of my ass. He massaged my flesh as though praising me with his touch for my treatment of our cocks. "Fuck, you know how to work a dick."

I loved everything about this—the feel of two thick cocks in my hand, the constant slide against him, knowing I was making him feel as good as I felt. It was a sensory high and a power trip all wrapped up in one heady hand-fuck, and I never wanted it to end.

He bit his lower lip, making it puffy, red, and slick. It drew my gaze with a power I couldn't ignore. Once again, I had the overwhelming urge to kiss him. To feel his mouth move against mine as we soared closer to the edge.

I groaned.

We didn't kiss. It was an intimacy too far. One that would make this more than two coworkers scratching an itch.

But God, it was tempting.

Alex's hips bucked at the same time his grip on me intensified. "Shit." The back of his head hit the door again. "I can't hold off. Your cock feels too damn good against mine. I gotta come. Tell me you're close."

The way he cared if I was there, too, made an unfamiliar gooey warmth spread through my chest. "Yeah," I rasped. "I'm fucking close. Do it. Come all over us."

"Oh fuck."

My eyes locked on his face as he jerked against me, and less than a second later, warmth filled my hand. Bliss overtook his expression, heavying his eyelids and giving him the hottest fucked-out look in his eyes. Damn, he was gorgeous when he came.

I used his load as additional lube, and two strokes later, I followed him over the cliff. Pleasure uncoiled from my center, shooting out my dick and joining the mess he'd made. I couldn't help but spread our combined release all over our dicks, coating us from tip to root. If it was too weird, too intimate, Alex didn't say. He merely sagged against the door with a satisfied grin.

"So this is a pretty sweet apartment you got yourself."

I threw my head back and laughed. "Glad you think so. The welcoming committee doesn't offer this VIP service to just anyone."

He tensed. Goddammit, I could have kicked myself. What the hell did I even mean by that?

After clearing his throat, Alex glanced down. "You, uh, gonna let me go at some point?"

I blinked. Shit. I still had our cocks in my hands like a fucking creeper or someone too enamored to let go. "Sorry," I said as I released them and took a step back.

"Mind if I use the bathroom to clean up? I got class in an hour and can't really show up like this," he said, indicating his sticky cock.

"Yeah, of course. Whatever you need."

"Thanks." He yanked his pants up high enough to walk, then headed off to my powder room without another word.

I took his vacated spot, resting against the door.

What the hell were we doing? What the hell was I doing saying things someone would say to a boyfriend? Alex was probably in the bathroom making himself vomit. If there was one thing I knew, it was that Alex might enjoy getting off with me, but he didn't like me. He'd made that clear for years, not that I didn't deserve it. However, the conundrum I found myself in now was that I did like him.

I liked him a lot.

Chapter Eighteen

Over the next few weeks, I made a series of poor decisions.

Every one of them involved Ryder and his cock.

I couldn't stay away. I'd become an addict, crawling back for another hit time and time again, despite the destructive nature of my actions.

The habit began the day I tagged along to sign Ryder's apartment lease. After he'd taken us both in hand and tugged us to an explosive finish, I'd realized two things. One, getting off with another man on the regular was a million times better than biting my lip as I hid under my covers to quietly take care of business alone, and two, I didn't hate Ryder like I used to.

In fact, I might even like him.

Once I'd cleaned our combined cum off my sated dick that day, I'd exited the bathroom to find him waiting in the hallway, jeans up but unbuttoned and shoulder propped against the wall. His eyes had been heavy with satisfied fatigue, and his half-smile had given me the absurd urge to press my lips to his. Only the fact that I'd come my brains out three minutes before kept me from reaching for him again.

"Truce?" He'd said as I'd walked up to him.

"What?"

He shrugged, then motioned back and forth between us. "This is fun. You're hot, and we're good together like this. We're not friends, but if we call a truce, we can quit hating each other's guts and enjoy fucking around."

I'd cocked my head and scanned his face for sincerity. "A truce, huh?" The offer was perfect. We could avoid any in-depth discussion about our past contentious relationship and keep hooking up. More importantly, I wouldn't have to admit the deep-seated hatred I'd harbored for him had evaporated. We could go on and skip any of the emotional bullshit I didn't have time for or interest in.

And I'd get orgasms.

He shrugged. "Why not?"

There were reasons. Many reasons, but none of them came to me right then. Probably because he'd drained half my brain power through my balls. "Works for me." I'd said with an answering shrug, all nonchalant as though my insides weren't throwing a party.

Since that day, we'd gotten each other off as often as possible anywhere we could. Granted, we usually only found time once or twice a week, but it beat how often I was getting it before by a mile. After work, before our shifts, in the back seat of his snazzy car, and one other time at his apartment. Whenever we could sneak away and not be missed or discovered, we took advantage.

But never in a bed and never more than quick blow jobs or rushed hand jobs. This wasn't a *thing*. We still weren't friends. We didn't talk or hang out beyond screwing around, but we'd stuck to the truce and enjoyed frequent orgasms.

Dominic had announced the last call about twenty minutes ago, which meant we'd be shooing customers out the door soon. Hopefully, tonight would be one of the nights Ryder and I ended up in the back of his car for a fun time. It'd be easy and far more comfortable to head over to Ryder's apartment once the bar closed, but that felt too boyfriendy. Meeting up at his apartment so late at night made it too easy for one or both of us to fall asleep afterward. The thought of accidentally waking up to the morning light in Ryder's giant bed was enough to keep me from accepting the occasional offer to drive there instead of jumping each other in the SUV.

Sneaking out of someone's bed while they slept sucked, but confronting Ryder after a night in his bed would be worse. He'd be all mussed and sleepy, probably naked or at least bare-chested.

He might have morning wood.

Shit.

I'd have to pretend to be unaffected, which was the real problem. The more time I spent with Ryder, the more I liked the guy.

And that was plain stupid.

"Hey, Ally…" Trevor jogged toward me, shouting over the music. His bowtie was askew, and a sheen of sweat made his gold glitter shimmer brightly beneath the lights.

I stopped collecting glasses onto my tray. The guys at my two tables were all from one bachelor party and had closed out a few minutes ago, not wanting to be caught in the rush of everyone leaving the moment the lights brightened. "What's up? Need help at your table?"

He shook his head, holding a phone out to me. "Your phone won't stop ringing. I'm sorry I went into your locker, but I remembered your combo from when you told me a while back. It was quicker than getting you first."

My stomach plummeted like a roller-coaster drop. Anytime my phone rang at work, I feared my mom was having a medical emergency. Parker had a strict no-cell-phone policy for his employees but understood my situation and wouldn't have a problem with me checking on my mom.

"No. Thank you, Trev. You did the right thing." I grabbed the phone from his open palm.

Six missed calls from Kenny.

"Fuck." I hit his contact and held the phone to my ear.

"I'll be closing out my tables. If you need me, come get me." He squeezed my arm before darting back to his area.

I couldn't hear the ringing over the loud music, so I hustled to the locker room. "Hello?" an unfamiliar voice answered as soon as I entered the staff room. "Kenny? Who is this? Where's Kenny?"

"This his brother?" The gruff voice was hard to make out over shouting and music in the background on his end.

"Yes," I shouted into the phone as though I'd hear him better at a higher volume. "This is Alex. Is Kenny okay?"

"Yo, man, you gotta come pick up your bro. He's fucked up, and he pissed some people off. Messed with the wrong guy. I don't want him here no more, but he's too fucked up to leave on his own."

Fucking Kenny. My heart slammed against my ribcage. I clutched the phone so hard I risked shattering the screen. "Is he hurt? Does he need an ambulance?"

"Fuck, I don't know. Nah, prolly not. He's just fucked up."

What the hell did that mean? Injured? High? Was he bleeding out or unconscious? "Can I talk to him?"

"Nah, he ain't making much sense... too out of it. Look, dude, you gotta come get his sloppy ass. I got 'im away, but they're gonna come looking for him soon."

Who? What the hell had Kenny done to have people searching for him?

"Should I call the cops?"

Wrong question.

"Fuck no!" the guy screamed, sounding clear as a bell for the first time since the call started. "Cops show up, I'll know it was you. You don't want that, man."

I grabbed a handful of my hair and tugged as I paced the small locker room. "All right. No cops. Promise. Text me the address. I'm leaving now to come get him."

"No fucking cops."

"You have my word."

"That don't mean shit to me," he said before the phone disconnected.

I swear my heart stopped in the seconds when I waited for him to text the address. Just as I was about to dive into a full-blown panic attack, my phone chimed.

"Thank fuck," I whispered.

"I heard." Trevor's voice at the door had me nearly jumping out of my skin. "Go. I'll take care of your tables."

I set my phone down and opened my locker, grabbing the first item of clothing I could reach, my sweatpants. "I gotta let Parker know."

Trevor waved my concern away. "I'll take care of you. You just concentrate on getting to Kenny. Once you're home and everyone is okay, let me know, okay? No matter what time it is."

I glanced up at him from where I'd bent over to tug on my boots. "Thanks, Trev."

"Of course."

He left, and I was alone to shove my arms into my jacket. I grabbed my beanie, phone, keys, and wallet, then ran from the room with my jacket flapping open and my boots untied.

Sprinting through the crowded club was never easy, but using the employee entrance made it faster than going through the main entrance.

"What the hell? Where are you going?" Ryder stared at me, incredulous, as I darted past him, fully clothed.

I couldn't spare the time to stop and tell him, so I waved a hand in the air. "Trevor knows."

"Are you okay?" he shouted, but I didn't answer. I just

continued running toward the door with visions of Kenny dying rolling through my brain. I couldn't imagine having to tell my mom something happened to her youngest son. It would destroy her.

My boots crunched over half an inch of freshly fallen snow. There wasn't time to properly clean off my car, so I used my sleeve to clear the windshield enough to see through it. My heart pulse thundered in my ears as I slipped into the frigid car.

With shaking hands, I shoved the key in the ignition and started the car. The engine turned over twice, then sputtered and died.

Nothing new, but now was not the time.

"Come on. Come on," I whispered as I tried again.

And failed again.

And again.

And another five times.

"Come one, motherfucker. Start."

It didn't.

"Goddammit!" I shouted, slamming the heel of my palm against my steering wheel. "Fuck!" I gripped the wheel with all my might, resting my forehead on it as I screamed through clenched teeth. "Fuck," I whispered. "What do I do?"

Uber. I'd have to get an Uber, which would take longer. And would they even let me put Kenny in the car? It might depend on the state I found him in. I refused to even think of what the car repair bill would be. Perhaps it would be better to find a new old car to drive.

"I'm fucked," I whispered.

A knock at the window had me jumping so hard that I whacked my knee on the steering wheel. The adrenaline coursing through my veins made it so I didn't even feel the collision.

Ryder stood at my window, bundled for the weather and

so damn handsome it should be criminal.

"What?" I barked as I manually cranked down the window.

"Get in my car. It's on, and it's warm. I'll take you wherever you need to go." His breath wafted out in a white cloud of steam.

I blinked. "I…" Ryder was bailing me out of trouble. "Really?"

He grinned. "Yes, really. Don't be stupid. Please get out and hop in my car. You seemed like you were in a rush."

"I was. I am." I scrambled out of my vehicle, remembering at the last second to lock the doors, though if someone stole it at this point, they'd be doing me a favor. "What about your closing duties? Your shift isn't over."

He waved away my concern. "Trevor's covering it. I owe him a steak dinner."

We slid into his SUV at the same time. Warmth immediately surrounded me like a full-body hug. The heated seats were a treat I'd never experienced. Normally my ass froze everywhere I drove.

"Where we going?"

"Um, one sec." I pulled out my phone and rattled off the address the caller texted me a little while ago. "Not sure exactly where it is." But I knew it wasn't anywhere we wanted to spend much time.

Ryder's eyes widened when the route appeared on his phone.

Yeah. Shitty side of town. Ryder probably never dreamed of venturing over there, let alone driving his eighty-thousand-dollar car through that neighborhood in the dead of night.

"All right. Let's go. We'll be there in eight minutes at this time of night. Or should I say morning?"

I nodded as he drove out of the lot, but my attention was

five steps ahead on what state we'd find my brother in. "Yeah."

I stared straight ahead, willing each light we neared to remain green. For his part, Ryder kept quiet, but I could feel his frequent glances my way. Anxiety for Kenny had me gnawing my lower lip and bouncing my leg like a spring rested beneath my heel. Every terrible scenario I could think of ran through my mind, from Kenny murdering someone to some drug slinger kidnapping him for a ransom I could never pay.

"Hey..." Ryder's large hand landed on my thigh, squeezing.

I stopped bouncing.

"I have no idea what's going on, but it's going to be okay, Alex. Whatever it is, I'll help you out. I've got your back."

I stared at his profile as he drove. He had a slight shadow under his eye, speaking to the late hour and long shift on his feet. He drove with confidence in his designer coat, looking like he belonged right there at the helm of his pricey vehicle while I sat in my thrift store jacket and big-box sweats. Still, he'd jumped to my aid, no questions asked. His hand remained on my leg as he drove, anchoring me to reality. Without it, I'd be lost in my head, continuing my journey down Worst-Case Scenario Lane.

Who was this man? We weren't friends. Would he do this for any guy whose dick he liked to play with?

"Wanna talk about it?" he asked as we pulled onto the highway. "I'm not trying to pry. You don't have to say shit. I'll take you wherever you need to go anyway, but if you want to bounce anything off me..." He shrugged.

I sighed. No, I did not want to talk about it, and it had nothing to do with who he was or wasn't to me. I didn't talk about my brother to anyone. Trevor was the only person in my life who'd met my family, and even he didn't know the extent of our trials. But the idea of unloading some of my burden in that moment of turmoil was too good to pass up. I could hate myself for this later.

"It's my brother."

His eyebrows jumped halfway up his forehead as he kept his focus on the road ahead. "I didn't know you had a brother."

Why would he? We didn't chat.

"Uh, yeah. He just turned nineteen, and… well, he's a total fuckup." I stared back out the windshield again. "My mom calls him a free spirit, but he's not. He's a selfish asshole who'd rather shoot up and party twenty-four-seven than contribute to our family." I winced. "Sorry, probably more drama than you want to hear about."

"Alex…" I faced him, and he spared me a quick glance before refocusing on the road. "I asked."

He had, hadn't he?

"You listened to me when I needed it. Let me do the same for you. No judgment. Just listening."

Had anyone ever made me an offer like that? I'd been judged. Hell, Ryder had been one of the guys to judge me from the moment he met me. It was why I remained tight-lipped about my family situation, even with my few friends. But the sincerity in his tone had me believing him.

"His name is Kenny. We live together with our mom. Kenny doesn't work or go to school. I have a suspicion he makes some money selling drugs because he has new shit sometimes, but he doesn't contribute to anything at home. He's always in some kind of trouble." I sighed.

Troubled eyes flicked my way. "Your mom doesn't get on his case?"

I shook my head. She couldn't get on his case. So much of her mental energy went to struggling through each day. She barely knew what he was up to and when. "I think she carries a lot of guilt since he was so young when she got si—" I cleared my throat. "Um, she has a lot on her plate, so we were mostly left to figure out our own shit. Every once in a while, I get a call like this to drag his ass out of some crap-hole in the middle of the night because he's too toasted to function."

"Wow, I'm sorry, Alex. That sounds... hard." He steered with his left hand and kept the other resting on my thigh. Not squeezing, not trailing up toward my cock, not stroking or trying to elicit a response, just the warmth of a human connection.

I frowned.

Should I shove him off? I wasn't accustomed to comfort, physical or otherwise. I had no idea how to accept it. What was I supposed to say or do with that hand? It felt nice, really nice.

Soothing, heavy, steady.

What did it say about that part of me who wanted to lay my hand on his and link our fingers together, deepening the connection? It would be weird, right?

I couldn't allow myself to get used to someone, especially Ryder, making me feel better in a time of crisis. There'd be no repeat of the insanity of this moment, but maybe, just this once, I could leave his hand on my leg and enjoy the feeling of not being so goddamn alone all the time.

No one would have to know.

"How ugly a situation do you think we'll be walking into?" he asked without removing his hand. Usually, the question would have had me bristling or spitting out an angry response, but his voice didn't hold any judgment or recriminations.

"Not sure, but whoever it was that called me made it sound bad. And there's no we. I appreciate the ride and the help, but you're gonna stay in the car while I go in and deal with Kenny and... whoever."

He grunted but didn't respond. I'd take that as an agreement. I couldn't imagine many rich boys would be eager to drag someone out of a crack house in the middle of the night, especially given the high likelihood that there could be some altercation in the process.

We passed the rest of the ride in silence. For his part, Ryder seemed calm and cool as ever, whereas I grew more disgruntled by the second. The next few weeks would suck. My mom had developed wounds under two of her toes from where they rested against her wheelchair's footplate all day. She'd been battling it unsuccessfully for months, and we were at the point where she needed surgery and possible toe amputations. She had a few appointments to clear her for the upcoming procedure.

But how could I do that now that I'd have a car repair bill to pay?

"Should be about three houses up here on the right." Ryder's voice broke through the silence, making me jolt. "You okay?" he asked as he slowed the car to a roll and finally removed his hand from my leg.

I mourned the loss immediately.

"Yeah, sorry. I zoned out." I ran a hand through my hair as he pulled to a stop before a small duplex. One side had peeling white siding and a boarded upstairs window. A rusted mailbox dangled from one screw on the house next to the door with the house number, 417, missing a seven where it had been tacked above the door. The second side of the duplex wasn't fresh and new, but it didn't scream of a neglected drug den either. It sucked for whoever had to live there.

I sighed, gripped the door handle, then peered at him over my shoulder. "I'll be as quick as I can."

Ryder rolled his eyes and reached for his door. "You're crazy if you think I'm letting you go in there alone."

"Ryder..." I shook my head. Earlier, the thought of him bearing witness to this part of my life filled me with shame. Now, the idea of him entering that piece-of-shit hovel had me in a near panic. How could I protect him and Kenny at the same time? The dealers in there would smell the money on him the second he walked through the door, and they'd pounce. He was fresh meat. A delicious meal for bottom feeders like the people Kenny hung around.

"This is not a game." I gave him a furious glare that didn't seem to register. "The people in there are serious. You're..."

His eyes narrowed, and his face contorted in a scowl. "I'm what? Too rich? Too soft? Too weak? Too fucking clean to be in there because I showered today?"

I pinched the bridge of my nose. "That's not what I mean."

"Fuck you, Alex. You might think I'm an asshole, and you're probably right, but I'm not enough of an asshole to send you in there by yourself with God knows what's waiting for you. So suck it the fuck up, buttercup, because I'm going in there with you."

Shit. His glare could rival mine. "Buttercup?"

He shrugged. "It rhymed."

I snorted a half-laugh. The tense moment seemed to have passed. Neither of us moved for a second as our gazes locked. "Thank you," I managed eventually.

He nodded once. "Well, if we're about to get our asses kicked, I guess we should get it over with, huh?"

Chapter Nineteen

Okay, so I'd never been in a physical altercation with another person. Never taken or thrown a punch outside of a gym and a heavy bag. Fighting wasn't my thing. In my world, money was a weapon far more powerful than fists. But I wasn't weak, I wasn't a coward, and I wouldn't abandon Alex no matter what he thought of me.

"Fine, but don't blame me if your pretty face gets fucked up," he said with his customary frown.

"Aww, Ally, you think my face is pretty."

"Don't call me that," he said as he shoved the door open and stepped outside.

After toasting my ass on my heated seats and being surrounded by the sublime heat pumped from the vents, the cold was a brutal smack to the face.

"Trevor calls you Ally." I followed him out into the cold, zipping my coat up to my chin. Any chill I could block out was worth the effort.

"Trevor's like a small rodent. Cute but annoying as fuck, and he does whatever the hell he wants."

I chuckled. "Oh, man, I'm so telling him you said that."

Alex's shoulders bounced even though his laugh was

quiet. Joking at a time like this might seem stupid, but a corny one-liner was the only way I could think of to distract him for a few seconds.

I left the car running in case we needed a quick getaway, but I made sure to lock it. The last thing we needed was to come outside and find my Range Rover missing. I pocketed my keys and followed him up the short, dark walkway to the front door. An outdoor light mounted to the side of the door should have provided some light, but it was either broken or not on because we had zero illumination besides the dim light of the thumbnail moon.

"Careful here." Alex stopped and turned around after traversing an uneven chunk of cement where a tree root had raised the walkway. Expression tight, he watched until I'd made it safely past the perceived danger.

I blinked at him, then cleared my throat. "Thanks." The word rasped out through my cold vocal cords. My insides turned to goo. The man who hated me had stopped in his quest to rescue his brother to ensure I didn't trip on a crack in a walkway.

He nodded. "Don't engage with anyone in there, okay?"

"Stop worrying. I'm a big boy, Alex... as you well know." I winked, which made him roll his eyes.

I'd call that a victory.

"All right, I'll stop with the mother-hen routine. I'm just not used to having another person to think about when I do this. Not that I'm not grateful, I am, but it feels like you're a bit of a wild card right now."

Now, it was my turn to roll my eyes. "What is it you think I'm going to do exactly?"

His shoulders moved up and down. "I don't know. Whip out your black Amex and start flashing it at anyone who looks at you."

My jaw dropped. "You are a dick," I said as I flipped him

off.

Snickering, he turned back around and continued to the door. I couldn't keep the grin off my face as I followed.

Before we could knock or even reach the crumbling front stoop, the door swung open, and a man in nothing but jeans and tattoos stood in the doorway. "Are you here for this guy?" he asked as he gestured with his vape pen to a man sprawled on the bottom step of a long, steep staircase leading to the second floor.

"Holy shit, is that Kenny?" Alex asked, concern marring his features. The guy on the step didn't so much as twitch.

"Yep." The man sucked from his vape and exhaled a plume of acrid smoke. "He ain't dead. Didn't overdose or nothin'. Think he's conscious, but he'll sure feel like shit tomorrow."

Alex walked toward his brother. I followed right on his heels until we reached the door, and he extended a hand to stop me from entering the house. Part of me wanted to argue, but to get close to Kenny, he'd have to turn his back on the guy who'd answered the door, and while he didn't seem outwardly dangerous, I'd feel better keeping an eye on him.

The guy eyed me up and down. "You boys in the market for any party favors tonight?"

"Why? So we can end up like him?" I gestured to Kenny.

Alex shot me a lethal glare.

"That ain't my fault. Kenny's a stupid fucker." The guy shrugged and filled the air with more smoke.

I wrinkled my nose and fanned the air, which only made him laugh.

"Shit." Alex's whispered curse had me stepping forward. He crouched down next to his brother. "Ken?"

A groan was the only answer he got.

Keeping one eye on the vaper, I stepped closer and glanced down at Kenny. "Oh fuck." Someone had beat the absolute shit out of Alex's brother. Both eyes were purple and swollen like chewing gum bubbles. Blood had crusted beneath his nose and over his mouth and chin. Even his hoodie was covered in blood, probably from when it sprayed out of his nose.

"Do you know what he took?"

The vaper shrugged. Goose bumps coated his scrawny arms and torso, but he seemed impervious to the cold otherwise. "The usual, probably."

"Do you know who did this to him?"

"Sure do, but I ain't telling you. Not about to put myself in a spot to get my ass beat like Kenny." He tugged at a thread near the pocket of his worn jeans. They hung low, giving us a view of zig-zag patterned boxers. "Think he stole from them. Either that, or he fucked somebody's girl. Can you just get him outta here before they come looking for his ass?"

"Yeah." Alex worked a hand beneath his brother's back and heaved him to a sitting position with a grunt. Kenny's head lolled to the side once, then bounced up straight. His puffy eyes opened to slits.

"Alex?" A goofy grin formed, showing his bloody teeth. "Hey, bro."

At least he wasn't feeling pain.

For now.

Later, he'd be in a world of hurt, guaranteed.

"Hey, Ken," Alex answered with a resigned sigh. "Ready to go home?"

"Nah, bro, we should party."

"Party's over for tonight, Kenny. Let's stand up."

"But you never party with me. All you do is work and school and school and work. So fucking *boooring*, bro."

A muscle twitched in Alex's jaw as he no doubt fought the urge to add to Kenny's colorful array of bruises.

I squatted down on Kenny's other side. "Let me help you get him up."

Alex blinked as though he'd forgotten my presence. Any other time, I might be offended, but the poor guy deserved a few breaks tonight. He nodded, then we each slid an arm around Kenny and hauled him to his feet.

He swayed heavily into Alex, who stumbled back a step to accept his brother's weight before we were able to steady him with our arms around his waist and his thrown over our shoulders.

"Who're you?" Kenny's morbid face turned my way. "You his boyfriend?" he asked in a sing-song voice.

"No," Alex barked. "He's not. Let's walk to the car."

We half-walked, half-dragged a staggering Kenny out of the house. Thankfully, he was a slender guy. It was hard enough to keep from tripping over his wandering feet—if he'd weighed more than Alex or me, our little trio would have crashed to the ground trying to maneuver through the doorway. As it was, we had to turn sideways and guide him as if he were a wobbly toddler.

"Tell him he ain't welcome here no more," the vaper said as we struggled through the doorway.

"I'm sure he'll be devastated," Alex muttered.

"I would be," I mumbled. "This place is great."

That had him snorting a laugh that made my insides soar. If I could make one minute of this shitty situation more bearable for Alex, I'd consider it a win. No one should have to carry this burden alone. My chest ached thinking about how many times he'd had to bail his brother out without a lick of support.

Where was their mother?

Hadn't Alex told me they lived with her?

Maybe she didn't care. Maybe she'd given up on her youngest son and left him to be Alex's problem.

"Kenny, you have to at least try to walk," Alex said with a grunt as the three of us listed sideways, thanks to Kenny's inability to walk in a straight line.

"This way, man." I tightened my arm around his waist and tried to get him to bear more weight my way since he seemed determined to bowl Alex over.

A bloody-toothed grin flashed my way. "You know he's gay?" Kenny said.

"For fuck's sake, Ken."

I grinned back at him. "Good to know. Hope that means he didn't mind when I sucked his dick like a lollipop the other night."

Alex's eyes widened so fast I worried they'd pop out of his head and onto the frozen ground.

Kenny, on the other hand, burst out laughing, which only made it harder to control him. "Bro!" He drew out the word for at least four seconds. "Dude, you finally got some. Congrats. It's been like for-fucking-ever." He lifted his arm from around my shoulders and attempted to hold it out for a fist bump from Alex.

When Alex did nothing but try to murder his brother with his glare, Kenny giggled like a, well, like a person high off their ass.

We finally made it to my SUV without any significant issues. "You got him?" I asked, shifting the very wiggly package to Alex's arms. There wasn't time to worry about Alex's silence. We needed to get Kenny in the car and get the hell out of there before anyone we didn't want to run into showed up. I dug through my pocket and retrieved the keys. My car chirped as I unlocked it and opened the back passenger door.

Somehow, we managed to usher Kenny into the car even as he worked against us. Alex only swore seven times and threatened to finish the job the dealers started on Kenny twice. All in all, a successful rescue mission.

Alex climbed into the back seat after his brother. He

reached across Kenny's body and fastened the seat belt around him. I stayed by the door, waiting for him to exit, but he buckled himself in next to Kenny instead. "I'll just stay back here with him. In case…." He shrugged and wouldn't meet my gaze. His expression reverted to the one I'd seen so often after I began working at Top Shelf—annoyance, anger, and intolerance of my presence.

"Okay. Sure." I fought to subdue the wave of disappointment rising from my core. "Makes sense." What did it matter where Alex sat? Of course, he'd want to sit in the back with his injured and stoned brother to make sure he was all right. Who wouldn't?

Yet, as I climbed behind the wheel and glanced at the empty seat beside me, I couldn't help but feel rejected. I'd gone from savior to taxi driver in the blink of an eye.

"Where am I taking you guys?" I asked as I opened the map app on my phone.

Alex rattled off an address on a street unfamiliar to me. I glanced in the rear-view mirror to find Kenny already slumped against his brother's shoulder, passed out and breathing through an open mouth—breathing through a nose as swollen and bloody as his wouldn't be pleasant.

According to my app, the trip to Alex and Kenny's home would only take five minutes. They lived exactly one point six miles away. The idea of them living so close to this shithole had me frowning at my phone. I'd known Alex didn't come from money like most of us when we'd met at camp. Hell, it was the reason we'd given him the nickname 'freeloader,' but I'd never considered his family situation beyond our immature taunts. Thinking of him and his family struggling caused guilt to bring the way we'd treated him back then to the forefront of my mind. We'd been assholes, plain and simple.

No one spoke as I navigated to their home. Every few

seconds, I glanced in the mirror to find Alex staring out the window with an unreadable expression, while Kenny slept against his shoulder with audible exhalations, a combination of a snore and a pant.

What was Alex thinking about? The second we saw his brother, he'd transitioned from worried but reachable to downright closed off. Any progress I'd made drawing out a laugh or two vanished into an abyss of a mood I couldn't decipher.

Was he mad at me? Because I wouldn't stay in the car?

Maybe. But I didn't regret it.

I didn't know the man well enough to understand how his mind worked. I knew him well enough to be certain he liked it when I tongued the slit of his dick and how his eyes rolled back in his head when I sucked his balls. Or that he groaned every time I added a little twist of the wrist during a handy.

All too quickly, I pulled up in front of an older one-story house with peeling brown shingles, rusted gutters, and a dim porch light waiting for Alex's return.

"Thank you," Alex said the second I put my SUV in park. "I'm sorry we fucked up your night." He somehow managed to position Kenny so he wouldn't fall over while Alex climbed out of the SUV. Kenny slept on, blissfully unaware of the drama he'd caused.

"Alex…"

He stopped with his hand on the door handle. Our eyes met in the mirror.

"I was happy to help. Seriously."

A single, solemn nod was all I received.

"Let me help you get him inside."

"No!"

The answer came so quickly and with so much vehemence, I froze.

"I've got him. You've done enough."

The words expressed gratitude, but his jerky movements and pissed-off tone were unsettling.

"How are you—" Alex grabbed his brother under the arms and hauled him out of the car. Then, in a move that had my jaw dropping, he squatted down and hoisted Kenny over his shoulder in a fireman's carry.

His brother groaned. Dangling upside down with the blood rushing to his head couldn't feel good with his injuries, but it would get him in the house with the least fuss unless Alex collapsed under his weight.

I pushed my door open and stepped one foot out. "Alex, this is silly. Let me help."

He held up the hand not wrapped around his brother's legs. "I got it, Ryder. Really. You've done enough." He'd softened his tone some, but it still left no doubt as to whether he wanted my continued assistance or not. "It's late as fuck. Go home and get some sleep, and I'll see you at work tomorrow. Thank you again." With that, he walked toward his house with his brother slung over his shoulder like he weighed no more than a sack of feathers.

I couldn't help but gawk at the way his sweatpants stretched over his ass as his muscles worked harder than usual to carry the load. Sure, I knew Alex was strong. One look at the guy's size and shape, and anyone could see he had an impressive set of muscles, but damn, I didn't realize he was carry-a-grown-man-with-ease strong.

I waited until he and Kenny disappeared into the house. He clearly didn't want me inside his space. Despite the hour, a restlessness coursed through me. I didn't want to go home alone and sleep.

But what did I want?

With a sigh, I glanced at the seat Alex had occupied before we picked up his brother.

I frowned as my gaze landed on something black and

rectangular.

"Shit. His phone." I shifted the car back into park and grabbed the cell.

No one could function without a phone these days. If I waited to return it at work tomorrow, he'd spend the day stressing about losing it and could end up in a lurch, especially if he needed to Uber somewhere since his car crapped out.

"Dammit," I muttered as I exited the car. "He's not gonna like this." For whatever reason, he hadn't wanted me inside his house. Whether ashamed of where he lived or pissed at me for an unknown offense, he'd be grateful I returned the missing device.

Right?

I jogged up to the door, which he'd left cracked open, probably because his arms had been full of a passed-out man.

"Alex?" I called through the crack as I pushed the door open. "You left your phone in my..." The door swung open to reveal Alex kneeling in front of an electric wheelchair housing a woman probably in her late forties. He'd been in the process of dressing a gnarly wound on her massively swollen foot. Kenny lay on his side on a threadbare couch a few feet away with a trash can on the ground by his head. "Car."

Alex leaped to his feet with fire shooting from his eyes. He wore gloves on his hands and held a thick wad of gauze. "What the fuck are you doing in here?" he screamed. "I didn't invite you in. Get the hell out of my house!"

"Alex..." the woman admonished, eyes wide.

"I... I'm so sorry." The entire scene had my brain shutting down. Alex had a mother with a severe disability. Was he her caregiver in addition to attending school, working, and managing an out-of-control brother?

How did he do it? How did I not know?

"Get the hell out," he shouted again, making me jerk as though he'd hit me instead of merely yelling. The hatred in his voice jolted through me like a lightning strike.

"Sorry," I said again. "You... your phone." I held it up, then glanced around for somewhere to leave it. There wasn't any place by the door, so I set it on the floor before me. "I'm sorry."

Then I turned and fled the house back to my fancy car, where I drove to my luxury apartment, replaying the loathing in Alex's gaze and the murder in his voice while recalling how many times I called him a freeloader.

No wonder he hated me.

So much for whatever fledgling connection we'd formed.

Chapter Twenty

Shit.

My hands trembled as I stared at the door Ryder yanked shut behind him.

Cold sweat dripped down my spine, raising a trail of goose bumps in its wake.

Shit.

I squeezed my eyes shut as I blew out an unsteady breath.

It didn't help.

"Alex…"

I turned back to my mom, fighting to keep my face impassive, but one look at her disapproving frown, and time turned back to when I was ten and in trouble for throwing ice-packed snowballs at my neighbor's car.

"Alex…" she said again as I crouched down to redress the wound on her foot. This time, her voice held a disapproving bite I hadn't heard directed my way in ages.

"I know. I was a dick."

"I'm not sure who that boy was, but he helped you out at two in the morning."

I'd have chuckled at how she called Ryder a boy if I had an ounce of humor lurking in me tonight.

"That's a good friend, honey."

Friend. Is that what we were? Probably not after the way I screamed at him for daring to return my phone. The disappointment in my mom's gaze was nothing compared to my internal flagellation.

"I'll apologize to him at work tomorrow."

I avoided looking up at her while I placed the gauze beneath her toes, then wrapped it the way her surgeon had demonstrated. As detrimental as her neuropathy was, in times like these, I was grateful she couldn't feel a normal sensation in her foot. At least these twice-weekly dressing changes didn't cause her pain.

"Care to tell me why you reacted that way?"

"No."

Her silence hit harder than if she told me I was being a brat.

"It's nothing." I sighed. "Personal stuff. We have a bit of a complicated friendship."

There was that word again.

"Are you ashamed of me? For your friend to meet me? You never bring anyone around."

"What?" I jerked my head up, meeting her sad gaze. "No. Of course not. You've met Trevor."

She pressed her lips together as she nodded. "Yes, but he is the only friend we've met in years."

"I'm not ashamed."

Was I? I'd always considered myself protective, but who was I protecting, my mother or myself?

She patted my hand in a way that told me she didn't believe me but didn't harbor any resentment. "Good night, honey. Thank you for helping out your brother. Now you go and try to get some sleep." She cast a worried look Kenny's way.

"He'll be okay. He's on his side in case he vomits. Now he

needs to sleep it off." Her forehead wrinkled as she stared at him. "He's going to feel awful in the morning." Moisture glistened in her eyes, threatening to spill over her cheeks.

I snorted. "Good."

"Alex…" She sighed out a heavy, weight-of-the-world breath. Then she shook her head and squeezed my hand. "You're a good son and a good brother."

"Do you need help getting into bed?" I asked as she turned her wheelchair and started down the hallway.

"No. I can manage tonight. I've had a lot of nervous energy since you got home with Kenny."

She'd been dozing in her chair when I burst through the door with my unconscious brother over my shoulder. Of course, she hadn't been asleep in bed. Nothing had gone my way tonight, so why wouldn't she be present to witness Kenny's state while passed out and bloody? Her tears broke my heart and fanned the flames of fury at Kenny's thoughtlessness and stupidity.

"Goodnight, Mom."

"Goodnight, honey. Don't forget to make things right with your friend tomorrow."

"I will," I whispered as she rolled down the hallway, then into her room. The door clicked shut, and my shoulders slumped. Suddenly, the weight of the night came crashing down on me with so much force that I almost collapsed to my knees.

I'd had to leave work early.

My car broke down.

Kenny was a mess.

Mom was upset.

I'd have to fix all of those things. It's what I did. Each task represented time, energy, and money I didn't have to spare.

Worst of all, I'd screamed at the one person who'd been on my side.

I was an asshole.

Kenny's gentle snores reverberated through the otherwise quiet house. He'd be safe there on the couch until he awoke feeling like trash.

As I stood in the center of the living room with my arms limp at my sides, a numbness washed over me. Shame over upsetting my mother left, anger over my out-of-commission vehicle faded, and worry for Kenny evaporated. Even guilt over the way I treated Ryder vanished. My chest felt hollow, as though someone had scooped out everything inside.

I couldn't move.

As awful as those other feelings had been, this was a hundred times worse. I was empty. I didn't even feel human.

And I hated it.

My gaze drifted to my cell phone, lying face down on the floor near the door.

Kenny uttered something unintelligible in a nasally mumble.

The walls began to close in, shrinking down until it felt like I was in a box so small I couldn't move. I couldn't breathe.

I couldn't be there.

After glancing at my brother, I grabbed the phone and ran from my house.

Chapter Twenty-One

Why couldn't I shake what happened at Alex's house?

His enraged screams to leave his house played on repeat in my head while I saw nothing but the fury in his gaze, even with my eyes closed.

Fatigue tugged at me as I stood at my kitchen island, head bowed and palms flat against the cool surface. I needed a shower but couldn't muster the energy for the task. Instead, as soon as I'd returned home, I shed my clothes in favor of a pair of soft, flannel pajama pants, brushed my teeth, and washed my face.

But I couldn't climb into bed. My limbs wouldn't obey. History told me I'd stare at the ceiling until dawn, and I couldn't stomach the thought of lying there wide awake for the next few hours, obsessing.

So I'd opted to obsess standing up in the kitchen instead.

Made sense.

Why did it grate on me so much? Alex hating me wasn't anything new. It was our status quo. So why did his words and tone put a sick feeling I couldn't escape in the pit of my stomach? Why did they feel as though they'd invaded me on a cellular level, throwing off my entire world?

A soft knock at my door had me lifting my head. Who the hell would be darkening my doorstep at this hour?

Shit. My spine straightened. It could be my sister.

Barefoot, I jogged to the door. Despite the late hour, I had the presence of mind to check the peephole before yanking the door open to an unknown visitor. I peered into the hallway, only to freeze, not even daring to breathe.

Alex stood at my door with a defeated posture. He stared at his feet. Was he there to yell at me some more? To berate me for entering his home uninvited?

I frowned as I took in his sweatshirt and sweatpants—the same outfit he'd worn home from the club, only without a winter jacket. And how the hell had he gotten to my house without a car? Did he pay for an Uber?

Curiosity won out over common sense. I unlocked the deadbolt and opened the door.

His head came up, gaze meeting mine.

"Ryder..." Remorse bled from him in waves so strong he didn't need to say anything else. The sadness and guilt in his gaze were more than enough apology for me. In the thirty minutes since I left him, he seemed to have deflated. Dark smudges beneath each eye put a pinch in my chest.

He needed sleep.

And he probably needed food.

Who cared for him while he was busy meeting his family's needs?

And going to school.

And working.

Christ, just thinking about his mountain of responsibilities had me exhausted. How did he do it every day? And why did the thought of being the one he turned to have my cock plumping?

Rather than invite him in, I grabbed the front of his hoodie and yanked him flush against me. We'd yet to kiss, and the move put his lips in line with mine with mere inches separating us.

"It's okay," I whispered. His breath held a hint of expensive tequila, the only shot I'd seen him take all night, hours ago.

He shook his head. "No," he whispered back. "It's not. I was awful to you. I was a dick. And after you help—"

I rolled my hips into his, leaving my rapidly stiffening cock nestled against his, making him gasp and his eyes flare.

"Well…" I whispered, barely a breath away from his lips. "I guess it's a good thing I like dick so much."

He trembled. His hands landed on my sides, holding me against him. "Kiss me, Ryder."

I groaned. There wasn't anything I wanted more than to know what his mouth tasted like. I'd fantasized about it nearly every time we fucked around recently.

With his hoodie still fisted in my hand, I hauled him to me, crashing our mouths together. The instant his tequila-laced flavor hit my tongue, I was a goner. His taste, sweet with notes of caramel and spice, beat any thousand-dollar liquor hands down.

A sliver of my brain registered the door slamming shut, so I shoved him back against it for some leverage. He groaned as he opened his mouth and let me delve my tongue inside.

Alex let me hold him against the door, but he did not play a submissive role. He sampled me with the same enthusiasm as I attacked him. He sucked on my tongue and lips, nipped then soothed, and never let me come up for air. I fed off his groans and shared my own as he invaded all my senses.

As we made out, I rubbed my entire body against him like a needy feline. His soft sweatshirt tickled my nipples while his hands roamed over my bare back, blazing a fire path everywhere they touched.

My cock ached, making a mess inside my flannel pants.

Grinding against him wasn't enough. I needed a hand or mouth to give me relief before the need drove me insane, but I couldn't fathom separating our lips long enough to ask for it. Nor could I unwind my hands from where they'd settled in his hair, holding his head for my attack.

I grew dizzy—whether need, lack of oxygen, or pure intoxication on Alex didn't matter. I'd have happily never inhaled again if it meant more time kissing this man.

Eventually, physiology won out, and we had no choice but to come up for air. Alex broke away, quickly kissing my lips a final time before resting our foreheads together. We panted, sharing the air between us.

"Christ, Ryder," he said between breaths. "That was…"

Wild? Sexy? Explosive?

"Yeah," I managed. "Safe to say you're completely forgiven."

Our weak chuckles mingled in the air between us. We kissed again, quickly and desperately.

Then one more for good measure.

I loved the way his lips felt against mine—soft but confident and unyielding.

His hands left my back as he straightened. I barely had time to mourn the loss of his touch before he captured my chin in his large hand, holding me a fraction of an inch away from those incredible lips. "Take me to bed, Ryder."

I stilled with my heart thumping a heavy rhythm against my ribcage. "Yeah?"

He nodded. His dark eyes were on fire with the same need I felt deep in my core. A need that could only be satiated by one thing.

Us together—in my bed.

"You wanna fuck, Alex? Is that it?" I asked, grinding our covered dicks together.

"Yes," he said with a gasp. He rocked into me, making me

dizzy.

I moved my mouth to his ear, tracing the shell with my tongue. Every place I tasted on this man made me crave him more. The way he shivered against me while asking for entry to my bed would fuel my fantasies for weeks. "You wanna fuck me?"

He stilled, and I drew back to look in his swirling eyes. "No," he answered. "Not tonight."

What? I frowned. His words and touch gave the impression he was as into this as I was. Had I misread the situation?

Then it dawned on me, and my lips curled. The need in his gaze wasn't to take control of my ass tonight but to give up his own. I couldn't have stopped the self-satisfied smirk for all the riches in the world. "You wanna be fucked, Alex? Is that it?" I asked with a husky voice I'd never heard from my mouth. It couldn't be helped. Though I was vers, I tended to bottom more often than I topped. Much more often. When I'd fantasized about sleeping with Alex, it always included his dick deep in my ass, but the thought of burying into his tight hole for our first time had me frantic with desire.

He nodded. "Yes." The word came out as a hoarse rasp.

Hungry.

"Fuck." I pressed the heel of my palm over my dick, biting my lip to keep from coming by his words alone. "Let's go." I yanked him along, practically dragging him to my bedroom like a caveman bringing his conquest back to his lair.

"A little eager?" Alex asked with a chuckle as he stumbled into me.

His dick brushed against my ass cheek, eliciting a low groan from deep in my gut. "You have no idea."

"Yeah. I fucking do." We staggered through my door into my bedroom, where I released him, but not before another few minutes of wild kisses and groping.

"Christ," I said as I forced myself to release him. "Get your fucking clothes off." Another night, we could take our time and peel each other naked, layer by layer. Tonight, I needed skin-to-skin contact as quickly as possible.

Thankfully, Alex seemed to be on the same page. We tore at our clothing, tossing fabric in every direction. Since I wore nothing but flannel pants and briefs, I stripped down faster than he did. Once naked, I watched as he rid himself of his boots, socks, and jeans. The second he kicked his boxer briefs off his foot, we flew toward each other like two opposite magnetic poles.

"Fuck yes," I said as our naked bodies lined up from our heads to the tips of our toes. Every inch of the warm, smooth skin that taunted me every night we worked was finally mine to touch, lick, and enjoy.

"God, you feel good." He mouthed at my pulse point while we ground our dicks together.

"This ass is what feels good," I said against his hungry lips as I grabbed a cheek in each hand. The firm flesh overfilled my palms. I squeezed and molded his ass like I was a master sculptor with fresh clay.

"I like your hands on me."

"Yeah?"

"Yes, I fucking love it."

"Mmm." I crept my fingers inward toward his crease, then spread his ass, massaging as I exposed him.

He bucked in my arms, then dropped his forehead to my shoulder.

"It's been a while," he said, clinging to my sides. "A long while. I don't bottom often. I'll need some solid prep."

"My pleasure." And it would be. I couldn't wait to work him open on my fingers to prepare him to take my dick. I shouldn't be so turned on by the fact no one had been inside him for a long time, but I fucking loved it.

Unless…

"Wait," I said as an unfamiliar bout of uncertainty crawled up my spine. I didn't release him, but I stilled my hands on his ass. "You're not just doing this because you feel bad about earlier, right? Because—"

He huffed a half-laugh, then lifted his head, meeting my gaze. "No, Ryder, I'm not doing this because I feel bad for acting like a dickhead. I'm asking you to fuck me because I want your cock so deep in my ass it throws off my heart rate."

"Oh fuck." I looked to the ceiling with a groan. The tip of my dick was already wet as I leaked from his sexy words. "Who knew you were such a poet?"

He chuckled, but it turned into a moan when my fingers resumed their journey, playing up and down his crack.

"Get on the bed."

Nodding like a bobblehead doll, Alex scrambled onto my king-size bed, giving me a prime view of his meaty ass. The one I'd be deep inside soon. I moved to my nightstand, retrieving a condom and a fresh bottle of lube. When I turned to the bed, I found Alex on his back, lightly stroking his hard cock. His face was flushed and eyes glassy as he stared at my dick, where it jutted from my body.

"Hurry, Ryder. Get me prepped. I—" He swallowed and allowed me to see the vulnerability in his eyes. A vulnerability he didn't show to anyone. "I need it."

I tossed the supplies on the bed, then crawled up and over him. "You take care of so much. Tonight, I'll take care of you. And, baby, I'm gonna make it so good you'll never want to leave my bed."

His eyes flared at the pet name, but he didn't comment.

"Spread your legs."

He did, drawing up his knees. I kneeled between his thighs, reaching for the lube. He'd slowed his hand on his cock to an occasional stroke, nothing to ramp him up, just a little fondling to take off the edge.

We stared at each other as I coated two fingers in lube. He sank his teeth into his lower lip, letting me see his apprehension without words.

I warmed the lube between my fingers, then batted his hand out of the way. "My turn."

He cursed as I sucked the head of his dick between my lips. By now, after weeks of hooking up when we had the time, his scent and taste were familiar.

And intoxicating.

As was the recognizable moan when I slipped my tongue under the tip and pressed upward.

"Fuck yes." He slid his fingers into my hair, petting me. It was another thing I'd become accustomed to and looked forward to each time I sucked him.

I spent the next few minutes working him over with the back of my throat. When groans upped to shouts of pleasure, I released his cock and dipped my head to take his balls into my mouth.

"Christ." His hips arched off the bed, and my scalp stung from the tug on my hair as I massaged his sac with my tongue. "I love that."

The whispered words said almost reverently had me smiling against his balls.

"You are so fucking good at this," he said, panting between the words.

Who knew Alex would turn out to be so good for my ego?

I snuck my slippery fingers up and behind his sac, where I rubbed my thumb over his taint.

He groaned long and loud from deep within.

"Ryder, you gotta put something in me. Just... fucking do it."

I lifted my head, catching his heavy-lidded, strung-out

gaze. His hands flopped to his sides.

"Ryder..."

I wanted my mouth on him as I prepared him for my cock, but I couldn't tear my gaze away from watching the pleasure play out across his face. He tensed when I found his hole, but only for a few seconds.

"Relax for me. Let me in."

He nodded and blew out a breath. The effect was immediate. His hole softened beneath my finger. I spent a few minutes playing in his crease, gently rubbing circles over the tight flesh and reintroducing him to a touch he hadn't experienced in a while.

His cock had deflated to half-mast at my first touch but grew once again, letting me know he'd adjusted. With our gazes locked on each other, he nodded once, so I pressed forward, nudging my finger into the tightest asshole I'd ever had the pleasure of entering.

"Oh... fuck..." He arched his back and gripped the comforter in his fists. "Ryder..."

"Good?" I kept my finger still, waiting for feedback.

"Yes. It's good. Keep going."

Grinning, I began to move my finger. I kept my movements gentle, circling and curling until he began to squirm on the bed.

"Another," he croaked. "Give me another."

I withdrew, then added a second finger.

"Fuck, that burn..."

Not everyone loved the burn in their ass from being stretched. I sure as fuck did, and the wonder in Alex's tone had me thinking he didn't mind it either.

And then he started to move, fucking himself on my digits.

"That's it, baby. Take what you need. God, Alex, you're so damn sexy." I worked my fingers in and out, scissoring to loosen the snug ring of muscles. Once his head began to thrash back and forth, I added a third finger and hunted around for my prey.

"Holy fuck!" Alex screamed when I found that magical bundle of nerves. His neck arched back, revealing the long, muscular lines of his throat. I wanted my mouth there to suck a mark everyone would see at work.

"Shit." I reached for my cock, stroking furiously as I continued finger fucking him.

He was moaning consistently now, riding my fingers like he'd been born for it. My hand on my shaft felt fantastic, but I wanted to feel him squeezing around me, so when he yelled, "Stop! Ryder, I don't wanna finish like this. Please let me come on your cock," I nearly passed out.

It was the hottest sentence ever uttered.

I withdrew my hand, loving the way he growled at the loss, then grabbed the foil packet I'd dropped next to him. Alex stared as I used my teeth to rip it open. "How do you want it?" I asked as I rolled the condom down my erection. I was so hard and full that the latex had to stretch wide to accommodate me.

"Like this. I want to s… like this."

I want to see you.

I swallowed a lump of emotion that had no place rising in my throat, but I couldn't stop myself from whispering, "I want to see you too." I wanted to witness every second of pleasure pass through his eyes.

Alex drew his knees toward his chest, exposing his softened hole to me. It glistened from the generous amount of lube I'd slicked into him, yet I still grabbed more and coated my dick. There were times when prep didn't need to be so thorough. Hell, I lived for the burn and stretch that accompanied penetration, but the first time in a while was not the time to cut corners.

I stroked my hands up the backs of his thighs, then rubbed

my thumb around his loosened rim, making him shudder.

"You're killing me, Ryder. Fuck me. Now."

I grabbed the base of my slippery dick and lined up with his hole. "Ready?"

He scowled.

"Guess so," I said as I gently pushed into him, taking care not to rush the process.

"Oh, shit," he said as I breached him. "Ryder..."

Lights danced before my eyes as I slipped through the first ring of muscles. I gripped his thighs, probably hard enough to bruise him. "Alex, oh fuck. Alex, you're so goddamn tight."

His nostrils flared as he inhaled through his nose. "I think you're just huge. Ryder, oh my God, I'm so full. I've never..." He shook his head.

"You okay?" Every ounce of strength I possessed went to not thrusting hard. No matter how much my body screamed at me to do just that, I refused to risk hurting him. He'd let me know when he was ready.

"Yeah, yeah. So good. Keep going. Slowly."

Inch by inch, I tunneled deep into Alex until my entire dick was encased in the hottest, tightest ass I'd ever had. He clenched, rippling his muscles along the length of me. "Wait!" I cried. "Fuck, don't do that yet. Don't move. It's too good. I'll come."

He chuckled.

"So not funny," I rasped, letting my head hang as I tried to breathe and think of snakes and spiders to keep my balls from erupting. "I've got a reputation to uphold."

Warm fingertips coasted up and down the sides of my spine. "Ryder, nothing you could do would make this anything less than the best experience of my life."

His words shot straight to the center of my chest, blooming out in a starburst of gooey warmth. His cheeks flushed bright red as though embarrassed he'd said something so sweet.

"Thank you," I whispered.

He smiled, and it only expanded whatever was happening inside my chest. "Y-you ready?"

"Hell, yeah. Give me everything you've got. I want the whole club wondering why I'm walking funny tomorrow night."

That was exactly the command I needed to bring me back from the brink of dangerous emotions to the burning need to make us come.

I withdrew, then snapped my hips forward, making us moan. Alex was no pillow princess. He worked his hips in time with mine, devastating my dick with a vise-like clasp each time I bottomed out.

I fucked him hard like he asked. With each passing second, he grew louder, groaning, moaning, and babbling nonsense encouragement for more and harder, which I did my damnedest to oblige. When he arched his neck and bared the line of the throat I'd been lusting after earlier, I allowed myself to feast. I trailed hot, open-mouthed kisses from his jaw to his collarbone and back up, pausing to suck at his pulse point. It fluttered wildly beneath my lips, which only made me suck harder like a starving vampire.

Alex grabbed my ass, sinking all ten fingers into my flesh as he urged me to keep fucking him. "Right there, right there," he cried. "God, Ryder... oh fuck."

After a final hard suck, I released his neck and grabbed his dick, jerking with near-violent strokes. Alex shouted and thrashed beneath me. A sheen of sweat glistened on his forehead, and his grip on my ass slackened.

He was close.

"Ryder..."

"I know, baby." Again, with the pet name. I couldn't stop it. I didn't want to. "Come for me, Alex. Show me how good my dick makes you feel." Three more tugs and two thrusts later, his back bowed, and he let out a string of curses so filthy I nearly blushed. Cum exploded from his dick in thick spurts, coating his abs. I fucked him through the intense spasms, then slowed my strokes despite being a hair's breadth away from the finish line myself.

Some guys hated being fucked after they finished, and I refused to spoil this experience by making assumptions.

"Keep going," he said between harsh gulps of air. "Finish in my ass. Keep fucking me, Ryder."

I stared at his blissed-out expression and knew precisely what would catapult me to the stratosphere. "Kiss me," I said in a voice too close to begging.

"Yes." He gripped the back of my neck and yanked me down to his mouth. I thrust like a madman as we devoured each other. It couldn't have been longer than one more minute before I ripped my mouth away and roared out my release.

"That's it," Alex said as my pleasure stole my ability to reason. "You're fucking gorgeous when you come."

I collapsed onto his chest, smearing his cum between us, which would be revolting later, but I kind of loved it at the moment. You knew the sex was on another level when, instead of cleaning up afterward, you wanted to revel in the mess.

"No more than you," I mumbled against his sweaty chest.

Alex closed his arms around me, locking us together. His heart knocked beneath my ear, still galloping a wild rhythm. My dick was still halfway in his ass, slowly softening. I did need to take care of the condom, but all I wanted was to lie there, surrounded by Alex's warmth and scent.

The next words out of my mouth shocked me as much as they must have stunned him.

"Do you want to stay?"

Chapter Twenty-Two

Too many sensations bombarded my post-orgasm brain for me to process at once. My skin buzzed with electricity, extra sensitive as sparks danced along the surface. My ass ached already, but that one I'd expected after spending long minutes with Ryder's thick cock tunneling into a hole that hadn't been used in a long time.

A *long* time.

Not since my senior year of high school when I'd thought the constant desire to fuck my boyfriend meant we were in love and not just horny teenagers. I figured it out when we broke up two weeks into college, each agog at the number of men we could meet and sleep with.

My current life was a series of near disasters I managed from the time I awoke to the time I finally crashed at night. Kenny called me a control freak, but I had to be. If one thing went awry, the ripple effect made our lives difficult. Take my car breaking down. To some, that was an isolated event, an annoyance they'd take care of and then resume their regularly scheduled programming. For me, it meant I couldn't get to work, take my mother to her appointments, or drive to class. Missing one day of work meant not buying groceries, paying utility bills, or meeting tuition deadlines. And the consequences grew from there. So, yeah, I tried to keep rigid control over my life, but as a necessity rather than a personality quirk.

Or so I told myself.

Bottoming represented a loss of control. It meant giving myself to someone who could make the experience unpleasant or painful. I didn't do it often, especially since I typically fucked random guys few and far between. Tonight, though, I'd needed to get out of my head. I'd needed someone else to take the reins and relieve me of the need to think and plan.

Ryder and his impressive cock gave me that.

And he gave me a full-body orgasm the likes of which I'd never experienced. It shook me to my core. Moving forward, it would be hard to keep myself from dropping my drawers and bending over every time I saw him.

"Alex?"

"Hmm? Sorry," I said as I stroked up and down the smooth, damp skin of his back.

"I asked if you wanted to stay." Ryder propped his chin on my chest and stared at me with a satisfied grin and heavy eyes. "I can give you a ride home in the morning."

What a terrible idea.

No. Say no.

"Sure."

His smile expanded, and the damn thing must have been contagious because I found my lips curving in much the same way. We grinned at each other like idiots for a few seconds before Ryder whispered, "That was…" He shook his head. "I don't think I even have words."

"Yeah." I swallowed as a lump rose in my throat. Clearly, I had a spectacular way with words as well.

"You okay? Did I hurt you at all?" Uncertainty crept into

his voice.

I might suck at these conversations, but even I wasn't enough of an ass to make him worry for even one second. "No," I said with a huff of laughter. "You did not hurt me. You destroyed me, but uh… in the best way."

Why did I suddenly feel nervous? Wasn't that supposed to happen before we fucked for the first time? I'd been too damn needy to feel it then, but now I didn't know what to do with myself.

His smile turned wicked. "Really?"

Leave it to Ryder to cut the tension with his ego. "Yes, really." I pinched his firm ass, laughing at his yelp. "I'm sure I'll regret telling you this later, but that was better than, well, any other time."

His head is going to expand right before your eyes.

But it didn't. Instead of gloating, he gave me a soft smile and stretched to peck my lips. "Good," he whispered. "That's what you deserve."

No puffing his chest. No joke about the power of his dick. It was just a sweet comment I had no idea how the hell to handle.

He kissed me again. "Let's get cleaned up. It's fucking late, and you've got to be exhausted."

I was. The kind of exhaustion that invaded every cell in my body and made the thought of moving unbearable.

With a burst of energy he shouldn't have had at three thirty in the morning after recently climaxing, he pushed up and off me. Our eyes met as the last inch of his soft dick slipped free from my body. My ass clenched in protest, and a tiny groan slipped free.

"Yeah, I liked it much better in there too."

Another sweet statement I couldn't process, so I didn't bother to try. Mustering what little oomph I still had, I began to sit up, only to have a strong hand on my chest push me flat down.

"Stay. I got this." Then he slid from the bed and walked—no, strutted—toward the bathroom, making it impossible for me to look anywhere but at his stellar ass. I groaned again. Next time, I had to get my cock between those luscious round cheeks.

Next time? Would there be one? Did I want one?

The water ran, and rummaging sounds made their way from the bathroom. A few seconds later, Ryder appeared with a damp cloth. Clean now, he strode across the room naked. His satisfied cock hung between his muscular thighs, big and beautiful.

Yes, beautiful.

My mouth watered at the sight. By now, I'd had him in my mouth several times, but he'd always been rock-hard before I feasted. The thought of going down on him like this, soft and sleepy, while he grew to full length between my lips had my fatigued dick attempting to rally.

He rested a knee on the bed, tilting his head. "You don't stop looking at me like that, I'm going to forget all my good intentions to let you sleep."

"Like what?"

He grunted. "Like you're imagining sucking my soft dick to its full potential."

Busted.

My cheeks heated, and he grinned. "Ah, so you were imagining that."

Rolling my eyes, I reached for the washrag. "Give me that."

He shook his head, batting my hand away. "Nope." He crawled onto the bed and over to me.

Was he going to—

Yep.

Ryder kneeled beside me, running the warm, damp cloth

over the mess on my stomach, then down, cleaning my dick, then—

"I can do that," I said before he got to my used hole.

He quirked a blond eyebrow at me. "You're not very good at letting someone take care of you, are you?"

That had me barking a laugh. "I don't even understand the concept."

Shit, why the hell did I say that? Ryder's expression went from playful to sad in the blink of an eye.

"Ignore me," I said, waving a hand. "My brain is already asleep."

He pressed his lips together, and my stomach dipped. He wasn't going to let it go. But then he lightly smacked my thigh. "Bend your knees."

I did, with my face burning the entire time.

"Ryder…"

"Shh. This is how you let someone take care of you, Alex. You zip those sexy-as-fuck lips I often prefer wide open." He winked. "But for now…" he mimed zipping his lip.

So I shut my mouth, and Ryder proceeded to clean the lube off my ass. Hot humiliation washed over me. Who knew why? Ryder had been all up in me not long ago, but somehow, this act felt more intimate than him shoving his cock inside me. After a few seconds, my discomfort and embarrassment morphed into something deeper, something almost pleasant.

He stroked the back of my thigh with his free hand as he rid my stomach of cum and lube. Warmth spread from under his hand up to my chest. It was then that I realized I had grown to like it. I liked his hands on me, the concentration on his face as he made sure to be thorough, and the gentle way he tended to me.

When he finished, he folded the washrag and tossed it on the floor. It landed with a wet splat. I couldn't tear my gaze away as he crawled back up the bed and then lay on his side facing me. His skin was so smooth and tanned even in January in Boston, thanks to the Caribbean trip he'd taken at Christmas time. I'd never been to the Caribbean. Hell, I'd never been to a real beach, only a lake when I was a child.

Before Mom got sick.

"Thank you," I whispered, feeling heat rise to my face again.

Thank you for so many things.

"Anytime," he said with a wink. He scooted closer until our mouths were close enough to share air.

This time, I was the one to lean in and kiss him—nothing too long or meant to ramp us back up, but a lingering press of lips. If I couldn't put my complete gratitude into words, maybe he would feel it from my kiss.

I pulled back when my cock started to take interest. As much as I'd love to go for a second round, chances were, I'd fall asleep mid-fuck.

"Roll over, away from me," he said before sneaking a final kiss.

I did as he asked. Maybe later, I'd wonder why I so easily followed his every order, but for now, not having to be the one to orchestrate every decision felt incredible. As soon as I landed on my opposite side, he snuggled the length of his body against my back. We fit perfectly, tucked together in all the right places. His cock nudged against my ass, maybe half hard again, but Ryder made no move to indulge it.

His lips touched the back of my neck as he wound his arm around my waist and pulled me even closer before burying his face between my shoulder blades. "Sleep," he whispered. "Shut your brain down and sleep. We'll figure everything out tomorrow."

We?

Who was this man I once hated?

"Okay," I mumbled, positive it would never happen.

But I found myself lifting my top leg and letting him sneak one of his between mine as I pressed my hand over the top of his. Lulled by the warmth of Ryder's naked body, with the gentle thrumming of his heart against my ribs, I surrendered to the comfort of his embrace. The racing thoughts I dealt with all day, every day, vanished, and I fell headlong into a deep, restorative sleep.

The next moment of awareness came in the form of a hot, hungry mouth trailing down my spine toward—*oh shit*—my well-used ass.

Any lingering fog of sleep evaporated in a sharp wave of pleasure as Ryder nipped my ass cheek. I found myself prone in the center of Ryder's bed, with my dick rapidly hardening between my body and his opulent mattress.

Strong hands grabbed my cheeks, pushing them apart, and before I had a chance to react, a warm tongue slid over my hole.

"Jesus... Ryder."

I humped the bed like a damn dog as he slicked me with incredible skill. The man knew exactly what he was doing as he played with my rim, alternating quick flicks and long, maddening licks. But when he slipped inside, giving my most vulnerable place a deep tonguing, I nearly lost my mind.

"How can you be so devious and so amazing at the same time?" I cried before pressing my forehead into the pillow, nearly screaming my pleasure.

Ryder chuckled. His tongue slipped from my body. I immediately mourned the loss of pressure, but only for a second because his talented mouth trailed up my spine. He kissed, bit, and licked his way to the back of my neck, where he paused to suck and make me squirm against the bed.

"Again," he rasped against my ear with a sleep and lust-roughened voice. "Let me have you again." He settled his weight on top of me, slotting his lead pipe of an erection in my spit-slicked ass crack.

"Christ..."

"Please," he whispered before licking the shell of my ear and biting the lobe. My entire body shuddered beneath him. "Next time, I'll spread for you, and you can fuck me until your balls are dry, but please let me in one more time."

There was no way in hell I could refuse an offer that good. I didn't want to refuse. He didn't need to beg for entry. Hell, I was two seconds from begging him to fuck me as hard as he had the night before despite the soreness reminding me we'd done this only a few hours ago.

"Yes." I turned my head so my cheek lay flush against the pillow. "Yes, Ryder. Put it in me. *Now*."

"Mmm... let's see." He remained mostly flat against my back, only tilting his hips to worm his hand between our bodies.

Thick fingers probed my hole. I flinched at the first touch, tender from the epic fucking I'd received, but within seconds, the discomfort morphed into need. He slipped a fingertip inside, and my ass clenched, trying to suck him farther into my body.

"Too sore?" he whispered as he nuzzled his nose against my bristly cheek, making an audible rasp.

"No. Never."

He spent a few minutes fingering me open with slippery fingers, I somehow missed him slicking up. I tried not to grind against the bed, but it felt so good, and my cock was so hard and wanting. "Ryder..."

"Fuck, Alex, you're still soft and slightly loose from last time. I don't know why that's so hot, but it is. I want you so bad, I can't even let you fully recover from the last time."

I whimpered.

"Do you like that?" he whispered against my ear. "Like

that you have me so hot for you that I need to be inside you right this second?"

It was overwhelming to think of being desired with such ferocity. Overwhelming and fucking incredible. "Yes. Fuck, yes, I love that."

We kissed. The angle was awkward with my head on the pillow, but neither of us cared. Our mouths met in a sloppy dueling of tongues without finesse or chill. All I cared about was feeling him inside every part of my body I could get him in. Our stubbled chins abraded sensitive skin with a rough scratch. It was raw, powerful, and unrestrained.

It was hot as fuck.

As we continued to attack each other's mouths, he withdrew his fingers and then shifted above me. I immediately felt the flared head of his cock seeking entrance.

"Do it," I said against his mouth. "One fucking thrust."

"Fuck." The position wasn't difficult. Ryder had to lift off me somewhat, but I remained flat on the bed with his hand gripping my side in a brutal hold. He did as I asked, shoving deep in one slow plunge.

"Oh shit, you feel so big like this." The pressure was unreal in this position, with my legs pressed together and my torso flat on the bed.

He chuckled. "I am big."

There's the arrogance I used to hate, but now it turned me on so hard.

"But you're also tight as a goddamn vise."

A perfect fit.

The revealing statement hung from the tip of my tongue, but then Ryder shifted back, yanking my hips with him. I was dragged to all fours with him behind me. As he pulled me back, he thrust forward, drilling me with his cock. My eyes crossed from the intensity of the movement as I scrabbled for purchase on the bed.

Ryder barely gave me two seconds to stabilize before he began hammering into me like he was trying to rocket me across the room. His fingertips bit into my hips as he grabbed my shoulder with his other hand, giving him an incredible amount of leverage and complete control over the pace and depth of his thrusts. Balancing on my knees and elbows, I rocked back to meet him each time he hammered forward. The filthy sounds of slapping skin, which couldn't be mistaken for anything else, combined with our ragged breathing and erotic moans to fill the room with a sexual symphony.

"Shit," he said after a few minutes of pummeling my prostate. "I'm gonna come. It's too fucking good."

"Do it."

"Not yet," he ground out as he squeezed my hip. Then the feel of his hand disappeared, only to return two seconds later, wrapped around my cock in a firm grip.

"Yesss," I hissed as he shuttled his fist along my slick cock with expert skill and a singular mission to shatter my control. An intense tingle brewed in my balls three strokes in. I continued to pump my hips back onto his cock as he jerked me closer to the finish line. Within seconds, the tight coil of need in my core snapped, and I came with a shout that Ryder's neighbors might report to the cops.

"That's it," he hollered as I lost the rhythm of my convulsing muscles. "Squeeze my dick. Fuck, this ass… goddammit." He curled over my back, snarling and cursing as he lodged himself deep in my ass and came.

We rode out our climaxes together, the only sound a chorus of heavy breathing. My shoulders trembled, and as Ryder's weight on my back grew, I collapsed onto the mess I'd made all over his bed. We both groaned as he slipped from my ass, though my groan was in part due to landing in the damn wet spot. As he somehow managed to throw himself to the side and avoided crushing me into said damp spot, I experienced the oddest twinge of loss over our separation.

I'd never had sex without a condom, yet a craving to feel his load dripping out of my ass hit with so much force it stole my breath. I wanted part of him left behind, as deep inside me as he could get. What the fuck was wrong with me? That was some high-level commitment shit I'd never entertained in my life. And to want that with Ryder?

Insane.

Of course, we'd used a condom. "Oh shit... wait... when did you glove up? I didn't even think of it." The thought hadn't crossed my mind in my desperation to feel him inside me again.

He kissed my shoulder, then chuckled as he rubbed my upper back. "Before you even woke up."

I turned my head on the pillow to find him lying on his side beside me with a satisfied gleam in his eyes. "The first thing I saw when I woke up was you sleeping on my pillow." A mischievous grin curled those swollen lips. "Being the deviant that I am, I peeked under the blankets. Your naked ass was right there, and I instantly got hard. So I wrapped this bad boy. This way, I wouldn't have to pause once we got the party started."

I chuckled. "And if I'd said I was too sore to fuck again?"

"I can pivot. There are plenty of ways to get each other off." He winked.

"Ah." I cleared my throat. "Well, thanks. I'm glad one of us was thinking."

One blond eyebrow curved to a perfect arch. "Hmm, am I sensing a bit of disappointment in your tone, Alex?" he asked, voice thick with seductive suspicion.

"What? No."

Yes.

Ryder scooted closer. "You sure about that? You sure you

don't like the idea of me emptying my balls in your ass without anything between us?"

My face heated. Fuck yes, I loved the idea. I just didn't know why. "I..."

"Because I gotta tell you, the thought of pushing your thick ass cheeks apart and watching my load drip out of your hole after fucking it raw is very—"

"Jesus, Ryder." If he finished that sentence, I was likely to roll over and beg him to do just that. "That's too fucking much."

His wicked grin grew. "I don't think you mean that, but okay." He kissed me. "I'll back off. So, it's Sunday. Do you have anything going on today?"

I blinked. How the hell did he switch subjects so easily? My entire body was on fire again, and that fire had roasted my brain to a charred, unusable organ. "Uh... two study groups on campus. One at noon and another from two until three."

He nodded. "How about we grab some breakfast, then I can drop you at home after so you can get ready for your study groups. Then maybe I can pick you up after, and you can come with me to the LGBTQ+ youth center."

The question slipped from him without hesitation, but he averted his eyes, and tension passed from his body to mine. Funny how he could talk about fucking without condoms no problem, but inviting me into his life made him uncertain.

Did I want to spend a large part of the day with him? Shower, get dressed, go out to breakfast, then reconvene to get a glimpse into something important to him? Something he didn't seem to share with others.

The same warm feeling I'd been experiencing recently spread throughout my chest.

"Yeah." I refused to acknowledge the thickness in my throat or the way his eyes lit up at my agreement, but it did give me the courage to say, "I'd really like to do all of that with you."

Chapter Twenty-Three

After a lengthy shower in which we wasted plenty of water getting each other off again, Alex and I made the frigid walk to a trendy café two blocks from my apartment building.

He reached the entrance first and grabbed the door, stepping aside to hold it open for me. My stomach fluttered at the considerate gesture. "Thanks."

As we stepped inside, warmth and the mouth-watering scents of cinnamon and coffee surrounded us, making my stomach growl.

Grunting out a laugh, Alex stomped the snow off his boots onto the rug and then walked toward the short line of customers waiting to order. "Hungry much?"

"Yes." Trailing after him, I had to press my lips together to keep from whistling at the sight of that gorgeous ass in his sweatpants. "I'm fucking starving."

He glanced over his shoulder and arched an eyebrow. "Sure, you haven't had enough to eat?"

"Never."

He grinned. Lighthearted Alex didn't poke his head out to play too often, especially not around me, so I lapped up that easy smile like a thirsty dog. "What are you thinking?" I asked as we moved to the on-deck spot in line.

Alex craned his neck to see the glass display cases housing rows of delicious pastries and breakfast treats. He said something, but my attention was locked on the deep purple bruise rising from the collar of his winter coat. My cock twitched. Damn, he looked good with my mark on him. I'd sucked a few hickeys in other places as well. Too bad I'd been too horny in the shower to think about enjoying them up close and personal because the love bite on his neck was so sexy. I wanted to lick it right there.

Again.

"Ryder?" Alex's forehead wrinkled. "Did you hear me?"

I blinked. "What? Sorry, I got distracted. What were you saying?"

He gave me a skeptical look before shaking his head. "Coffee cake. That cinnamon scent is driving me wild. I'm getting the coffee cake."

You're driving me wild.

"That sounds good, but I think I'm going for the bacon, egg, and cheese sandwich. Need the protein, you know?" I said with a wink.

Alex chuckled as a customer in front of us shifted down the counter toward the order pick-up sign. He stepped up to the counter before me because my brain was still admiring the mark I'd left on his neck.

"Good morning, gentlemen." A curly-haired barista with an ear full of diamond studs and a tiny septum ring beneath her nose smiled at us. She wore a navy-blue apron with an embroidered coffee mug in the center of her chest. "Welcome to Brewed Awakening. What can I get for you two today?"

I opened my mouth to order, but Alex beat me to it. "Can we get a large Americano with two shots, a large regular black coffee, one slice of coffee cake, and a bacon, egg, and cheese sandwich?"

Whatever the barista said next was lost on me as I scraped my jaw off the floor. How on earth did Alex know my coffee order? Not just know it, but know it perfectly. He glanced my way with a shit-eating grin.

"How?"

He snickered. "Remember that time Parker bought coffee for everyone?"

"Yeah."

Shrugging, he said, "I remembered." Then his cheeks turned pink, and he glanced down as though suddenly realizing it might be strange that he memorized my coffee order after hearing it once.

Strange or not, the gesture made it hard for me to swallow. I liked that he knew that about me. Something so simple yet personal.

"Okay, gentlemen, that'll be twenty-six dollars and forty-three cents. And is that for here or to go?"

"Here," I answered, tapping my credit card against the reader before Alex had the chance to wiggle cash out of his wallet. He frowned, and I shot him a wink while the machine charged my card.

"And a name for the order?"

"Ryder."

"All righty, here is your receipt. Enjoy your meal, guys." She handed over the short slip of paper with hands adorned by two-inch-long neon green nails.

"Thank you." I nodded at the barista, then turned to my scowling date. "Stop pouting and move down to get our food." Smiling what I hoped was my most charming grin, I ushered him down to the end of the counter, where a few others mingled around waiting for their food.

"Ryder, I could have paid for that."

"I know."

"I'm serious."

"I know," I said again, bumping my shoulder to his. "I see how much you make in tips. You know, if you hold that grumpy facial expression for too long, your face might freeze that way."

Finally, he snorted a laugh. "Who are you, my mom from fifteen years ago?"

"You were even grumpy as a kid?"

He nodded. "I prefer to think of it as serious."

"Maybe, but you can be serious with a smile."

"Ryder!" Another barista, a man with salt-and-pepper hair and a manager tag, stood by a tray with our food.

Alex lurched forward to grab the tray before I could, as though he thought it would compensate for not paying. There wasn't anything to make up for, though we should probably talk about it once we sat.

We had a number of things we needed to talk about.

"Here, good?" Alex asked as we approached a small two-person booth in the back corner of the café next to the emergency exit.

The air held a bit of a chill from the glass emergency exit, but the tables surrounding us would be empty.

Looked like I wasn't the only one who realized we had to chat.

We shed our coats before sitting—I'd lent him one since he'd showed up at my house without—and I grabbed my drink off the tray, then took a long sip. The hot liquid warmed me from the inside and had me sighing in pleasure. "Nothing better," I said as I leaned back in the seat. "Well, almost nothing better."

Alex also drank from his mug with a grateful expression as though thanking the caffeine gods for the gift of energy. "Yeah, that's good," he said as he set the mug down. Then his eyes widened. "Oh, shit. I forgot I need to call a tow truck."

I stilled as I watched him fish in the coat pocket for his

phone. After seeing his reaction to me buying a single coffee and pastry for him, I realized I probably should have asked before making decisions on his behalf. This had the potential of blowing up in my face.

Would it matter that I'd had pure intentions? That I'd only wanted to make things easier for him?

"Um, wait," I said as I reached across the small table and gently nudged the phone away from his ear. "Don't call."

Frowning, he lowered his arm. "Why not?"

"Well, there's a chance I already took care of it." I held his gaze. This felt like a pivotal moment for us, and I refused to back down.

His eyes narrowed to suspicious slits. "What do you mean there's a chance you took care of it?" He pushed away his fork, his coffee cake forgotten.

Well, I didn't forget a crumb of my breakfast. Fucking Alex twice in a few hours had me ravenous for food, among other things. I took a bite of my sandwich, chewed, and swallowed before answering. "I had your car towed to an auto shop. They texted while you were getting dressed. Your car will be ready this afternoon. And no, I refuse to accept any money, so you might as well deal with it."

Here it came, the fury, the lecture about overstepping my bounds and throwing my money around. I rested back in my chair as I tried to prepare for whatever caustic words he'd throw my way.

But they didn't come. Instead, he shook his head with a furrowed brow. "Why would you do that?" The genuine bewilderment in his voice and confusion in his dark eyes broke my heart. Had no one ever done something nice for him?

"I did it because I wanted to, Alex. For you. I wanted to do it for you, to help you out and make today a little less shitty for you."

His shoulders sagged. "But... but *why*? Ryder, you can't stand me."

I barked out a laugh so loud and so incredulous that it drew stares from halfway across the coffee shop. "Seriously?" I asked, leaning in. "You still think that after last night? Hell, after the last month?"

His eyebrows drew down, giving that gorgeous face the glower I'd come to expect. I'd seen him wear every expression imaginable, from fury to ecstasy, but this serious, slightly irritated one had to be my favorite.

"I... no. The last month has changed things for me too."

I sighed. Beating around the bush wasn't my style. Saying most things didn't come easily to me would be a blatant lie. With money came privilege, and with privilege came safety. I was used to asking for what I wanted and getting it, and I'd be damned if that didn't happen here, even if I didn't have an inch of a safety net in this situation.

I rested my forearms on the table, leaning in as far as possible. My heart rate accelerated, making me feel like I'd chugged four mugs of double espresso in minutes. I was about to hand Alex a lot of power.

The power to hurt me.

The only people who'd ever had that power were my family. Given the state of my relationship with my father, I wasn't feeling too confident about giving another person influence over my emotions. But I had no choice. Alex couldn't continue thinking I didn't like him, not when I wanted him so fiercely and for more than just our physical chemistry.

"I'm just going to lay it all out there, Alex. I do not hate you. Never have. There's no denying I was a dick to you. I didn't... I never thought beyond showing off for my buddies back then. I have no excuses. It was shitty of me. I own that, and I'm so sorry for it. I made snap judgments without knowing anything about you or your life. And now—"

"I don't want your pity." His eyes narrowed with suspicion.

"And you don't have it. I promise."

He nodded.

"But I... care. So I feel like shit for how I treated you, and I don't like knowing you struggle." I shrugged. "But it isn't pity. It's just... giving a shit." God, I was bad at this. Could I blame my parents for not being able to express my feelings well, or was that all on me?

For whatever reason, my bumbling apology seemed to work for him. He gave me a half-smile. "There's a small chance I was a dick to you as well," he said, copying my words from a few moments ago.

"Yeah, well, I know we like to one-up each other, but I think you're going to have to concede the win to me here. I was by far the bigger asshole."

"Yeah," he said with a teasing glint in his eyes. "You were."

We stared at each other across the table, both grinning. All around us, people carried on with their lives, enjoying breakfast, chatting, and working. But we might as well have been completely alone for all the attention we paid anyone outside the bubble of our table.

I reached out and covered his hand with mine, where his rested on the tabletop. Never before had I felt the need to have a physical connection with someone, but the second he flipped his palm and wrapped his fingers around my hand, my heart steadied.

"Last night was amazing—"

Alex grunted. "The last part was amazing. The rest..."

I shook my head. "No, the whole thing. I really liked helping you out last night. We solved a problem together. We worked as a team. You let me in and let me see parts of your life no one else does. It was special." My cheeks heated as the words left my mouth, and I averted my gaze, finding something very interesting on the top of my sandwich. For all I know, he'd laugh and call me childish for interpreting things in such a way.

"Ryder, look at me," he said in a soft tone I'd yet to hear from him. "I felt the same way the night you talked to me about changing your career goals. Special, I mean."

We stared at each other for a few moments, probably looking like two fools mooning over each other.

"So now what?" he asked.

"Now, we hang out more *alone*. And we learn more about each other. Maybe we learn everything about each other." I held my breath, realizing just how much I wanted to be with him.

"I..." He swallowed. I loved the way his throat moved and would have loved to lick over his Adam's apple as he did it. Maybe he'd let me later. He stroked his thumb over my wrist, raising thousands of goose bumps along my arm. "I think that sounds perfect."

Pounds of tension whooshed from me in a long exhale. His agreement made me feel like I could fly out of my seat and soar above the entire city.

My smile hurt my damn cheeks.

"And we fuck." His voice dipped to the seductive tone I'd heard from him last night. "We fuck a lot."

I groaned as my dick responded to the enticing statement. "Yes. We definitely do that. A lot."

"So..."

The smooth pad of his thumb continued to draw circles on my wrist. Somehow, it soothed and ramped me up at the same time. I wanted to reach across the table and kiss the hell out of him. "So?" I asked.

"Does that make us..."

I arched an eyebrow.

He rolled his eyes. "I mean, I'm not interested in anyone else, so I guess I'm asking if we'll be exclusive."

"Yes," I answered so fast he snorted a laugh.

"Okay then."

"Is that what you want?" I held my breath, not daring to disrupt the air around us until I got the answer I wanted.

He nodded. "Yes. I'm feeling a little possessive where you're concerned."

Damn, that was nice to hear. "Same. I almost punched a customer at the club last night for staring at your ass. Not that I can blame him. Your ass is a work of art."

That had Alex rolling his eyes again, this time with an adorable flush to his cheeks. "Last question, does that make us..."

"Boyfriends?" My heart fluttered at the word. Why did it sound so good falling from his lips?

His face scrunched as though he'd gulped sour milk. "Does that sound stupid?"

Hell, no, it didn't sound stupid. I shook my head. "No. Not stupid. I think it sounds pretty damn good. I've never had an official boyfriend. Hookups and a few fuck buddies, but nothing more."

"Me neither." A glimmer of teasing shone from his eyes as he smirked. "Unless you count Jared Poznic, who I dated for three days in the seventh grade."

I laughed hard. "No. We're not counting that fucker, whoever he is. I like the idea of being your first."

"Hey, don't knock that special time in my life. For half a week, we were super serious. He carried my books to class and everything," Alex said with a wink.

God, I loved it when he shed his rigid outer shell and got playful with me. When he let down his guard and allowed me to see the man he shielded from everyone else. Sure, he laughed, joked, and smiled with his VIP customers at Top

Shelf, but now that I'd spent enough time with him to see beneath his hard exterior, I realized what a performance he put on at work. None of those smiles were real. They were an act to garner tips. We all did it.

"Fine," I said with an exaggerated sigh. "Guess I'll have to settle for being your second. At least I know I'll be the best."

Instead of laughing like I'd been going for, he grew serious. "Yeah, I think you will be." He climbed out of his side of the booth and scooted in next to me.

Being a table designed for two, we barely fit on the single-occupant bench together. Not that I minded, he could press up against me anytime he wanted. Alex rested his chin on my shoulder and whispered, "I'm sorry for screaming at you last night when you came into my house. Last night would have been horrible if you weren't with me, and I repaid you by being an asshole. I'm sorry."

I turned my head until our lips were almost touching. "It's okay, Alex. I'm not mad." Sitting this close with his hand on my thigh, it was impossible for my body not to react. I wanted him. My cock wanted him and grew accordingly.

"I was embarrassed." Though no one was close enough to eavesdrop on our conversation, he spoke low as though he didn't want the universe to overhear. "Our lives, our worlds are so different, Ryder. You have so much, and I'm a mess. I have noth—"

I kissed him. Not the wild, hungry kind of kiss I'd have taken were we alone, but a soft press of my lips to his meant to stop him from disparaging himself. "I don't want things from you, Alex. I just want you. Things I can get. I've always had *things*. But I haven't had you, and that's what I want. Just you. Okay?" Maybe I was already getting better at this sharing-my-feelings thing.

"Ryder..."

We kissed again. And once more.

"Yes, my family has money," I said when we broke apart. "We have stuff. That doesn't mean we're not a fucking disaster in other ways. I know the things I harassed you about in the past make it seem like I look down on you and your family, but I don't. Alex, I respect the hell out of you for all you do for your family. You carry so much on your shoulders, and while they are big, strong, and very sexy, they must be getting tired."

"I have a lot of responsibilities. If I don't work, we don't eat. My mom has medical bills, equipment, and tons of doctors' appointments. My brother…" He shrugged. "Well, you met him. They take up so much time. I might have to cancel plans on a moment's notice or miss out on them altogether. What happens when you get tired of my obligations?"

The vulnerability in his voice was like a knife to my heart. "Is that what happened with your father?"

"Yeah. He fucked off exactly one week after my mom was diagnosed with multiple sclerosis. I was ten, sitting at the breakfast table. She'd fallen the previous day because of weakness in her leg. I couldn't get her up by myself, so I called him to come home from work. He came, but the next day, while I was eating breakfast, he came out of his room with a bag over his shoulder. He told me he'd signed up to be a husband, not a nurse. Then he ruffled my hair and walked out the door. Haven't seen him since."

"Jesus." How did his family survive so much devastation at once? I'd wondered why his mother used a wheelchair but didn't know if I should ask. His opening up on his own felt incredible. I turned, as much as possible, wedged between the wall and Alex's hard body. Our food and coffees were forgotten as we focused on each other. Now that we were deep in a serious conversation, I wish we'd stayed in my apartment. This way I could tackle him back into my bed and tell him how serious I am about us with true privacy.

"I can promise you I am not that man. And I know words are just… words. But I'm coming into this with my eyes wide open, Alex. Your family is important to you and requires a lot of your time and attention. But that's what makes you, you. It's what makes you honorable, trustworthy, and so damn special. I hope that we'll grow closer, and I'll become an important part of your life, which means I'll share the load with you. Not today. I realize that will require a lot of trust on your part, but someday."

His brow wrinkled in confusion, and I couldn't help but reach out to smooth a finger down his forehead. "But… why? We're not your problem, Ryder. Why take this all on, knowing it could be hard at times? You could hook up with anyone."

Well, that was an easy one. "Because you're worth it, Alex. Yes, I can hook up easily, not with anyone…" I shrugged. "But sure, without sounding too arrogant, I don't usually have a problem finding someone to hook up with."

He chuckled and squeezed my hand. "Don't start pretending you're not arrogant now."

"You know what I can't do easily?"

He tilted his head and searched my eyes.

"I can't find someone I connect with. Someone I can hook up with again and again and have it be better each time, and when we're done, want to see that person across the table at breakfast. Or be excited to work with them at night. Or want to do whatever I can to make their life easier. Or want to learn every single thing about them and have them know everything about me."

"Ryder… shit," he said with a watery laugh. Then he pressed a hand to his chest. "You're taking my damn breath away."

My heart soared as I leaned in. "So, we're doing this?" I

whispered.

"We're doing this."

Alex grabbed the front of my shirt and sealed the deal with a kiss that probably made half the café blush.

Chapter Twenty-Four

I floated my way through the entire afternoon. Study groups? I think I went to them, but don't ask me what we talked about. Hopefully, the notes our group leaders emailed were comprehensive because I didn't absorb a damn word.

Ryder's words from that morning replayed over and over in my mind.

My life consisted of school, work, taking care of my family, and the minimal spare time remaining, I usually spent stressing about those other three things. A social life? What was that? Aside from the occasional quick lunch with Trevor or mandatory fun with my coworkers, I didn't have one of those.

Yes, I knew I had a prickly personality ninety percent of the time. Life had fucked me without lube or prep more times than I could count. Of course, I'd built six-inch steel walls around my heart and head. Who wouldn't? A therapist would probably help, but who had the money for one of those?

Not me.

It would take a damn saint to be willing to chisel through my bullshit, yet Ryder had done it, and that man was far from a saint. Ryder was, well, a man. Flawed and prone to mistakes, same as me. In my desperation, I'd let him climb a few of my walls and glimpse the mess on the other side.

And he hadn't run away. Instead, he claimed to want more. And he'd fucked me like he'd meant those words. But he'd said the words after fucking me.

God, did he fuck me good.

And there I went, daydreaming about Ryder and his talented dick again.

My phone rang, dragging me away from my latest we'll-have-to-try-that-later fantasy.

Diamond Auto Shop flashed across the screen. "Hello?" I said as I brought the phone to my ear.

"Good afternoon, this is Darla with Diamond Auto Shop. I'm looking for Alex Morgan."

"I'm Alex." I slowed to a stop near where I'd agreed to meet Ryder.

"Fantastic. Well, Mr. Morgan, your car repairs are complete, and it's ready to be picked up at your convenience. We're here until eight tonight and open at seven thirty tomorrow morning."

"Wow, that was fast. Thank you."

"You are very welcome, Mr. Morgan. We pride ourselves on fast and quality service."

"And the bill?" I asked, though I knew what she'd say.

"Is taken care of." Her cheery tone had me rolling my eyes.

"Of course it is," I mumbled. "Um, could you tell me what the cost was?" If it were crazy expensive, I'd—what? What the hell would I do? I couldn't pay Ryder back. At least not in a timely manner. Maybe he'd take a payment plan.

In blow jobs.

"No, I cannot," she said with a tinkly giggle. "I have strict, written instructions not to let you know anything about the invoice amount. "In fact, someone wrote an exact script for me. Nice try, you stubborn, sexy man. Now go find Ryder and give him a kiss as a thank you."

"Oh my God," I said as my face heated to the equivalent of a tar road in the desert sun. I pinched the bridge of my nose, shaking my head. Thank God, no passersby could hear her side of this ridiculous conversation.

Darla giggled again. "Sounds like you got yourself a very sweet man there, Mr. Morgan."

Her statement had my hand dropping to my side. "Yeah." My throat dried up, leaving my voice a rough croak. "I'm pretty sure I do."

"Have a good day, sir. We'll see you when you pick up your vehicle."

"Yeah… thank you."

She disconnected the call, leaving me standing beneath a bare oak tree once again, thinking about the man who'd shaken my entire life and stirred up emotions I'd locked in a box, all in less than twenty-four hours.

It was a gorgeous day. Even as the sun dipped closer to the horizon, the bright ball heated the chilly air to a beautiful fifty degrees, much higher than the average for the year. I closed my eyes, allowing the warmth to kiss my face while I inhaled. Without Ryder, today would have been a mess of anxiety and stress. I'd have probably missed my study group and freaked out over how to pay for my car repairs. He'd eliminated that obstacle for me, and as much as I should probably feel guilty over it, all I felt was grateful.

I couldn't wait to show him how grateful later. And, shit, now I was soaking up the sunshine with a growing erection.

A sharp wolf whistle cut through the air, making me jump. I opened my eyes to find Ryder sitting behind the wheel of his Rover. He wore aviators and a leather jacket—thank you, warmer day—that probably cost more than my car repairs. Damn, did he look hot. The dark jacket contrasted with his beach-boy blond hair in a way that made my mouth water.

"Hey, sexy," he called out as he pushed his aviators up to his head. "Need a ride?"

My smile grew so fast that my cheeks ached with the force of it. This funny, gorgeous, intelligent, and generous man was all mine. At least for the time being, and I wasn't going to waste a second of having him in my life.

I sauntered toward the car. When I reached it, I folded my arms and rested them on the open window. "My car is in the shop, but I'd hate to put you out," I said with a wink. "I'm happy to get an Uber." Holy shit, whatever fancy cologne he wore, I wanted to take a bath in it, or better yet, rub my naked body over every inch of his marking myself with his scent.

"Sure, that's one option." His grin grew wicked. "But will your Uber driver suck your dick?"

I pursed my lips, then shrugged. "I mean, if I play my cards right, maybe..."

Ryder barked out a laugh. "Smartass," he said as he lowered his sunglasses. "Get that sexy ass in my car before I'm forced to get out and show this whole damn campus who you belong to."

Like he had any competition to worry about, but still, the possessive words turned me on and made my heart flutter. Damn, all these new emotions. Now that I'd let them in, they seemed determined to stick around.

"Well, now I don't really want to get in," I grumbled as I opened the door and climbed into the passenger seat.

Ryder laughed as he leaned over the center console. "Promise that wasn't a one-time offer. I plan to do all sorts of nasty things to you later, and I'm sure hoping you'll do plenty to me too. It's my turn to feel your dick in my ass."

"Jesus." I pressed down on the very interested dick he'd mentioned, fighting the urge to hump into my hand as I leaned toward him for a proper hello.

He was smiling as he pressed his lips to mine in a quick peck that wouldn't cut it after the teasing. I grabbed the back of his head and held him there as I probed my tongue against the seam of his lips.

He opened for me at once, allowing me to plunge inside for a deep taste. The groan rumbling from his chest did nothing to calm my cock.

"Shit," he said against my mouth after at least a solid three minutes of devouring each other. "Let's skip the community center. I need you to fuck me."

It was my turn to groan. As much as I wanted that, and as much as I was risking my cock's fury, I knew he'd feel guilty if we bailed on the kids. They counted on him being there, and he'd given them his word. What kind of jerk would it make me if I caused him to back out of a promise to a bunch of struggling kids?

"You can't skip it." I grabbed the lapels of his leather jacket and held him close as I inhaled the intoxicating combination of his cologne and the leather.

"Are you smelling me?"

"Yes, I fucking am." I drew in another sample sniff. "Tonight... after the community center, I want to fuck you wearing only this jacket."

A tremble ran through him. "Hell yes," he whispered. "Thank God Top Shelf isn't open tonight."

So true.

"Okay," he said with a sigh. "Take your hands off me so I can function."

Chuckling, I released him, but not before sneaking a final kiss from those addictive lips.

We were both grinning and adjusting the tight fit of our pants as we faced forward. As Ryder pulled the Range Rover away from the curb, he rested his right arm on the center console. Without thought, I reached out and threaded our fingers together. He flicked his gaze my way with a smile, then tightened his grip. The need to touch him, to be connected physically, rode me hard, and if we couldn't get naked and have some fun, at least I could hold his hand, something I'd never done with another man. Not even Jared Poznic.

We passed the twenty-minute drive to the community center, chatting about our favorite television shows. It turned out we had similar tastes in comedy and drama, but Ryder loved horror, whereas I tended to nerd out over science documentaries.

"Aww," he teased with a chuckle as I shuddered over his recounting of *Terrifier*. "Is it too scary for you?"

I flipped him off. "No. It's not too scary. It's too dumb. I'm too intelligent for that shit."

He laughed harder. "Don't worry, big guy, you can snuggle up close when we have a marathon of the whole trilogy."

"Fuck that." No way, no how.

"Come on." He slowed to a stop at a red light, then leaned over and whispered in my ear. "How about a trade? For every horror flick you watch with me, I'll geek out on a documentary with you."

"Not hap—" Huh. That wasn't a bad deal. "Throw in a blow job, and I'm in."

"Well, fuck yeah. I'll take a BJ from you any time. You don't need to watch a horror movie to blow me."

What? Was he for real? I scowled. "That's not what I meant!" I glared at him only to find his stupidly handsome face screwed up as he failed to hide his laughter.

"I knew what you meant," he finally managed after the ridiculous guffawing ceased. "I just enjoy flustering you."

"Really?" I asked as I rolled my eyes. "Never noticed."

The light turned green, and he drove two more blocks

before veering into a small parking lot in front of a one-story cement building.

A large hand-painted rainbow arched from the ground on one side of the door to the ground on the other side, originating and ending in a painted fluffy cloud. To the left of the door, a sign read *True Colors LGBTQA+ Youth Center. All Welcome.*

"How'd you get involved here?" I asked as he backed into a spot as far from the entrance as he could pick.

"A friend of mine volunteered here in college." His face lit up as he spoke. "I tagged along one day when I was bored and have been coming ever since. Missed the fuck outta this place while I was gone."

It didn't mesh with the high school boy I'd known who called me *freeloader*, but it jived with the man I'd come to know today—the generous, non-judgmental man who'd helped my family and me without question. Despite living in wildly different tax brackets, he hadn't batted an eye at where I lived and didn't seem to think less of me today. It was exactly what I needed to shed any lingering hold our past had on me.

He killed the engine, which I had no idea how he remembered to do since his electric vehicle didn't make a damn sound, then turned to me. "Ready?"

A sudden drenching wave of nervousness washed over me. "Yeah," I said with all the confidence I could muster. I was shit with kids—wait, was I? Maybe not, but I had less than zero experience with them, so who knew? But I'd basically raised Kenny, and look how he turned out. He certainly wasn't a ringing endorsement of my skills in mentoring the youth.

"Ready."

"Great. Let's do it." He climbed out of the car as comfortably as if he were heading into his apartment. I followed suit with a bit less enthusiasm, but I tried to keep the terror off my face.

"Alex, relax," he said with a chuckle. "You're not going in for a root canal. They're just a bunch of kids."

"That might be easier," I muttered.

Laughing and shaking his head, he took my hand and tugged me across the parking lot. "Come on, Mr. Anti-Social, imparting some wisdom to the youth of our city will be good for you.

"I'm not anti-social," I said, refusing to melt over the way he still held my hand. I guess this was one of the perks of having a boyfriend. "I socialize my ass off four nights a week."

"That's not socializing. That's work."

Touché.

As we reached the door, I wondered what he'd do if I dropped his hand and raced back to the car like a world-class pussy. But as I prepared to loosen my grip, Ryder abruptly stopped and turned to face me. "Thanks for coming with me, Alex. This is… well, this is important to me, and it means a lot to share it with you." A lightning-quick flash of uncertainty crossed the face of this self-assured man, whose confidence frequently crossed the line to blatant arrogance. "Even my family doesn't know I volunteer here."

This was a big deal to him. He let me into the most private and sacred part of his life.

I cleared my throat before I did something unthinkable, like choke up, then said, "We better get in. They might fire you if you're late."

He grinned and squeezed my hand, seeming to understand the subtext for the sappy excitement over the invitation that it was, even if I worried I'd embarrass the hell out of him by crashing and burning with the kids.

Ryder pulled open the heavy door and gestured for me to

enter before him. When I narrowed my eyes, he laughed, then whispered, "You got me. I'm not just a polite boy. Sue me for wanting an extra peek of your ass."

My eyes widened, and I elbowed him as I passed—that devil. Now, I was going to be walking into a youth center fighting an erection. Perfect.

I stepped in, and a rush of warmth spilled over me like a rolling wave. The air smelled faintly of vanilla and fresh paint. A low hum of laughter, music, and muffled conversations blended, creating a gentle atmosphere of controlled chaos.

A mural stretched along the main wall—another radiant rainbow stretching across a clear blue sky dotted with plush white clouds. Bold, encouraging affirmations decorated the wall above and below the arc of the rainbow.

You are loved.

Your voice matters.

Be proud.

There were at least a dozen other mantras to empower the kids in a way I never had been. Sure, I was damn lucky my mom never gave me grief about my sexuality, but that was more because her days were consumed with her illness. I didn't begrudge her that, and I'd take mild apathy over belittlement from a parent any day, but it would have been amazing to hear some of these declarations as a confused teenage boy.

Cushioned benches lined the walls of the open space. Some were scattered with mismatched but plush pillows in every color imaginable. Teens and tweens clustered around a wide, low coffee table in the center of the room, playing an intense game of Uno while another group leaned over a half-finished jigsaw puzzle, and another group sat at a table, completing what appeared to be homework. On the far side of the room, a rainbow flag draped across a doorframe led to a cozy lounge area, where a few kids curled up with books or tapped away at their phones.

A bulletin board covered in flyers stood by the front desk with announcements for art classes, movie nights, basketball games, and support groups. Above it, a banner in shimmering gold letters read, *Welcome Home*.

I imagined this place literally saved lives.

My shoulders relaxed almost immediately. The anxious knot in my stomach began to unwind. If this center was a safe place for these kids, it could be for me as well.

A volunteer, a young woman with a shaved head and pierced lip sat behind the desk, mouthing along to the overhead song as she typed something into her dinosaur of a computer. She wore a royal-blue polo shirt with a rainbow and the center's name over her heart. An enamel pin reading, *Here For You*, dangled from the collar of her polo.

Somehow, we caught her attention, and she glanced our way only to have a radiant smile break out across her face. "Ryder!" she practically shouted. "Micky mentioned you were coming today."

The second Ryder's name left her lips, heads popped up all over the room. Two seconds after that, screeches, whoops, and shouts of "Ryder's here!" went up throughout the center. Then, before I had a chance to process the incoming tsunami of teenagers, Ryder's hand ripped from mine as a gaggle of gangly arms and legs wrapped around him from all angles.

He sent me a rueful grin that I waved away right before turning his attention to the kids.

"Micky! What's up, my man? Hey, Kimber, love the new hair color. TJ, can't wait to hear how your school debate went," and so on until I was beyond impressed with his memory and recall of each child and something personal from their lives.

My cold heart melted a fraction while I watched him

display a monumental amount of patience as the teens and tweens began to pull him in all directions. "Ryder, you owe me a basketball game. Ryder, will you play Minecraft with me? Ryder, I need help with my math homework."

"Whoa, whoa, whoa." He lifted his hands in surrender. "Did they give you each ten sugar packets when you walked in the door today? Let me introduce you guys to someone before we do anything else."

What felt like a million curious young gazes turned my way.

"Hey." I lifted a hand for an awkward wave like the social superstar I was.

"Guys, this is Alex. He's a pretty special dude, so go easy on him and don't tell him any bad stories about me, okay?"

"Is he your boyfriend?"

"They were holding hands!"

"I wanna see you guys kiss!"

"Does he have a big di—"

"Do not finish that question!" Ryder shouted above the roar of nosy kids. He shot me a bemused look. "So much for going easy on you."

My face burned. I now completely understood the idiom 'fish out of water.'

"Yes, you meddlesome monsters, he is my boyfriend, but that is the only question I'm going to answer about him. And no, you cannot see us kiss." He winked at me. "But we sure like to."

A chorus of *awws* went around the center until Ryder rolled his eyes. "Simmer down, you guys. Okay, I'll try to get to everyone, but I'm telling you now, whoever needs homework help, Alex is your guy." He pointed to me as he spoke. "My man is wicked smart."

My damn face couldn't get any hotter. Ryder seemed determined to have me combust into a pile of ash at this point.

A gentle hand tugged at my wrist. I glanced down to see a waif of a girl looking up at me with wide, jade green eyes. "Can you do math?"

I chuckled as I nodded. "I can."

"Will you help me? I suck at math." Her sweet face crumbled. "I'm in the remedial class for sixth grade."

A boy at least a foot taller, threw an arm across her shoulders with a fierce scowl. "She struggles in math, but she is not dumb," he said with all the ferocity of an older brother protecting his sibling. It also seemed to be a warning to me not to upset her.

"I'd never think you were dumb. I bet you just haven't found the right method that works for you. I'd love to help with your math homework."

The protective boy studied me for a moment, then nodded and stepped aside. I guess that counted as his seal of approval.

"My stuff is set up over there," she said, pointing to a table.

I cast a glance at Ryder, who was already involved in a serious debate over which pizza restaurant was the best in Boston, so I followed the girl to her table.

Math, I could do. Math came easy to me. Hopefully, I could help this girl, whose name I still needed to learn.

The afternoon passed in a blink. One by one, kids came to me for assistance with their homework after my new friend, Alyssa, left with excitement and a newfound understanding of integer equations.

Ryder was the hit of the entire center. Each kid vied for his attention, gobbling up his smiles and praise like their favorite candy. Every so often, our gazes would meet, and he'd send me a wink or a private, pleased smile that made every ounce of nerves I'd felt worth coming here.

We were about an hour in when I realized I was having

fun. A lot of fun. These kids were funny, sweet, and full of so much energy that I could barely keep up. But what took the afternoon from fun to spectacular was watching Ryder. He was in his element working with these kids. The career change to education made perfect sense. My *boyfriend* was a natural and belonged in an environment working with kids. He truly cared about every kid here, giving them his full, sincere attention. When a few hours in, he mouthed thank you, I couldn't stop myself from blowing him a discreet kiss like some sappy romance movie character.

If his father saw him in action, there'd be no way to deny this was where Ryder shone. As his new boyfriend, I'd make sure to not only tell him that but also stand by his side when his father fought against it. Nothing, not even parental pressure, should keep him from achieving this dream.

Chapter Twenty-Five

Over the next few weeks, Alex and I became the subject of endless workplace teasing and pranks. At first, we'd tried to keep our relationship on the down-low, but that plan crashed and burned after only four days when Trevor walked into the staff room to find me shoved up against the lockers with Alex's tongue down my throat.

Okay, so maybe we hadn't been trying that hard to keep things private, but what the hell was I supposed to do when he prowled into the staff room while I was on break, looking all sweaty and glittery from that damn gold body paint Parker insisted we wear on Saturday nights? The man should be categorized as a lethal weapon. I'd had no choice but to allow him to slam me against the lockers and kiss me brainless. It was only after Trevor walked in and shrieked like a damn banshee that I realized boners and Top Shelf uniforms didn't mix.

Since that day, we'd suffered a series of juvenile pranks, routine invasive questions about our sex life, and constant ribbing. I loved every second of it. Each time Trevor begged to know our favorite positions or Dom ribbed me for doing a shitty job covering up a hickey—Alex was a biter, and I did not hate it—I got a secret thrill. Alex was mine, and my coworkers talking about it as though they had nothing interesting in their own lives only reinforced that fact.

At first, Alex worried about how Parker would react to the news of our relationship. He couldn't lose the job and feared our boss would have a problem with our relationship. It turned out the fear had been unfounded. Parker was a great boss and told us that as long as our relationship didn't interfere with our job performance, he didn't care. So, we kept things friendly while serving drinks and entertaining customers, though our level of flirting with customers took a nosedive—another thing I didn't hate. I quickly found out I had a bit of a possessive side I struggled to squash when men hit on my guy right in front of my face.

Which was how I found myself bent over, palms flat on a VIP table with two of Alex's tremendously talented fingers buried deep in my ass twenty minutes after closing on a night Parker trusted us to lock up.

"So?" Alex asked as he pegged my prostate and made me see stars. "What do you have to say for yourself?"

He'd only yanked my shorts down far enough to free my cock and access my ass. I was harder than I'd ever been and leaking all over the damn VIP table. If the Department of Health sent an investigator tomorrow, we'd be royally fucked. Though I was hoping to get fucked a lot sooner than that.

"You're not talking." Alex twisted his fingers and grabbed the base of my cock at the same time, sending a riotous jolt of lightning through me while denying me the release my body already craved.

"Alex…" I whined, slapping the table. "Fuck me already."

His dark chuckle settled low in my stomach, twisting the coil of need tighter. "Not until you tell me what I want to hear."

God, he was going to be the death of me in the most erotic way possible. "Fine," I managed as I panted through the near-painful pleasure his hands wrung from me. "I didn't like it."

"Didn't like what?"

He was determined to make me spell out every damn word. Fine. That's what he'd get. "Your customer came on to you. He wanted to fuck you. He wanted to fuck what's—" I needed to shut up now.

But Alex had no intention of letting me. He stroked my cock as he continued fingering my ass and driving me insane. "Keep going."

"Goddammit, Alex, he wanted to fuck what's mine. You're mine, and he was hitting on you right in front of me. Yes, I was goddamn jealous. I fucking hated it. You happy now?"

His fingers disappeared, leaving me feeling so empty I couldn't help the pitiful whine that left my throat. I'd pissed him off. Alex was more concerned than I was about what our coworkers and Parker thought of us. He hated PDA, even if he was an animal in private.

He stroked my cock twice then his hand vanished as well. Just as I was about to beg for something, a mouth, more fingers in my ass, his hand back on my weeping cock, something, I heard the rustle of a condom package.

Oh yes.

Two seconds later, the thick head of his cock nestled against my entrance.

"Fuck yeah, I'm happy."

He shoved into me in one long, smooth, forceful thrust that had my back arching and my sweaty hands slipping on the table. I loved being filled by him. Nothing beat the feeling of his cock in my ass. Well, maybe mine in his—no, it was a clear tie. I had to admit, I was more of a slut for ass play than Alex was, though he bottomed, demanded to bottom, more than I'd assumed. Still, I fucking loved his dick in my ass. I'd take him every morning, noon, and night if I could.

Once he buried himself as deep as possible, he curled over my back and spoke in my ear. "Tell me what you saw."

"Move."

"Not until you tell me what you saw."

Damn sadist.

I sighed. What could I say? I'd grown up the only boy of very wealthy parents. Sharing wasn't my strong suit. "He touched you. That bastard flirted with you, asked you out, and touched you. He grabbed your fucking ass. *My* ass."

"Mmm, and what did I do in response?"

"I—" He sucked my ear lobe, making goose bumps erupt all over my skin. "Shit, um, I couldn't hear what you said, but I saw you grab his wrist and remove his hand."

"Mm-hmm. I told him I wasn't interested in him the first time he asked me out. The second time, I was a little less polite. And when he grabbed my ass, I told him I'd break his hand if he touched me again."

"Fuck." Why did that turn me on so fucking hard? My cock was making a mess all over the table. A table I served four nights a week and would never look at in the same way again.

"I. Don't. Want. Anyone. Else." He punctuated each word with a short, hard thrust. I moaned. It was so good. "Are you hearing me?"

I whimpered as he stopped moving again. "Yes. Yes. I hear you. You're so mean. Fuck me, Alex." I tried moving on his cock, but he clasped my hip in an unbreakable grip, immobilizing me, speared on his thick cock in simultaneous ecstasy and agony. "Please."

"I only want you, Ryder," he whispered against my ear. Shivers ran up and down my spine. "For fuck's sake, I think about you all damn day. I'm practically useless because I can't think of anything else."

Something primal surged in me as I failed again to move on his dick. "Alex, you're killing me. Please move."

The maddening sexual control freak ignored my pleas. My ass was stuffed full of his cock. It rippled around the thick intrusion as though goading him into moving. Each second that passed without movement drove me one step closer to madness.

"As sexy as you look when you're jealous..." he rumbled against my ear, "... I don't want you getting in some guy's face. It's not worth it. They're not worth it. Your safety and future are too important to risk by starting a fight with a man I'll never want."

For whatever reason, I clung to my last thread of pride. "I wasn't jeal—"

His dark chuckle made my ass clench around his length. "You saying you weren't ready to rip out that guy's throat for touching me?"

"Which fucking guy? I caught more than one staring at your ass."

"Any of them. I will stop any man who tries to touch what's—"

"Mine?" I held my breath. Please say it.

"Yeah, Ryder," he whispered against my ear. "I'm yours. I'm so yours I don't even notice anyone else."

Oh fuck, those words turned me on even more than his cock in my ass. My dick was creating a puddle on the table beneath me.

"Now admit it?" He flexed his hips in the tiniest undulation imaginable, but the effect flowed through me in a delicious wave of pleasure. That's it. I couldn't play the game any longer. I needed more, and I needed it now.

"Okay!" I shouted as he did it again, making my eyes cross. "I was jealous. I wanted to rip his heart out and stomp on it right there. You happy? Now, fuck me, Alex. Put me out of my damn misery and fuck me."

My words set off something in him, and he snarled behind me. "Yeah, I'm fucking happy," he said the instant before he attacked without mercy, slamming my ass with brutal force.

I shouted at the intense shock of pleasure. My sweaty palms were no match for his power. I slipped on the third pump of his hips, landing flat on the table in a pool of precum. The cool wood was a balm to my heated cheek, but the cock destroying my ass was pure heaven.

Alex gave me no time to catch my breath, not that I wanted it. He pounded into me like it was his last fuck. I used my trembling leg muscles to power into him each time he plunged. The effect was rough, ball-slapping thrusts that would have sent the table scraping across the polished floor if it weren't bolted down.

"God, I love fucking this ass," Alex mumbled with wonder. "Fits so damn tight."

"Perfect," I managed around my labored breaths. "Always perfect."

Alex grunted and yanked my hips back, freeing my cock from its prison between my body and the sloppy table. He wrapped one of those huge hands around my cock in a choking grip and stroked like his life depended on it.

"I can't hold back," he said, panting. "Your ass is too good."

"I'm there. I'm there. I'm the… oh fuck me." The orgasm ripped through me, unloading my balls with powerful spurts all over the damn table. Just as the climax hit, Alex's fingers dug into my hips, and he held his cock deep in my ass as he roared out what sounded like a spectacular release.

I smiled as my energy drained away, leaving me a satisfied pile of limp limbs. Just as I was about to drop back to the table in a lake of my mess, strong hands hauled me up beneath my shoulders and spun me around. Before I could react, Alex wound a strong arm around my waist and the other around my neck, hauling me flush against him. Then he stole my lips in a slow, languid kiss that muddled my mind more than any illicit substance. It went on and on, drugging me into a lethargic, blissed-out state as the pleasure of his mouth compounded the potent orgasm.

"Jesus," I said when we finally broke for air. Our foreheads and noses touched as we shared precious oxygen between us. "That was…" How to even describe it?

This close, it was hard to see Alex's blush, but I could feel the heat rising to his cheeks. "I don't know what came over me," he said with a light chuckle. "I always thought it was annoying when someone had a possessive boyfriend—"

"Gee, thanks."

He laughed again. "But tonight… your eyes. Fuck, Ryder, knowing how badly you did *not* want that guy to touch me got me so freaking hard. I was afraid I was going to tear through my stupid uniform."

"Well, if my snarling at twinky college boys is going to pull that reaction out of you, I might start hiring them to hit on you in front of me."

His eyes narrowed. "Don't you dare. As much as you hated watching it, I hated feeling it."

I kissed his nose. "You say the sweetest things."

Alex peered over my shoulder with a wince. "Shit, looks like we have some cleaning to do."

"You don't think we should leave it like this for Parker to find tomorrow morning?"

If horror were a picture in the dictionary, it'd be the expression on Alex's face right then. His eyes nearly fell out of his head, and his jaw hit the floor while he shook his head so fast, his sweaty hair flopped side to side.

"Relax," I said as I playfully shoved him off me. "I would

never."

We used the napkins on the table to clean our dicks as best we could then hiked up our pants. Once relatively decent, I said, "We sanitize, then head over to check on your mom?"

He nodded. "If that's okay."

I rolled my eyes. "When is it ever not okay with me if you check on your mom?"

"Never. I just—"

I stepped up to him and kissed his frowning lips. "I know. You just worry it's too much, and I'll get annoyed. Well, it's not, and I won't. I'm more than happy to check on her any time of day or night. Okay?" It'd become somewhat of a ritual for us to stop by Alex's house after shifts at Top Shelf. Some nights, his mom was sound asleep in bed, cell phone on the pillow next to her in case of an emergency. Sometimes, she was on the couch, having been too fatigued to get into her wheelchair herself, so we'd help get her settled for the night. And sometimes, she was snoozing in her chair or watching television. Never once had I complained because it genuinely didn't bother me at all. I was dating Alex, and he came with important responsibilities.

No problem.

Yet he always got this apologetic look on his face as if he needed to make up for burdening me in such a great way. Hopefully, one day he'd realize I didn't view his mother as a burden. His brother, on the other hand, well, I'd like to kick that little shit's ass. Never once did he help Alex or even offer to lift a damn finger or toss a dime toward the family's finances. The guy was the definition of a lazy mooch, and it pissed me the fuck off. So far, I'd kept my lips zipped and my opinion to myself because Alex didn't need me telling him. He knew it and resented it. But what could he do? Though he paid ninety percent of the bills, with a tiny amount of assistance coming from his mother's disability stipend, it was technically her house, and she didn't have the heart to boot Kenny out on his slothful ass.

"Okay," he said with a rueful smile, though I knew it wouldn't be the last time I had to reassure him. "Thanks, Ry. She was feeling a little under the weather earlier today, so I want to make sure she's not getting a cold."

I grabbed his hand as we walked toward the supply closet to grab the industrial-strength disinfectant. That stuff was strong enough to strip the freckles off a redhead, so it should have no problem removing the lovely cum mess I'd made on the table.

"Should we stay there tonight?" I asked as Alex glanced down at our joined hands with a smirk.

Yes, I liked to touch him all the time, even if we were walking fifteen feet to get some cleaner. Sue me.

"Would that be all right with you?"

I rolled my eyes. "Yes, Alex, it would be all right with me. It's always all right with me."

"Okay, yeah. I think it would be a good idea."

Another point of stress for Alex was sleeping at his place. He'd convinced himself his house wasn't good enough for me, and I shouldn't be sleeping there. It'd taken a week of twice-a-day blow jobs for me to wear him down enough to let me stay over the first time. We mostly stay at my place. Yes, it was more comfortable and more private, but I was happy to stay at his house any night. Even if he didn't have people who needed him, I'd be glad to sleep there. Clearly, I needed to do something to convince my boyfriend I wasn't the hoity-toity snob he seemed to think I was.

Huh, maybe I should be offended by his opinion on how I'd react to anything less than luxury. Now, on the flip side, I'd be a big fat liar if I didn't admit how much I loved to spoil Alex. I had to be careful with it because he was as stubborn as they came and disapproved of me spending money on him, but I had my ways.

I wouldn't say money was an *issue* between us, but it was a minor sticking point I strove to keep from becoming a problem.

"Great! Let's do it. And in the morning, I'll order breakfast from that place your mom loved. What was it?"

He narrowed his eyes at me. "The French place where a croissant costs twenty dollars?"

Yep, that's the place. I shrugged. "Don't know. I just know she loved it. You can't have a problem with me wanting to do something nice for your mom. I want her to like me." I gave him the most persuasive grin I could muster at two in the morning.

"Oh, she loves you, trust me. She's ready to toss me out on my ass and have you take my place at this point."

We both knew that wasn't true, but I did love the way his mom had taken to me. "Well, then, I'm definitely buying breakfast from the French place. I gotta keep my status as favorite."

Alex grunted and pulled me in for a slow kiss. "Fine," he said with a half-smile when we pulled apart. "We'll sleep there, and you can buy her breakfast."

And if the expensive French café also happened to be my boyfriend's favorite breakfast spot, we'd chalk it up to a happy coincidence.

Chapter Twenty-Six

For nearly two months, I've had a boyfriend, a serious one, it seemed. One who chose to stay at my rundown house and sleep in my fifteen-year-old double mattress bed when he had a brand new pillowtop king mattress in his luxury apartment just fifteen minutes away.

Why did he do it? Why did he stay on my side of town when he could have been sleeping on his thousand-thread-count sheets and stepping on his heated tile bathroom floor?

He did it because it made my life easier. Frequently staying at my house allowed me to take care of my mother and keep an eye on my wayward brother while still spending multiple nights with my boyfriend.

Ryder's willingness to bend for my comfort boggled my mind. Who did that? Who freely put themselves in an uncomfortable situation for someone else, no, not someone else, for me?

Someone who really likes you, you idiot.

Like I said, mind-boggling.

But also pretty damn wonderful. So much so that I got a warm, squishy feeling in my stomach each time I woke up to find him still asleep beside me in my old bed.

For the first few weeks, I spent most of my free time waiting for the other shoe to drop. Whenever Ryder and I weren't together, which admittedly wasn't too often since we became an official *thing*, I tried to prepare myself to be dumped the next time I saw him. I thought for sure he'd get sick of my grumpy attitude, my inability to pay for anything beyond the occasional cheap fast-food meal, or my needy family.

But he didn't. He smiled and rolled with the punches in the genial way he had, which made everyone like him.

Well, maybe not everyone saw the amicable side of him. There were a few guys at Top Shelf who ended up on the receiving end of his surprising possessive streak. And, God help me, I should find his jealousy off-putting, but instead, watching him snarl at someone blatantly hitting on me made me so hot I'd thrown him down and fucked him senseless each time.

What could I say? I was a sucker for how much he wanted me.

Especially since I wanted him just as much.

The morning of my mom's foot surgery, my alarm blared before the sun had risen. I was supposed to drive her to the hospital by seven, and of course, Ryder insisted on joining us, no matter how much I warned him it would be a long, boring day.

As I reached out to slap the snooze button for nine more precious minutes of relaxation, the strong arm around my waist tugged me against a naked chest while a set of warm lips went to work on the side of my neck.

"Good morning, handsome," Ryder whispered as he kissed his way up my neck.

My body responded instantly with shivers zipping down my spine to my interested dick. "Mmm, morning." I turned in his arms until I could fasten my mouth to his. Morning breath be damned, I'd take his kiss anytime, anywhere.

We made out for a few minutes, our hands roaming, our legs entwined, and our kisses sleepy. I'd have given my left nut to be able to spend the entire morning in bed doing just this, but my life was never that simple or relaxing.

"You ready for today?" Ryder asked as he cupped my ass and ground me against his morning wood.

I groaned. God, that felt good. "I think so," I managed to say as arousal tried to take over. "This, uh, this is the first time she's had this kind of procedure, so I'll have to learn how to change her dressings and clean the wound afterward, but she'll have a home care nurse for the first few weeks to make sure we're handling everything okay."

He nipped at my chin, then kissed me before saying, "I'd like to learn, too, if that's okay with your mom."

I pulled back a few inches. "You would? What for?"

Chuckling, Ryder shook his head. "So I can help you. Why do you think?"

My hard-on wilted. "Ryder, that's sweet, really sweet, but you don't have to. You're already doing enough by driving us to the hospital. None of this is your responsibility."

There were so many fun things he could be doing with his day. Soon, he'd be back in school. He should be enjoying his final few weeks off, not playing nurse to my mother.

"Alex," he said, drawing out my name as he gave me a little shake. "We've talked about this. Why is it so hard for you to accept that we're a team? That I'm not helping you out of some misplaced obligation but out of a desire to be your partner? You're busy as hell. I'm not right now. Let me help."

I bit the inside of my cheek. Was it really that simple? If the tables were turned, I'd be offering the same thing to him. Of course I would. So why was it so hard for me to accept what he claimed?

"I know you're used to doing every little thing on your

own. I know you haven't had anyone you could rely on for a long time, if ever." He tapped the side of my head gently. "But try to get it through this thick skull of yours that you don't have to anymore. I'm not going anywhere. Your life is not scaring me away."

Those words, simple at their core, meant more to me than any grand gesture or romantic display. Yet, I still struggled to embrace them. Maybe it was time to look into therapy. Time to admit my father's leaving gave me a mountain of abandonment issues, and the major responsibility of taking care of my complicated family from a young age warped my view of family and responsibility.

When I tried to turn away, he grabbed my chin, forcing me to search his eyes, where I found sincerity, heat, and maybe even more. Maybe something I'd be terrified to reach for, especially because I might be feeling it, too, so I put it on the back burner for another time.

"Okay, you're right," I said, which made an enormous smile break across his face.

"Who doesn't love those words?"

Chuckling, I shoved his shoulder. "Always so arrogant." Then I sobered. "I'm trying, okay? I promise I'm trying to change my thinking and stop worrying that my family's problems will become too much for you and you'll run away."

"Babe, I guarantee my family will implode at some point, and I'll need you to jump in and peel me off the ground. The only reason it hasn't already happened is because I'm avoiding them right now."

Huh, knowing I could repay the favor of support in the future lifted some of my anxiety. "Deal."

He nodded once, then pinched my ass. "Let's get moving," he said as I yelped and rubbed the spot.

"I think I liked it better when we hated each other."

A strong hand cupped my dick. "Really? You sure about that? I was about to offer you a blow job in the shower. Guess I can rescind the offer if you prefer it the way it was when we hated each other."

I rolled my hips, pushing into his palm as I fought to keep my eyes from rolling back in my head. I'd never been with anyone who brought me from zero to ready-to-fuck so quickly. All I had to do was see, hear, or smell him, and I wanted him. Then, when he touched me? I instantly and powerfully wanted him.

"I take it back," I said with a gasp as he scraped his teeth across the tendons in my neck. "This is better. Please put your mouth on my cock."

"Get in the shower, now," he whispered with a final squeeze of my dick.

I shot out of the bed so fast you'd think he'd announced a bedbug infestation.

Ten minutes later, after removing a mountain of adaptive equipment from the bathroom, I was under the hot spray with my dick buried so far down Ryder's throat I'd have worried I'd never get it back if I had any working brain cells. He grunted and groaned like a damn porn star as he drained my balls with a skill that amazed me every damn time he got his mouth on me.

I returned the favor with just as much enthusiasm, starting with a hungry dick suck and ending with a tongue fucking that had him biting his bicep to keep from scarring my mother with his cries of pleasure.

Fifteen minutes later, we stumbled out of the bathroom, dressed, sated, and ready to caffeinate so we could survive a long day of hanging around the hospital waiting room.

The hallway already smelled of coffee, which meant my mom had been able to get up and into her wheelchair by herself. It had been getting harder for her as the wounds on her feet progressed. Ryder pressed a kiss to my cheek and winked as though he understood without words what the delicious smell meant.

"Morning, Mom," I said as I stepped into the kitchen, only to stop and frown at the scene before me.

Mom sat in her wheelchair at the table wearing the matching lilac sweat set I'd gifted her for Christmas. Her hair needed to be brushed, but that task had become difficult over the past few months, so I typically needed to help. Kenny sat at the table with her, wearing a wrinkled wife-beater and black flannel sleep pants. The bruising he'd suffered at the hands of a furious drug dealer had finally faded. That didn't mean he looked good. Over the past weeks, he'd lost a lot of weight and had permanent dark rings under his eyes from long nights of drugged-out partying, minimal sleep, and crappy nutrition.

"What's going on?" I asked as I took in the way they glared at each other across the table. Most of the time, Mom stayed out of Kenny's messes. I tried to protect her from his antics as much as possible, but whatever she heard, she ignored for the most part, claiming he'd grow out of his 'rebellious streak' one day. To see her shooting daggers at him with her eyes had my stomach twisting. "Hello?" I said again when no one answered me. "What is going on?"

Ryder stayed quiet but didn't leave. Maybe some would have thought he should have stepped out to give our family privacy, but the way he slid his hand against mine and linked our fingers, giving me his silent support, would forever stay in my mind. He was there for me, by my side.

I squeezed his hand as I said. "Someone needs to start talking right now."

Mom shifted her gaze away from Kenny. "Your brother got arrested last night."

My eyes widened. "Wha—"

"Again."

"Oh shit," Ryder whispered as my jaw hit the floor.

"What do you mean again?" I stared at my brother, who rolled his eyes like he was fifteen and caught staying out past curfew, not nineteen and spending time in jail. "Kenny, what is she talking about?"

He huffed an indignant sigh. "It's nothing. The cops are fucking assholes. They have it out for me."

My mom flinched at his language but didn't interject.

I pinched the bridge of my nose. "What did you get arrested for?" Maintaining an even tone required considerable effort.

Ryder guided me to the table, pulled out a chair, and gently nudged me into it. Then he went to the coffee machine, where he pulled two mugs from the cabinet above our decade-old drip machine.

Kenny snorted and shook his head.

"Got something to say?" I asked as I narrowed my eyes.

"Excuse me. I'm going to finish getting ready." Mom wheeled her motorized chair away from the table and down the hall toward her bedroom.

Part of me wanted to scoff and call her out on how she fled the scene every time her son caused a problem, and we needed to have a challenging conversation with the nineteen-year-old man-child who contributed jack squat to our little family. But as usual, I bit my tongue. She had enough on her plate without me pressuring her to discipline her adult son, especially on a surgery day.

But I never had a problem putting Kenny in his place. Not that it mattered to him. "Well?" I said as I folded my arms across my chest while Ryder sat next to me, setting my coffee in front of me. He'd picked up on how I drank it—one packet of sugar, no cream—before we'd even started dating and never failed to hand me the perfect cup. He, on the other hand, preferred a million shots of espresso, something we did not have in my house, but he'd never once complained about a mug of Folgers.

"Why's he always gotta fucking be here?" Kenny asked with a near snarl. "Tired of hearing you two licking each other's fucking assholes."

My face burned, and anger simmered in my veins. "Jesus, Ken…" I knew this was his deflection, lashing out to keep us from talking about the real problem—his arrest. But still, I'd rather knock his teeth out than have Ryder subjected to this."

"Alex can make his own damn coffee," my brother continued as though I wasn't two seconds away from punching him in the face. "Don't let him treat you like his fucking bitch. What the fuck are you doing slumming with us anyway, rich boy?"

"Kenny!" I snapped. I started to rise, but Ryder's hand landed on my thigh, keeping me in place. The warm contact immediately settled me from a raging boil to a low simmer, though if Kenny continued to run his mouth, I'd make sure he regretted it.

Ryder tilted his head as he stared at my brother with a neutral expression. Only the narrowing of his eyes and the tension in his shoulders hinted at his anger over Kenny's nasty words. "You know what, Kenny? I've been trying to give you the benefit of the doubt for Alex's sake," Ryder said, his voice controlled but razor-sharp. "But I'm starting to think you're not worth the effort."

Kenny smirked. "Oh, did I hurt your feelings? Go cry about it in your fucking Range Rover."

"My car?" Ryder laughed, but there was no humor in it. "That's what you're fixated on? Jesus Christ." He leaned forward. "I'm not 'slumming' anywhere. I'm with Alex because he's the best fucking thing that's ever happened to me. Something you'd understand if you weren't so busy getting arrested or getting your ass kicked. You're welcome for helping you out, by the way."

"Fuck off," Kenny spat. "You don't know shit about me."

"I know enough." Ryder's grip on my thigh tightened. "I know you've been leeching off your brother for years. I know you've got every excuse in the book for why you can't get your shit together. And I know you're too damn selfish to see what it's doing to your mom or Alex."

Kenny's face flushed with anger. "This is family business. You're just—"

"Family?" Ryder cut him off. "Pretty sure I've been more family to your brother and your mom in the past few months than you have in years."

A knot formed in my throat. I should step in, but Ryder was saying all the things I'd been thinking for so long.

"That's rich coming from you." Kenny sneered. "Playing house with my brother like you give a shit. We both know you'll be gone as soon as you get bored with your little charity case."

I gasped—bullseye right to my biggest fear.

Something dangerous flashed in Ryder's eyes. He stood slowly, palms flat on the table. "Listen carefully because I'm only going to say this once," he said, his voice dropping to a near whisper that somehow felt more threatening than if he'd been shouting. "Alex isn't my charity case. He's my boyfriend. The man I'm building something with. And unlike you, I do give a damn about him." He straightened up. "So, you can call me whatever names you want. You can mock my car or how I like to make him coffee or whatever the fuck else makes you feel better about your own failures. But don't you *ever* imply that what I feel for your brother isn't real. And for the record..." he said with a wicked smirk, "... there's not a goddamn thing you could say or do to make me stop licking his ass, so keep your fucking opinions to yourself." The kitchen fell silent except for the hum of the refrigerator. Kenny stared up at Ryder, his expression wavering between rage and something that almost looked like respect.

This was the moment where one right word from Kenny could turn his life around. Where he could ask for help, apologize, or just not be a dick. But instead, he rose from the table with so much force that his chair clattered to the floor. "Fucking douchebags," he muttered under his breath before storming out of the kitchen.

I flinched at the sound of his door slamming, then found Ryder's gaze.

He leaned back in his chair, staring at me as he ran a hand over his stubbled face. "Shit, Alex, I'm sorry. I was out of line, yelling at your brother like that. He jus—"

I grabbed the front of his cashmere sweater as I shook my head. "No, you were perfect."

Then I slammed our mouths together, kissing him with all the feelings I was afraid to voice.

Chapter Twenty-Seven

When tearing Kenny a new asshole, I might have gone overboard, but the way Alex had tried to dive down my throat afterward let me know he didn't mind my aggressive approach at all. Someone had to put that little punk in his place, and I knew the situation was complicated for Alex due to his mother's feelings on the matter. The funny thing was, I didn't balk at saving Kenny's ass from violent drug dealers, and I would have bailed him out of jail in a heartbeat if he'd shown an ounce of remorse and asked for help. But instead, he'd run his mouth. What I wouldn't tolerate was him talking shit about Alex.

Not a fucking chance.

After Alex kissed me senseless, he helped his mom finish getting ready to head to the hospital. Since they didn't have a modified car with space for her motorized wheelchair, he had to help her into a manual chair, then into my car, where he folded the chair and stowed it in the trunk.

All before seven a.m.

It was exhausting, both physically and emotionally, but Alex never complained.

And Kenny never came back out of his room.

And Alex couldn't figure out why I liked doing things for him, why I wanted to spoil him.

No one deserved it more.

The weather had changed, bringing the warmth of spring, which made getting around easier. I no longer had to worry about Alex driving on snow and ice in his old beater of a vehicle. For some reason, he wouldn't let me buy him a new car, no matter how many times I asked.

Stubborn man.

When we arrived at the hospital, we wheeled her to the OR check-in window. From there, she was whisked away to prepare for surgery, and we had a few hours to kill.

"Want to grab a coffee at that little shop on the first floor?" I asked after saying goodbye to his mom.

Alex nodded. "Unless you need to go. You don't have to stay with me."

I resisted the urge to roll my eyes. "I know."

"Okay, then coffee it is." He bumped my shoulder, then took my hand, making me smile.

I got it. This relationship thing was new to both of us, and he needed to make sure one final time that I wanted to be here.

Which I did. Over the past few weeks, I'd discovered I'd happily sit on a trash heap just to be next to Alex.

Throwing my arm around his shoulders, I tugged him to me as we strolled down the hallway. "Or we could find a supply closet and reenact what went down in the shower this morning," I whispered against his ear before kissing the side of his head.

He glared at me with the same scowl that used to annoy me. "Jesus, Ryder." He shifted his hips as he walked.

"Something wrong?"

"Yes, something is wrong. I'm fucking hard in the middle of the damn hospital."

"Mmm, I love making you hard, especially when you grow on my tongue. Wanna know what my favorite thing is?" He didn't respond, but the furrow in his brow told me he couldn't decide whether he wanted to strangle me or push me against the window and fuck me. "My favorite thing in the whole goddamn world is taking you in my mouth in the morning when you're still soft and sleepy. I love the way you get so fucking hard on my to—"

He stopped so abruptly that I stumbled, but the way he shoved me against the wall of windows prevented me from falling. "Shut up," he said with a growl as he slammed his palm over my mouth. "Just shut the fuck up."

I smirked beneath his hand.

"You cannot say shit like that to me in the hallway of a hospital."

Since I couldn't speak, I raised an eyebrow. *Why?*

He stepped into me, letting me feel his erection pressing along the length of mine, which went hard in a flash. My eyes fluttered closed. Oh, how I loved that feeling.

"Yeah," he whispered. "That's why." He removed his hand and whispered, "Because now I want to fuck when I have to sit in a hospital waiting room for hours."

I opened my mouth, and he shook his head with a laugh.

"No, I'm not fucking you in a hospital supply closet, you deviant."

He'd do it. If I pushed, I could get him to the point of no return where he'd drag me off like a caveman to the nearest dark corner. A shiver ran through me at the delicious thought, but I backed off. I'd succeeded in taking his mind off today's stress.

"Then I guess I'll have to settle for coffee."

As he laughed, my phone buzzed from my pocket. A quick check showed my mother's name at the top. We hadn't spoken in weeks since the blowup with my father when I'd moved out. She texted a few times, but I'd left them on read. I silenced the phone and shoved it in my pocket.

"You're going to have to talk to them at some point."

"I know. Just not today. But I know I have to do it soon. My classes start in a few weeks so…"

The phone buzzed again. Another call from my mother. I frowned at the flashing screen.

"You should get it," Alex said gently. "It might be important."

"She's probably just trying to get my attention."

"Ryder…"

I sighed. "Yeah, I know." My mom wasn't the type to bomb my phone with calls and messages. She seemed perfectly happy to let our silence go on until I finally reached out. If she was calling, it had to be important. I pushed off the wall as I swiped the phone and lifted it to my ear. "Hello, Mother."

Immediately, sobs so loud they were nearly wails came through the phone. Alex grabbed my arm, clearly able to hear even though I hadn't put the phone on speaker.

"Mom? What's wrong? Are you okay?" I clutched the phone hard as my heart raced. "Where are you?"

"At the h-h-hospital. E-emergency R-room."

I met Alex's worried gaze. "She's here," I mouthed.

He still held my arm, but now his thumb rubbed back and forth in a soothing motion.

"What happened?" I was yelling now. Alex and I started jogging in the direction of the Emergency Room.

"I-it's your father. H-he had a-a stroke."

I stopped dead in my tracks. "What?" I whispered. A cold wave washed over me, numbing my entire body.

"It's bad, Ryder." Her meek voice pierced through my heart, and my stomach bottomed out. "Can you come?"

The teary question zapped me out of my shock. "Yes. Yes, of course. "I'm…" My head spun. My stomach lurched. I was going to be sick.

Alex pulled me close and pried the phone from my clenched fist. "Mrs. Calloway?" he said as he lifted it to his ear. "I'm Alex. Ryder is with me in the hospital right now, waiting for my mother to come out of surgery. I'll bring him to you in the ER right now." He fell silent, rubbing his hand up and down my back as I leaned into him.

My father had a stroke. He was only fifty. He played golf all the damn time. He wasn't unhealthy. How had this happened?

"Yes, ma'am... okay, he'll be right there." Alex ended his call and slid my phone into my pocket while I stood there, useless, with my mind rioting. "Hey," he said as he cupped my face and forced me to meet his gaze. "Your mom said they're admitting him to the ICU. That's where she wants you to meet her, okay?"

I nodded. His big thumbs stroked over my cheeks in a move I'd have nuzzled into like an attention-seeking cat only seconds ago. Now, his touch was the only thing keeping me grounded as my world descended into chaos.

"Okay, all you need to do right now is keep breathing slow and steady. I'll get you there."

Of the two of us, Alex had dealt with more than his share of devastating medical news. Plus, he was rock steady. I had no problem putting myself entirely in his hands.

"Let's go," he said.

"Wait—" I caught him by his wrists before he could release my face. "I... we don't get along. Most of the time, I don't even like him. But this..." I shook my head as shame gripped my throat. "I'd never want something like this for him, but I'm still angry at him. What kind of person does that make me?"

"Oh, baby..." He yanked me into a bone-crushing hug, surrounding me with his warmth and strength, exactly what I needed. "Of course you didn't. I'd never think that of you for a second. Just because something tragic happened doesn't change who he was or that you had a complicated relationship. That's all still valid, but it doesn't mean you don't want the best for him. Okay?"

God, this man, how did he always know exactly what to say? What the hell would have happened if he hadn't been with me when I got the call?

"Thank you," I whispered.

"Always." He released me, then gave me a thorough once-over with his assessing gaze. "You ready?"

"As I'll ever be."

Hand in hand, we walked to a bank of elevators. I had no idea which floor he pushed or if anyone else joined us in the elevator. All I could do was stare at the slit where the doors joined and feel the strength of Alex's hand clutching mine.

"We're here," he said in a low tone when the doors slid open.

I felt numb, as though he was guiding me through a sensory deprivation tunnel while he led me out of the elevators and down a short hallway.

"Hey," he said, concern marring his voice.

I blinked. A set of closed double doors came into focus.

"I can't go in with you."

"What?" Panic clawed at my throat. "Why not?"

He pointed to a white sign on the wall above a mounted phone. It read *Two visitors at a time. Immediate family only. Use the phone to give the receptionist the name and room number.*

Shit.

"I can't—"

"Shh..." Alex kissed the side of my head. "You can. And I'll be right here when you're done, okay?" He pointed left, where a small waiting area with four vinyl chairs and a fuzzy television playing the local news awaited him.

I shook my head. "Alex, your mom. You can't—"

His expression hardened to the most serious I've ever seen from him, even as his eyes radiated with something profound. Something I was terrified to hope for because it might crush me if I misread him.

"I said I will be here, Ryder. I. Will. Be. Here."

I nodded, and he kissed me hard, then turned to the phone. A few seconds after, he picked it up and said, "Ryder Calloway for the patient in room six. I'm his son." Silence and then, "Thank you."

As soon as he hung up, the doors began to open at a snail's pace. My pulse pounded in my ears so loudly I almost missed his final, "You got this." But I could never overlook the press of his lips against mine.

I probably should have thanked him or reassured him I wouldn't collapse or puke all over the floor, but my mouth wouldn't work anymore. I walked straight through the double doors, feeling like a pirate's captive walking the plank to my doom. Every step I took brought me closer to a situation I didn't yet understand but knew would be bad.

The ICU had the distinct odor of disinfectant and despair. High-pitched beeping came from all directions, some short and staccato, while others were drawn out or in multiples. The air felt charged with anxiety and fear. I struggled to force my gaze to the left, where the rooms were, instead staring straight ahead at a bustling nurses' station. If I didn't look, I couldn't see anything devastating.

"Mr. Calloway?"

I startled, then glanced down to find a five-foot-nothing perky woman in maroon scrubs. She had her blonde hair tied up in a neat bun and hideous white rubber shoes. A medical mask hid most of her facial features, except for her eyes, which shone with compassion.

"Um, yeah. That's me. But you can call me Ryder."

"Come with me, Ryder. I'm Avery, and I'm the nurse taking care of your father until seven o'clock tonight."

I followed as she continued to speak.

"Your mother is in with him now. We're expecting the neurologist soon." She stopped outside a room with a sliding glass door and a pulled curtain. "It's always a little shocking for family members to see their loved ones in the ICU for the first time, so let me tell you a little about what you can expect."

"Uh, okay, thanks." Maybe a heads-up would keep me from freaking out when I walked in there.

"He has a breathing tube in his throat, but that is temporary. The neurologist will explain it more. Several machines are monitoring him right now, so don't be startled by the wires, IVs, and tubes. He is stable right now, and the neurologist will explain the plan when she arrives in a few moments. Are you ready?"

Was I ready? Hell no. Did it matter? Apparently not.

"Yes, I am." My right palm tingled. I'd give anything to have Alex there beside me, holding my hand and bleeding his strength into me.

She slid open the door and stepped into the room, pushing the curtain aside for me. The second I entered the small room, my gaze zeroed in on my father lying still in the mechanical bed in the center of the room. There wasn't anything else to capture my attention.

Though I'd been warned what to expect, my loud gasp ripped through the room. Avery squeezed my upper arm before moving to a computer mounted on the left wall.

My father lay on his back, completely still but for the rise and fall of his chest. A tube ran from his mouth to a loud machine, which I assumed pumped oxygen into his lungs.

Jesus.

Wires seemed to come from everywhere, leading to a

screen mounted near his bed. Multiple lines fed into two separate IVs, one in each hand. Another tube extended beneath the covers to a bag hanging on the side of the bed. It was halfway full of dark yellow liquid.

He looked small and vulnerable, nothing like the business mogul who ran a billion-dollar empire. Nothing like the man who disapproved of my choices and had no problem telling me.

He'd hate anyone seeing him this way. If a photo were leaked to the press, he'd ruin the life of the whistleblower. Strange as it was, he'd probably hate being seen in a gray hospital gown with the horrid geometric pattern more than anything else. The man hadn't left the house in anything but a bespoke suit or golf outfit in decades.

What now? Was I supposed to talk to him? Touch him?

A delicate throat clearing had me jerking my gaze to the right, where my mother sat in a high-back chair against the wall. She looked terrible—mussed hair, red-rimmed eyes, hands clenched on her lap. I couldn't think of a time I'd seen her looking anything less than perfect. She didn't even let her children see her without a full face of makeup and coiffed hair.

My father was—shit, is—her life.

"Mother—"

The curtain slid open, and a tall, willowy woman in a long white coat stepped into the room. "Good morning," she said in a soft tone. "I am Dr. Travers, one of the neurologists here on staff. Are you here to see Mr. Calloway?"

I glanced at my mother, who seemed near catatonic at this point. She didn't respond, so I stepped forward and held out my hand. "Yes, I'm Ryder, his son. And this is my mother, his wife, Sylvia. My sister is out of town, but I'm sure she'll be coming straight back." God, had my mom even called Vera?

Dr. Travers shook my hand. "Very nice to meet you, though

I'm sorry about the circumstances."

"Thank you."

"Mr. Calloway suffered an embolic stroke, which means a blood clot in his brain restricted blood flow, causing damage. We currently have him sedated to give his brain a rest and plan to remove the breathing tube in the next few days. Until then, we won't know the extent of the effects."

While I appreciated her no-nonsense competence, my head felt too stunned to process what she was saying. Later, I would probably think of a hundred questions, but for now, only one came to mind. "What do you mean, the effects?"

She nodded. "So, we can see on CT imaging that he experienced a profound stroke. Based on where the damage is, we can expect significant weakness or possible paralysis to his right side. He will most likely have difficulty speaking, which we call aphasia, and some level of cognitive impairment. It's impossible to know the severity until he's awake, and our speech, occupational, and physical therapists can then evaluate him. I will say, though, he most likely has a long road of recovery ahead of him. This is not to scare you, but I do want you to have realistic expectations."

Paralysis?

Aphasia?

Cognitive impairment?

Did that mean he wouldn't be able to walk and talk? What about feeding himself? Or even going to the bathroom on his own?

I wanted to ask, but was too terrified to hear the answer.

"I know this is extremely overwhelming. I'm going to give you guys a chance to process and think of some questions for me. I'll be back in a few hours."

She disappeared as quickly as she'd appeared. Maybe she wasn't the warmest and fuzziest when it came to her bedside manner, but I'd take her straight talk over coddling any day.

In a move that shocked me, my mom shot up from her chair and rushed over to me. She grabbed my arms and gave me a little shake. "The VanBuren merger," she said, voice panicked.

"What?"

"Your father was in the final stages of a huge merger with VB Corp."

"Okay, well, clearly, it will have to be put on hold." Why was she even thinking of business at a time like this?

"No." She shook me again. "Your father wouldn't want that. You know how important his work is to him."

Did I ever. "Screw work. Mom, he's not even conscious."

Acrylic nails dug into my skin through my thin sweater as she clutched me tight. "No, please, Ryder, you have to take over for him."

"What?" My jaw hit the floor, and I took a step back from her, shaking my head.

She pulled me back to her. "Please," she said, tears falling from her eyes. "You have to do this for him. He needs to know his company is taken care of while he recovers. It's the only thing he'll care about when he wakes up."

I scoffed. Pretty sure he'd want to be able to stand and shit on his own. I managed to keep those words in. She was probably right. All he'd care about was if his money grew while he was lying unconscious in a hospital.

"Please, Ryder. He needs you right now. You need to run the company for him while he is unable to do so. I'm begging you. You're his only son."

School would start in a few weeks. I was supposed to begin a new path, one I'd set for myself based on my own goals and desires, not those my parents laid out for me. We hadn't had a conversation about my switch to a master's degree in education, but my father must have told her about our blowup. My stomach turned over. I couldn't, didn't want to say yes.

"Ryder, it's time to stop playing around." Her voice shifted from that of a devastated wife to the socialite who made headlines with her lavish lifestyle. "We've let you be selfish long enough. It's time to grow up and do what your family needs. You need to step up and take your father's place until he is well again."

I stared down at her fresh tears. Were they for my father or for the fear of losing her status as the top one percent?

Or was she right?

Would it be selfish of me to step away from my father's business to pursue my dreams at this time?

Fuck, I wished Alex was with me.

Chapter Twenty- Eight

After Ryder disappeared behind the ICU double doors, I lowered into the stiff chair with my heart in my throat. In a matter of minutes, our roles had reversed entirely. Ryder kept me sane all morning, and with one phone call, his world exploded.

What shit timing, not that a family crisis could ever happen at a good time, but Ryder's relationship with his father fractured the day Ryder told his father he wanted a different future. One he'd devised for himself. Now, who knew what had happened to their chance to repair the rift?

Thinking of the mix of complex emotions Ryder must be dealing with had my heart aching—fear, guilt, shock, sadness, grief. I'd give anything to be at his side, holding him up in whatever way he needed, but having spent more than my fair share of time in hospitals, I knew there'd be no chance of getting beyond those doors. I'd have to suck it up and wait until he emerged.

So, I waited.

The first hour crawled slower than a slug through sand. I fucked around on my phone, watched the news report the depressing state of our nation, and counted ceiling tiles until my eyes blurred. By hour two, I'd given up on entertaining myself and stared at the doors, willing Ryder to appear.

My phone finally rang close to the top of the third hour. "Hello?" I said, recognizing the number for the recovery room.

"Hello, is this Alex?"

"Yes, it is."

"Hi, Alex, I'm Theresa, one of the PACU nurses taking care of your mother. I just wanted to let you know that she is out of surgery, awake, and doing very well."

The relief had my hands shaking as I tried to hang onto my phone. I could not have handled a second bout of bad news. "Thank you."

"You're very welcome. She'll be in here with me for about an hour before we send her up to a room for the night. You're free to come sit with her at any time."

"Um, thanks. Is it... may I speak with her?"

"Of course. I'm handing her the phone right now."

The line went silent for a moment before I heard a sleepy, "Alex?"

"Hi, Mom. How are you feeling?"

"Hi, honey, I'm feeling okay. Pain is under control. I'm a little groggy. What's wrong?"

I chuckled. Leave it to a mom to notice something had happened with just a few words. "Um..." The words lodged in my throat.

"Alex?" Her concern loosened my tongue. The last thing she needed was stress on top of trying to heal.

"Ryder's dad had a... um... he had a stroke."

"Oh, honey..."

"Yeah, I don't know much right now, but he's in the ICU."

"Oh, you can't even be with him right now. I'm so sorry, honey."

"Yeah, it sucks. I'm in the waiting room, just... waiting. I'll come to you as soon as I can, but I promised Ryder I'd be here when he came out. He was... rattled."

"Of course he was. Honey, I am fine. They are taking good care of me. You stay there and take care of your man, okay?"

"Are you sure? I feel—"

"Don't you dare say guilty, Alex. I am fine. Do you hear me? I am fine, and your man is not. Be there for him."

My throat thickened until I could barely squeak words out. "I-I love you, Mom," I managed.

"I love you, too, honey. I'll make sure the nurses get in touch with you to give you my room number when I'm moved out of here."

I blinked away a rapid rush of tears. "Okay."

We said our goodbyes and ended the call. I blew out a stuttered breath, shut my eyes, and rested my head against the wall behind me.

And then I heard the whir of the double doors swinging open. I flew out of my seat so fast my head spun.

Ryder strode through the doors and stopped a few feet away from me. He looked devastated and gorgeous simultaneously. My heart leaped into my throat as we stared at each other. I'd had three hours to prepare, and yet I couldn't think of the best thing to say.

In the distance, someone's phone rang, snapping us out of our trance. We moved at the same time, practically throwing ourselves at each other. The second we crashed together, I wrapped my arms around him in a vicious hold, and he did the same.

"Thank you," he whispered.

And then I realized my words didn't have to be said in any special way. All I'd done for Ryder was sit in a chair and wait for him, and that was enough. I was enough, just as he'd told me dozens of times.

"Are you okay?" I asked as we clung to each other.

He shook his head. "I don't know. It's bad, but we won't know how bad for a few days. They have him sedated right now."

"Your mom and sister?"

"Can we sit? I feel so drained."

I released my hold on him. "Of course." Wrapping an arm around his waist, I guided him to the supremely uncomfortable chairs that had been my home for the past few hours.

"Um…" he said once we were sitting, facing each other as best we could. I took his hand and held it tight. "I talked to Vera. She's in Canada with her friends but is trying to get back. She's probably on a plane now. My mom is a mess. She's freaking out about business shit mostly."

Something in his tone had uneasiness slithering down my spine. "Okay…"

He closed his eyes and blew out a breath. "She asked, no, begged, me to step into his shoes at the company until he can return."

I sucked in a breath. Everything in me powerfully revolted against that idea. Ryder didn't want that. He had plans, dreams, goals, and a clear path to achieve them. My instinct was to tell him how I thought the idea was complete bullshit, and he should tell his mother so in no uncertain terms.

But I held back because I knew this man, and I knew he couldn't leave his family in a lurch during a crisis.

"What… what did you tell her?" I asked as dread filled me.

He seemed to shrink before my eyes, transforming into an unhappy man I didn't recognize. My Ryder was full of life. He was arrogant, snarky, and called me on my shit. I'd fallen in love with that man and—

Oh shit.

The realization slammed into me like a wrecking ball.

I fucking loved this man.

He blinked glassy eyes. "I told her yes," he whispered. "Oh, God, Alex, what have I done?"

I grabbed him in a fierce hug, ignoring the plastic chair's arm digging into my stomach. "We'll get through it, Ryder," I whispered in his ear. "I'm not going anywhere, and we will get you fucking through this together."

"Promise?" he whispered in an insecure tone so un-Ryder, it broke my heart.

"Yes, Ryder. I promise."

*Thank you for reading **Shaken and Stirred**. Get ready for the second half of Alex and Ryder's story, **Heavy Pour**, coming in the fall of 2025! Read on for an excerpt from The Duality of Swans, another M/M contemporary romance by Lilly Atlas!*

The Duality of Swans

"Will you hurry up already?" Randy hollered as he kicked a spray of dusty rocks down the dirt path. He spun, cupping his hands over his mouth and shouting, "Next time, I'll bring that broken-down stroller in front of Old Man Hinkle's trailer so I can roll your slow ass. At least we'd get there faster."

Randy back-walked along the dirt road a good thirty feet in front of Tate with a forty of Budweiser sticking out from his back pocket. His hair, the same dark blond as Tate's, was buzzed short as always. He constantly teased Tate for leaving it a bit longer and shaggier, calling him a girl and asking if he wanted pink bows for his birthday.

Tate rolled his eyes. His damn brother wasn't breathing if he wasn't acting dramatic or ragging on someone. "Where's the damn fire?" he yelled back. "Pretty sure you've never given a shit about the county fair before. It ain't going nowhere for five days. Why you gotta rush me? It's too hot to walk fast."

"The fire's in my fucking pants," Randy said, jiggling his crotch as he waggled his eyebrows. "Whit's gonna be there. She told Ginger if I find her 'fore Daryl, she'll blow me, but if he gets there first, he's gonna get his cock sucked insteada me. So fucking move it."

Oh, for fuck's sake. Tate slowed his pace, shooting his brother a smirk. "Has Whit seen those pubes on your face? Cuz if she has, it won't matter what time you show up. She ain't gonna blow you if she sees you looking like a walking ball sac."

"Fuck you," Randy said, stroking his new, patchy goatee. It grew darker than the rest of his hair, making him look stupid as hell. "Ma said it makes me look like a movie star."

Snorting, Tate slowed to a snail's pace. "Should probably do the opposite of what Ma recommends. In case you haven't noticed, she's strung out ninety percent of the time. Probably can't see shit right."

Randy flipped him the double bird. "Shut up. I look good. And can you just walk faster, loser? You're doing this shit on purpose cuz you're jealous. No chick wants your knob."

Tate rolled his eyes again. Annoyance, not jealousy, had him messing with Randy. He didn't give two shits about having some chick slobbering over his dick. Two years ago, Randy started calling him all sorts of names for not showing much interest in girls, so he talked the talk, but he'd yet to walk the walk. Not that Randy knew. Tate could spin a tale like nobody's business, and he'd let Randy think he was getting some.

"Run ahead! What the hell do you need me with you for? Need me to cheer you on so you can get hard for Whit?"

"Fuck no." Randy blinked, then laughed. "But, shit, you're right. What am I doing waiting on your stupid ass? Later, loser." He took off at a jog, shaking up that warm Bud hugging his ass. There'd be an unpleasant surprise if he offered the beer to Whitney after the poor girl blew him. At least something would erupt for her, though it'd be the last blowie she offered up. His brother needed a few more brain cells. Tate didn't hold out much hope of him finding any.

He took his sweet time, strolling past cornfield after cornfield on his way to the county fair. Carnivals weren't his scene, but he had a few extra bucks from the tile job he'd helped his neighbor, Jim, with last weekend. Jim gave him a hundred fucking bucks for two days' work. Tate hadn't ever had his hands on that much cash at once. He spent eighty of it on groceries and saved twenty. The good groceries too. Frozen peas instead of the kind that came in a can and some bacon. Spending that last twenty on some funnel cake and a few rides at the fair would make this the most exciting night he'd had in ages.

By the time he reached the event, the sun had dipped into the horizon, leaving the whole fairground shadowed in twilight. Tate didn't bother looking for his brother. The last thing he wanted was to walk behind some booth and find him getting blown by Whitney, the easiest girl in their high school. She was cool, though. She was always nice to Tate, which he couldn't say of all of Randy's dipshit friends.

At eighteen, she and Randy would graduate in a few weeks, while Tate had a few more years to go. Fifteen, but some days, he felt like forty. Guess that's what happened when your old man was a damn deadbeat, and your mother couldn't make it through the day without pumping something into her bloodstream. Some days she made it to her job waiting tables at the local truck stop diner, but it was a crap shoot. The only reason she hadn't been fired was pity. The owner had known his mother since childhood and felt fucking sorry for her.

Someone bumped his shoulder, jostling him from his thoughts. Tate blinked the fair into focus with a muttered apology. He glanced around at the bright, blinking lights and the crowds of townsfolk. Shit, he'd wandered halfway through the fairgrounds without paying a lick of attention to where he was walking.

322

Where was the damn funnel cake booth? He'd had a craving for the stuff since he'd seen the first fair flyer a few weeks ago. There was not much better than some warm, fried, sugary goodness.

As he glanced around, movement from a stage to his left caught his attention. Performers moved all over the stage, but what had him walking closer was the music that seemed so out of place for a state fair. Behind him, obnoxious carnival music blared from the rickety Ferris wheel, while in front of him, something slow and elegant played for the performers he now realized were ballet dancers.

What an odd thing to have at the fair. Last year, the main event was pig races, and this year a ballet? Maybe someone was trying to class up the place. Tate snorted. They'd have had better luck getting lipstick on those racing pigs.

Still, he took another step closer to the show out of what he'd later call morbid curiosity.

The stage, like everything else at this hick fair, had seen better days, made of rusted metal with what looked like plywood layered on top. Rows of folding chairs held maybe fifteen scattered audience members despite the crowds at the fair. It seemed like most people were as confused as he was to see a ballet performance at the county carnival. Either that, or they were too busy puking their guts out on rides.

Or getting blown like Randy.

Girls who seemed to be around his age danced across the stage in pink tutus with flowers in their hair. They pranced and leaped on the tips of their toes with identical smiles plastered on their faces. Tate watched for a minute before boredom set in. As he was about to resume his search for a fried treat, a new dancer practically floated onto the stage.

Tate froze.

His skin prickled, starting at the nape of his neck and spreading through to the tips of his fingers.

Air whooshed out of his lungs like it did when Randy socked him in the gut.

The guy on stage danced with a fluidity that almost seemed fake like a person shouldn't be able to move with such grace.

Grace? When the hell had he ever used the word *grace*?

When the male dancer leaped, his long legs extended as straight as an arrow. When he twirled, Tate held his breath, sure no one could possibly spin that fast and that many times without toppling over.

This was the first ballet Tate had seen, and his brother and friends would rib him to no end if they saw him gawking like a fool, but he couldn't turn away. He couldn't even blink for fear of missing a second of the guy's routine.

Sweat broke out across Tate's brow as he watched the play of muscles in the guy's bare chest while performing a move that required a flexibility Tate couldn't fathom. The dancer's lower half was covered by a pair of light gray tights that were so fucking snug he could make out each individual ass muscle as the guy danced.

Or he could have if he was looking.

But he wasn't.

He especially wasn't looking at the way those tights cupped the guy's crotch.

No fucking way.

Tate swallowed.

Fuck, I'm looking.

Staring.

His heart raced.

Completely transfixed.

The dancer held a final pose, and the sparse crowd cheered. Tate should have clapped, but he still couldn't move. If it wasn't for the fact he stood seventy feet from the stage, he'd have sworn the dancer's gaze met his.

His gut tightened.

God, he couldn't fucking breathe. Nothing in the world had captured his attention the way this dancer had. The entire fair could erupt in flames, and he'd never notice. It felt like live wires were popping and crackling under his skin, making him crave *something* he couldn't put his finger on.

He swallowed a painful lump down his arid throat.

The guy's body was like marble, crafted to perfection—smooth, hairless planes, rippling abs, sculpted arms, and that muscular ass. Were he closer, Tate wouldn't be able to keep from reaching out and touching—

Oh fuck.

No. No, no, no.

His stomach cramped. Forget the funnel cake. He couldn't eat to save his life right then.

I can't be. It's not possible.

The weird feelings were nothing more than admiration for someone who worked hard at their impressive skillset. A skillset Tate would never have but could appreciate the sacrifices it would take to get there.

No way in hell was he attracted to the guy on stage. This was probably from all the girls in their tight costumes. He tried to shift his attention to one of the perky ballerinas, but his damn eyes wouldn't cooperate.

No.

His stomach lurched.

A heavy weight slammed into his back, making him stagger forward with a grunt.

"Here you are, you fucking slowpoke." Daryl, Randy's best friend since they popped out of the womb, hopped on Tate, piggyback-style. "What the fuck are you watching this shit for?"

Tate tore his gaze from the stage where the ballet troop bowed for their meager applause. He forced himself to turn toward the rest of his friends.

Randy laughed. "Look at that. One dude dancing with all those bitches."

Still hanging off Tate, Daryl snorted. "That ain't a dude. It's a fairy. That why you are watching them, Tatey boy? You got a thing for fairies?" He ruffled Tate's hair.

A crushing pain bore down on his chest, making it impossible to speak.

Randy's laughter increased. "You better not be a fucking fairy, Tate. I ain't living with a homo."

"Fuck off," he grumbled, bucking backward.

Daryl yelped as he flew off Tate's back. His ass hit the dusty ground. "What the fuck, Tate? Rude."

Whitney, standing under Randy's arm, giggled. "Maybe you're the fairy, Daryl. Always jumping on Tate's back and rubbing his head."

Randy's eyes widened. "Oh shit, you two fucking?"

Was this what a heart attack felt like?

Tate's face burned hotter than the damn sun.

"Fuck off," he mumbled again.

"I ain't no fucking fairy," Daryl said, all humor gone. "I'll fuck you right here right now, Whit."

"I'd rather die," she said with a smirk.

"C'mon." Randy kicked Daryl's leg.

"Ow! What the hell, Whit? You'da blown me if I got here first, right?"

She shrugged.

"Quit it, you two. I want some fucking funnel cake," Randy announced.

"Oh, me, too," Whitney cooed, running her hand up Randy's torso.

Daryl hopped up. "Let's do it."

The three of them started for the food tent. Tate still couldn't move. Chances were high he'd need CPR in the next few minutes.

"You coming, asshole?" Daryl shouted, walking backward next to the others.

Tate risked a final glance at the stage. It stood empty and quiet, and any onlookers had disappeared into the crowded fair.

He shuddered and blew out a breath. "Yeah. I'm fucking coming," he said as he forced himself to jog after the group. Whatever had happened a few moments ago had been a damn fluke. Maybe he'd had a mini-stroke or needed some damn water.

Dehydration fucked people up, right?

Whatever. It didn't matter. All that mattered was that he knew for certain he hadn't been attracted to that dancer.

No way, no how.

They passed the next few hours laughing, eating, riding rides, and making general fools of themselves, not attempting to leave until they were stuffed and a little nauseated.

"I gotta take a leak before we walk home," Tate said as they approached a restroom.

"Hurry," Randy said. "I hate waiting."

"What do you care? Didn't you already get blown?"

Whitney, Daryl, and a few of their other friends snickered.

"I'm young," Randy said with a shrug. "Time to go again." He slung an arm around Whitney's shoulders.

"Poor Whitney," he muttered as he strode into the restroom.

Not more than a minute later, he emerged a few ounces lighter. Of course, his loser friends were nowhere to be seen.

"Jackoffs," he muttered, starting for the fair's exit. Whatever. It wasn't as though he needed them to find his way home. As he reached the edge of the building that housed the bathrooms, jeering and a familiar laugh caught his attention.

"The fuck? Randy?" he called as he followed the sound around to the back of the building. His brother had a unique laugh, and Tate loved to bust his balls over it. When he really got going, his laugh sounded like a six-year-old girl, high-pitched and giggly.

"Dude," Randy called, waving him over. "Look at this shit."

He pointed, and Tate craned his neck to see past his friends. What he saw had his stomach twisting.

Two guys with dark hoodies and bandanas over their faces huddled over someone curled in the fetal position on the ground. They whaled on him, kicking, shouting homophobic slurs, and laughing. The sight made him sick. Tate could hold his own and had been in a crap load of fights in his fifteen years, mostly with his brother, but he didn't enjoy it, and he'd never go after anyone for shits and giggles.

"What the fuck?" Tate said. "Why are you standing around watching this shit?"

Daryl jumped up and down, practically giddy. "It's that guy. The sissy from the ballet."

"What?" Tate whispered, blood turning to ice.

"They're teaching him a fucking lesson," Randy said.

"Damn straight," Daryl agreed. "Bet he'll think twice before prancing around on a stage in this town again. We do not need his kind spreading their fairy dust all around."

Tate didn't hear what else was said. His feet acted of their own accord, propelling him toward the fray. "Hey!" he shouted.

Randy caught his arm. "What the fuck are you doing?"

Tate whipped around while still walking. He jerked his arm from Randy's hold. "They're gonna kill him," he shouted, gesturing toward the beating.

Scoffing, Daryl shook his head. "Who the fuck cares?"

Jesus. He spun back. "Get the fuck off him!" he screamed,

charging forward.

The assailants were big, and two-on-one odds were never good, but Randy and Daryl would have his back. They might not be eager to save a gay guy's life, but they wouldn't let Tate get his ass kicked.

"I said, get the fuck off him." He reached one of the guys, grabbing the back of his sweaty shirt.

The guy stopped kicking the dancer and whirled on Tate. "What the fuck?" he shouted in a lethal growl

"Tate!" Randy hollered.

"Fuck this," Daryl yelled. "I'm out of here."

"Let's go."

Randy's voice.

Guess Tate was on his own. He cocked his arm and rammed it into the attacker's face. Blood spurted beneath the bandana, but he didn't go down. His buddy stopped kicking the dancer and spun toward Tate.

Shit, I'm so fucked.

He fought as hard as he could, but the dudes were huge, and before long, he was bruised and bloodied, but so were the attackers.

The dancer lay curled up on the ground, twitching every so often but unable to get up and run away.

Tate dodged a fist coming at his nose and kicked out, but his foot only met air. Another fist collided with his stomach, making him double over and nearly tossing his funnel cake.

"Hey! What the fuck is going on back here?" The new voice came from twenty or so feet away.

The fight stopped instantly, and all three of them faced the voice. A rent-a-cop rounded the corner of the building and jogged their way.

Without another word, the two attackers took off in opposite directions.

"Stop!" the guard shouted as he raced after one of them.

He grabbed his radio. "I need an ambulance behind the bathrooms. Cops too!"

He had to get the hell out of there before he was arrested. An ambulance was coming. The dancer would be taken care of.

Go, go. Run.

But he didn't move. Instead, he gave into the driving urge to peer back at the dancer on the ground. He'd managed to sit himself up. Blood trickled from his nose and mouth, and his dark hair had twigs and dust throughout the strands. He cradled his arm against his chest and trembled. He seemed to be struggling to breathe.

"T-thank you," he whispered.

Tate froze, unable to speak. Even battered, the guy captured his attention in a way no one had before. He wanted to rush forward, wrap his arms around the dancer, and promise no one would hurt him ever again. He wanted to chase after his brother and beat the shit out of him for watching and laughing.

He wanted to kiss the tears right off that devastated face.

No.

A siren sounded, closer than was comfortable. Red lights flashed, providing the electric jolt he needed. Help was on the way. Instead of responding, he fled.

He ran until his legs burned, and his lungs screamed at him to stop. He ran straight through the cornfields, ignoring the stinging cuts from the coarse leaves slicing his skin. He ignored the blood and bruises on his face and body.

He had no idea how much time or distance passed before he tripped and landed hard on all fours, panting like an exhausted dog.

Fuck.

He couldn't be gay. He could not be gay.

I'm not gay.

He'd be next. The next guy on the ground protecting his vital organs as giant feet slammed into him again and again.

I'm not gay.

A flash of the dancer holding a beautiful pose flitted through his mind, and his heart skipped a damn beat.

Oh God.

I'm not gay.

He vomited all over fallen ears of corn.

Thank you for reading SHAKEN AND STIRRED. If you enjoyed this book, please leave a review on Amazon or Goodreads.

Other books by Lilly Atlas

M/M
The Duality of Swans

Bottle Service Boys
Shaken and Stirred
Sip Happens (Coming fall 2025)

M/F
No Prisoners MC
Hook: A No Prisoners Novella
Striker
Jester
Acer
Lucky
Snake

Trident Ink
Escapades

Hell's Handlers MC
Zach
Maverick
Jigsaw

Copper
Rocket
Little Jack
Joy
Screw
Viper
Thunder

Hell's Handlers Florida Chapter
Curly
Spec
Tracker
Frost
Jinx
Lock
Ty
Pulse

Mayhem Makers Series
Solo Rider

Blue Collar Bensons
First Comes Loathe
Shock and Aww

Audiobooks
Audio

Join Lilly's mailing list for a **FREE** No Prisoners short
story.
www.lillyatlas.com
Facebook
Instagram

TikTok

Join my Facebook group, **Lilly's Ladies** for book previews, early cover reveals, contests and more!

About the Author

Lilly Atlas is an award-winning contemporary romance author. She's a proud Navy wife and mother of three spunky girls. Every time Lilly downloads a new eBook she expects her Kindle App to tell her it's exhausted and overworked, and to beg for some rest. Thankfully that hasn't happened yet so she can often be found absorbed in a good book.

www.ingramcontent.com/pod-product-compliance
Lightning Source LLC
Chambersburg PA
CBHW072121250626
47159CB00007B/2531